Meaghan Wilson Anastasios spent her formative years in Melbourne before travelling and working as an archaeologist in the Mediterranean and Middle East. She holds a PhD in art history and cultural economics, has been a lecturer at the University of Melbourne and was a fine art auctioneer. More recently, Meaghan has been seduced by the dark side and now uses her expertise to write and research for film and TV. She lives in inner-city Melbourne with her husband and their two children. *The Water Diviner* was her first novel, which she co-wrote with her husband Andrew. *The Honourable Thief* is her first solo novel.

Also by Meaghan Wilson Anastasios
(with Andrew Anastasios)

*The Water Diviner*

# THE
# Honourable
# THIEF

## MEAGHAN WILSON
## ANASTASIOS

MACMILLAN
Pan Macmillan Australia

First published 2018 in Macmillan by Pan Macmillan Australia Pty Ltd
1 Market Street, Sydney, New South Wales, Australia, 2000

A catalogue record for this book is available from the National Library of Australia

Typeset in 13.5/16 pt Granjon LT by Midland Typesetters, Australia
Printed by McPherson's Printing Group

The characters in this book are fictitious and any resemblance to real persons, living or dead, is purely coincidental.

MIX
Paper from
responsible sources
FSC® C001695

The paper in this book is FSC® certified.
FSC® promotes environmentally responsible, socially beneficial and economically viable management of the world's forests.

*To Andrew.*
*For the history we have made together.*

# Prologue

A trickle of earth from the vaulted stone ceiling showers down, the tranquil chamber echoing with a sound like rain on a tin roof.

As Benedict Hitchens scratches and hacks at the soil in the world above, he pictures it in his mind's eye, as if he might conjure it from thin air by will alone. He has been searching for it his entire life and knows its contours better than the face of a loved one.

It is said to have been born in the fires of the club-footed god's forge. Ingots of silver, brass, tin and solid gold rolled and beaten, turned and shaped by hammer upon anvil. The giant disc is a cosmology showing the earth, the heaven and ocean; the blazing sun, the full moon's orb; every starry light above the earth's curved surface. In delicate tracery it tells the tales of the world of men, played out beneath the arching heavens. A city at peace; a city at war. A harvest – ploughshares cleaving the soil. A hunt – dogs and men tearing flesh from bone. A marriage – the joyous groom leading his bride to bed.

Legend holds that no one who carries it into battle can be felled by mortal means. Yet the man who carried it had perished in the war that would be remembered for all time. For three thousand years, poets have sung of his valour.

The sepulchre preserves his secrets.

A beam of light cuts through the darkness. The hero's slumber is disturbed.

# PART I

# I

## Istanbul, Turkey, 1955

The man sat on a rush-bottomed chair, long legs crossed and extended in front of him. He leant back against the lime-washed stone wall and waited. A lifetime of experience had taught him the value of patience. Feline eyes squinting in the midday sunlight, he held a hand-rolled cigarette between two spider-leg fingers and lifted it to his lips, inhaling deeply then exhaling, watching the whorls of smoke twirl towards the ceiling.

Something caught his eye in the crowd outside. There. Leaning forward, the man took stock of an approaching couple. *They couldn't be more obvious if they had a neon sign above their heads*, he thought to himself. With a swift move, he snuffed out his cigarette and leapt to his feet, whipping around and shouting over his shoulder.

'Yilmaz! Come!'

From the back of the shop came a sudden thud and the soft-shoe shuffle of leather soles on stone paving. His assistant swept back the beaded curtain and stumbled into the sulphurous light, betrayed by his bleary eyes. It wasn't the first time Yilmaz had sought refuge from the stuffy, shoebox-sized shop by indulging in a nap on the cushiony piles of kilims and carpets in the back storeroom.

He stood, blinking, bracing for the expected onslaught. 'Ilhan *Bey* . . . I'm sorry . . . the inventory. It's difficult. There are many artefacts I don't . . .'

'Shush. It doesn't matter now. Time to test what you have learnt. Out there.' Ilhan Aslan tilted his chin towards the two foreigners negotiating their way through the lunchtime melee in the open square.

'Quickly. What do you see?'

The sixteen-year-old boy sidled towards the plate-glass window and peered out.

'Tailored clothes. Very well cut. And his Panama . . . from a milliner. Made to measure. Her heels – she can't walk far in those . . . they came in a car. No parking nearby, so it was a chauffeured one. Money. Lots of it. They are wealthy.'

Unsatisfied, Ilhan clipped the boy over the back of the head. 'You're wasting my time. Anyone can see that. I need more. Quickly! Where are they from?'

The boy squinted, taking stock. 'Lipstick – red. Too much makeup. And long fingernails painted red. Her dress – flashy. She wants to be noticed . . . admired. His suit – blue linen. New. Open-necked shirt. But not Savile Row . . . no tie. And he walks with a swagger. Certainly not British. Italian? No – too tall. And too broad. And she has that blonde hair. But they are not pale enough for Germans.' Yilmaz paused, weighing the options. 'They walk as if everyone around is watching them. They are American. Yes – definitely American.'

The older man prodded the boy's shoulder. 'East or West Coast? It's important. To seduce them, you must know them. Quickly, boy. In one minute they'll be on our doorstep.'

'Pale hair but brown skin. Her smile – so wide. And those teeth – white and square. Like *tavla* tiles. So much gold jewellery. And those sunglasses the size of ducks' eggs . . . she swirls her hips and wiggles as she walks – like a movie star. And his shoes – no laces. Boat shoes . . . West Coast. Or Texas. Maybe . . . oil money?' Yilmaz looked up at his patron hesitantly.

Ilhan nodded, biting the inside of his cheeks to disguise the smile of pride that rose to his lips. An ability to measure up a potential customer meant everything in his business. What tone of voice would be most effective – familiar or respectful? Which vocabulary would they respond to – colloquial or formal? Were the visitors looking to be wooed – seduced – by the salesman, or would they prefer a swift and efficient transaction? Most important of all, how much could they afford to spend – or, as was so often the case, how much would they be willing to part with? Ilhan was a chameleon who became exactly what each of his customers needed the minute they walked in the door. As his apprentice, one day he would need Yilmaz to do the same. And the boy was a natural. But Ilhan never left anything to chance when he could avoid it. Thanks to Umut's phone call that morning, he already knew everything there was to know about the American couple short of their birth weight. But he wasn't about to let the boy know that.

He clapped Yilmaz affectionately on the back. 'Good. But they are not oil money. See the man's eyes? No wrinkles. If he was an oil man, he'd have crow's feet around his eyes from the sun. No . . .' Ilhan paused for dramatic effect. 'The movie business.'

The couple paused on the opposite side of the road, peering nervously at the shopfronts like spring lambs on market day. Along the cobbled street, small clusters of men sat on low stools outside their stores, flicking *tesbih* beads between manicured fingers and gossiping. Spotting the new arrivals, they rose as one; half-smoked cigarettes stubbed out and stored for later use, beads tucked into trouser pockets, and heavily pomaded hair patted down.

Ilhan lightly pushed Yilmaz between the shoulder blades, urging him towards the front door. 'Go! Now! They have come here to see us. So get out there and grab them before those vultures swoop and steal our prey!'

Spreading his hands in an expansive gesture, Ilhan took a step forward and bowed his head gracefully: a conductor acknowledging the audience's applause. He addressed his visitors in impeccable English. 'Sir. Madam. My name is Ilhan Aslan. It is an honour to welcome you to my humble gallery. To have come here such a distance . . . Los Angeles is a world away.'

He was pleased to see their eyes widen with surprise. Startled, the woman turned towards her husband. 'But, how did you . . .?'

'If you'll excuse me, madam, one of my favourite pastimes is to visit the movie cinema. And the minute I saw you crossing the square, I knew at once that you must be a Hollywood star of the screen.'

The woman flushed, raising her hand in protest but obviously pleased by the compliment. 'Oh, no. Not me. You must be mistaking me for someone else. Though my husband *is* in the business.'

Teeth on edge and with broad shoulders squared, the tall man took his wife's hand and hooked it through the crook of his elbow. 'Now, sweetie. That's enough of that. Don't need to share *all* our secrets with the locals.'

Ilhan smiled and nodded his head. 'You must both be weary. And it is so hot in Istanbul at this time of year. The boy will get you a refreshment. *Çay* . . . Turkish tea? Or a cold soda?'

The statuesque blonde woman glanced at her husband, who answered for her. 'Er . . . something cold would be super. Thank you.'

'Yilmaz!' Ilhan clapped his hands. '*Iki soda*!'

The bell above the door jangled as Yilmaz bolted up the road to the tiny *büfe* that supplied the myriad stores lining the street with the obligatory hot and cold drinks that lubricated the Turkish commercial world. Without these beverages, the wheels of business in Istanbul would grind to a shuddering halt.

For all their outward confidence, the stately couple were unsettled, unsure where to position themselves in the tiny, and very cluttered, space. Countless ornate brass lamps hung from the ceiling like grapes from a vine. Teetering piles of lustrously painted ceramics were stored along narrow shelves, and stacks of folded carpets and kilims leaning against each wall reduced the already restricted floor space. The air was hot and heavy, and the greasy scent of raw wool in the rugs made the room stuffier still. A languidly spinning ceiling fan did little to dispel the heat.

Sensing his guests' discomfort, Ilhan indicated an upholstered banquette at the end of the shop. 'Please. Do you wish to take a seat? The boy will be here with your drinks in a minute.' He drew aside a curtain and lifted out an electric fan that he turned on and directed towards the seat. 'This will help.'

The woman looked to her husband for direction. He nodded, and she lowered herself onto the banquette with evident relief. Her husband took a seat beside her, taking a silk kerchief from his breast pocket to mop a sweaty brow.

Ilhan's customers could be as skittish as nervous young colts or as aggressive and suspicious as sacrificial rams being led off to the imam at Bayram. This couple, he suspected, would be a challenging combination of both. Conditions were less than ideal. Ilhan could tell already that the man would be the one making the decisions. He would determine whether or not the Turk would turn a profit today. But the American was hot and out of sorts. This was going to require a deft touch.

The doorbell jangled again as Yilmaz returned bearing a copper tray carrying two small, clear bottles of *gazoz* with striped paper straws, and for Ilhan, a tiny, waisted glass full to the brim with tannin-dark tea. The two Americans reached eagerly for the bottles of Turkish lemonade. Ilhan held the scarlet red and gilt-painted saucer delicately in one hand, and dropped one small sugar cube into his tea, stirring it with a silver spoon.

'If I may ask,' Ilhan spoke gently, soothingly, 'what brings you to my city, Mr and Mrs . . .?' He paused, brow furrowed. Of course Umut had already provided him with this information. But this was all part of the act.

The man leant forward, extending his hand. 'Van Buren, Mr Aslan. Charles Van Buren. And this is my wife, Marilyn.'

Ilhan grasped his hand, careful not to exert too much pressure. Or too little, for that matter. 'Please. Call me Ilhan.'

He turned to Marilyn Van Buren and took her hand, raising it gently to his lips. 'Charmed.' He raised his gaze, aware of the effect of his exotic good looks on foreign women, and looked deeply into her startlingly blue eyes. '*Maşallah*,' he exclaimed. He turned to Van Buren. 'Forgive me . . . it's your wife's eyes.'

Marilyn's high cheekbones flushed pink. '*Maşallah*? It's the darnedest thing – you can't imagine how many times I've heard that word since we arrived. What on *earth* does it mean?'

Reaching into a wooden box that rested on the counter, Ilhan took out a small charm and held it aloft. An indigo-blue circular disc no more than a quarter of an inch in diameter was set with a small white glass circle with a tiny black droplet at its centre. It was surrounded by a hand-beaten rim of silver surmounted by a tiny loop through which was threaded a turquoise ribbon and a small silver pin. 'This is the *nazar boncuk* . . . an amulet to ward off the evil eye.' He stood and moved towards Marilyn, glancing at Van Buren as he indicated his intent to pin it on Marilyn's yellow sundress. 'May I?'

The American nodded. 'Of course.'

Ilhan continued his explanation. 'The evil eye amulet is always blue. And so, in Turkey, to have blue eyes is very lucky. *Maşallah* – a blessing from God.' As he slid the pin through the shoulder strap of Marilyn's dress, his fingertips brushed her bare skin. She shivered imperceptibly, and he could see tiny goose bumps form on her nut-brown shoulder. She glanced up at him through thick black lashes.

Van Buren was reaching into his pocket for his wallet. 'OK – how much?'

Raising his hand in protest, Ilhan shook his head. 'Please. No. You are blessed to have such a beautiful wife. It is my good fortune to bestow a gift upon her.'

Head cocked to one side, Van Buren looked proudly at his wife. 'Yup. She's a doll. Thanks, Ilhan. Appreciate it.'

And, just like that, he knew he had them. He smiled to himself. It was too easy.

Seating himself on a low wooden stool, deliberately placing himself at a level lower than his customers, Ilhan rested his elbows on his knees and clasped his hands before him. Van Buren and his wife reclined comfortably on the banquette, visibly relaxed.

'Now. Mr and Mrs Van Buren. How did you hear about my humble store?'

'Well, it's a long story. Marilyn here has been at me for years every time we travel to Europe. "I just gotta see Constantinople, Charlie",' he mimicked. 'Isn't that right, sweetie?'

Marilyn leant forward, extending an elegantly turned ankle towards Ilhan and displaying her generous cleavage to excellent effect. 'When I was a little girl, my favourite story was *Ali Baba and the Forty Thieves*. There's just something about Arabian stories. And this place is even more romantic than I ever imagined. We went up to Topkapi yesterday to have a look around, and, gee, I'll tell you what. That place is *something*! If my dreams came true, I'd be a princess in the Sultan's harem.'

Laughing loudly, Van Buren patted his wife's knee. 'Well, honey. That'd never do.' He turned to Ilhan. 'So, seeing as how I'm not going to let this little lady become a sultan's concubine, I figure I'd better buy her something special to remember the place. We have a private guide showing us round the city – Umut Atalar – and he recommended you as a man who could show us some unusual treasures.'

'Umut is – in my humble opinion – the best in the city. He is a very capable guide. You chose well.' *And*, thought Ilhan to himself, *Umut is also very capable when it comes to lining his own pockets*. 'It would be an honour to help your beautiful wife find a souvenir from our city. I have many exquisite things worthy of such a woman.' Ilhan clapped his hands. 'Yilmaz!' His assistant entered the room and bobbed his head. Ilhan addressed him brusquely in Turkish. 'Don't bother with the rubbish. Start with the good silk carpets and a few of the large antique kilims. But no antiquities. Not yet.'

Yilmaz nodded his head. '*Evet, efendim.*' He turned and hefted a folded carpet from a pile at the back of the shop. With a practised flick of his wrists, Ilhan's assistant unfurled it with a flourish so that it billowed like a silk parachute across the floor. The intensity of the colours and intricacy of its design were breathtaking. Whorls of cobalt blue entwined with ruby red danced across a surface as lustrous as burnished copper. Intending to dazzle the Americans with the display, Yilmaz unfolded carpet after carpet, each more beautiful than the last.

'These are the best examples you will find anywhere in Istanbul. Of that, you have my word. Unfortunately, the only thing I don't have to show you at the moment is a flying carpet,' Ilhan quipped.

The Americans laughed out loud, Van Buren slapping his thigh with genuine delight at Ilhan's well-worn joke. He turned to his wife. 'Well, honey, what do you think?'

'They are simply darling. And everyone says you should buy a carpet when you go to Turkey. But we do have so many rugs already, Charlie.' She turned to Ilhan. 'Actually, I had my heart set on some jewellery.'

'Ah, of course. But you must tell me what you have in mind. I have Nomadic jewellery that is very popular with tourists to this city. Lapis lazuli, jet stone, turquoise and hand-beaten silver. It is not so expensive, but very lovely.' He paused. 'Or, if you are looking for something a little more . . . how can I put it? . . . special, then I have just acquired a piece that is quite unique. Like you, madam, it is one of a kind.'

The dealer turned and lifted a flat, lidded box from the top of the counter. He knelt at Marilyn's feet like a supplicant before a queen, and carefully opened the hinged box.

'This is from the eighteenth century. It was worn by one of the Sultan's wives.'

The American woman drew her breath in sharply. 'Oh, Charlie! This is stunning!'

Nestled in the box and set against black velvet was a necklace made of shiny silver discs chased with elaborate gold and black filigree. Hanging from the centremost disc was an inverted crescent embellished with teardrop ruby pendants, each the size of a lemon pip. Ilhan had no idea whether or not it had ever actually graced a royal décolletage. But, he justified to himself, if it hadn't, it certainly should have. He stood and lifted the necklace from the display box. 'Yilmaz! The mirror!'

Marilyn held her long blonde hair atop her head as Ilhan secured the necklace around her throat. She turned to appraise her reflection in the mirror held aloft by Ilhan's assistant. 'Oh, wow.' She spun around, letting her hair cascade back across her shoulders. 'Honey . . . what do you think?'

'Well, sweetie, I may regret it once Ilhan here tells me the damage. But you look magic.'

'Please, let us not concern ourselves with such mundane details, Mr Van Buren,' Ilhan protested, knowing instantly there would be no need to show the American couple the cheaper alternatives. 'Let us simply enjoy the view.' He paused. 'It has only taken two hundred years, but I think, at last, this treasure has found a woman who is worthy of it. She would put a queen to shame.'

As his wife continued to preen in front of the mirror, Van Buren turned to Ilhan. 'Now, buddy. Let's get serious here. She's found her trinket. But I want to see what you've got stashed under the counter.'

Ilhan feigned ignorance. 'Mr Van Buren, everything I have to sell here in my gallery is on display. There is no reason I would have anything hidden away.'

Standing, Van Buren took Ilhan's elbow and led him into one of the corners of the store, lowering his voice conspiratorially. 'Look, this other stuff is great. But, let's face it, I haven't seen anything yet that I couldn't find at any of the other shops in the Bazaar. Umut told me that you were the go-to guy if I wanted things that might be . . . well . . . a little harder to get my hands on.'

'I'm not sure what Umut was referring to, Mr Van Buren. But if I did have access to certain things, what might you be interested in?'

'Well, Ilhan . . . it's one of the few things Marilyn and I have in common. When we travel, we both like to pick up a souvenir or two to take home with us. She,' a tilt of his head towards Marilyn, still admiring herself in the mirror, 'has put together a mighty fine collection of jewellery. And me? Well, I've got a thing for antiquities. Do you think that's something you can help me with?'

The ceiling fan whirred, stirring the humid air. Van Buren dabbed beads of sweat from his brow as Ilhan stood stock-still, waiting and watching the desire mount in the American's eyes.

'Well, Mr Van Buren. As you are no doubt well aware, here in Turkey we have the greatest archaeological heritage of any land. Thousands of years' worth of treasure buried beneath our feet. Everywhere, the ground is full of precious things.' He drew a deep breath, gazing into the distance for dramatic effect. 'When I was a child, I grew up on my family's farm on the Aegean coast. Near Pergamum. You know Pergamum?'

Van Buren nodded. 'Sure. That temple – that's quite a place. Best thing I've seen since Mount Rushmore.'

'Well, in the fields around Pergamum, ancient artefacts lie as thick on the ground as snow in winter. So, as a child, I began collecting the things I found. It became something of an obsession with me. Now, when I visit the villages in the mountains and plains of Anatolia, sometimes the families who sell me carpets also find beautiful objects they wish to sell. The farmer's lot is hard in this country. This is one of the only ways they can support their families. And I feel it is my duty to assist them.' He looked down at his hands and smiled. 'I would also rather these treasures are with me than with someone who won't love them as I do.'

'So, what you're saying is that you do have some other things to sell that aren't out on display?'

Ilhan shook his head. 'No. What I am saying is that, although I do have a collection of antiquities that I store here, they are not for sale. They belong to me.'

Van Buren would not be deterred. 'Could I see them?'

Running his fingers through his thick, dark hair, Ilhan shook his head. 'Well . . . this is a personal issue for me, you understand?' He laughed wryly. 'This is my own collection of souvenirs.'

Marilyn had tired of admiring her own reflection and joined the two men. 'What are you fellas talking about?'

'Well, sweetie, Ilhan was just deciding whether or not to show us his antiques.'

Reaching out to clutch Ilhan's forearm, Marilyn moved towards the Turk, batting her eyelashes theatrically. 'Oh, Ilhan. Pleeease. Charlie here just *loves* old things. *Pleeeeease* show us?'

Sighing heavily, Ilhan capitulated. 'How can I refuse the queen? Yes, you can see my collection.'

He turned to Yilmaz, who stood patiently in the corner still clutching the oval mirror, and directed him in Turkish. 'Now it gets interesting. Get the Hacilar figurine and pottery, and the Greek urn. Oh, and the Neolithic bulls from Eskitepe.'

Yilmaz nodded. '*Evet, efendim.*'

Ilhan turned to the Americans and addressed them gravely. 'You must understand that these artefacts are not for sale.

14

They are my personal property. I am showing you because you are connoisseurs of beautiful things.'

Reseating himself on the banquette, Van Buren leant back and winked. 'Sure thing, Ilhan. Whatever you say.'

'Oh, honey. It's just like the ones we saw in the museum . . .'

Van Buren held the goddess figurine reverentially between his thick fingers. He turned her in his palms, caressing the waxy patina of the clay and feeling the swell of her hips and pointed peaks of her weighty breasts. He shook his head. 'No . . . this one's much better. She's an absolute beauty. Seven thousand years old?'

'You have a good eye.' Ilhan watched the American closely.

'But, Ilhan, man to man . . . How do I know this is the real deal?'

'Mr Van Buren, two years ago I was in the south-east buying kilims when I heard that an old man had stumbled on a Neolithic gravesite in his field. He showed me the burial . . . he dug it out with his own hands.' Ilhan leant over to take the figurine from Van Buren. He placed it back in its velvet-lined box on the shop's counter and resumed his seat. 'But, anyway; its authenticity should be of no concern to you because it's not for sale.'

The bell above the door jangled as someone shouldered their way forcefully into the shop. Ilhan leapt to his feet and swooped with hawk-like efficiency towards the Hacilar figurine. Cheated, the statuette was snatched away from beneath his outstretched fingers.

A bull of a man stood in the centre of the store, legs braced in a fighter's stance. Taller than Ilhan by a head, a crumpled corduroy jacket hung from his broad shoulders.

He cradled the ancient goddess in suntanned hands the size of baseball mitts. The man drew a deep breath and then spoke in English. 'Aslan . . . You are a dog and a thief.' The interloper brandished the figurine, clutching it tightly in an upraised fist. 'You have no right to this! None at all. Not something this important. It should be in a museum.'

Ilhan crossed his arms defensively in front of his chest and addressed the stranger calmly. 'Benedict Hitchens. Return my property and get out of my store.' He glanced over his shoulder and switched to Turkish. 'Yilmaz! Fetch the police!'

Ilhan's white-faced assistant nodded and darted out the front door. The Van Burens stood stock-still, dumbstruck.

Jutting his jaw forward aggressively, the man confronted the dealer. 'And what will you tell the police?'

'The truth. That figurine is my property. I purchased it, and it is a part of my personal collection. I was just showing it to my friends here. And as long as it remains in the country, I am breaking no laws.' He extended his hand. 'But you already know that. Now, if you please, give it back to me.'

Benedict Hitchens' bluster began to falter. Reluctantly he handed the goddess back to Ilhan. 'You have no right. No right at all. When you do this, you steal from the people of Turkey.'

Ilhan placed the figurine back in its display box. 'I fail to see how that is possible, Mr Hitchens, given that I, myself, am a Turkish person. I can hardly steal from myself, now, can I?'

The man directed his impotent rage towards the Van Burens. 'And you people . . . thanks to you, scum like him stay in business.' He pointed at the ancient goddess nestling serenely in her velvet bed. 'I assume you realise smuggling is a serious offence in Turkey? These Neolithic figurines are disappearing as quickly as they can whip them out of the ground.

They're priceless, and this example is the best I've ever seen. Believe me, I'd know. And no one person should be allowed to own her.'

The archaeologist's suntanned brow creased deeply above sea-green eyes and he shook his head in disgust, lifting his hand in a failed attempt to smooth a lock of unruly sandy-blond hair from falling into his eyes. He fired a parting salvo at Ilhan, jabbing his finger angrily towards his chest. 'You think you're so bloody clever, don't you? But one day you'll slip up, and – mark my words – I'll be here to cheer as you fall.'

He turned and stamped out of the shop, slamming the door behind him.

For a moment the three people left in his wake were silent. Ilhan drew a deep breath. 'What can I say? Other than to offer my sincere apologies for that man's behaviour.'

Van Buren stood transfixed, watching the archaeologist's imposing profile as he disappeared into the crowd. 'Benedict Hitchens. That name . . .'

'Mr Hitchens originally hails from your part of the world. For a while he was the most famous archaeologist on the planet. But he has been operating under something of a cloud of late – he was caught up in a major antiquities theft. And now he is on a personal crusade to drive honest dealers like me out of business.' Ilhan sighed deeply. 'The man is quite out of control. I am terribly sorry you were exposed to that ugliness.'

Walking towards the counter, Ilhan lifted the box containing the figurine and moved to close its lid. 'He was right, though. It *is* illegal to take antiquities out of the country.' He gestured towards the necklace resting against Marilyn's throat. 'Even that "trinket", I'm afraid, madam.'

He glanced at the couple. Marilyn's fingertips caressed the strands of the Ottoman necklace hungrily, and Van Buren's jaw was clenched, his eyes fixed on the box in Ilhan's hands.

The American held out his hand. 'Whoa, whoa. Now, wait just a minute there, Ilhan. Don't be so hasty. I haven't taken orders from anyone since I was in the army. And I'll tell you this for free – I'm not gonna start today. Now. Where were we?'

Ilhan smiled.

# 2

## Istanbul, Turkey, 1955

B enedict Hitchens sat in the first-floor bay window of
the *lokanta* opposite Ilhan Aslan's store, eyes fixed on the
entrance; waiting.

Before him sat a half-eaten dish of *mantı*. The tiny beef-
filled parcels of dough soused in minty yoghurt sauce were
usually enough to tempt his appetite out of hiding. But today
was different. Picking at the food unenthusiastically, his mind
was elsewhere.

The open square outside the restaurant was teeming with
life. Men in suits sauntered between their workplaces and the
innumerable tiny kebab salons and *lokantas* that serviced
the businesses in and around the Grand Bazaar. As was
common in Middle Eastern societies, many of them walked
companionably in pairs with their arms linked. Beneath the
shadow of Constantine's Column, the Çemberlitaş Sütunu,
tourist buses idled, having surrendered their passengers to
the eager tour guides who gathered in a swarm along the
Divan Yolu end of the square.

He was always struck by the irony any time he found himself in Çemberlitaş. The monumental porphyry column was erected in 330 AD by Emperor Constantine as the city's focal point when he nominated his eponymous metropolis as the new capital of the Roman Empire. These days, the burnt stump of the mighty monument was nothing more than a convenient meeting point for tourists from across the seas, come to pick over the bones of this once great city. Kemal Atatürk had rung the death knell for Istanbul when he shifted the capital of the modern Turkish state to the windswept and dusty central Anatolian town of Ankara in 1923. After that, the ancient city on the Bosphorus lost its meaning and its purpose. These days, 'New Rome' had the air of a soon-to-be decommissioned amusement park. Like the disintegrating column, Istanbul in 1955 was a sorry sight.

Picking at a thread coming loose from the worn cuff of his corduroy jacket, Ben smiled to himself, all too aware of his hypocrisy. He was in no position to be criticising anyone or anything for being a little frayed around the edges. Drawing a soft pack of cigarettes from his breast pocket, the American sighed deeply and struck a light from a matchbook lying on the tabletop. Flicking ash into the ashtray with one hand, he caught a glimpse of his reflection in the plate-glass window and tried unsuccessfully to recall the moment he had begun to transform into a caricature of his former self.

More than twenty years spent working outdoors in the unforgiving sun of the Middle East had left him with deep lines at the corners of his eyes and a furrowed brow permanently etched into suntanned skin. He gazed at his worn lace-up brown brogues and threadbare chinos, stained grey about the knees from years spent kneeling in the dust. Yes, he was a walking cliché.

It was convenient to use the Turkish police force as a scapegoat for his downfall. And it was true that their unrelenting scrutiny made it difficult for him to reinvent himself. He glanced up. His two minders for the day were perched at a table at the rear of the shop. It was a little insulting that they no longer made any attempt to hide from him.

At first the men following him had made a sincere effort to blend into the crowd and remain unseen, so it had been some months before he noticed. The first time he'd suspected he was under surveillance was when he observed the same two men who had been seated behind him at a *lokanta* in Pera queuing for the same ferry bound for Kadıköy. He had climbed the stairs towards the upper deck of the boat to gaze out over Istanbul's iconic skyline. Standing on the opposite side of the deck, the two men self-consciously and pointedly looked in every direction other than towards him. He dismissed this as a coincidence until the same men reappeared at the *meyhane* where he was dining that evening. Despite the deliberately convoluted route he took home, they continued to trail him, arm in arm and feigning interest in the contents of a window display of wedding gowns when he paused to tie his shoelace in an attempt to catch them out. The next day, a friend spoke with a contact in the police force and confirmed he had been under surveillance for three months. Ben didn't bother to ask why.

He butted out the dying embers of his cigarette, glancing towards the antique store across the plaza. He could see movement within, silhouettes edging towards the doorway.

The American couple stepped out onto the cobbled street, the man clutching a small carpet tied into a tight roll and tucked under his arm. With her arm hooked through his, the woman flicked her golden mane nervously over her shoulder and glanced skittishly around her, guilt emanating from her like rays from the sun.

He wondered why people had to be so depressingly pre-dictable.

Standing and pushing his chair back with a clatter, the American threw enough change down on the table to cover his bill, and strode towards the stairs. Passing the undercover policemen, he addressed them in fluent Turkish, 'Please . . . stay and finish your tea. I'm just going back across the road to the antique store. I won't leave till you're done.'

The two men blinked, aghast. Before they could respond, he was gone.

He barrelled across the square, aware of the disapproving glances shot his way by the predominantly Turkish crowd. Undignified haste was not considered proper in this city. But it had been a long time since Benedict Hitchens had cared much what anyone thought about him.

A sleek black limousine pulled up outside Ilhan's store. A chauffeur in a peaked cap leapt from the driver's seat and opened the back door with a flourish. The man and woman ducked their heads and disappeared behind tinted windows. The car sped away into the labyrinthine network of alleyways that crisscrossed Sultanahmet's steep hills.

Across the street, the door of Ilhan Aslan's shop was shut. A small sign hung from a brass chain. *Kapali*. Closed.

Striding across the cobbles, Ben banged on the glass with a clenched fist. 'Come on . . . Come on!' he muttered beneath his breath.

A curtain at the rear of the store moved as someone peered out. Ilhan appeared from the gloom and unlatched the bolt on the front door.

'"Scum"? One day, you will go too far, Ben. I might take offence.'

Stepping into the store, Ben clapped Ilhan on the shoulder. 'It was intended as a term of endearment. Far be it from me to pass judgement upon scum.' He paused. 'So, judging by their faces when they left, we had another success?'

Reaching into his breast pocket, Ilhan withdrew a fat bill roll and peeled off a thick wad.

Ben counted out some of the notes. 'Send this off to Crete for me, will you? Same address. If I keep it all, I'll just piss it up against a wall.'

'It's been a long time. When are you going to do more than just send money? You could deliver it in person, you know.'

As always, the thought of Crete and the mess he had left behind made Ben want to curl in on himself like a dying moth. 'That wouldn't be doing anyone any favours. And not to put too fine a point on it, Ilhan . . . but it's none of your bloody business. I'm doing my best.'

Eager to change the subject, the American tucked the remainder of the money into his wallet. 'Don't you ever feel slightly uneasy about taking so much money for something so completely worthless?'

'Not for a moment. Do you?'

'No. Philistines like that? They deserve it. The real thing would be wasted on them. As Petronius put it: "*Mundus vult decipi, ergo decipiatu*" – "The world wishes to be deceived, so let it be".' He seated himself in the path of the cool air circulated by the fan and leant back against the velvet banquette, arms stretched out along the plump cushions.

'I notice you have yourself some new friends today. Haven't seen those two before.' Ilhan gestured outside to where the undercover policemen had relocated themselves to a bench seat opposite the store.

'Swarthy complexions, thick moustaches, terrible suits . . . they're all starting to look the same to me.' Ben smiled. 'I've been meaning to ask – how is it that those gentlemen always have me in their sights when we complete one of our transactions? Yet they never try to stop it. They must know what's going on in here. So why are they giving me such a hard time while you get to do whatever you want?'

'No great mystery, my friend. I pay them. You don't.'

'Well, perhaps if you paid me more, I could do something about that.'

'Speaking of which – and by that I mean addressing your state of abject poverty – Raphael is finished. He's expecting us. We need to be on the next ferry to the Asian side.'

A sickening rush of what was either dread or anticipation rushed through his guts. It was disappointing to realise he could no longer distinguish between the two sensations. He took the coward's way out and changed the subject. 'Reminds me of something funny I overheard the other day. A couple of Englishmen were talking – one was telling the other he was keen to visit the Asian side of the city because he wanted to try Chinese food. Bloody tourists. Idiots.'

Ilhan ignored him. 'Didn't you hear me? It's done.'

Ben sighed. There was no avoiding it. 'Finished? Already? He's good.'

'That's what I've been telling you. He is the best. But he is also an impatient shit. Now come on. You know how he is when we keep Turkey time.'

'Sons of whores – you keep me waiting!'

Ben and Ilhan ambled up the steep street behind the Kadıköy markets towards a wild-eyed gnomish man standing on the stoop of a three-storeyed *yalı*, waving his hands in the air as if he were signalling an aircraft coming in to land.

The ramshackle terrace house was held together by little more than a thick layer of peeling paint, a girdle of tangled ivy and a lot of good luck.

Striding up the slumped steps, Ilhan clapped his hands on the small man's shoulders and kissed him on both cheeks. 'You are the only Italian I have ever met who cares so much about time, Raphael. Besides, we're only thirty minutes past the hour.'

'So that is thirty minutes more you keep me waiting before I retire to my salon.'

'Salon? Is that what you call it?'

'*Testa di cazzo*!' Raphael Donazetti mumbled under his breath. He turned to Ben and embraced him. 'These Mohammedans. Pleasure they do not understand.'

Ben laughed. 'If you knew Ilhan as I do, Raphael, you wouldn't say that. He's usually the last man standing. And he gets the girl more often than not.'

The Italian raised his eyebrows sceptically and shrugged. 'They choose him over you? No! I will not believe that! *Impossibile*!' He stood back and opened his door, waving them into the house.

No matter how many times Ben made the journey across to the Asian side of the city to visit Raphael Donazetti, stepping across the threshold of the Italian's workshop remained an overwhelming experience. The ground floor was a halfway house for every imaginable ancient artefact. Even for Ben, identifying which among them were authentic was next to impossible. A pair of marble Graeco-Roman wrestlers struggled for breathing space beside an Egyptian sarcophagus lying in repose atop an elaborately carved Byzantine reliquary. Cabinets set against the walls were jammed full of cardboard boxes containing what looked like Neolithic stone and bone tools, animal figurines and Bronze and Iron

Age spearheads that could have been thousands of years old, but were just as likely made only yesterday. Orthodox icons stared mournfully from the walls, cheek by jowl with erotic wall panels showing Indian deities entwined in dauntingly gymnastic sexual positions.

When he'd first visited Raphael's workshop, the Italian had explained to Ben that it was an important part of the forger's art to study originals with a degree of scrutiny not permissible in the great museums of the world. Early in his career, he had discovered that the security guards at the Louvre did not look kindly upon people who climbed barriers to examine at close quarters the teeth marks of tools used by the sculptors who made the *Venus de Milo*. After a rather uncomfortable encounter with the director of the museum in which he only just managed to charm his way out of a visit to a Parisian jail cell, Raphael decided it would be best to acquire his own, original, artefacts to study.

Manoeuvring through the room, Ben squinted to see through air hazy with a fog of plaster dust and tobacco smoke. What spare wall space was not covered in works of art was hung with large sheets of butcher's paper emblazoned with Raphael's scribblings recording the ingredients and chemical formulae that were the tools of his trade. Any time he paid Raphael a visit, the Italian had a pot or beaker of something bubbling away on a gas burner. As he told it, given time, he could replicate anything; world-class forgery was as much science as it was art.

A shallow dish balancing on a column of dusty archaeological journals caught his eye. Roughly the same size as a dinner plate, its surface was covered with a buff-white slip and over-painted with dark umber geometric designs. Ben picked it up, tapping the fired ceramic with the signet ring on his pinkie finger to test it for the right resonance. Tilting it on an angle in a shaft of direct sunlight, he examined the consistency and distribution of the paint as it lay on the dish's chalky surface.

'Mesopotamian. Ubaid II, 4200 BC or thereabouts.' He searched for the clues the craftsman had left on the base. 'Probably from the Persian Gulf settlements.' Its form and design were instantly identifiable to anyone who knew anything about Near Eastern archaeology.

The Italian stood at the other side of the room, black eyes sparkling and arms crossed. He was clearly enjoying himself.

'At least that's what it *looks* like. The baked clay has the right biscuity consistency, that's for sure. Jesus, Raphael.' He laughed. 'I can't tell if I'm looking at an original or not.'

Raphael raised his hand above his head with a flourish. 'You and every curator *per tutta l'Europa*. You never believed me, but you name a museum – all have on display my "homages".' His eyes gleamed with pride.

'The Met?'

'. . . a Neolithic carving – is pride of its collection. *Magnifico*!'

'The British Museum?'

'. . . too many Old Master drawings to count. Of those I am very proud.'

'The Louvre?'

'. . . gold and silver Graeco-Roman coins. Perfect.'

'The Hermitage?'

'Ah, well the Iron Curtain blocks my view, *sì*? Maybe I will never know, eh? But even the communists, I am sure they cannot resist the beauty of my work.'

A scornful expression contorted Raphael's features. '*Pezzi di merda*! Art experts. With their "connoisseurship", their "expertise". Dancing from one side of room to other, little berets on little heads, big cravats on chicken necks, pointy noses up in air, lips pushed together like cat anus. They think they know everything. Pah! Is one thing only they do well.

*Fare una sega* . . . you know, Ben?' The little man cupped his hand in the air at his groin, jerking his wrist feverishly in a disturbingly accurate simulacrum of self-abuse. 'Is why I stop making my own art. My dealer in Rome, she say, "Raphael, you will be bigger than Picasso! More famous than Michelangelo! The world, it will be falling at your feet!" *Fica stretta!* They want I should be one of them. *Non mi rompere i coglione!* Better I should make love to my own sister. Now, I make the art to make of them all a donkey's *culo*.'

When it came to curses, Ben's Italian vocabulary was sadly lacking. But the vehemence with which Raphael spat out his words made translation unnecessary. The venom in the Italian's face said it all.

During Raphael's impassioned rant, Ilhan had been sidling his way towards a door on the other side of the room, hands pressed to his chest and hips swivelling to maintain clearance from the impressive accumulation of dust lying upon every surface. He made it to the threshold with his neatly pressed dark pants and slim-fitting suit jacket virtually unscathed. Turning to face Ben and Raphael, he spread his hands expansively. 'Gentlemen, our time is limited. Shall we inspect the fruits of our labour?'

Clapping his hands together, Raphael rose on his toes. '*Sì! Basta!* Enough! Come. I show you.'

'Raphael, this is perfect. Absolutely perfect.'

Turning the Cycladic idol in his hands, Ben felt the heavy, creamy marble cool against his skin. The statuette was as long as his forearm. Its flat, shovel-shaped head was featureless apart from a long, fine nose. The elegantly modelled face tilted heavenward and sat atop a swan-like neck emerging from broad shoulders. On the idol's torso, deeply carved geometric incisions indicated arms crossed beneath small, pointed breasts and above two lines forming a v-shaped pudendum. Several hair-fine fracture lines filled with a stark white adhesive where the statuette had been repaired were all that marred an otherwise pristine – and utterly bogus – example of one of the most desirable ancient artefacts on the market.

The Italian bowed. 'It is my pleasure to be introducing you to the three treasures of the Avi Steigmeier collection. Bought in Athens at Apollonia Galleries in 1923. Lost since Nazi *puttane* send Steigmeier to ovens and fat *porco* Göring steal away his collection. Now, is miracle! They are found! Or so we say, yes?'

In one corner of the crowded room stood a tall, lightly muscled and youthful figure carved in marble, hands clenched into fists at his sides, hair falling about his shoulders in intricate braids, and a beatific smile illuminating his face. At his side stood a voluptuous female figure, the marble chiselled masterfully to replicate translucent folds of diaphanous fabric falling over full breasts, gently swollen belly and fleshy thighs. She was sadly bereft of a head.

'They are quite extraordinary, Raphael,' Ben said.

Placing an affectionate and paternal hand on each of the two monumental statues, the Italian beamed with pride. 'I am just craftsman. Is the secrets you gave me, Ben, that makes these *perfetto*. The *kouros*, he made from marble from Thasos – same quarry used by Archaic Greeks two thousand five hundred years ago. Hellenistic Venus, you tell me to use marble from Paros like genius sculptor Praxiteles. I do. And our *bella* goddess from Cyclades? I find beautiful white stone on Naxos. See it sparkle like diamonds? Is most beautiful stone I ever see!'

'And that's why everybody wants the real, four and a half thousand year old Naxos figurines.' Ben continued to fondle the pitted surface of the Cycladic statuette, marvelling at the convincing patina. 'Exquisite. And it's aged so perfectly. Raphael, you are an evil genius.'

'*Grazie*. But it is not so difficult. I tell you. First I break them – that is hardest part. Is not easy for my soul. My beautiful work in pieces. But is necessary so breaks also look old. Never you find statue this big in one piece. Then quick bath in acid makes wear on the stone. Next, some time sitting in sand at the bottom of a river.' He laughed. 'But not a fast river, I learn in my early days. *Merda*! The time I use a river in winter . . . I not think of what happens with water in spring when snow melts. I go back . . . all my work gone! You wait! One day a *finocchio* with good luck, he will be finding the Sumerian king figure I lost that day. Ha! It will be changing history. Archaeologists like you, Ben; they will wonder, "How is it? Sumerian statue on Aegean coast? No! It cannot be!" I think of this, it make me laugh! I think, now is worth losing statue to make such a big joke!' Raphael slapped his thigh with glee. 'But this time, no problem. I put in locked crate made of metal grille and tied with chain to post on shore. After six months, I pull up crate, I make jigsaw and stick together. *Finito*!'

Raphael lifted a manila folder from a cluttered desk and brandished it above his head. 'But your work in here, Ben . . . your work, she make all of us rich men. All your research. Without this, these "homages" we make, they no more than just pretty things. These papers – these so-called "provenance". Is what *figli di puttana* experts want. *Idioti del cazzo*! They think we cannot make forgery of bits of paper too?'

Ben carefully extracted a sheet of flimsy paper from the file. The Italian explained. 'I do what you tell me. I make letter from Professor Hedley Moore comparing our *kouros* with one in Athens National Museum. Also, letter from Director of British Museum asking Avi Steigmeier to loan Venus for exhibition.'

'And what if someone thinks to ask them?' Ilhan stood by the desk, arms crossed tightly at his chest.

'To ask them, they need to find, how you say . . .? Gypsy woman who speaks with spirit world . . . Both men now dead, you see. Nobody know they not write these letters. I find paper from 1920s, use Remington typewriter – also from 1920s. And receipts from Apollonia Galleries. I take original you find, then make print block to copy letterhead, print new receipts. The numbers you find in Apollonia archive, I make them match numbers on these receipts. Anybody looks, they find description in archive of real Steigmeier statues. Evidence is perfect and nobody suspect nothing.'

The Steigmeier collection had been an easy target. During his lifetime the Jewish collector had been notoriously paranoid about keeping details of his vast holdings of priceless antiquities out of the public eye. Although his collection had been meticulously catalogued, Avi Steigmeier refused to allow it to be illustrated and so unwittingly created what amounted to a forger's manual; it contained physical descriptions, detailed provenance and scholarly essays about each work. But they had not been seen in public for decades and without any images, no one could ever really be sure what the artworks looked like.

'My statues – they probably better than originals. With these papers, is perfect. And, the Steigmeiers? Hitler – that *faccia di cazzo* – he make sure no Steigmeiers are around to say differently.' The Italian crossed himself. '*Riposa in pace.* But, is good for us.'

'Yeah. I suppose.' Ben's stomach clenched at the thought that they were exploiting the Steigmeier family's grim end for financial gain. He was relieved to know he had yet to lose the last shreds of humanity still dangling from the frayed edges of his soul.

'And . . .' Raphael took a second file from the desk. 'Here is other documents you ask for. I do exactly like you say. So-called provenance for your artefact? Is also perfect, like all my work. But, Ben – is hard for me to understand. Why so much trouble for something I think is – forgive me, I no try be rude – not worth much money?'

Ben inspected the pieces of paper. The Italian was right. They were faultless. 'It's hard to explain, Raphael. All that matters is that your paperwork here draws the attention of the people I need to see it in the auction.'

'You sell authentic antiquity, Ben. Not like my work . . . you no need no papers.'

'As I say – it's difficult to explain.'

Ilhan chuckled. 'I wish I could enlighten you, Raphael. But most of the time I, too, have trouble understanding what motivates this sorry excuse for a man.' He patted Ben affectionately on the shoulder. 'Now, enough of the self-congratulatory celebrations, you two. Let's not forget – how would you have brought this coup to pass without the copious amounts of cash I have injected into the venture? All those visits to idyllic Greek islands, Raphael. It's surprising it took a whole month to find one piece of marble on Naxos. You can't have been looking very hard.'

The Italian glared at the Turk, curled his right arm, flattened his hand, and flicked the underside of his chin with his fingertips. '*Se ti prendo ti faccio un culo cosi*! *Vaffanculo*!'

Unaccustomed to playing the role of diplomat, Ben stepped between the two men. 'Gentlemen, gentlemen. It is getting late, and we all have other places to be.' He turned to Ilhan. 'So you have all you need?'

Ilhan's eyes were fixed on the Italian. 'Yes. If it doesn't inconvenience the maestro too much, a representative from Sotheby's is here to escort these back to London and ensure nobody gets cold feet. They'll be arranging it sometime in the next day or two. As far as they're concerned, I'm an intermediary for a dealer who bought the statues after the war and wants to remain anonymous. They've used the catalogue descriptions I sent them and the provenance you created, Ben. There wasn't time to photograph them for the catalogue, of course. That took some explaining. But, in the end, they didn't care. The catalogue should be arriving any day.'

Ben turned to face Raphael. 'So, you're confident they're ready to go?'

'They are perfect.' The Italian clapped his hands together. 'So. Gentlemen. We are done. Madame Thuy and her pipe wait for me. Now that the business it is finished, I invite you to join me in the chasing of the dragon.'

Ben raised his hand in protest and shook his head emphatically. 'Not for me, thanks. I don't need to add opium to my growing list of vices. My organs couldn't deal with another poison.'

The Italian shrugged his shoulders theatrically. 'It is the loss of yours, *amico*.'

The taxi dropped Ilhan and Ben in Divan Yolu. The sun had passed its zenith, but had lost none of its bite, grilling the edges of the chestnut leaves brown and singeing black shadows onto the cobblestones. On the street, pedestrians moved languidly in the shade cast by an umbrella of soaring branches.

The two men stopped outside Ilhan's store.

'So, now things move quickly.' Ilhan plucked at Ben's threadbare jacket. 'And perhaps, at last, we can do something about updating your wardrobe. It doesn't reflect well on me to be seen in public with you. You look like a beggar.'

'If you're so ashamed of me, let's get inside. Or are we just going to stand out here baking in the sun? What about the famous Turkish hospitality?'

The Turk shrugged. 'No time for that now, my friend. Yilmaz is looking after the shop for the rest of the day. I have business to take care of.' He patted his breast pocket, still plump with the Van Burens' money. 'You should see it! There is a new shipment of antiquities just in from the south-east . . . Authentic ones, this time . . . You should come with me.'

'You're trying to get me tangled up with outright theft now? No thanks!' Ben shook his head and laughed wryly. 'Forgeries are bad enough. I'm struggling to hold on to the few scruples I have left. But how about we catch up later tonight . . .?'

'You've forgotten already? Ah, *abi*. That wonderful brain of yours. I fear you're pickling it. Keep drinking as much raki as you do, and your skull will become a bowl of *karışık turşu*.'

'Pickled vegetables, you say? You never told me you were planning a career change. Comedian now, is it?'

Ilhan ignored him. 'The representative from Sotheby's. I thought it would be best to meet somewhere informal – share a meal. Not that they're going to suspect anything, but it would be advisable to be somewhere we can relax. But not too relaxed, remember. Don't disgrace yourself. Or me, for that matter. You're only there as window dressing.' He looked the American up and down. 'Shabby as that dressing may be.'

'Is that what you call being "brutally honest"?'

'No. It's what I call "self-preservation". I've invested too much time and money in this to see it turned on its head. Speaking of which, don't forget to bring –'

'Yes, yes. I know. I'll have it.'

'I wasn't joking before, Ben. What you're doing doesn't make sense. It's been such a long time. You've held on to that thing for so long. Why risk exposing yourself now?'

'It's my only chance, Ilhan. If it leads me where I think it's going to, I'll finally be able to show those morons I wasn't lying. Not to mention, I need to find out what happened to her.'

'So be it. But you know this won't work out well, don't you? She wasn't what I'd call your lucky charm. Not that you ever take my advice.' His friend shrugged and glanced at his watch. 'So I won't waste any more of my time. Speaking of which, I'd best be off. See you tonight.'

Walking along the narrow street leading down the hill away from the square, Ben negotiated the groups of men who gathered on the pavement outside stores provisioned to tempt the tourists. One glance told the touts that Benedict Hitchens was a complete waste of time.

He knew he should be excited that they were nearing the culmination of many months' work, and that the outcome would be a financial windfall that came at very little personal cost to himself. He was far enough removed from the process that he felt relatively detached from the elaborate deception he, Raphael and Ilhan had concocted. But Ben was also strangely bereft. It was a response that could only be attributed to the dawning realisation that he was about to relinquish the one remaining tangible link he had to her.

He was deeply conflicted every time he thought of Eris. Ilhan was right. It had been a long time, although the guilt and pain caused by her loss still weighed heavily in his gut. But she had left him the one thing that could be his salvation and for that he would always be grateful to her. It could also be Ben's downfall – the proverbial nail in a coffin that was already halfway into the grave. Summoning up the eternal optimist within, he chose to ignore that side of the equation.

In the streets around him, the daily rhythm of life in the ancient city continued unchecked. In the courtyard outside Nuruosmaniye mosque, *hadjis* went through the motions of ritual ablution as they prepared for prayer. Perching on low stools, they bathed their hands and feet in the clear water gushing from brass taps at the base of a blindingly white marble fountain. Whispery hair and age-spotted scalps were topped with finely embroidered white skullcaps showing that those old bones and bunioned feet had undertaken the arduous pilgrimage to Mecca and attained the fifth pillar of Islam.

Downhill, away from the orbit of the tourist buses, were the markets frequented by the locals. Fraying canvas sunshades extended into the street from storefronts, providing shoppers with shelter from the fierce summer sun. Ben sidled past groups of women haggling with traders as they tested the quality of silk between their fingertips from colourful bolts stacked in piles to the roof.

Watching the women of Istanbul negotiate with the stall-holders reminded Ben of the exchange with the American tourists earlier in the day. A disturbingly familiar surge of guilt brought the bitter taste of bile to his tongue. Sometimes he wished he could emulate Ilhan's laissez-faire attitude to fleecing wealthy foreigners. But there was some comfort to be had in the knowledge that not everything he said to the

Van Burens had been an outright lie. The Neolithic figurine was the best he had ever seen – the original version, that was. And – thanks to his efforts – the seven-thousand-year-old prototype for the forgery that he had excavated in Eskitepe what felt a lifetime ago *was* in a museum. She was proudly displayed in Konya, many hundreds of miles away from Istanbul and unlikely to be on the Van Burens' travel itinerary.

He tried to convince himself that he had actually done them a favour. If the goddess had been a genuine Neolithic artefact rather than a convincing replica produced in Raphael Donazetti's workshop less than a month ago, there was a fair chance that the Van Burens would have been challenged at customs as they attempted to smuggle the goddess out of the country. The antiquities police kept a close eye on the city's dealers, and the arrival of a wealthy American couple at the business premises of a known smuggler would have sounded alarm bells if they hadn't also known that Ilhan would never be caught selling an authentic antiquity in his store. He saved that trade for the black market. If he had sold the Van Burens a genuine ancient artefact, the wrath of the Turkish police would have descended on their well-coiffed heads. Instead, they had experienced an adventure they would dine out on for the rest of their lives.

Nonetheless, Ben would rather have found another way to earn a living.

Did he feel guilty? Absolutely. Did he have any choice? No.

In the scheme of things, his scam with the Van Burens was loose change. The magnitude of the hoax he had embarked upon with Ilhan and Raphael was another thing altogether. That was fraud on a grand scale. He glanced over his shoulder at the two men trailing him. They had followed him over to the Asian side of the city, and he could only assume Raphael was well known to the antiquities police. Even the densest officer on the force would be able to figure out what was going on. He just hoped that Ilhan was paying them enough to keep their mouths shut and that he was protected by the same umbrella that kept Ilhan dry.

All those years of research and back-breaking work gone to waste, his expertise now employed to deceive and swindle. The knowledge that he had only himself to blame didn't make him feel any better.

The footsteps of the two men behind him echoed off the rough cobbles.

He wasn't proud of what he had become. But he also knew that until he could clear his name, he had little choice. Not as long as he was under constant police scrutiny. He could only hope that the dangerous game he was playing might yield some fruit.

He continued to stroll down the street towards the cacophony, chaos and noisome aromas of the docks at Eminönü.

A thought struck him. Wind back time . . . get the chance to do it all over again, would he do anything differently?

Ben sighed. Oh, for the wisdom of hindsight.

# 3

## Eskitepe, Southern Turkey, 1950

The telltale line of white fibres appeared and his heart began to race. He didn't know what, exactly, he had found. The rush of adrenalin coursing through his veins told him there was something there, and that whatever it was, it was going to be good. Years in the field had taught Ben to trust his gut.

Lightly scraping the long edge of his trowel across the surface he removed another thin layer of dust, and what had been little more than a sprinkling of fragile hair-like filaments merged into a solid band about a quarter of an inch thick. To one side of the line of plaster, the texture of the earth was different. When he tapped it lightly with the trowel's wooden handle it was as hard as baked clay and rang hollow.

*Mudbrick. Perfect.*

He picked up his brush and gently swept the surface. The rectangular profile of the bricks showed up like a chequerboard against the pale dust. Most other excavators repeatedly struck barren ground, or trenches intersected by inconveniently placed stone walls. Luck of the draw, they'd say. But not him. He would walk the site carefully – trance-like – before sinking his trench markers. He couldn't explain it, but he always knew exactly where to start – it was as if the things hidden beneath the soil were speaking to him. Time and again he plotted trenches that revealed something extraordinary. Among his peers, his uncanny ability to dowse archaeological sites had earned him the nickname 'the water diviner'. But in the superficially polite yet competitive profession where excavation permits were given to those who had the most to show for it at the end of the season, his gifts, and infamous lack of modesty, won him few friends.

'Done it again, Hitchens you old dog,' he murmured to himself under his breath.

The line of the mudbrick wall corresponded almost exactly with the string line pegged along one side of his trench. The plaster lining was an interior surface. He was digging right in the centre of a large room.

'Hey! Come!' Ben beckoned his team of workers in Turkish. Five young men who had been waiting patiently at the edge of the trench shuffled towards him, shovels, picks and buckets clunking together against their legs.

For many thousands of years, human beings had chosen to live in the exact same spot by the banks of a river in this fertile and hospitable valley. As one group of occupants moved on or were forced out, another arrived and built a new town on top of the ruins of the last, often reusing building materials left behind by earlier settlements and repurposing any worthwhile architectural edifices that remained. Layer upon layer accumulated over the millennia, creating an artificial mound – a tell, or *tepe*.

The modern town of Eskitepe clung to the tell's steep sides like a cluster of barnacles growing on a ship's hull. Those houses that were at the very centre of the settlement had been dug into the *tepe* and their unplastered interior walls offered a layer-cake view of human history. For decades, the ancient treasures poking out of the soil had been pillaged by the villagers, who saw it as their God-given right to exploit the riches lying beneath their feet. It was a steady and lucrative trade, and a welcome supplement to the meagre income they earned by toiling in the fields.

When the Turkish government gave the British Institute permission to excavate the site, they were expected to employ the local boys to work as labourers in order to feed some income back into the village. It was hoped – in vain, as it turned out – that the money would discourage the residents from conducting their own, illicit, excavations after the team left each evening to return to their hotel in Konya. They also paid the local village chief a salary to act as custodian of the site.

Ben had found that these well-intentioned tactics were about as effective as trying to bribe a dog not to lick its balls. Any time he called for a well-earned day off for the team, they returned the next day to find great holes gouged into the hillside. When he questioned the *mukhtar*, the old man shook his head dolefully. 'It was the Syrians, Ben *abi*. They came over the border in the night. They were looking for Armenian gold.' This was a bald-faced lie, and they both knew it. The Syrian border was over three hundred miles away across a virtually impassable mountain range. Ben had no choice but to bite his tongue and nod his head sympathetically; loss of face meant everything in this part of the world and he could not challenge the *mukhtar* without grave consequences for their ongoing relationship – a relationship he had to nurture to retain access to the site. It was a delicate, and often infuriating, balancing act. Diplomacy was not one of his defining characteristics.

As blinding white heat beat down on his head, he turned to address the eldest of his five workers. 'Here, Ferit.' He pointed at the line of white, now standing out starkly in the midday sun. 'This is a wall. Here? Do not dig. This is mudbrick. Don't touch it. Do you understand?' The boy nodded. 'And here,' poking his trowel at the fill that packed the room, 'here – dig four inches of dirt.' The American held out his hand flat, running it horizontally across the surface. 'Make a flat surface. Then clear the dirt with the buckets.'

He passed the boy a large canvas bag. 'Put any pieces of ceramic you find in here.' He retrieved a potsherd the size of a matchbook from the ground. 'Like this . . . this is ceramic. If you find anything else, tell me. If the soil changes – its colour, or the way it feels, stop digging and call me. Immediately. Understand?' The boy nodded again. Ferit's eyes were as animated as a puddle of sump oil. If it had been permissible to ignore Turkish social conventions, Ben would have put the youngest boy in charge of the team. Hamit was just fourteen, and had shown himself to be observant, resourceful, and whip-smart. But this counted for little in the village's rigid social hierarchy. Ferit was the eldest, and the son of one of the most important families in Eskitepe; it would have upset the natural order of things if Ben had promoted the younger boy. And so, he was forced to make do with the slow-witted Ferit.

As his team set to work chipping away at the packed soil, he took a tape measure and began plotting the wall top and plaster line in his notebook. Nervously tapping the toe of his boot against one of the stones, a roiling tangle of tension churned in his gut. This stage in the excavation was unbearable. There was no place for hustle and expediency in archaeology. He was expected to document every piece of detritus he found in case he missed some clue vital to understanding the history of this place. He understood that, but at moments like these, he hated it.

The sun continued to sweep a path across the sky, burning through his worn cotton shirt and casting hard-edged shadows on the stones beneath his feet. Beads of sweat rose on his shoulders, coalescing into a stream that trickled down his spine and soaked the waistband of his trousers. He looked up towards where the village boys were making slow progress through the trench.

'C'mon, c'mon,' he hissed through gritted teeth.

Standing on the summit of the *tepe*, he listened to the gurgle and slosh of the river far below. Unhooking the canteen from his belt, he took a swig of utterly unsatisfying lukewarm water and grimaced. As the workers had cleared more and more of the fill from the room, with nothing much to show for it other than a growing pile of bags overflowing with nondescript pottery fragments, he began to question himself.

The wall was now exposed to a depth of three feet. The plaster surface was blindingly white but utterly featureless. He had no idea how far they would have to dig to find the floor, but it was now a race against time. On an archaeological site like this, the earliest deposits were at the bottom. If someone dug into a deeper, earlier level, and brought older objects into a more recent context, it disrupted the site's chronological sequence. In archaeological terms, it was a disaster. Now the sun was sinking towards the horizon. It wouldn't be long before the light disappeared, and Ben knew the looters would be hovering like vultures. There was no doubt this room was important, and they would know it too. They would focus their attentions on his trench and by tomorrow whatever secrets it held would be gone.

Walking slowly along the wall, he examined the point where it vanished beneath the dun-grey dust, desperately seeking a hint of what might lay beneath. Something caught his eye. A wire-thin shadow ran along the base of the wall where it met the dirt. It wasn't much – just a foot or so in length.

*Probably nothing*, he thought to himself.

Heart pounding, he dropped to his knees and ran his fingers carefully along the wall. Where it emerged from the packed earth, a plaster-covered lip curled back and away from the surface of the wall. It was too narrow to be a door or a window, but it certainly wasn't an accidental breach in the wall – it was neatly finished and thickly coated in plaster, just like the rest of the room. It was deliberate. Too narrow for a door or window meant just one thing – it was most likely the top edge of a niche set back into the wall. And one thing any archaeologist knew was that the only reason a niche was made in a wall like this was to create a prominent showcase for something important.

Ben considered his options. The 'by-the-book' approach would be to recall his resting workers and get them to continue removing carefully measured spits of fill across the entire trench, exposing the niche in stages.

Too laborious, and too risky, he concluded. *If I don't get this done now, the 'Syrians' will be back tonight to finish the job for me.*

It was an easy choice. With the tip of his trowel, he scraped a line delineating a smaller area within the trench, the niche at its apex, and began to dig.

Word spread quickly around the site after his workers returned from their tea break to find him on his knees, carefully scraping, brushing and digging to remove the packed earth from an inset in the wall. The alcove was the size of a large shoebox.

As the chisel-shaped top of a headdress appeared above the dust, and beneath it almond-shaped eyes and an aquiline nose, a buzz of excitement galvanised the spectators. They cast shadows across the wall as they pressed closer, blocking the sunlight. Ben spun round, shouting in frustration. 'Back! Get back! I can't see!'

Illuminated by the sunlight and liberated from the earth that had protected her for seven thousand years, she gleamed. Using a dental pick to break apart the clods of soil clinging to her curves and brushing the loose dirt away with a paintbrush, Ben revealed narrow shoulders, pendulous breasts, a wasp-thin waist and bountiful hips. At about eight-and-a-half inches in height, she was as perfect an example of Neolithic artistry as he'd ever seen.

'You are beautiful . . .' he murmured.

Careful not to expose her fully yet and risk having her topple over onto the earth that encased her and kept her upright, he continued to chip and brush away at the packed soil that filled the niche as the workers looked on, fascinated.

'Steady on there. Trying to put me out of a job, are you?'

A gentle touch on his shoulder. He turned, shielding his eyes from the sunlight.

Ada Baxter stood with one hand on her hip, a Nikon camera raised jauntily at shoulder height. As the official photographer for the excavation, Ada was expected to make a visual record of the discovery. She leant forward, eyes squinting as she examined the figurine. 'God. She's stunning.

Looks like the ones from Hacılar . . . Fifth millennium BC, do you think?'

'Maybe even earlier.' Ben continued to brush away the dust. 'Won't know until I can examine her more closely. Right now, my biggest concern is getting her out of here without damaging her.' The sun was descending rapidly towards the horizon and he had no intention of leaving this treasure behind for the looters. But the ancient clay was friable and fragile. If he wasn't careful, he'd leave one of her limbs behind in the densely packed earth.

Ada bumped him playfully with her hip. 'C'mon, Ben. Out of the way. Let me do my work. I'll be quick.'

He stood and brushed the dust from his knees. 'Sure you're not just doing this as an excuse to be near me?'

She held her camera to her eye as she checked the light levels. 'You're currently the least interesting thing in this trench. *She's* the one I'm here to see.'

As he edged past her, he lightly cupped her waist and whispered in her ear. 'So I'm not interesting, then? Should I feel used?' Ada flushed, her high cheekbones glowing pink under olive-brown skin. 'Ben! Shush!' Turquoise blue eyes flickered towards the assembled workers. 'They'll hear!' Ben laughed. 'Yes, they may very well. But unless they have been secretly attending English classes, they won't understand a word of it.' He clapped his hands together. 'Now, I beg of you! Please hurry up! I have to get this done before sunset.'

Ada went to work. As the sun cast long shadows across the trench she turned to the assembled workers, calling to two in fluent Turkish and directing them to hold reflectors over the niche to cast a better light on the subject. As she bent forward to set a small scale next to the figurine, her shapely form strained against her light cotton pants. Ben's hands flexed involuntarily at the thought of the night before, recalling her soft skin beneath his touch.

If he'd been so inclined, every season he had an array of excited and excitable young students to pick from. It wasn't really a fair competition, though. And he knew it. He had no desire to play with what he knew was a loaded deck. Tall, strong and lean, his face wouldn't have been out of place in a magazine ad for a manly fragrance. Coupled with an outdoorsy charm and a position of authority as excavation director and academic of international renown, he was a fairly irresistible package. Ben spent much of the excavation season fending off attempted seductions by the novice female archaeologists under his supervision. Their approaches ran the spectrum from sweet and subtle to utterly brazen. He knew the lifecycle of the dig romance all too well from his younger days as an oversexed and overconfident graduate student and he no longer had the stomach for it.

Ada was an exception. For a start, she was his peer – a professional archaeologist and photographer who had been working in the field long enough to know how to conduct a relationship with an inbuilt termination date. She was clever, intelligent and had a raucous laugh with a decidedly dirty edge to it. She was also an enthusiastic lover who didn't seem to want anything from their relationship other than her own physical satisfaction. And that suited him perfectly.

Ada changed lenses and leant in to take a close-up of the Neolithic goddess. 'Ben, she is perfect . . . what a find.'

His eyes skimmed over the Englishwoman's perfectly formed behind. He smiled.

*Couldn't agree more*, he thought.

The day ended in a heady rush of euphoria. As his team crowded round, slapping his back and lauding his discovery, Ben soaked it up. His decision to expose the idol by excavating a single, isolated spit of soil within the trench had been unconventional, to say the least. The risk of compromising the integrity of the site's stratigraphy was significant. If his instinct that something major was buried there hadn't paid off, he would have had some explaining to do when his excavation journal was examined at the British Institute in Ankara. Instead, he had another important discovery to add to his growing list of achievements. Now, the only thing that occupied Ben's thoughts was getting back to the hotel quickly to celebrate. With Ada. Alone.

She was still warm from the shower as he inhaled her scent and loosened her white robe. Beneath the folds of silk, her skin was glistening and pink. He ran his hands down her torso, skimming her erect nipples with his rough palms. As he rested his hands on her small belly, lightly brushing her shimmering honey-brown hair, she shuddered with anticipation.

'So . . . not interested in me, you were saying . . .' His voice was thick with desire as he wrapped his arms around her waist and drew her towards him, nuzzling her breasts and running his tongue around her nipple.

'In general, no.' Ada's voice was husky. She leant in, pressing her hips against him. 'But I may have one use for you.'

Slipping his fingers between her legs, Ben felt her; wet, warm and swollen. 'Really? Just the one?' Her scent and the touch of her satiny skin were intoxicating. He was hard, pulsing and throbbing, as he slid his fingers inside her. 'Something along these lines?' Ben murmured. She groaned and began to ride his hand, steadying herself against the desk and pressing her pelvis against him. She licked her hand and grasped him, pumping and squeezing. Straddling the chair, Ada lowered herself onto him. She slipped her groin against his, moving faster and harder, finding a rhythm. He cupped her face between his hands and kissed her deeply, probing her mouth with his tongue as he slid inside her with long, slow strokes. Running his hands down to the small of her back, he squeezed her waist, thumbs pressing into the little dips at the top of her hips. Blood pounding in his ears, he felt a hot tightening in his groin. Moving faster, he clenched his teeth and moaned as he felt Ada pulsing and contracting. She pressed her breasts against his chest and buried her face in his neck to smother her cries. He exploded inside her.

Ada collapsed forward against him and looked up through thick, black lashes, her blue eyes gleaming. 'Well, seems you're not so uninteresting, after all.'

She dropped her head back against his chest, her cheek falling against a silver coin hanging from a fine chain around his neck. She lifted the pendant in her fingers. 'Now I've got you at a weak moment, tell me about this.'

The pendant glinted in the late afternoon sunlight. On one side was the profile of a noble male head; on the other, a woman in pleated robes holding a shield aloft. 'This? It's Achilles,' he answered. 'And on the other side – Thetis, his mother, bringing him his armour. See there, on the shield? "AX". Achilles' monogram. It's from Thessaly – fourth century BC.'

'Achilles? Because . . .?'

'Obsession of mine. Why him, you ask? Half man, half god – and his own worst enemy. My kind of man.' He laughed.

'It doesn't come as any surprise. Always suspected you had something of a god complex,' she said.

'You've got it all wrong. It was his heel that interested me. Now, if poor Thetis had found some way of making him invincible other than dipping him in the River Styx by the ankle, the poisoned arrow that felled him would have bounced right off that heel. Poor Thetis – she tried her best. She was a goddess, you know?'

'Yes, I am familiar with the story, thank you very much. You're not the only one who has studied Classics, remember?'

'Ah, yes. Heaven forbid I should forget your exceptionally fine education. So you'll understand why the metaphor has always intrigued me. Achilles was just about perfect other than that one tiny chink in his armour. Got him in the end, though. Plus, he could be a morose and sulky bastard. Fascinating character. Very human. Which is my point. I'm certain he was a real man.'

She dangled the pendant from the silver chain. 'It's beautiful. Where did you get it?'

'A gift from a woman. When I finished my thesis.'

'Should I be jealous?'

'No. It wasn't that good a thesis.'

She slapped his naked thigh. 'Not that, you fool! The woman.'

'Ah . . . I see.' He flinched, then dropped his head and kissed her brow to disguise his reaction. 'No. Nothing to worry about there. She's long gone.'

'Just one of many in the long parade of broken hearts stretching from your door, then?'

'Something like that.' Ben pressed his lips into Ada's hair and inhaled so deeply he thought his ribs might shatter. He held his breath until the tears threatening to tip over his eyelids subsided.

Ada drew back and looked at him, head cocked and brow furrowed with concern. 'Ben? Are you all right?'

'Me?' He rose from the chair and dropped back onto the bed. 'I'm fine. Big day. That's all.' He hooked his arm around

50

Ada's waist and gently pulled her down by his side. 'But thanks for checking.'

She rested her hand on his chest and watched it rise and fall with his breath. 'If you ever find a chink in that armour and feel like letting someone in . . .' Ben kissed her. She smiled sadly and nuzzled her head into the crook of his shoulder.

As slumber took hold, Ada's eyelids dropped and her lips parted. He held her tightly in his arms and felt his own head sink back into the pillow.

The pendant lay on his chest and rose and fell with each breath. It wasn't there to remind him of the woman who had given it to him. There was no risk he would ever forget.

4

## Crete, Greece, 1938

A meaty hand whacked Ben between the shoulder blades. 'Christ on a cross, Grigoris! If I drop this bloody thing, my life won't be worth living!' He gingerly placed the priceless clay disc on his desk, surrounded by his scribblings and notes.

Sitting at a table in the corner, surrounded by the day's finds, Professor Ethan Cohn shot daggers at the two men. The director exhaled theatrically, his frustration at the disruption palpable as he painstakingly recorded their discoveries. He worked with the single-minded focus of a man with no life outside his work.

The site at Parthenia was a textbook Minoan site. It was yielding enough Bronze Age material to keep the dig's overseers at the British School at Athens happy, but not so many surprises that it placed too many demands upon Ben's time and attention. It was straightforward archaeology. Once the work on site concluded at the end of each day, he would

52

retreat to the tiny dig house to undertake his own research towards his doctorate at Oxford. He knew it irked Ethan that he didn't work by his side to process the site's finds. But Ben was thinking of the long term. The less time he spent on his doctorate, the longer it would be before he would be permitted to lead his own excavations.

Grigoris leant over Ben's shoulder and with his forefinger poked at the artefact Ben was studying. 'You are worried about breaking this? But it's a child's scribbling. It means nothing.' Grigoris' boulder-like head perched atop shoulders as broad as a ship's beam. If he had a neck, Ben had never seen it. His wide mouth split into a smile and jet eyebrows as extravagant as ostrich plumes shot heavenward. 'This thing, Ben – it's nonsense. Just shapes. You foreigners get all excited about nothing.'

'You couldn't be more wrong.' Ben traced his fingernail along the spiral of seemingly random abstract shapes pressed into the ancient clay. Italian archaeologists had discovered the Phaistos Disc in 1908 in the ancient palace site of Phaistos. A circular disc of fired clay, it had been stamped with hiero-glyphic symbols radiating from its centre in a spiral. Its meaning had baffled archaeologists and linguists for decades. 'I'm close to cracking this. It's like a code – once you identify the patterns, deciphering the meaning is easy. You see here?' He indicated a cluster of symbols. 'I've worked this out. It reads "Idomeneus". And why is that important?' He began to pontificate, as if he were holding forth in a lecture theatre. 'The Italians found it in the Minoan Bronze Age levels at Phaistos, so it's from the same era as the Trojan War. Who's Idomeneus, you ask?'

'Actually, I didn't,' quipped Grigoris.

Ben ignored him. 'Idomeneus was King Minos' grandson and commanded the Cretan troops at Troy. He was also one of Agamemnon's closest advisors, and one of the men who breached the walls of the city in the Trojan Horse. So here he is – in black and white and just as real as you and me. And if Idomeneus was a real person and not just a figment of Homer's imagination, then why not all the other characters in *The Iliad*? One day I'll pin down the greatest prize of all. I want to find Achilles. I *will* find Achilles.'

'Always with the Trojan War, Ben. Why not just believe Homer and be done with it?'

'Because I want to find evidence. Proof.'

'Some things are just about belief, Benedict,' the Greek countered. 'You'd try to find evidence of the Bible stories, too, I suppose?'

'And many archaeologists do. But if people can believe the Bible is historically accurate, why can't Homer's stories be based on fact, too?'

Grigoris sighed heavily. 'You need more faith, my friend.'

'And when we stop searching for truth and meaning, we'll be little more than animals.'

'Truth I can't help you with. But meaning, I can. And your life needs more of it.' The Greek nudged the leg of Ben's chair with a heavy boot. 'Get up! Outside, dusk is falling. You work too hard. And tonight, it's my nephew's christening. You will join us.'

So that was Grigoris' caper, then. It was to be an abduction. Ben had wondered what he was doing when he returned to the site. Grigoris had excused himself from his duties as trench supervisor to attend the family celebrations. The Greek community's festivities were anything but sedate, and as one of the leaders of the village Grigoris was expected to play toastmaster. He approached his role with an admirable diligence; Ben had chalked up more than his share of grim hangovers thanks to his friend's committed revelling. An informal invitation to join the party earlier in the week had been extended, and under other circumstances, he would have seized the opportunity to unwind with the villagers. But the Italians guarded the Phaistos Disc jealously, and it was only after calling in many favours and manoeuvring his way through a Gordian knot of bureaucracy that he was able to secure its loan. Like a bridegroom on his wedding night, now it was in his hands he wasn't going to let it go. Besides which, he was seized by the manic fixation that took hold when he was in pursuit of intellectual quarry. Nothing could drag him from his desk until physical and mental fatigue rendered him insensible.

He made a feeble attempt to decline the invitation graciously. 'Να σου ζήσει! Best wishes to you and your family, Grigoris. But I just can't leave. I'll be at it until the wee small ones, I'm afraid.'

The Greek frowned and placed a commanding hand on Ben's shoulder. 'It wasn't a question, Ben. It was an order. You *will* join us. Professor Cohn? You won't miss him for the evening, will you?'

'Miss him? Not bloody likely. You'll get no objections here,' the older man scoffed. 'He's no help to me, anyway. I could do with a hand classifying these potsherds. But he's too caught up in his own research – as futile as it is.'

'So my quest is quixotic, but your own obsession with alchemy – a field dismissed by most sensible people as nonsense – is rational?' Ben fought the hot surge of anger that swelled in his chest. 'You've seen my translations of the Hittite tablets, Ethan. The names of King Priam, Prince Hector and the city of Troy written there as clear as day. Not as myth. Not as legend. As historical fact. And this inscription here – it's based on Luwian script. I swear it. The same language used in Troy.'

'Yes, yes. You are a very clever boy, Benedict. One day your hard work will make quite a mark. But right now, you need to take a break before you spontaneously combust. Besides – you've taken to whistling to yourself while you work. Off-tune. And it's making me crazy. Barely out of your teen years and you're already behaving like a doddery old man.' Professor Cohn spoke slowly, patronisingly, as if addressing a dim-witted child. It only fuelled Ben's anger. But he bit his tongue. He knew from bitter experience that no good came of crossing his mentor.

Cohn spread his hands benevolently. 'So your timing is perfect, Grigoris. What this young man needs is a drink and a night off. I give you permission to drag him out of here, kicking and screaming if necessary.'

'But –' Ben objected.

'Enough! I don't wish to see hide nor hair of you until you've let off some steam.'

'Fine!' He threw his hands in the air. 'I surrender. Lead me astray, Grigoris.'

In years to come, he would have many an occasion to reflect upon how it is that the most random and inconsequential of moments can shift the path of a man's life.

When they arrived in Grigoris' village, the bucolic night did little to lighten Ben's mood. Crickets chirruped merrily beneath the velvety purple night sky as hissing lanterns cast a pool of golden light upon a crowd of revellers dancing to the trilling Cretan *lyra*. The smell of pine and wild thyme mingled with the fragrant smoke billowing from the charcoal pits, where slabs of lamb and goat meat grilled and sizzled on slow-turning spits.

Ben willed himself to relax, but his mind kept dragging him back to the cramped wooden desk where he laboured every night. The disc, and the secrets it concealed, called to him.

His obsession with the Trojan War had taken hold when he had been transcribing a series of four-thousand-year-old Hittite cuneiform tablets at the British Museum as part of his studies at Oxford. The ancient documents were an important historical find; a villager from the town of Eskitepe in southern Turkey had unearthed them in a single cluster, hinting at the likelihood there would be others found and that they may be part of a much larger ancient archive. Interpreting the inscription became a high priority for the museum.

Ben's precocious linguistic gifts had captured the attention of his teachers and he had been entrusted with a task that would usually have been the purview of far more advanced students in the archaeology program. But winning the appointment hadn't been easy. The memory of the ferocity with which Ethan Cohn had advanced his name to secure him the internship at the museum still made him cringe. He had been mortified to learn how shamelessly his mentor had exaggerated his qualifications and experience – Ethan saw his protégé's standing as a reflection of his own, and he was damned if he was going to be diminished by a less than stellar sidekick.

Although he had never expressly sought it, over the years the curmudgeonly older man had earned Ben's deep gratitude and respect, but Ben never felt completely at ease with him. He was a fierce friend but a vitriolic enemy, and it was not easy to distinguish the line between the two camps until after it had been crossed. Despite his contrary ways, Ethan had scaled the walls of academia and entrenched himself in an impregnable eyrie that few dared attack. Even his more eccentric theories about the ancient science of alchemy found scant detractors. And so his endorsement secured Ben a place in the program at the British Museum over many other applicants who were – on paper, at least – far better qualified. No one had been more relieved than Ben when he'd vindicated Ethan's faith in him by quickly deciphering the Hittite inscriptions.

As the balmy Mediterranean breeze swept up the craggy mountains and cast its shadows in the leaves above Ben's head, he recalled the moment he had realised the magnitude of his discovery. He would never forget the sensation; the prickling of the hairs at the base of his skull and blood pounding in his ears. Against most measures, it was an unremarkable tablet – nothing more than a list of taxes and tributes paid to the Hittite treasury over twelve hundred years before Christ's birth. But it was its ordinariness that made it all the more extraordinary. Because there, pressed into clay, was the name, King Priam of Troy. With that, Ben knew he had found his calling. He would hunt down and translate every written text dating to the time of the Trojan War, until he found irrefutable proof that Homer's account of the war in *The Iliad* was based on fact. The Phaistos Disc was one more piece in the puzzle, and it was the reason he had found his way to Crete.

Grigoris broke into his reverie as he joined him on the low stone bench and handed him a tumbler of honey-gold *retsina*. 'So. I bring you to a party and you sit on a wall by yourself and sulk. I don't understand you Englishmen.'

'Just enjoying the night air, Grigoris. And for Christ's sake – I'm *American*.' He raised his glass. '*στην υγειά μας!*'

'English . . . American. All the same. Dull bastards, every last one of you. But good health to you, anyway, you tiresome son of a whore!'

They watched as hoary-headed, toothless old men cackled and women wearing delicate lace mantles nodded their heads together, smiling at the spectacle of the young folk of the village flirting under their parents' watchful eyes.

'You should join them.' Grigoris nudged his friend. 'Will you feel more sociable if you have a companion here with you? Shall I fetch your girl from town? What's her name? Is it Elsa?'

Ben laughed. 'No. That was last season. I can't quite make up my mind this year. So far it's a choice between Maysie and Dianne. Though my ambition is to make it through the season without *having* to make a choice. And to invite one of them here would send the wrong message.'

'Ah, Ben. So many hearts broken.'

'You're looking at it all back to front, Grigoris. I'm doing these girls a favour . . . giving them a romantic Aegean diversion, the memories of which will get them through many long, grey British winters wed to a straight-laced marrying-type.'

Long ago he had decided that the life of the lone wolf suited him. If anyone threatened to get close enough to unpack their emotional baggage, he recoiled as if from a branding iron. It had always struck him as a peculiar – and not particularly appealing – aspect of his personality that although he had learnt to use his copious charm to win friends and gain influence, even when he was the centre of attention he chose to remain an outsider.

Benedict Hitchens knew that nature had been kind to him. He had been blessed with a potent combination of good looks, confidence and charm. But it was the slight air of menace that hovered about him that made him irresistible. Somehow it made even the most sensible girl lose her common sense. He treated them well and loved them as best he could. Then at the end of the season he packed them up, drove them to the airport for the return flight home, mopped their tears with his rumpled handkerchief, and never gave them another thought. He had no time for their hurt feelings and saccharine dreams.

Now he had reached a point in his life where he was able to appreciate how liberating this could be. For two months, he and the other archaeologists lived and worked in the closest of circumstances. They ate, drank and slept together. Then those who were not employed full-time at the site returned home. For most archaeologists the short lifespan of the dig and the inevitable termination of relationships at season's end could be traumatic. He found it reassuring. Ben knew he could have maintained long-distance associations with his newfound friends and lovers if he wished. But he never did. He had conditioned himself to enjoy emotional isolation and believed it made him a stronger person. He could not, he pondered, imagine that changing any time soon.

It was only at moments such as these, as he watched the inhabitants of the small village of Asos join together to welcome a new member to their congregation, that a deadening wash of melancholia suggested he was depriving himself of an important dimension of human existence.

'Grigoris!' a woman snapped from across the square. 'I need you to bring another wineskin from the cellar.'

And just like that, the life he thought he had mapped out for himself evaporated like so many of the very best intentions. The girl walked over to them with economical steps, studiously ignoring the handsome stranger sitting on the wall. Her black hair was arranged carelessly in a rough bun at the nape of her neck which allowed tendrils to escape in a messy cascade across her high cheekbones. She carried herself with a grace and nonchalance that demanded attention, even as she appeared to be scorning it.

'Ah, Karina.' The Greek stood and extended an arm. 'This is my good friend, Benedict Hitchens. Benedict . . . my sister, Karina.'

For the first time in his life, he was lost for words in the presence of a woman. She was tall, like her brother, and high-waisted, with long, slender legs that whipped against the soft folds of her white skirt. Her full breasts swelled immodestly above the lace-edged neckline of her closely fitted bodice, and her lips – though set in a stern, straight line – were full and rosy red. Ben fought an overwhelming and highly inappropriate urge to embrace her.

'Friend, you say?' She regarded him with cool, grey eyes. 'So you're the man who keeps my brother working past sunset.'

'It's a pleasure to meet you,' he responded in fluent Greek. His wits were returning to him. 'I see where all the looks went in your family, Grigoris.'

'Your nectar won't tempt any butterflies in this village, Grigoris' friend. Only wasps. And beware our sting.' Despite the frosty words, her lids dipped ever so slightly over her eyes and the corners of her mouth twitched conspiratorially. She paused before turning on her heel and left a snapped command in her wake. 'Brother! Now!'

'Yes, yes. I'll be right there.'

Heart pounding, Ben watched her retreat through the crowd of revellers. 'And why have you been keeping her hidden from me?'

'Why? You can ask me that? With the cartloads of women who find their way to your door? You think I want my angel of a sister to be one of them?'

'She's different.'

'Yes, she is. Very different. And she is not for you.'

'You don't think?'

'No, Ben. I don't think. Anyway, I know my sister. And I can tell she doesn't like you.'

'That's only because she doesn't know me well enough yet.'

Grigoris guffawed. 'No – it's because she is an excellent judge of character.'

Ben watched her sidle through the crowd, hands on her waist. She seemed more conscious of her movements, swivelling her hips and gyrating provocatively; was it for his benefit? Was she aware of his eyes upon her? Wishful thinking, perhaps. Either way, his mind was made up.

'Grigoris – despite your understandable misgivings, would you give me permission to woo your sister? I promise I have it in me to be a good man.'

'You ignore my wishes then.' He shrugged. 'It's your funeral. My parents have tried to arrange five marriages for her already. The last sap was so heartbroken after she gave him his marching papers that he kept marching and joined the army. She is wilful and . . . particular.'

'I can be very persuasive.'

'I've seen you being "persuasive" with those English floozies. And I'm warning you – keep your "persuasion" in your pants when you're around Karina.' The big man shook his head gravely and placed his hands on Ben's shoulders. 'As we are friends, I must warn you. If you do not treat my sister respectfully, I will stab you.'

Ben laughed. 'You'll have to catch me first.'

'I am not joking, Ben. I will hang you from the rafters by your intestines and you will die. This will be necessary for Karina's honour, even though it will hurt me.'

'Not half as much as it will hurt me.'

'Yes,' the Greek nodded sagely. 'That's true.'

So commenced a protracted period of fruitless seduction. It was an unfamiliar state of affairs for Ben. Night after night he would question his sanity as he walked back to the dig house from the village after yet another failed attempt to spend time with Karina alone, stymied by a seemingly endless parade of chaperones bent on defending her honour. That, and the fact that Karina showed little interest in him, fed a brimming well of frustration.

As he trudged through shadows cast by the white light of the moon, gravel crunching underneath his tread, he pondered the thought that perhaps, after all, Grigoris was right and he was wasting his time. At such moments he considered the likelihood that it was the impossibility of the task that kept him coming back. He had never had to expend any effort at all in romantic pursuits. Women generally landed in his lap – figuratively and, occasionally, literally. Although he found Karina's indifference peculiarly beguiling, he had no way to know whether or not he was making any headway.

Day would break and with it the temptation of succumbing to one of the generically appealing female students working by his side who made no secret of their desire for him and, most of all, their availability. But then he would recall the proud tilt of Karina's head and cynical sweep of black brows that might have appeared insolent if not for the humour in her eyes, and he would deflect their advances. And so as the sun set and gilded the mountains with light, he would return to the small village in the Cretan foothills to dine with her family and be ignored by her.

As the evenings progressed, he whittled away his time exchanging small talk with Grigoris and the other menfolk over pitchers of *retsina* and hand-rolled cigarettes until a hazy cloud of intoxication settled over his senses and rendered him mute. But then he would glance up and catch her looking at him through the thick black lashes that fringed her icy blue-grey eyes, and his breath would catch in his throat. As she strode purposefully about her small home, imperiously issuing orders to her many brothers and distributing affection to her elderly aunts and the young cousins who nipped at her ankles, Ben's regard for her grew from infatuation to admiration and, finally, something he thought approached love. He watched her and knew she would never abide his self-pity or indulge his self-regard.

He began bringing small gifts with him that she accepted politely but with complete disinterest. She would peel the corner of the paper back from a carefully wrapped silk scarf, selected by Ben to complement her eyes from the array on display in Heraklion's finest women's clothing store, and smile tightly before placing the parcel, still wrapped, on the kitchen table. Her aunts would cluck and coo approvingly, but Karina was unmoved.

Her stony demeanour became a burr beneath Ben's heel, bothering him to distraction. He upped the ante, hoping to shatter her apathy with extravagance. Draining the bank account filled monthly by his family's trust fund, he bought her a delicate tiered gold necklace and presented it with much fanfare in an embossed leather case in full view of her family. At the sight of the golden threads glittering in the lamplight, she tilted her chin up, lifted one magnificently arched ebony brow, and murmured beneath her breath, 'Ευχαριστώ.'

'"Thank you"! That's it? "Thank you"! Hah!' Grigoris doubled over with gales of fruity laughter. 'I warned you, friend. My sister is not easily won.'

The following afternoon when Ben arrived in the village on his nightly pilgrimage, Karina's grandmother greeted him at the door of the family home wearing the necklace above the black folds of her widow's garb. The old woman preened and beamed broadly at him with a toothless smile, her black eyes shining in folds of ancient skin like currants pressed into an Easter bun. She patted the necklace with wizened hands and pinched his cheek with spidery fingertips.

'It looks beautiful on you, *γιαγιά*.' He smiled through gritted teeth. 'Where's your granddaughter?'

Clucking and grinning, she ushered him out into the cobbled courtyard beside the kitchen. Karina stood with her back to him, sleeves rolled above her elbows and hair secured beneath a red scarf trimmed with white lace. She raised her arms above her head, fingers cupped beneath the head of an octopus whose flaccid tentacles were as thick as her wrists. As Ben watched, she slammed it violently onto the stones.

'Is that what you did to your last suitor?'

She dropped the dead creature in a glistening heap on the stones and turned, clamping hands slippery with marine slime onto her hips. 'That's what you're doing, is it?'

'What's that?'

'Courting me?'

'I was joking, Karina. Not about courting you, I mean. About your suitors. But my gift – that wasn't a joke. It was intended for you.'

'What need do I have for such things? Save them for your English girls who can adorn themselves with jewels and fine cloth as they eat cucumber sandwiches and drink tea and go punting in London.'

'There's no punting in London.'

'How could I know that? I don't care, anyway. The lifestyle of spoilt women with their silly men means nothing to me! I am a Cretan woman. We are draught horses pulling ploughs. We work in the fields all day with dirt in our mouths and thorns in our hair.' Her arms shot out before her, hands splayed like starfish, her fingernails stained black with octopus ink.

'Look at me! I am not made for gold and fine things! Will my goats give me more milk if I adorn my neck with gems? Will my cheese set faster if I'm wrapped in finery? No. But γιαγιά – she spends all day in the house, God bless her, spinning wool and knitting our clothing. Your "gift" gives her great pleasure, and, unlike me, she won't lose it in a bale of straw or bundle of firewood. After she dies, perhaps she will return it to me and I will sell it and use the money to buy something useful.'

She angrily took hold of the octopus and resumed her determined battery.

Her scorn would have sent many a lesser man skulking away with his tail between his legs. But Ben resolved to go down fighting.

As he watched her heft the mighty beast above her head and slap its dead weight onto the stones again and again, he had an idea.

Mastering the unwieldy gearshift on the John Deere Model A tractor took some practice, and the financial outlay drained his coffers dry. But as he guided the gleaming green chassis into the apex of the tiny πλατεία where Karina's home stood and he saw her mouth drop open with disbelief, any doubts he had disappeared.

The engine's thumping gurgle echoed through the village. Timber doors slammed open as curious neighbours emerged to discover the source of the racket. The bravest among them – children and old men, in the main – approached cautiously. Ben doubted any of them had seen a tractor before, though none of them would admit it. And so whiskery grandfathers strolled around the chugging vehicle, nodding sagely and wincing as they burnt their hands on the blazingly hot exhaust pipe.

Karina stood in the doorway of her home at her brother's side, her normally inscrutable expression a scramble of delight and shock.

Grigoris broke the silence. 'You know, this is a very impractical way for you to get around the island, Ben. It's surely too slow.'

'It's not for me.' He swung his legs over the side of the driver's seat and dropped to the ground. 'It's for your sister.'

'Then it's an impractical way for *her* to get around the island. What will she do with such a machine?'

'I'm sure she'll work something out.'

All eyes turned to Karina, who stood silently in the doorjamb, arms crossed at her chest. She smiled and a constellation sparkled in her eyes. 'Now *that* is a useful gift for a Cretan woman.' And he knew he had won her.

Ben's parents didn't attend the wedding in the tiny, white-washed church. They didn't see Father Nikolaos place garlands of sweetly fragrant citrus blossoms on the bride and groom's heads and lead them in the Dance of Isaiah as flinty-faced Byzantine saints watched from the walls in serried ranks.

It wasn't that Marshall and Lily Hitchens declined the invitation. They were never invited. In the hollow corridors of their palatial Boston home, they never knew that their only son had given his heart to a village girl under an indigo Aegean sky. If they had, Ben knew they would dismiss it as a folly; the crowning achievement of a life spent disappointing them and shirking family obligations.

Village life gave Ben all the things his upbringing had lacked. In his new home, a door was an invitation to enter, rather than a way of keeping people out. Privacy was a foreign concept and any thought of keeping a secret from the village laughable. It was quite a novelty. He came from a world where to simply 'drop in' on a neighbour was social suicide and a calling card was an accessory de rigueur.

He was surprised by the speed with which he adjusted to living under a microscope, even if he did have occasion to question the rashness of his decision. The turning point came in the earliest days of their married life together. One of Karina's widowed aunts materialised unannounced in their kitchen in a clucking cloud, smelling of talcum powder and soured milk and seeking her favourite niece's companionship. Ben cursed silently as his plans for a romantic, candlelit meal capped off by a languid exploration of his new bride's nubile body in their marital bed disintegrated before his eyes. Bitter disappointment made his throat tighten. What was he thinking? How could he imagine that infatuation with his wife would sweep aside a lifelong preference for solitude and emotional disengagement?

As he wrestled pique to the mat, he distracted himself by stoking the ancient wood stove and brewing Greek coffee for the two women. Auntie Sophia didn't disguise her delight, marvelling at how fortunate her niece was to have found herself a man who didn't regard it as a slight to his masculinity to serve his wife. Ben thought it was the least he could do, given he was hoping his wife would reciprocate and serve him in another way later that evening.

When Sophia was leaving, she presented Ben with a freshly baked tray of *καλιτσούνια Κρήτης*, the fried crescent moon–shaped pastries filled with cinnamon-scented sweet cheese that were his favourite. She smiled widely and pinched at his trim waist. It was a conspiracy. The women in the family were contriving to add a paunch to his well-muscled but lean frame. She patted him on the cheek with a hand as rough as the bark of an ancient olive tree. 'She is lucky, my niece. As are you. I see it in your eyes. You have much love for each other. And you are now my son. I will look after you as long as God permits me.'

He had never been versed in the lexicon of unconditional love. It was a foreign language to him. But as he savoured Sophia's warm acceptance he was struck by a melancholic realisation of what had been missing from his life. He kissed her powdery cheeks and vowed never to take his new life for granted.

After their house guest departed, the two newlyweds stumbled into their bedroom in a feverish tangle of limbs. Between cool cotton sheets, his wife's long legs wrapped around his and she drew him deep inside her, eyes heavy with desire. Later, sated, they lay entangled together and listened to the quiet sounds of the night, their bodies slick with perspiration.

Karina ran her fingers across his chest. 'Ben – I'm worried. The other women were talking today about that stupid little German with the moustache that looks like a coffee stain on his top lip.'

Ben laughed. 'Hitler?'

'Yes. The newspapers say he wants to fight with England. Is that true, do you think?'

'It's possible. But if it is, the war won't come to Asos.'

'Why not?'

'Even the Great War stayed away from this island.'

'Yes, that's true. But there have been many other battles fought here. That's not what concerns me. What if your country goes to war? Will you leave me and go home to defend your family?'

He cupped her cheeks between his hands and kissed her eyelids. 'You don't understand, do you? This is my home now, and you are my family. And that is the way it will always be.' He guided her head to his shoulder and wrapped his arms around her.

'If anyone threatens you or this village, I promise I will give my last drop of blood to protect you.'

# 5

## Crete, Greece, 1939

Self-important men in suits blustered and cajoled and fired diplomatic salvos from one side of Europe to the other, herding the world closer to war.

On the island, it was easy to ignore the chaos. Months whirred by in a golden, pastoral haze. By day, Ben laboured on site at Parthenia, working like a man possessed to finish his work before the sun plunged beneath the horizon. Despite the political foment in Europe, the British School at Athens seemed oblivious and continued to fund the excavations on Crete. Although he was certain the time would come when changing circumstances would force the closure of Parthenia and the other sites on the island, for now Ben's employment was secure. Now that his future was tied to the island, he could only hope that any disruption caused to the excavation by the trouble in Europe would be short-lived.

Purple shadows carved abstract shapes in the gravel road as he dashed towards his home in Asos. At night, long after Karina had gone to sleep, he would sit and write at the kitchen table as moths fluttered dusty wings against the lantern's smoky glass. He barely noticed, transported as he was in his mind's eye to the plains of Ilium, where Greek chariots cut deep troughs in Trojan soil as the city's defenders unleashed a sharp-toothed shower of death upon their heads.

His dissertation, once it was submitted to examination, was a reflection of himself – brilliant but incendiary. The examiners hummed, hawed and harrumphed, publicly at odds with Ben's contentious theories about Achilles and the heroes of *The Iliad*. 'Bugger them all!' he cried one morning as Ethan handed him a directive from the university asking for elaboration on various points they deemed too speculative. The salvo he shot across their bows was a file box stuffed to overflowing with transcripts of all his translations, delivered with a scathing letter of support penned by Ethan employing a level of invective even Ben, familiar as he was with the older man's acrimony, found daunting.

He learnt that he had been awarded his doctorate when the postmaster arrived in Asos clutching a telegram in his clenched fist. Ben was fanning the coals beneath an obscenely spitted pig carcass and an equally prone whole lamb. Grigoris sat beside him, nonchalantly spinning the spit by hand between swigs of potent aniseed-flavoured *tsikoudia*.

'I have to call you Doctor Hitchens now, do I?' Grigoris took his hunting knife from the scabbard at his waist and cut himself a chunk of sizzling lamb fat. 'Now you are a doctor, maybe you can help me . . .' Eyes sparkling with mirth, he played with his belt, threatening to lower his pants. 'I've got this boil on my arse. It's the size of a duck's egg. If you could just drain it for me . . .'

Ben threw his hands over his mouth in mock revulsion. 'Urgh. Don't think so, Grigoris. Not that kind of doctor. Sorry. Boils I can't help you with. But ancient things . . .'

'Ancient things? You came to the right place, then. Plenty of them around here. You can start with Auntie Sophia.'

The two men laughed. Serious now, Grigoris patted Ben on the back. 'Go and tell your wife. She'll be proud.'

'I will.' He prodded at the gleaming coals. 'But later. Today's feast belongs to others.'

They resumed their companionable silence. In the village square, tables had been set with blindingly white linen table-cloths and placed in the shade of the plane trees standing at attention in each corner of the πλατεία. Families arrived carrying immense platters of food – vegetables in garlic and olive oil; flaky pastries soused in runny honey; great slabs of white cheese dripping in brine; plump black olives the size of a man's thumbnail, and fat chunks of pink-tinged octopus floating in red wine vinegar and emerald-green oil. Ben marvelled at the bounty as his empty stomach struck up a discordant refrain.

Today was a twofold celebration. It was one of the infinite number of saints' feast days. Which one? He strained his memory. One of the 'E's. Evagelos? Efrasios? Eliana? Efthalia? Yes. that was it. Efthalia. He had trouble keeping track of the tiny, jet-haired and barefooted multitude that seemed to own the village streets and lanes. But he was sure there were at least two children among them named Thalia and Euthaleia who would be honoured today.

Judging by the clamour at the entrance to the village square, the other guest of honour had just arrived.

News that a wealthy Frenchman had taken up residence in the substantial manor house beyond the outskirts of the village had been greeted with varying degrees of suspicion.

The two-storeyed home and its orchards and fields had been left to the brambles and thistles after the previous owner fled the island when government troops moved through Greece purging communist sympathisers. The more optimistic villagers were cautiously hopeful that the new resident would return the estate – once the pride of the village – to its former glory. Other, cagier, residents were apprehensive. A perfumed foreigner taking possession of the village's best land? It wasn't right. Grigoris fell in the latter group, and Ben suspected the new arrival faced a Sisyphean task in convincing him of his good intentions.

Ben was reserving his judgement. He had no reason to mistrust the Frenchman. But something about the situation just smelled a little off. Why would a European man of great wealth establish himself here in one of Crete's backwaters? It would make sense to buy up one of the huge mansions on the waterfront and build himself a marina for his pleasure craft and a private beach for his bathing beauties. But what man would choose to retreat to the ragged foothills with only bleating sheep and poison-tailed scorpions for company? Yes, he could see the hypocrisy in doubting another foreigner's reasons for choosing this town above all others. He glanced up to where a straight-backed Karina busied herself about the tables. *No questioning my motives, though*, he thought to himself.

'Well, no more avoiding it.' Grigoris lumbered to his feet and drained the last of his drink. He brushed the coal dust from his hands. 'Manolis is over there getting in his ear. I'd better go and make my presence felt. Lay down some ground rules. Want to join me? Look this μαλάκας square in the eye?'

'Plenty of time for that later. This is the first time I've been entrusted with the meat. If I burn it, it'll be me on the spit.'

'Suit yourself.' Grigoris shrugged.

Ben watched as his brother-in-law sauntered over to where a tight cluster of village men surrounded the Frenchman. Formal gestures of greeting – handshakes and introductions – followed. He could see little of the foreigner other than a straw homburg with a black band about the rim placed upon an immaculately coiffed head of peculiarly orangey-red hair.

As the group of men spoke, the villagers' body language transformed. Square-set shoulders relaxed and arms crossed in front of chests dropped to a position of ease by the men's sides. Was that a slap on the back he saw? He couldn't hear what was being said, but whatever it was, the Frenchman was breaking down their defences. Too quickly for Ben's liking. *What's put you on guard?* he berated himself. *Nose out of joint because you're no longer the most exotic local? Well, you'll have to get over that, quick smart.*

A stout, broad-shouldered man moved to the front of the group. Manolis – the nominal village headman – clapped his hands loudly. 'Ladies! Gentleman! Your attention!' He waited as the chattering ceased and the musicians lifted their bows from the *lyra* and *laouto* strings. 'I would like to welcome to Asos our newest resident. Monsieur Josef Garvé.' In response to Manolis' urging, the Frenchman stepped forward.

Garvé's face was wide and bland, its features fleshy and indistinct, with the contours of what might once have been a potent jawline disarmed by a soft dewlap beneath his chin. In contrast, his lips were so thin that his mouth seemed little more than a slash cut into a badly risen lump of raw dough.

'Neighbours – I trust it's not too presumptuous to call you that.' As one, the villagers of Asos tutted their approval, taken by the Frenchman's fluent grasp of their language.

'I know it must be unsettling to find a stranger in your midst. I understand your concerns about foreigners coming to take your land. But I want to assure you that I am here as a friend. I am a wealthy man and I am not here to take from you what is rightly yours. I will not take anything more from the soil other than what I need to survive here. I have spoken with Manolis and told him that you can use my fields and orchards and, notwithstanding the produce I need to put aside for my own consumption, the remainder can be distributed among yourselves as you see fit.' Ben knew Garvé had chosen his mark perfectly. He had won the battle for Asos without firing a shot.

'I also have need of a housekeeper. I have taken Manolis' suggestion that the widow Ilena would be a good choice. She and her daughter Agape will be taking up employment in my home.' Another crowd-pleaser. It had been eleven years since Ilena's husband was killed by a rockfall while tending his flock in a remote mountain ravine. He left behind a wife and a newborn daughter, who survived on the goodwill of neighbours and extended family. Taking up the village's favourite needy cause would be a popular move.

Garvé's face had been expressionless. But now his mouth strained, flaccid cheeks puckering and opening to expose a row of round-edged and alarmingly white teeth.

'All I ask . . .' he spread his arms; a benediction to all those gathered before him, '. . . is that you welcome me into your hearts.'

Too much. Surely. Ben looked at the adoring faces turned towards the Frenchman. *Christ on a pushbike! Whatever he's selling, they're buying.*

Any sense of obligation he felt to hurry over and introduce himself disappeared. He spun the spit and watched fat drip and sizzle onto smouldering coals.

'That's where you're hiding!' When Ben heard Grigoris' jocular greeting, he knew there was no more avoiding it.

'Not hiding. Just making sure I don't crucify our dinner.'

His brother-in-law made a big show of ushering the guest of honour towards him. 'Josef Garvé, may I present Benedict Hitchens. Benedict Hitchens, Josef Garvé. You're both not from around here, so . . .' he flapped his hands, '. . . I'm . . . ah . . . sure you'll have lots to talk about.'

Garvé extended his hand. The Frenchman addressed Ben in impeccable English. 'Pleased to meet you.' His voice carried the mark of his Gallic heritage and was unctuous as engine grease.

'Likewise,' was all Ben could manage. He was damned if he was going to roll over as easily as his neighbours.

'Is that a Boston accent?' he enquired, taking a seat.

'Yes. Via Oxford.'

'Ah. An Oxford man. What did you read?'

'Archaeology. Just awarded my doctorate.'

'You don't say?' Garvé's eyes were lifeless black pits. They scanned Ben impersonally, like a shark determining which limb would yield the tastiest flesh. 'Seems we have at least one thing in common, then. I'm what you might call an amateur enthusiast.' Glancing down, he flicked the back of his hand along the crisp edge of his buttery linen lapel, brushing away an invisible blemish.

'It's a relief to find you here. I thought I'd be stuck in this village without any literate company.'

*Well, he opened the door*, Ben thought. 'Now that you mention it – I was wondering . . . what's the attraction?'

'Attraction?'

'Why here?'

'If you mean Crete, it's no secret – there's a storm brewing in Europe. It's only a matter of time before war breaks out. I don't know how much you've heard about me . . .'

'Nothing,' Ben interjected.

'. . . but I own a shipping company. Atlantis Maritime. Much of my trade passes through the Suez Canal. This is good a place as any to keep an eye on it. I'm also a keen student of the Minoan Bronze Age. I'm hoping to add to my collection of artefacts while I'm here.'

Dust haze rose in the square as the men and women danced, arms linked and legs weaving in dizzying arabesques to the harried sound of the *lyra*. On the outskirts of the spinning dancers a small group of young girls mimicked the adults, laughing and clipping each other's heels as they attempted to keep pace with their elders.

'Quaint, isn't it? Being a learned man and a student of human history, I'm sure you'll agree with me – it's hard to believe these people are the heirs of one of the world's most advanced civilisations, isn't it?' Garvé locked his eyes on Ben, watching for his reaction. 'No doubt you've heard of the latest theories in Europe – that Ancient Greek culture was actually an offshoot of a far older Aryan civilisation . . .'

Ben scoffed. 'Theory? Fantasy, more like. Himmler's *Ahnernerbe* is an absurdity! The ancient Greeks were Nazis? It's bloody preposterous!' He had first heard of Heinrich Himmler's propaganda campaign through his peers at Oxford. German expeditions were crisscrossing the globe in search of evidence to prove the Aryan race was the progenitor of all major ancient Western civilisations. In Oxbridge pubs and student common rooms, the pseudo-scientific theories of the *Ahnernerbe* – the Ancestral Heritage Organisation – had been the butt of innumerable jokes, most of them off-colour.

Garvé flicked a string of silver worry beads – an irritating affectation. 'I have well-educated friends in Europe who put great stock in these hypotheses.'

'With all due respect, your friends are bloody idiots.'

'Well, for the sake of civility, we had best leave that topic aside, then.' A frosty smile tugged at the corners of the Frenchman's mouth. 'A change of subject. Why are *you* in Asos?' The calculating black orbs scanned Ben's face.

'My wife and her family live here. Grigoris – he's my brother-in-law.'

'A wife?' Garvé's eyes widened. 'You don't say? Which one?'

Karina was standing by a table ladling syrup onto a tray of baklava. Sensing Ben's eyes upon her, she looked up.

'Ah. She's beautiful. You chose well. But to marry one of them? That's quite a commitment.' Flick. Flick. Flick. The incessant clicking of the κομπολόγια seemed to be tugging at Ben's eyeballs, worming beneath his skin. 'I assumed you were just slumming.'

Ben's fists clenched. 'Slumming? What do you mean by that?'

The Frenchman locked Ben in his deathly gaze. 'Apologies. My English vernacular sometimes fails me. I meant enjoying the favours of the locals. A diversion before you return home to civilisation.'

*Stay calm, Ben*, he said to himself as a hot red tide of fury began to rise in his chest. *Stay calm. Give him the benefit of the doubt. He doesn't know what he's saying.*

'It's like watching circus monkeys perform, isn't it?' Garvé gestured at the villagers spinning and twirling around the village square.

Ben shook his head, refusing to credit what he had just heard. 'I beg your pardon?' *Keep a lid on it, Ben. It's a cultural misunderstanding. That's all.*

'Monkeys. Dancing monkeys. Such simple people ...' The Frenchman picked at his teeth with a manicured forefinger. He tilted his chin towards Karina. 'I suppose you can leave once you tire of her. There's no shortage of willing women on the island, after all.'

Garvé rose to his feet and fixed his eyes on the young girls dancing in the square. Bending at the waist he whispered conspiratorially in Ben's ear. 'There's another thing we have in common, it seems – a taste for Greek women. Though I prefer a greener vintage. Yours has held on to her looks. Unusual . . . beauty in this part of the world is usually the preserve of the very young. Once these girls reach full maturity their bodies thicken and their flesh grows pendulous – not to my liking at all. Now, if you'll excuse me . . .' Garvé strolled into the centre of the square and took the hand of Ilena's eleven-year-old daughter Agape. The young girl blushed and laughed then led the Frenchman into the line of dancers where he joined their dips and spins.

Ben was dumbstruck. If he had heard such sentiments expressed about strangers he would have been alarmed. That they were directed towards people he loved shook him to the core.

The Frenchman prowled among the frolicking villagers, a wolf among the flock.

As the crowd thinned and groups of people peeled off and retreated to their homes, Grigoris wandered over and joined Ben by the smouldering coals and now-naked spit. The shock of his exchange with Garvé had rendered Ben mute. How could he broach such a topic with anyone, least of all his volatile brother-in-law?

Grigoris handed him a glass of *tsikoudia*, full to the brim. 'This Frenchman, he is going to be good for the village. He's going to pay me to harvest his crops. It's money we need.'

'Do you have to take it from him, Grigoris? You know I'll always help if you need it.'

'And what would that mean if I put my hand out for money from you? What would that say about my balls? No. It's my job to take care of my family. Save your money for my sister.' He lowered his voice. 'Besides, he's also letting Grandma keep grazing her goats on his pastures by the river. I didn't want to worry her, but if he'd wanted them gone, I don't know what we would have done. Those goats are more important to her than her own fucking children.'

Ben cursed beneath his breath. *Bloody hell. He's set himself up as the resident Messiah. And these people need him too much.* 'I don't trust him,' he protested feebly.

'Ah, you foreigners . . . you're all too suspicious.' Grigoris slumped his arm across Ben's shoulders. 'He's a difficult man to dislike.'

Ben sighed. 'Well, I'm going to make it my mission to try.'

'You worry too much, brother. If you join the dance circle, you must dance. Everything's going to be fine.'

'I hope so.' *Either way*, he thought to himself, *I'll be watching him*.

# 6

## Crete, Greece, 1941

The fog of war smothered Europe in a dense cloud, and for the briefest of moments it seemed it would be as Ben predicted and Asos and her residents might escape the bedlam. News of death and wanton destruction in distant cities reached the shores of the island but for a while nothing much seemed to change. The sun rose and set and the sheep gave milk as they had for as long as anyone could remember.

The return of Karina's cousin, Dimitri, in 1940 had been the first sign that the tide was turning in the village. The little Ben knew about him had been relayed in fractured chapters by *retsina*-loosened tongues. It wasn't exactly that Dimitri had been banished. He was family and would never be spurned in Asos, but the path he had chosen meant his brethren couldn't be seen to support him. Not in public, anyway. Although nobody would deny that the smuggling enterprise he ran between the rocky islets of the Aegean was illegal, Ben suspected that much of the village was secretly proud of his well-deserved infamy. Certainly the fact that he made sure that Asos was well supplied with tobacco and illegal imports didn't harm his popularity.

Dimitri's reappearance answered the question that had been nagging at Ben ever since Josef Garvé had selected this spot as his *pied-à-terre* in Crete. The two-storeyed home and its outhouses had been restored to their former glory and it had become a delightful place to live. Villagers worked round the clock, doing everything from plastering walls and repairing thatching to embroidering new curtains and bedspreads, and were compensated handsomely for their labour. The fields surrounding the house had been brought to heel, and where once a patchwork of brambles and unruly fruit trees had flourished, now goats and sheep grazed in green pastures beneath neatly pruned branches heavy with ripening peaches and apricots. But still, Ben was puzzled. There was no shortage of beautiful estates on Crete, most of them located in far more accessible places. Why Asos?

As it turned out, the isolation of the village was its primary appeal. That, and its association with a well-connected and preternaturally gifted smuggler. Garvé and Dimitri had business to do, and Asos provided them with the perfect hideaway, far removed from the scrutiny of those who wanted to put a stop to illegal activities on the island. The villagers had become plump and content with their newfound affluence and so willingly turned a blind eye to the convoys of trucks arriving at the Frenchman's gates in the small hours of the morning under the oversight of Dimitri and his men. Goods were unloaded and repacked before being dispatched to the capitals of Europe, where wartime parsimony meant legs were going without silk stockings and lungs were pining for tobacco. In a time of prohibition, Josef Garvé knew that voracious men and women would pay unconscionable prices for luxury goods and had repurposed his shipping fleet to serve those appetites. Garvé's only ideology was greed. He had no loyalty or political allegiance whatsoever and was an opportunist who would be found on whichever side promised him the greatest profit.

His stock in trade also provided him with the means to cultivate friendships and curry favour in Crete's insular high society. The British had garrisoned the island in October 1940 after Italy attacked the Greek mainland, and Garvé had turned his attention to servicing the needs of the troops and their officers. It irked Ben beyond reason to see the expat community applauding the Frenchman for boosting the morale of the boys in uniform. Huzzah! The man's a patriot, they cried. A loyal and true ally! But Ben had looked Garvé in the eye and knew that the only master he served – the only loyalty he felt – was to himself.

The change in Asos' fortunes and its dependence upon Garvé's largesse meant that despite his desire to see the man tarred, feathered and driven out of town, Ben had to keep his mouth shut. But that didn't mean he had to like it. Avoiding Garvé in the village hadn't been difficult. He had confected a plausible excuse any time a planned event was looming where he knew that crossing the Frenchman's path would be inevitable. But Garvé had been doing the rounds of the island, so it was only a matter of time before his malignant shade crossed the threshold at Parthenia.

Even though he had been anticipating it, when Garvé appeared at the excavation at Ethan Cohn's invitation, Ben felt violated. Ethan entered the dig house holding aloft a gleaming glass flask of honey-gold liquid. 'Ben! Imagine! Chanel No. 5!' he crowed as the Frenchman walked in behind him. 'Really, Monsieur Garvé. I insist on compensating you for this. It's too much. Certainly more than Esther deserves.

Though there's no doubt she'll be impressed!' Cohn lowered his voice. 'Always at me about the gifts her friends' husbands buy them; the holidays they take to Capri and the Côte d'Azur. "You knew what you were getting into when you married an academic!" I tell her. "Better if you had married the banker your father lined up for you." She just goes on and on . . .'

'Really, Professor Cohn. It's my pleasure. And I'm the one asking you a favour. It's very gracious of you to give me a tour of the site given the demands on your time. Think of this as a small gesture of thanks.'

The Frenchman's lifeless gaze panned across the room and settled upon Ben, who sat in the corner at his desk, hunched over the Phaistos Disc. The one immediate benefit of the outbreak of war had been the frantic departure of the Italian archaeologists, who had no choice but to leave one of their most precious ancient treasures in the hands of the enemy. With all the demands on Ben's time, there had been scant opportunities to study it since. But now that the closure of the excavation at Parthenia seemed inevitable, he was determined to make a final, desperate, attempt to crack the Disc's code.

'Mr Benedict Hitchens. It's been a while.'

*Not as long as I'd like*, thought Ben. 'Garvé.'

'You gentlemen know each other?'

'We're neighbours.' Garvé edged through the cluttered room. 'Your comrade is the only one of the villagers I seldom see. You must be keeping him busy.'

'Ben is determined to catalogue and pack everything. He's certain the Germans are going to invade the island and that we'll lose all our work.' Cohn shrugged, untroubled. 'I'm not so sure. Why would they bother?'

It was a source of ongoing frustration to Ben that neither Ethan nor any of his peers at the British School showed any desire to protect the Minoan treasures as war edged closer to their shores. There was enough money in the coffers to keep the bar at the School well stocked with Tanqueray Gin and single malt whisky, but they had cried poor when Ben went to them with a proposal to ship the most important artefacts to a safe zone.

'If you'll forgive me, he may have a point, Professor Cohn.' Garvé bent over Ben's shoulder and ran his finger across the disc's pitted surface. 'This, for instance. The Phaistos Disc, isn't it?'

'I'm impressed, Mr Garvé.' Ethan nodded his head approvingly. It was rare to meet anyone other than a trained archaeologist who knew anything of the field.

The Frenchman dipped his head with what Ben knew to be false modesty. He wouldn't classify self-abnegation as one of Garvé's failings. 'Anyone with even the most basic background in Cretan history would recognise it immediately, Professor. And I can assure you, it would be quite a prize in Berlin. Himmler's convinced there's a connection between the symbols on this disc and Nordic runes. He would use it to prove his theory about the connection between Aryan peoples and the ancient Greek civilisation.'

'Which – as I have already said – is patent nonsense.' Ben edged the artefact away from Garvé's probing fingers. 'I'll die before I let that Nazi scum get his hands on this. Shipping it to safety should be easy – I've been speaking with a contact in the navy who thinks he may be able to secure us some space on a military transport. At no cost.'

'You don't say? I would have thought the military would be more concerned about transporting things that are essential to the war effort. Particularly with the Germans on their way.' Garvé swept the seat of a chair with his hand-kerchief and gingerly sat on its edge, knees pressed together.

'It's only a matter of time.' He considered Ben with blank eyes. 'Undoubtedly you know something of my business by now, Ben. I share your veneration of these objects and it would be an honour to use my vessels to transport them somewhere safe. Also at no cost, of course.'

Ethan Cohn slapped his thigh. 'There you go, Ben! Sounds like a solution. I told you there was nothing to worry about!'

'It is a very generous offer.' Ben's teeth clenched together and hot darts of pain shot through the muscles in his jaw. 'But I'll see how I go with the military . . .'

'Still,' Garvé paused, eyeing the Phaistos Disc. 'The offer stands.'

*Over my dead body*, Ben thought.

The sun had set and night creatures held court in the surrounding trees and shrubs as Ben stamped along the winding gravel road. In the distance, the glittering lights of home hovered like a constellation against the ragged mountain backdrop.

He was furious. Raging.

As the months progressed there was no more pretending that Crete could avoid the growing conflict. His manic attempt to document all the material unearthed at Parthenia had devolved into a frustrating exercise in triage rather than salvage. Days were spent fighting a hollow sense of loss as he was forced to focus his attention on the things he knew to be most important at the expense of those less remarkable.

No matter how hard he worked, they were running out of time. And despite Ben's objections, Ethan Cohn had begun to make moves to entrust the most precious of their finds to Garvé, who had promised to ship them to safety in Egypt before the island came under serious threat. Ben's intransigence had come across as irrational and petulant. And unless he found another alternative, Cohn and his cronies at the British School would hand the fruits of his labour over to a man Ben despised.

*No way on living earth will I hand everything over to that bloody vulture!* he swore to himself. *Better to lose it all than that! We're all too far in his debt already. And the man's a goddamned snake. Wouldn't trust him as far as I could throw him . . . probably not even that far!*

As he approached his home, two heads were silhouetted against the white cotton curtains veiling the kitchen window. One he recognised immediately – noble forehead, full lips and determined chin. Karina. The other was unfamiliar. A woman. Older. Stringy hair piled in a furry clump atop her head. Head bowed. Not one of the aunties. As he reached for the front door handle, he saw Karina reach out and rest her hand on her companion's shoulder.

The two women looked up, startled, as Ben entered.

'Ilena . . . I wasn't expecting to see you.' The older woman's head was bowed, the back of her hand pressed to her mouth. She nodded, acknowledging his greeting. But her eyes were downcast and she said nothing.

He locked eyes with his wife, questioning. Karina squeezed her eyes shut, shook her head sharply and gestured at the door with her chin. There was no mistaking the unspoken command. Whatever there was to be explained, she would tell him later.

'Ah . . . I need to pop over to see Grigoris. To . . . just . . . ah . . .' He left the explanation hanging. They weren't listening to him anyway.

When he returned two hours later Karina was sitting alone in the kitchen, her fine brow creased with concern and long fingers tangled together in her lap. He crossed the cold stone floor and rested his hands on her shoulders. 'Tell me.'

She lifted a hand to her hair and twisted at a jet-black ringlet that had fallen from the thick braid snaking down her back. 'It's Agape. I can't . . . it's too shameful. Ilena came to me because she trusts me. She knows I'm not one of the circle of gossiping hens who cluck all day by the village well, pecking and scratching over everyone else's secrets.'

'Is it money? If it is, we can help her, Karina.'

'No.' She shook her head brusquely. 'Money can't help. Poor Agape. No father. No one to protect her.' A fat tear fell from her eye and dropped to the floor. 'And now, it's too late.'

Ben took his wife in his arms. 'Karina . . . tell me.' He felt her shoulders shudder as she leant against his chest.

'That man . . . the Frenchman. The old cat desires tender mice,' she whispered.

A shard of chill fury pierced his chest. 'Garvé? He's . . . interfered with Agape?'

Her silence was the only answer he needed.

'I'll kill him!'

Karina's hands shot out, grasping his wrists. 'No, Ben! You mustn't! Then everyone will know and Agape will be disgraced.'

'He's a worthless maggot. He can't get away with this.'

'That may be, Ben. But you can't make this about you and your anger. If you attack him, you will also destroy her.'

'It sounds like that bastard's way ahead of me there.'

'You don't understand! You live here among us, but you don't learn.' She stood, eyes flashing and hands clamped onto her waist. 'One day, that man will leave. And as long as Agape's shame stays a secret, she will marry and have children just like all the other young girls in the village. But if you make this known, she will carry its mark on her back for the rest of her life.'

'Well, you can't expect me to do nothing!'

'And you think so little of me that you believe *I* will do nothing about this?' Karina snapped. 'Then you don't know me very well at all, husband!'

'That's not what I mean . . .'

'I would hope not!' She turned and sat on the edge of the table. 'What we need to do is work out how we can take that poor child away from that revolting Frenchman without the rest of the village knowing why. Ilena is desperate. She is only staying there because they need the money.'

Ben shook his head. 'Surely she doesn't need it so badly that Agape has to be a whore for that filthy pig.'

Karina winced. 'It's not for us to pass judgement on them, Benedict. It's our job to help. You mentioned your money . . .'

'*Our* money,' he corrected her.

'No, Ben. It is your money. Your parents' money. The parents I've never met.'

'You're not missing out on anything there, I can assure you.'

'Regardless, maybe there is something useful we can do with it. Auntie Sophia. She is getting older, and her arthritis makes it difficult for her to clean her house and do her washing in the river. You could pay Ilena to help her.' She smiled sadly. 'The only danger Agape would have to face with Sophia would be death by cake.'

Until now, Karina had never asked Ben for anything. After they married, her pride wouldn't allow him to spend his family money on her. That she would choose to use it to help an orphaned child just made him love her more. 'That's perfect. You're brilliant,' he took her hand and raised it to his lips. 'And you're also the most generous soul I've ever met.

How did I ever manage to convince you to throw your lot in with me?'

'You are extremely lucky. And, yes I am generous. I married you, didn't I?' She lowered herself onto his lap and kissed his cheek. 'You must have caught me at a weak moment.'

# 7

## Crete, Greece, 1941

In April 1941, news reached the island that the Greek mainland had fallen to Axis troops. A torrent of ragged Allied troops beating retreat crashed upon Crete's shores. By the beginning of May, Crete was the only Greek territory that had not been crushed and subdued by the enemy. The arrival of King Georgios and his government on their flight into exile confirmed the inevitable. It was now a question of when, not if, the island would be attacked.

Ben became desperate in his search for an alternative to Garvé's smuggling operation to save his archaeological treasures. But it was a quixotic endeavour. When he approached the Australian officer who had suggested they might be able to find space for his shipment on one of the transports ferrying troops and supplies between Crete and Egypt, the soldier looked at him in disbelief.

'Listen, mate. That was then. This is now.' Ranks of canvas tents crowded Chania's green pastures, sheltering row after row of canvas stretchers bearing the sick and wounded. 'Now? You've got Buckley's chance. My only concern is getting these poor bastards off the island before the Hun turns up.'

In Asos, the villagers prepared for war. While women built up stores of food and wine in darkened cellars, the men led heavily laden donkeys up into the mountain range's farthest reaches to hide caches of weapons and ammunition. They resurrected ancient strongholds in the caves and crevices along hidden networks of meandering pathways high in the island's central massif that had sheltered generations of islanders from unwelcome visitors.

Amidst the chaos and frenzied activity, Ilena settled happily into her new position with Auntie Sophia. For her part, Sophia had assumed a quaintly patrician air by virtue of being the only woman in the village with domestic help on call. As Ben let his belt out one notch, he attributed it to the time Sophia now had on her hands to exponentially increase her output of baklava and honey cakes.

Agape was now free to be a child again. She joined the swarm of youngsters playing in the street from morning till dusk and gave every outward appearance of being untouched by the trauma she had experienced. Ben was quietly pleased that he had the capacity to help Ilena and her daughter, and although she'd never admit it, he knew Karina was, too. But until the night he and Karina were roused from sleep by a frantic knocking at their kitchen door, they had no way of knowing the extent of Agape's suffering.

On the threshold, light from the oil lantern cast deathly shadows across Ilena's ashen face.

'Please! Please help me . . .'

A frail silhouette hung like a pendant from the bough of a gnarled olive tree. Icy moonlight glittered where she had bound her hair into a thick braid falling to her waist.

Hands and feet protruded from the heavy embroidery of her nightgown, still youthfully plump and soft. But Agape's skin was drawn, her lips pallid and lifeless.

As Ben took the girl's pliant body in his arms he was shocked by how light she was. She had no more substance than a bundle of kindling. With one hand he reached up to where the coarse rope had cut a livid welt into her soft-skinned throat and eased it away. As he gently lifted the noose from her neck, Agape's head slumped unnaturally forward onto his shoulder. His heart constricted with grief. Behind, a guttural moan sounded as Ilena's knees gave way.

*Why?* was all Ben could think. *Why now?*

'She was carrying his child . . . My girl . . . She was so ashamed . . .'

Ilena began to keen, a wounded animal's cry. Karina sobbed, but her strong arms held firm as she enfolded the older woman in a gentle embrace and helped her find her way to the earth.

He laid the dead child at her feet. Ilena fell forward and buried her face in her daughter's hair, fingers clutching at skin now frozen by death's chill grasp.

'Ben, we have to help.' Karina brushed the tears from her cheeks with the back of her hand.

'Help?' Through the veil of shock and disbelief, all he could think was that Agape was now well beyond help. 'How?'

'If it's known she took her own life, the priest can't bury her.'

Christ! Religion. The opiate of the masses. The one comfort Ilena might take from this would be to see her daughter afforded a decent Christian burial.

He could see only one way out of it.

Convincing Ilena to leave the body of her only child was no easy task. Karina sat with her in the dust as long moonlit shadows crept across the earth like ghostly fingertips. Ilena stroked her daughter's silken hair and cupped her face with weathered hands.

Dawn bled over the horizon, turning the eastern fringe of the sky pearly grey. Karina gently coaxed the girl's mother to her feet and led her along the narrow path towards the village as Ben took his knife and cut loose the rope from the tree.

The ravine was close by. A narrow path – little more than a goat track – skirted the cliff top. It was precarious enough that it was one of the few places deemed off-limits to village children who were otherwise free to roam the country-side. As Ben arranged Agape's lifeless body in a tumble of rocks and gravel in the bottom of the ravine, he knew no one would question how she died. Her mother was the only person who might ask how it was that a young girl could be found at the base of a cliff with rope burns around her neck and no obvious signs of a fall. But Ilena would be the last person to draw unwanted attention to these anomalies. Accidental death was far preferable to the alternative. If anyone had any doubt about what had happened here, they would be silent out of respect for a woman who had already suffered enough.

He tossed the rope into churning waters fed by mountain springs and watched to make sure it disappeared into the rapids, then bent to kiss the child's forehead. He was surprised to see fat teardrops fall from his eyes and pool on the dust caking her pale skin. When was the last time he had wept? he wondered. So long ago, he could barely remember.

As the sky blushed rose-gold, larks and swallows filled the air with their song. He turned his back on the grim *mise en scène* and felt the acid burn of remorse transform into molten rage.

Garvé. That son of a bitch.

The first arrows of light pierced the morning mist. On a rise above well-tended fields and neatly pruned fruit trees, the Frenchman's home stood sentinel.

'Garvé! Garvé!' he screamed in English, hammering at the timber doors with both fists. 'Open up, you bastard!'

A heavy tread on the stone steps behind him. 'You're wasting your time.' An expressionless and unfamiliar voice addressed him in Greek. 'He's not here.'

Ben spun on his heel, fists raised and ready to fight. 'What do you mean?'

'What I said. He's not here. He's in Cyprus. On business.'

A slight man stood before him, velvety black hair shaved almost to his scalp and jet-bright eyes glittering beneath heavy brows. 'You're Benedict. The Englishman. Married to my cousin.' The other man extended his hand. 'Dimitri. You've been avoiding me.' He wasn't a large-framed man, but his shovel-shaped hand bore the marks of a labourer, and the muscles in his forearm were ropey and well defined. 'I'm having breakfast. Join me.'

Without waiting for an answer, Dimitri turned and strode towards the stable. Ben followed mutely. The Greek tossed him a heel of fresh bread and gestured at a table set with an array of enamel plates. 'Cheese. Honey. Olives. Tomatoes. Help yourself.'

'I'm American.' The early morning chill made Ben shiver as he dug his teeth into the doughy bread.

'What?'

'You called me English. I'm American. Not English.'

Dimitri shrugged. 'Who cares? English. American. Not Greek. So what's the Frenchman done to you?'

'Not to me. To . . .' He paused, uncertain how much he should reveal. 'To a friend of mine.'

'I heard noises in the orchard before dawn.' He squinted against the morning sun's glare. 'Is it the girl?'

Ben wondered how much he knew. 'Girl?'

'Agape. The widow's daughter.' The Greek shifted in his seat. 'What he was doing here. It was wrong.'

'You knew! And you did nothing?'

'Do what? I'm not the girl's father. Not my place to interfere.'

The smell of wood smoke began to seep up the valley as fires were stoked in the village, cooking the day's fresh loaves and pastries. Ben's back was warmed by the rising sun, banishing the morbid chill that had seeped into his bones during the night.

Talking through mouthfuls of bread and golden honey, Dimitri continued. 'Thought you were angry because of the shipment.'

'Which shipment?'

'The crates we took from Parthenia yesterday.'

Ben's jaw dropped. Ethan. The stupid old bastard.

'Ah. You didn't know.' Dimitri laughed wryly. 'Not surprised. The Frenchman knew you'd be angry. It's all he talked about before I left. Shouldn't tell you, I guess.'

'So why *are* you telling me?'

'My time with this man's almost up. He needed me and my contacts. But I don't need him. Won't be long and I'll be back running my own show again. And with the Germans coming, it's time to choose. Sure as hell won't be the Frenchman and the Nazis. You're family.' He stretched his legs out in front of him and interlaced his fingers, cracking his knuckles. 'So. Garvé promised something you had at Parthenia to some bigwig in Berlin.'

The Phaistos Disc. It had to be. 'Berlin? Ethan wouldn't agree to that.'

'He doesn't know. Garvé told him only what he wanted to hear. The Frenchman's as smooth as a new-laid egg when it suits him. Wanted to see which way the wind blew. And now he knows. It's a German wind that's on the way. So now he'll do anything to keep the Nazis happy. That's why he's in Cyprus. Getting passage to Europe for the shipment. Only thing he cares about . . . his big promises. A little girl . . . To him, she's less than nothing.'

'That little girl? She's dead.'

'Dead?' Dimitri shook his head sadly. 'I'm sorry. Her father – he was a good man.'

'I want to punish him.'

'Punish him?' The Greek picked at his teeth with a filthy forefinger. 'Yes. We can do that.'

Waves sluiced up the stony beach as crickets chirruped and a lonely owl cooed from a pine bough. Scooting clouds crossed a bare-faced moon and cast feathery shadows on the waves. It was a serene evening. But crouched behind a fallen log, hunchbacked and bent double with knees cramped into knots, Ben was anything but relaxed.

Not for the first time that night he wondered what on earth he was thinking. At his side, a tethered donkey nickered and breathed hotly into his ear. He shifted uncomfortably on the spot, berating himself for being so easily duped. *Dimitri has played me for a patsy. I've been drawn out on a fool's errand.*

It had to be past the hour by now, he thought. Where were they? Why had he been so ready to believe that Dimitri wanted to help him? Ben felt like an idiot.

The plan had been quick and easy to conceive. The Parthenia shipment was only a small part of a much larger consignment of goods departing Crete that night. Dimitri had told him he would make sure the boxes were packed in the last truck. If all went to plan, the men would gather on the beach to wait as Dimitri summoned the boat waiting offshore. This would also be Ben's signal. While the men were distracted, he could remove the boxes from the back of the truck, load them onto the donkey, and spirit them away to a cavern in the mountains. Easy. And the benefits were twofold. A major loss of face for Garvé, and Ben would hold on to the Phaistos Disc.

Why, then, this feeling of dread in his gut? he wondered. *Dimitri flipped allegiances too quickly. That's what's bothering me. How can I trust someone who's so quick to betray his partner?*

He was about to stand and beat a humiliated retreat when he heard it. The unmistakable rattle and grind of a convoy of trucks descending the coast road. Christ! They *were* coming. No backing out now.

The trucks were driving without headlights, the smugglers relying on moonlight alone to navigate roads they could have negotiated blindfolded. With a screeching of brakes the trucks rumbled to a halt in the cove. Doors opened and the men jumped out, two from each cabin, their heavy work boots crunching across the shale towards the water's edge. Murmuring below their breath, matches flared as they lit cigarettes and stood on the beach. A lone figure turned on a torch and flashed a signal across the water.

*That's it. Now.*

Ben ran, crouching, towards the back of the truck at the end of the convoy. He moved as silently as he could, but the brittle stones beneath his feet snapped and broke with each step. He could only hope the rolling waves and the men's own movements would disguise the sound of his passage.

A canvas flap hung from the canopy covering the back of the truck. Heart pounding, Ben flipped it aside and crawled in. As promised, the four boxes from Parthenia were stacked at the rear of the tray. The smallest of the four, which Ben knew contained the Phaistos Disc, was at the top of the stack. Relieved, he reached for it.

Suddenly, out of the corner of his eye he saw movement. A black silhouette materialised from the truck's darkest recess. His gut clenched and he balled his fists as the hairs on the back of his neck stood on end.

'Shh!' The figure moved towards him, hands outstretched in submission. 'It's me! Dimitri!'

'What the *hell* are you doing?' Ben hissed. 'You're lucky I didn't lay into you!'

'Before we left, the Frenchman sent a message. Thought we were going to be ambushed. Wanted the Parthenia crates guarded. The man's a devil. I swear he can read minds. So I volunteered. Figured it was the only way.'

'But your men . . .'

'. . . need to think I was attacked. You'll have half an hour. That's how long the boat will take. Once it's here, we don't have much time on the beach. Have to shift the cargo before sunrise. No time to chase off after a small-time thief. So – hit me.'

'Hit you?'

'That's what I said. Hit me. Then tie me up. There's rope over there.'

'Are you sure?'

'Got a better way?'

'Thank you, Dimitri.' He drew back his fist. 'And – I'm sorry.'

'You owe me one. Or maybe I owe you a punch in the face.' He squinted his eyes shut and clenched his teeth together. 'Come on. Do it. And make it convincing.'

Any doubts Ben might have had about the wisdom of ambushing Garvé's shipment were put to rest the day of Agape's funeral.

Before the altar stood a gleaming open casket trimmed with shining brass fittings and lined with pure white satin. Agape's sweet face lay in repose, all signs of violence gone, her tiny limbs clad in a gossamer gown edged with the most delicate lace.

He whispered in Karina's ear. 'That dress – the casket . . . They're expensive . . .'

'Garvé. Doing everything he can to comfort the widow Ilena.'

'Has the bloody man no shame?'

'No, Ben, he doesn't. But we knew that already.' She took his hand in hers.

Garvé appeared at the church entrance bearing a bouquet of white flowers so enormous he could scarcely make it through the doorway. When she saw him, Karina glared at him with eyes narrowed into slits, her fingers clamping, vicelike, onto Ben's hand. 'If we weren't in a holy place, I'd . . .' she hissed beneath her breath.

'. . . You'd control yourself, because it's not going to help Ilena's grief if you make a fuss, my darling.' Ben was surprised to find himself playing the peacemaker.

After the service, as mourners departed the cool, white-washed interior of the church mopping at tears with embroidered handkerchiefs, Ben found himself alone with Garvé.

'I was hoping you would be here, Benedict.' The Frenchman backed him into a corner. 'It's a terrible day. Terrible. That poor girl.' He shook his head with feigned grief. 'But life goes on, does it not? And I am afraid I must add to your woes. You see, I have some very disturbing news. Professor Cohn called on me for assistance – I don't believe he had time to consult you. With the Germans coming, there was no time to waste in getting your treasures off the island.' Fingers entwined at his chest, his face contorted into something resembling regret. 'But while my men were transporting your finds from Parthenia, the trucks were robbed and the boxes containing all the pieces stolen. Even – and this grieves me – even your precious disc. All gone.'

'I see.' Through gritted teeth Ben smiled. 'Well, we're at war. Shit happens.'

'I'm surprised to hear you so cavalier . . .' Garvé paused, drew breath. 'You're not as . . . disappointed as I thought you might be.' Raptor-like eyes locked on Ben's face. 'I'm curious – you don't know anything about it, do you?'

Ben could no longer restrain himself. 'You – you're a parasite of the foulest order! Just breathing the same air as you . . . it turns my stomach.' He spoke in a snarl. 'I know what you did to that girl. And it's taking all my self-control not to grind your self-satisfied face into the dirt!'

'I see.' The Frenchman looked across at Agape's coffin. 'Perhaps I should explain. You see, nature announced to me that Agape was ready – she was menstruating and had started to develop breasts. The hair on her private parts was thick . . .'

'You're a pig, Garvé. She was a child. No man of right mind –'

'Many men have, and many will continue to do so. You look at the world through the lens imposed on you by a small-minded society, Benedict. Only in the West is physical union between a girl of age and an adult man forbidden. Besides, as you well know, in this village it is not unusual for girls to be betrothed at a very young age. Sometimes to men much older than themselves.'

'It's not the same thing –'

Garvé ignored him. 'I never wanted it to end like this. I was terribly sorry to learn of her death. I had grown fond of the girl, in my own way.' He gazed at Ben dispassionately. 'You know, you might consider trying it one day.'

'Trying what?' asked Ben, afraid of the answer.

'Lying with one so young. Their flesh is like satin, their cunts so tight . . .'

Ben grabbed the Frenchman by the collar. 'You fucking son of a bitch . . .!'

'You won't hit me here, Benedict. Not in the house of God, with all his saints as witnesses! What would your family say?' He brushed Ben's hands away. 'Speaking of family, you would be advised to tread carefully. The life you have known on Crete is nearing an end. It would be a terrible shame if your actions – or presence in this village – drew the attention of the German authorities.'

Garvé turned to walk through the arched doorway into the blinding midday sun. Over his shoulder he offered a final retort. 'You have a choice, Benedict. And I advise you to choose wisely. This island is about to descend into hell. And I can do more to protect your peasant family than you ever will. Or, if it pleases me, I can destroy it.'

Scraps of tattered cloth hung like raggle-taggle bunting above their heads from the prayer tree's gnarled boughs. Ben took a linen handkerchief from his pocket as instructed by Karina and knotted it to a bare branch. She followed suit. They stepped back and admired their handiwork.

'There. Now we will be safe.'

She said it with such certainty that, for a moment, the ritual banished the grim apprehension gripping his heart.

He would never leave Crete – not with Karina here. Although America wasn't at war with anyone yet and on paper, at least, he wasn't an enemy of Germany, he had no doubt it was only a matter of time. To stay in the village with the impending arrival of Nazi troops put his wife and her family at risk. And then there was Garvé's implicit threat. There was only one thing he could do.

When he told his wife he was joining the growing ranks of the Resistance in the mountains, she had been philosophical and not at all surprised. Eyes downcast, she spoke in a whisper. 'Of course you must.' If it would put her mind at ease during the long months ahead, joining her to make an offering at the ancient tree on the outskirts of the village was the least he could do.

He felt for her hand and held it tightly.

'I have one thing for you, τα μάτια μου.' She reached into her skirt's deep pocket and took out a small velvet bag. 'A gift.'

'What for, my love?'

'Christos. The jewel maker in Heraklion. I asked him to make it for you. To celebrate your success now you are a doctor. You have worked so hard . . .' She pressed the pouch into his palm. 'With everything that has happened . . . it has never been the right time to give it to you. But now, we have no more time left.'

He undid the fine cord holding the pouch shut and tipped

the contents into his hand. *It can't be*, he marvelled. *Where on earth did she get her hands on this?*

Hanging from a finely wrought chain was a coin. One side depicted a noble profile of a stately youth. On the other was a woman bearing a shield astride a hippocampus – the mythical creatures attendant to ancient Greek water deities.

She pointed. 'Achilles. And his mother, Thetis. Bringing her son the shield made for him by the god Hephaestus. He is so important to you. Sometimes it feels like all I ever hear from you is Achilles this, Achilles that! With all the attention you give him, sometimes I think maybe you should have married him instead of me!' Her eyes gleamed. 'The coin – it was made three hundred years before Christ was born,' she said, voice lifting with pride.

'I know this coin well. Made in Larissa Kremaste. Thessaly. Achilles' birthplace. They're almost impossible to find! How did you . . .?'

'Dimitri.' She shook her head, halfway between disapproval and admiration. 'I don't think there's anything he can't get.'

'Karina . . . I don't know what to say.' He wrapped her in his arms and held her tightly. His heart ached at the thought of leaving her. Burying his face in her satiny hair, he kissed the crown of her head as he slipped the chain and medallion into his pocket. 'Thank you, *ζωή μου*.'

'No!' She retrieved the coin and looped the chain over his head. 'This is to wear. Not to keep in your pocket.'

'Wear it?' He felt the metal, cool and heavy against his skin. 'It's not very – er – *manly* to wear a necklace, is it?'

'Not manly? I dare you to say that to Father Philippos. He wears his crucifix with pride.'

'A crucifix isn't quite the same thing.'

'Why not? You're an apostate – and, for you, this is as close as you will get to a religious icon. Besides, as long as you don't undress in front of anyone, no one will ever know it's there.'

He smiled as he played with the chain around his neck. 'I'll have to make sure I leave my clothes on then, won't I?'

'But how will we lie together in the mountains, then?'

'Karina . . .'

'I'm coming with you. It has been decided.'

'Decided? By who?'

'By me.'

'No.' He reached out and cupped her cheek with his hand. 'Karina – it's too dangerous.'

'Dangerous?' she scoffed, batting his hand away. 'And you think I'll be safer in the village with those animals arriving here any day?'

'But if anything happens to me – I just don't want to put you at risk.'

'Well, if something happens to you, I will no longer have any appetite for life. So best we both go at the same time. I will not be a widow.'

He knew there was no point trying to dissuade her. He also knew he would be less concerned about her safety over the grim months that lay ahead if she were by his side. But that did little to dissolve the cold vortex of anxiety spinning in his gut.

A light breeze scooted up the hillside, bringing with it the briny smell of the sea and setting the villagers' hopes and prayers fluttering like tiny pennants among the tree's emerald-green leaves. Amethyst light from the setting sun reflected in Karina's eyes.

'Ben?' She placed a hand gently on his chest. 'Breathe.'

She knew him so well – could sense the turmoil within even when he presented a brave front to the world.

He kissed her cheek and wished that a breath alone could banish dread.

# 8

## Eskitepe, Southern Turkey, 1950

'Shit!' Ben smashed the phone back into its cradle. '*Morons*! Goddamned petty, small-minded *morons*!' He balled his hand into a fist and slammed it down on the table.

'Something wrong?' Ada stepped out of the bathroom rubbing her wet hair with a fluffy white towel, blue satin dressing-gown fastened around her waist.

'Those phlegmatic morons at the British Institute of Archaeology in Ankara. I put a call in to Hector McNeil himself. Thought my best chance was to go straight to the top.'

'McNeil? Was that wise? Doesn't he despise you?'

He had never been able to work out exactly why the director had taken such a set against him. He could only assume it had something to do with Ben's meteoric rise in the profession and the public attention his discoveries attracted. As far as he could gather, McNeil's greatest achievement in the field was to excavate a Neolithic hunter-gather site that added nothing more to the archaeological record than to show that some people once lived there for a bit. Since then, he'd dedicated his life to the Institute, where he claimed a great deal more credit for the discoveries that took place under its auspices than was his due. It was no consolation to Ben that whatever ill-will McNeil felt towards him was more than reciprocated.

'Yes, he's not my greatest fan. But he was so thrilled to hear about the figurine, I thought it would be a good time to hit him up for some more funds. It's just too good an opportunity. The Hittite levels are going to be something else. I just know it! That's why I came to this bloody shithole – pardon my language. I've followed their rules – excavated the levels they want exposed so I can have my turn at trying to find the Hittite archive. I don't need much – just enough to employ a few more workers and open an exploratory trench . . . Bloody short-sighted idiots!' he said.

'So he didn't think much of the idea, then?'

'You could say that. God forbid that McNeil and his cronies might change their thinking . . . "I say, Hitchens, old chap. Let's just keep our mind on the job, shall we? Focus on the Neolithic. You've got a veritable goldmine there. No need to spread things too thin. Sure to be something going on down there in the Bronze Age. But it can wait. Been there a long time! It's not going anywhere, is it?" He thought it was hilariously funny. Jesus wept.'

He slumped back down into his desk chair. 'He's got no idea. Those tablets in the British Museum. They were found here, and I know there's more. I just know it. But if those cretins won't loosen the purse strings to pay for some more workers, there's nothing I can do.'

'I can understand McNeil's fixation with the Neolithic, I must say.' Ada rested her hand lightly on his shoulder and leant past him to where the terracotta goddess lay on Ben's desk. She ran her fingers across the corpulent form. 'She is delicious. No doubt about it. It's odd, though, isn't it? The changing standards of beauty. Times must have been tough when someone picked up a handful of clay and brought her to life. Obesity as a physical ideal – it's evidence of indulgence and success. If you're out hunting and gathering or ploughing the fields from dawn to dusk, you don't have much opportunity to build up fat stores like that. The impossible becomes desirable.'

He squeezed her delicate waist affectionately. 'So . . . your lean physique attests to your restraint and self-discipline. By your reckoning you'd be from a society of plenty, then.'

She laughed. 'I suppose. Something like that, anyway.' She extricated herself from his embrace. 'And on that note, I'd best be going. For one thing, I have work to do. For another, I want to avoid Doğan's evening shift.' The hotel's cleaner, Doğan, was a ferrety man who, if the toilets were anything to go by, spent more time patrolling the halls attempting to catch degenerate foreign guests in flagrante delicto than he did cleaning.

She kissed Ben chastely on the cheek. 'Till tomorrow then.'

And with that, she was gone. In her absence, embers of fury flared to life within Ben's chest.

Short-sighted, narrow-minded bureaucrats stymieing his plans. He couldn't believe it was happening again.

A solitary ice cube clunked dolefully against the glass as he swirled what remained of his Scotch in a low tumbler. Lifting it to his lips, he drained the last mouthful and relished its toasty burn at the back his throat.

Alcohol was his oil on troubled waters. In a futile attempt to dispel his frustration after the conversation with Hector McNeil, he had sought refuge in the room that passed as the

Hotel Sefer's bar. He called over the hotel's manager, Fatih. The man worked without pause, took what little shut-eye he managed to catch on the couches in the lobby, and also served as bartender.

The hotel had made a half-hearted attempt to transform a tiny alcove just off the foyer into a cocktail lounge. To distinguish itself from its competitors and justify its claim as an 'international' hotel, the management of the Sefer had contrived a bar to service foreign guests. Ben was also fairly certain that it accounted for at least one of its two-and-a-half stars. But it was a fairly feeble effort. Four stools upholstered in faded blue velvet perched awkwardly beside a narrow bench covered in unconvincing mahogany laminate. The only source of light was a pendant lamp set with a smoky glass shade hanging from the ceiling at a height that made it a peril for anyone above five feet four inches in height. The room was hidden from the street by a heavy timber screen to shield its guests from the prying eyes of religiously observant passers-by.

The offerings on display in fly speck–spattered bottles set along the bar looked to have been chosen for their decorative qualities more than anything else: sickly blue curaçao, egg yolk–yellow advocaat, poisonously green crème de menthe and ruby-red Campari featured in the line-up. It was only after some cajoling that Ben had convinced Fatih to invest in a case of Bowmore single malt Scotch whisky on the undertaking that he would personally ensure that it was all consumed during the course of his residency. The Turkish government–owned company, Tekel, had a monopoly on the production and sale of all alcohol in the country. Importing booze was hideously expensive, which was why the small number of bars in town only sold the local varieties. But as far as Ben was concerned, most of the locally produced alcohol was as kind to the palate as paint stripper, and although he happily embraced the diverse wonders of the Turkish cultural landscape while excavating, he refused to abandon his favourite tipple. They were six weeks into a twelve-week season, and according to his calculations, there were just four bottles of Bowmore left.

*Have to continue to supplement my diet with more raki, or I'll run out before we finish here*, he thought to himself as he watched Fatih pour a generous slosh of Scotch into his glass. *Perish the thought.*

Footsteps signalled the arrival of another barfly.

'Isn't there a saying about he who drinks alone?'

Ben glanced over his shoulder.

'I am not drinking alone. I am simply throwing a very exclusive party . . . invitation list: one.'

The man indicated the bar stool to Ben's right. He was medium height and slim with pomaded black hair slicked back from a high forehead. Dark brows topped golden eyes and an aquiline nose. 'May I join you?'

Ben shrugged. 'It's a free country. Relatively speaking, that is.'

The new arrival extended his hand. 'Ilhan Aslan. You, I presume, are Dr Benedict Hitchens.'

The American laughed scornfully. 'Well, how about that? Of all the gin joints in all the towns . . . I was wondering when I'd get to meet you, you bastard. You are goddamned shameless! I'll give you that.'

'You have heard of me, then?'

Rebuffing the Turk's extended hand, a familiar red fury began to buzz like angry horseflies behind Ben's eyes. 'Like the rest of the town, you'd know this is where the team is staying . . . yet here you are. I don't know whether to be shocked or impressed that you dare show your face here.

Thanks to you and your filthy money, every day we have to clean up the mess left by the villagers hacking into the *tepe* looking for things to sell you.' He turned to the hotel's proprietor. 'Fatih, this man is not a guest of the hotel. I would like him to leave –'

Ilhan dropped his hand. 'That is why I am here, Dr Hitchens. I regret the problems I have been causing you. Can I please buy you a drink? I hope that we can rearrange things so that your excavation runs more smoothly from now on.'

Fighting his naturally combative response, Ben weighed up his options. 'Well, most days I'd say the only rearranging I'm interested in would involve your features. But it's been a long day and I just can't be damned. So tonight, you're in luck. Fatih, one double. And he's paying.'

Eyes deliberately turned from his drinking companion, Ben stared fixedly at the faded tourist poster hanging above the bar advertising the lush splendours of the Turkish Aegean coastline. Not for the first time he pondered its incongruity, land-bound as they were in the arid southern Turkish plains, many, many miles from the sea. Ilhan talked and he listened, determined to appear noncommittal.

Ilhan stopped, drew breath, and raised his glass. 'So, Dr Hitchens. Do we have a deal?'

Ben was silent. It was an audacious idea. But it broke every rule in the book. He also knew that if the men in Ankara holding the purse strings didn't keep hamstringing him, he wouldn't even be considering Ilhan's proposal.

'Dr Hitchens? What are you thinking?'

'Let me get this straight. You'll pay me for any unimport-ant artefacts I find on the *tepe* – those I know will just end up gathering dust in cardboard boxes in the museum's basement. And you'll make sure the entire site is protected. *Properly* protected.'

'That's correct, Dr Hitchens. No more "Syrian" incursions, I can assure you. My men will make sure of it.'

'What about the government . . . the museum staff? My excavation permit is conditional on my handing over everything I find on site to the museum.'

'Yes, there are a few people who might notice once you start sending them fewer objects. But – and believe it or not, it pains me to say this – it won't cost me much to convince those people to look the other way.'

'It has always bothered me, all those beautiful things going to waste. It's not as if I can take any of them back to England with me. More's the pity.'

'I know. And I agree. After all, what has happened to the tens of thousands of pottery fragments, broken vessels and animal figurines you've unearthed over the past few years? Only a handful of the very best objects are on display in the museum. All the others? They may as well be in the rubbish bin.' Ilhan shook his head. 'It's such a waste. Better that they are in the homes of collectors who will cherish them.'

It was hard to fault the man's logic. And it was even harder to turn down the prospect of money that would allow Ben to achieve what he wanted here without going cap in hand to his myopic overlords in Ankara. 'What if I don't find enough to sell you? Then it won't be worth my while.' As he spoke, he felt as if he was watching himself from a distance. He couldn't believe he was negotiating with the dealer.

'You make a good point.' Ilhan paused, brow furrowed in thought. 'There might be another way. Do you have access to the goddess you unearthed today?'

'Today? How did you . . .?'

'Nothing happens at Eskitepe without me hearing about it. That young worker of yours – Hamit. He is an extremely observant – and ambitious – young man.'

Hamit. Of course. *Might have known he was too good to be true*.

'So. The figurine. What do you have in mind?'

Wrapped in her tissue paper shroud, the goddess weighed heavy in Ben's palm.

'Just a cast, you say?'

'That's right. I have an artist working for me in Istanbul – as he's always at pains to remind me, he's something of a genius. He will make replicas from the cast and I will sell them as genuine antiquities. Not that I'll be advertising the fact, of course. And the people who buy them won't want the authorities to know. So the fakes will be circulating on the black market only. There's no risk anyone will know you have allowed her to be copied.'

'You don't have to send it to Istanbul for that, do you? There's no way I can cover her absence for that long.'

'No, no,' Ilhan reassured him. 'I'll take the cast myself. Tonight. I will return it to you tomorrow morning.'

'How can I be sure you'll bring it back?'

'For one thing, I certainly don't want the police looking too closely at my business. I presume that would be your first call if I were to disappear. For another, I plan for this to be a long and very profitable relationship. And it wouldn't be very prudent of me to launch our business relationship with a betrayal, would it?'

'No.' Ben handed the package over, albeit reluctantly. 'I suppose it wouldn't.'

Ilhan extended his other hand. 'So now we are business partners, Dr Hitchens.'

The burning frustration that had lingered since his conversation with McNeil evaporated, replaced by a peculiar euphoria. He grasped Ilhan's hand. 'Yes, I suppose we are. And you'd better start calling me Ben. Let's drink on it.'

He called out to Fatih, who had resumed his vigil at the hotel's front desk. 'Fatih *Bey*, might we have two more drinks? Raki, please.' Despite their new alliance, he had no intention of sharing his dwindling supply of Scotch with the Turk.

'You've been in Turkey too long if you drink "lion's milk"!' Ilhan laughed. 'Not many foreigners take a liking to it.'

'Got the taste for it – well, for *tsikoudia*, I should say – when I was in Crete.' Fatih poured a generous measure of raki into tall, narrow tumblers and added blocks of ice, topping it off with cold water which turned the clear liquid milky white.

Ilhan smiled. 'Raki . . . ouzo . . . *tsikoudia*. Same thing.' The two men clinked their glasses together and took deep draughts. 'Turks and Greeks . . . we have so much in common. But like jealous brothers we still squabble over our toys. So . . . Crete then. You were there during the war?'

'Moved there when I was studying at Oxford in the '30s and never managed to leave. I'd been working on the Minoan sites. I was living there in a small village in the mountains when the Germans arrived. I thought I could just blend into the background. Go native. No such luck.'

'From what I've heard, it was hell on that island after the invasion. You fought with the Resistance?'

'When the Brits started parachuting in, they were running blind. I knew the island, knew the people. Spoke the language. As close as you could get to being a local without being a Greek, I suppose. So, yes. I fought with my countrymen.

How could I not? The Germans were fiends.' Ben winced and shouldered shut the door to purgatory that rasped open any time he thought of Crete.

Ilhan was silent for a moment. 'Why are you here now? Why not back in Greece?'

'Too many bridges burnt . . . literally and figuratively. And as you say, Turkey and Greece – two sides of the same coin. It wasn't difficult to switch to the other side of the Aegean.'

Ilhan raised his glass. 'Well, I can thank the Greeks for sending me such a pragmatic man. I think this will be a long and fruitful friendship.'

'One man's pragmatic is another man's corrupt. My comrades at the Institute would have me hanged, drawn and quartered if they knew about this.' He threw back the last of his drink and shoved guilt to one side. 'But I'm not going to let bloody pencil-pushers fuck things up again. I've had enough of that to last a lifetime.'

# 9

## Eskitepe, Southern Turkey, 1952

When a person is engaged in an activity he or she knows to be wrong, there's a point at which post-rationalisation and positive benefits begin to outweigh the sense of guilt. For Ben, that moment came when he had accumulated enough money from his dealings with Ilhan Aslan to employ more workers on site. When he sank the first pick into virgin soil to open an exploratory trench in the Hittite levels of the *tepe*, right on the spot he knew the farmer had discovered the British Museum cache of tablets all those years ago, any sense of wrongdoing quickly disappeared.

He was conscious of the fact that what he was doing with Ilhan would mean the end of his career if discovered. Worse, he could end up in jail if the police were involved. But it also contravened every unwritten rule in the archaeologists' playbook. He was duty-bound by the terms of his excavation permit and honour-bound by an ethical code of conduct to protect everything he discovered. He was expected to study, analyse and publish the results of his research, and submit to the museum every human relic unearthed – not just out of respect for Turkey's proprietary claim over the things that lay in its soil, but to preserve cultural heritage and knowledge for generations to come.

All that became secondary as his activities began to bear fruit. As his workers came down on the tops of master-fully crafted and well-reinforced walls, he knew this had been a strongly defended and important city. The wealth of cultural material yielded day after day confirmed that this was a major Hittite site – and certainly large enough to be an administrative centre that would have housed an extensive archive of documents. Whether or not there had been a destructive fire in ancient times hot enough to bake the tablets and ensure their survival remained to be seen. Without adequate heat to vitrify the clay, there was a good chance the friable material would have just melted back into the soil from whence it came. But the material he had studied at the museum gave him hope that other documents had survived and that here, entombed in the satiny Anatolian dust, he would find unequivocal evidence to prove the existence of the Homeric heroes he had pursued for so many years.

As the months and then the seasons passed, he persisted, knowing he was on the right track. When Hector McNeil questioned Ben about how he could afford to open new trenches, he lied and attributed it to good fiscal management and creative budgeting. The Neolithic trenches were progressing as before, revealing new and more splendid evidence of humankind's experiments in early urban living. The abundance of spectacular finds continued to draw the gaze of the world's press and capture the public's imagination. As far as McNeil was concerned, provided Ben's new excavation wasn't making further demands upon the Institute's coffers, he couldn't have cared less.

Over time, the Friday evening meetings with Ilhan in the Hotel Sefer's bar evolved from a hurried exchange that filled Ben with deep shame to a relaxed and often protracted affair involving long and impassioned conversations between the two men about everything from politics to philosophy and outer-space exploration. There was no hint that they were suspected of any misconduct, and so they became careless, communicating openly and without subterfuge, the tissue paper–wrapped parcel of misappropriated antiquities frequently sitting open on the bar as they downed drink after drink.

It fell to Ada to be the voice of reason. Ben had taken her into his confidence – largely, he suspected, because confessing his transgressions assuaged his guilt. She was far from happy to be complicit in his crimes. But although she was outspoken in her disapproval, he knew she would never betray his trust.

Everything was going to plan. And, yet, a troublesome whisper of guilt and fatalism fuelled by Ada's censure picked away at Ben's nerves.

It was, of course, too good to last.

It was a Friday evening and the end of a long and productive week on the *tepe*. Ben and Ilhan sat side by side at the bar, nursing generous tumblers of raki. Ben knew there was trouble when Ilhan glanced over his shoulder and the Turk's usually impassive eyes widened with a shock of recognition.

'Dr Hitchens?'

The voice wasn't familiar to him. He spun on his bar stool to face the interloper.

Standing before him was a tall man with a slim build draped in an expensive navy suit. 'Hasan Demir. Inspector Hasan Demir.' He extended a hand with elegant, manicured fingers.

Ben's stomach clenched. He stood and took the man's hand. 'Ah – pleased to meet you.' He indicated Ilhan, who sat, rooted to his chair. 'And this is –'

'No need for introductions. Ilhan *Bey* and I have encountered each other before. On more occasions than I would care to count.' He indicated the stool beside Ben's. 'May I?'

It was a rhetorical question. The man had already taken a seat. 'It's most fortuitous to run into you here, Dr Hitchens.'

'And why is that?' *There's only one thing I can think of*, Ben thought to himself. *And it's not good.*

'I'm planning to visit Eskitepe tomorrow.'

'Oh? Sightseeing?'

'No. I'm tasked with investigating major antiquities crime. Theft . . . smuggling . . . the like.' He fixed Ben with an inquisitive gaze. 'You see, it's usual to see a trickle of things on the market from this region. Farmers turn things up all the time and they find their way to Istanbul. We invariably intercept some of them. But I'm here because recently that trickle has grown to a deluge. And that concerns me. As it should you.'

'What are you suggesting?' Ben tried to sound shocked rather than defensive.

'I plan to interview your workers. That the increased illegal activity corresponds with the expansion of your excavation seems too much of a coincidence. Can't be too careful with some of the villagers. As far as they're concerned, it's their land and they have every right to exploit what they find in it.' He shrugged. 'Turkish law begs to differ.'

Out of the corner of his eye, Ben saw Ilhan edging his hand towards the bar, where his parcel of the week's finds sat, open. He wasn't fast enough.

'Strangely enough . . .' Hasan reached for the package, scooping it away from Ilhan's grasp. He reached inside and withdrew a horned clay ox no bigger than his thumbnail. '. . . This is exactly the type of object we've been finding. Small. Easy to transport. Not so expensive or important that it should draw too much attention.' His eyes flickered to Ilhan's face. 'Where did you find these?'

Ilhan drew himself up and faced down the policeman. 'As you say. From the farmers.'

'At Eskitepe?'

'No. Roundabout. Here and there. You know how it is. Little things like this turn up all over the place. I've been spending lots of time down here travelling from village to village. They know what's been happening at Eskitepe, and have started hunting for things themselves. Can't blame them for trying to make a living.'

Hasan ignored him, turning instead to Ben. 'And how do you know Ilhan *Bey*, Dr Hitchens? It does strike me as a curious friendship.'

'Just coincidence. We bumped into each other here at the Sefer – oh, it must be two years ago now.'

The inspector was silent.

Ben knew Hasan couldn't disprove Ilhan's claims. But his presence meant the site would be under enormous scrutiny. It was the death knell of their arrangement.

His heart sank. The sudden loss of illicit income was one thing. Even the thought that Hasan may uncover enough evidence to pursue criminal charges against him gave him only moderate concern. But the thing that made him feel as if the floor was falling away from beneath his feet was the realisation that word of Hasan's suspicions would find its way to Hector McNeil's receptive ears.

He could justify his actions to himself in as many ways as he liked. His experiences on Crete had made him wary of miserly and short-sighted men and the damage they could do. But that would mean nothing if it came to defending his reputation.

Now, thanks to what felt at this moment like the most moronic exercise in self-sabotage, it would take a miracle to save his career.

It was one thing to be able to pinpoint the events that shaped his behaviour. It was another altogether to let them destroy his life.

# IO

## Ankara, Turkey, 1952

Lurching stacks of books teetered on every flat surface, shedding dust into the grey light of the Institute Director's office. To a man accustomed to the immense plains and indigo cupola skies of southern Turkey, it was unendurable. Ben gazed at Hector McNeil's polished scalp with its frizzled comb-over of gingery strands as the director's cloying platitudes washed over him like tepid bathwater.

'I'm sure you understand. This whole thing – well, it's bigger than both of us, I'm afraid. The rumblings coming back to us – and, most importantly, to the Turkish government – are that you may have been taking some rather . . . ah . . . *unorthodox* approaches at Eskitepe,' he said. 'It's not that I'm unsympathetic, you see. But your relationship with this Ilhan Aslan fellow . . . it doesn't look good. And we think it's best that you make yourself scarce for a bit . . . Wait until things have cooled down.' McNeil smiled nervously at Ben. 'Now, I've had a word with our comrades at the British School in Athens, and there's still the most tremendous goodwill towards you over there after all you did for them in Crete. They would be delighted to have you back now that they're reopening the sites after the war.' McNeil paused. The air in the stuffy room quivered. Ben dug his fingernails into his palms to distract himself from the seething pit of anger in his chest.

The summons from the Institute to attend a meeting with the director in Ankara hadn't come as any surprise. Now he watched in silence, transfixed by McNeil's pendulous liver-spotted lips, a fleshy garland for a graveyard of yellowing teeth. 'Ah . . . Benedict, my man?'

'So. You are taking away my directorship. On the basis of rumours.' Ben inhaled, lungs filling with dusty, silverfishy air. 'Though I presume you're still happy to take credit for my finds. I'm rewriting human history for you down there. I get you headlines across the globe, and now you're going to take it all away from me. Without any evidence at all.'

McNeil flushed pink and fixed his eyes on a point somewhere above Ben's head. 'You know how the Turks are, Benedict. Guilty until proven innocent. It's only a temporary setback, old chap. We'll send Hopetoun over to run things until this all dies down. Give yourself a chance to clear your name.'

*Which would be well and good if I was innocent of the charges*, Ben thought. But if the Institute and Hasan Demir had discovered the full extent of what he and Ilhan had been up to at Eskitepe, he knew he'd be in prison already.

Ben knew he probably should have been grateful that it was only his career that was finished. But given it was the only thing left that really meant anything to him, the realisation that he had destroyed everything he had worked so hard to achieve burned his soul like acid.

He knew he had no one but himself to blame. But that was cold comfort.

*'Bir çay daha alır mısınız abi?'*

Ben flinched, brought to his senses by the tea boy's approach. He raised his head and gave a wan smile to the beacon-faced boy who stood before him, shining copper tray proffered expectantly. He handed the boy a coin. *'Alırım- sağol.'*

He held the tiny saucer between his blunt-ended fingers, feeling like Gulliver in Lilliput, and carefully dropped one sugar cube into the toffee-brown tea. The smell of tannin rose and he savoured the tea's caustic bitterness.

The overhead speakers crackled, announcing the impending departure of another train headed west. On the platform outside, passengers jostled each other in an awkward dance, positioning themselves for an undignified scramble to secure the better seats on board. It was the third train he had chosen to miss. He glanced up at the timetable, knowing it wasn't the last. It wasn't as if he had anything to hurry back to.

He felt a brief rush of guilt. Ada. She was there. Each year, their romance began and ended with the excavation season. They both knew it and it had suited them. But it had been three seasons and Ben suspected Ada was feeling more attached to him than she might have preferred, and certainly more than he felt for her. He enjoyed her company and relished the physical aspects of their relationship, but recoiled at the thought of it becoming anything more complicated. Although he cared for her, he suspected they were headed for a cul-de-sac that would end in her being hurt and he had no idea how to circumvent it.

It was all getting a little too much. He hung his head and tried to think. The searing heat of the Anatolian summer throttled him, sticking his cotton shirt to his back and making his scalp itch. He had no idea what to do next. He had never been one to retreat from a fight, but he was also canny enough to know when defiance would be a pointless waste of effort and energy.

His choices were limited. England had only ever been a staging post after he left America when he was still a teenager. He had fallen out with his family after making what had been deemed a treacherous decision not to advance his father's interests by sanitising the family's robber-baron fortune through a political career that had been carefully plotted out soon after his birth. He had always been a wilful child, unwilling to adhere to the rigid social conventions and mores that governed his parents' lives.

When he had been admitted to Oxford, his father assumed he would be studying law. He didn't tell his parents he had decided to read archaeology until the morning he was departing the family home. His mother wept silently as his father raged and swore that he would disinherit him. Ben turned his back on his past, his mother's tears burning a hole in his heart. And he had never been able to work out whether his decision was motivated by a compulsion to study ancient history and travel to exotic lands or if it had more to do with his disinclination to do what was expected of him.

Although he kept in irregular contact with his mother, he no longer felt any ties at all to the land of his birth. As for England, he did return to the university periodically to satisfy its teaching requirements, but he stayed no longer than he was obliged to. His life and work had centred on the eastern Mediterranean and the Near East for so long that he couldn't imagine living anywhere else. But if he was now professionally *persona non grata* in Turkey, there weren't too many options available to him. As McNeil had pointed out, there was always Crete. But the thought of returning to the island made him recoil.

A woman was seated on the opposite side of the waiting room, buffeted by the scrum of passengers swarming towards the doors. Her hand clasped the handle of a small leather suitcase that lay on the bench seat beside her. She half rose to her feet then sat down again, checking the time on a small wristwatch. Dressed modestly in a black dress that exposed delicate ankles and fine wrists, she toyed nervously with the fringe of a shawl covering her shoulders. A skein of glossy black hair was worked into a neat bun and held in place at the nape of her neck by an ornate wooden hair comb. She had been sitting in the lounge through the departure of several trains all heading in the same direction. Glancing up, she caught his eye. He smiled. She winced as if burnt and looked away.

The disembodied voice over the loudspeaker announced the departure of the 3:15 train to Eskişehir.

*Now or never*, he thought to himself.

He stood, swinging his small satchel onto his shoulder. On the opposite side of the waiting room, the woman also stood and moved towards the platform. She seemed hesitant, glancing back over her shoulder as she joined the queue of people lining for the train.

As the train clattered away from the capital, the endless wheaten plains of the Anatolian plateau whisked past its windows. Incandescent light bathed scenes that could have been lifted from a nineteenth-century French painting – a two-wheeled wooden cart clattering along a rough track through stands of sunflowers, casting rosy plumes of dust into the air; a group of women with their heads swathed in colourful scarves moving through a jade-green sea of apricot trees.

He smelled the loam and the dirt, shutting his eyes and ballooning his lungs to fill them with spears of pure oxygen and the snap of wood smoke. The rhythmic clatter as the train moved along the tracks was mollifying, easing the clenched fist of anxiety in his chest.

'Excuse me . . . the window . . . would you mind . . .?' A hesitant voice speaking accented English came from the row of seats behind him. He turned, and was surprised to see the woman from the station. She smiled apologetically, and lifted a small leather-bound book from her lap. As the wind blew through the cabin, the fluttering pages of the book were butterfly wings in her hand. 'I am trying to read. With the wind, it blows the pages. It is difficult . . .'

'Of course. I am terribly sorry.' He stood and pushed the window shut then turned and smiled. 'I'm disappointed that you spotted me as a foreigner. Is it that obvious?'

The woman lifted her chin, indicating his leather satchel on the hat rack above his head. '"Dr B. Hitchens". Not a very Turkish name.'

He laughed. 'No. You've got me there. What are you reading?'

*The Iliad.*' Eyes the shape of almonds and the colour of copper ingots gazed out at Ben from beneath arched black brows. He smiled and recited the opening line of the epic poem; 'μῆνιν ἄειδε θεὰ Πηληϊάδεω Ἀχιλῆος οὐλομένην . . .'

Surprised, the woman smiled and responded in Greek. 'Yes. "Sing, goddess, of the rage of Achilles, son of Peleus . . ." You know Greek and can recite Homer. That is very impressive for a man of medicine.'

'Not that type of doctor . . . Though it wouldn't be the first time someone has made that mistake. I studied Classics at Oxford and Achilles is a pet subject of mine – *The Iliad* is as close as you can get to a biography of the great man. So, yes, I know it very well.' He reached over the back of the seat and extended his hand. 'Ben Hitchens.'

The woman hesitated, then stood and placed her hand in his. 'Eris Patras.' As she leant towards him, the brocade silk shawl draped across her chest fell away. Ben's eyes fixed upon the golden pendant hanging from a delicate chain around her neck. She pulled back, attempting to withdraw her hand from his grasp as she clutched at the shawl, trying to rearrange it modestly across her chest. He gripped her hand, heart pounding with excitement.

'Wait! Wait just a moment. Please.' He leant towards her and pushed the shawl aside, slipping his fingers beneath the pendant and feeling its weight in his hand. It was heavy.

*Solid gold*, he thought to himself.

At the centre of the pendant, the figure of a man wearing a tall headdress was flanked by lotus blossoms. Arms outstretched, he grasped two geese by the neck. The tiny granulated beads of gold sitting like dewdrops along the lower edge of the pendant marked its origin.

He was stunned. *I can't believe it*, he marvelled. *It can't be. This is impossible.* 'Where did you get this?' he asked.

The young woman pushed his hand away and covered her chest with her forearms, defensive and confused as she retreated to the row of seats behind her.

He realised that to the young Greek woman he must look completely unhinged. 'I'm terribly sorry. Forgive me.' Sitting slowly, he raised his hands with palms facing outwards in a gesture of submission. 'Please. Let me explain. I'm an archae-ologist. That pendant . . . it's magnificent. Thought at first it was Minoan . . . But that's not right . . . Can't be certain without looking more closely at it, but I'd put money on it being Mycenaean . . . fifteenth century . . . three and a half thousand years old, I mean. If it is . . . well . . . it's beyond value! Where did you get it?'

The woman's eyes flashed as she gathered her possessions, as if readying to relocate to another carriage. 'That is none of your business,' she said in a quavering voice. She turned and reached for the handle of the glass door behind her.

'No, wait . . .!' Floundering, he sought a way to stop her leaving. 'I can prove who I am!' He tore open his worn leather satchel and rifled through his papers. 'C'mon, c'mon. I know it's here somewhere . . . Aha!' Leafing through the worn pages of a dog-eared copy of the *Journal of Near Eastern Studies*, he found what he was looking for. 'Here!'

She reached tentatively for the book as he jabbed excitedly at the page with his forefinger. 'There – see? That's me!' A black-and-white photo illustrating an article about the excavations at Eskitepe showed him kneeling in a trench, brushing away dust from an exposed skeleton.

'A photo in a magazine does not mean I have nothing to fear from you,' she said.

'No, but it does mean I know what I am talking about. So, please, tell me where you got the pendant. Did you buy it?'

The young Greek woman seemed to relax slightly. After a moment, she moved around to the bank of seats he had been occupying and placed her suitcase on the floor. 'No. My family has owned it for a long time. We've always known it was very old. Before we fled Asia Minor, my father had properties around Hisarlik. This is just one of many old things he found while he was planting and harvesting.'

'Hisarlik . . . Troy, you mean? Are you sure?'

'Of course I am sure.'

'When you say "old things" – do you mean ceramics . . . pots and things like that?'

'Some pots, yes, and sculptures and pieces of marble.' She paused. 'But there is also more jewellery. And other pieces of gold – cups, jugs. Statues. The jewellery . . . my father found that all in the same place.'

Ben was incredulous. 'Does it all look like this?'

The woman appeared nonchalant, shrugging her shoulders. 'Yes, the jewellery is the same as this. Rings, bracelets, armbands. All with these tiny beads on them. I think there is also a thing for wearing on the head.'

'A crown?'

'Sort of. More like a band. For around here.' She ran the tips of her fingers around her forehead. 'Like that.'

'Yes – a diadem. Do you still have any of the other pieces?'

Biting her lip, Eris hesitated. 'Why? Why do you want to know?'

'Because, if you have more gold like that pendant, it is very important that the world knows about it.'

Hisarlik . . . Troy. His heart was pounding. It seemed too good to be true. He had never seen the priceless hoard of Trojan gold Heinrich Schliemann discovered in 1873, but he had studied the records of it closely enough to know that the pendant nestling against Eris' tawny skin was just as ancient, and just as important. Schliemann had discovered his treasure in north-western Turkey and smuggled it out of the country soon after. But it had disappeared without trace from the Berlin Museum during the war.

He leant forward, hands clasped before him like a supplicant. 'If I come with you, would you be willing to show me the other pieces you have?'

Eris gazed out the window, gnawing at her lower lip. The sun was low in the sky as they passed long-limbed stands of poplar trees that cast flickering, spindly shadows into the carriage. She looked up at Ben. 'And what will you do if you see these things? If the Turkish government knows we have them, they will want to take them away from my family. We have been keeping them – saving them. Until we need to sell them. Now, we need money. We cannot have the Turks take them away from us.'

Ben couldn't believe his luck. If his instincts were right, this woman might hold the key to the greatest archaeological find of the century. If this had happened at any other time, it would have been extraordinary. That it occurred as he confronted a professional disaster was unprecedented. It was almost too incredible to believe. He had to convince her to cooperate with him.

'Miss Patras, please. Please let me see what you have,' he said. 'I'm sure we can find a way for this to work for both of us.'

'Ada? It's Ben. So, my plans have changed. I don't think I'll be back at Eskitepe for a while.' He paused; drew breath. 'A fair while, to be honest.'

There was no response from the telephone. As he stood in the booth on the platform he could hear only the crackle and hiss of the long-distance line. 'Hey . . . Ada . . . you there?'

Her voice echoed from the receiver. 'Yes . . . Yep. So what you're telling me is that I shouldn't sit around waiting for you. You do realise I'm leaving in three days, don't you?'

'Damn! I completely forgot.' *That'd be right, you prick*, he berated himself. 'I'm so sorry . . .' He paused. 'Look – can you delay your flight? Wait a day or two before going back to London? I can be back in Istanbul by the end of the week. Why don't you hole up at the Büyük Londra Hotel and wait for me there? We can do the rounds of the *meyhane* in Pera.

It'll be fun. I don't want you to leave without a proper farewell . . .'

Ada interrupted, businesslike. 'Don't think there's much point, Benny-boy. A good time, not a long time, right? That was what we said. The season's almost over, anyway.'

He tried to protest. 'Come on, now. It means more than that . . .'

'No. No, it doesn't. And that is absolutely fine. Never expected it to be otherwise. Same time next year, then?'

He winced. 'About that – I don't know when I'll be back on site. McNeil has got wind of my arrangement with Ilhan. No proof, of course. But enough to sideline me. They're sending Hopetoun down to run things for a bit.'

'Hopetoun? That arse?' Ada scoffed. 'Well, that's his usual modus operandi, isn't it? Swoop in and take the credit for someone else's work. Look, Ben – I hate to say "I told you so" . . . but it's irresistible. And I *did* bloody tell you. What were you thinking? Still, that's unfortunate.' She hesitated. 'So. What now?'

Further up the platform, Eris stood nervously, shifting her weight from one foot to the other as she clutched the handle of her small, worn leather suitcase. On the opposite side of the station the train that would have carried Ben south from Eskişehir to Eskitepe eased away from the platform. 'Something has popped up in İzmir. Not sure yet. But it looks good. Hey – keep in touch, all right?'

'Might just do that. If you're lucky.' Ada drew a deep breath. 'Take care, won't you? It's been fun.'

'Yep. You too,' he said. 'And, Ada . . .?' The line went dead. 'Thank you,' he mumbled beneath his breath.

On the platform, passengers were boarding the overnight train to İzmir. The parched summer heat of the Anatolian Plateau was dissipating as a lilac-hued dusk approached.

Nostalgia corroded Ben's resolve. Yes, he could return to Eskitepe for a few more nights with Ada, and be there to watch Christopher Hopetoun preen around the site like a bloated peacock. But really, he wondered, what was the point? A depressingly familiar and hollow wave of regret washed over him.

He placed the handset back in its cradle and edged through the crowd to where Eris stood waiting for him.

# II

## İzmir, Turkey, 1952

Peaky waves slapped against the hull of the small wooden boat. A bleary-eyed fisherman held fast to the tiller, tending to the congested outboard motor as it churned the inky waters. To the east the rising sun edged a craggy mountain range with a silver halo and pinpoint lights came on at intervals along the shoreline as İzmir began to wake from its slumber. Although the pre-dawn air was warm with the promise of what would be the furnace-like heat of day, Ben shivered as the sea mist's salty breath settled on his skin and hair.

Eris sat, rigid, on the bench seat at the stern of the boat, fighting the swell's rise and fall. After the night train had arrived at the station, she had negotiated transport to the harbour where she'd convinced a fisherman to carry them to a town on the other side of the bay. Barely a word had passed between them during their journey. She seemed troubled, her fingers plucking at the fringe of her scarf and her brow furrowed. He could tell she had no desire to indulge in small talk, and so he left her alone. There was too much at stake to risk scaring her off.

This might be his one hope for salvation. He didn't know exactly what the fallout from Eskitepe would be, but whatever the outcome, it wouldn't be good. Even if he managed to avoid official censure, vindictive colleagues would make sure word got out, and his reputation would be destroyed. But if Eris' treasure trove lived up to expectations, all would be forgiven, if not forgotten, in the deluge of acclaim that would be his after it was revealed to the world.

If he could show that a cache of Mycenaean gold had been found in the shadows of the great walls of Troy, he would be one step closer to proving that the heroes of *The Iliad* were real men, and that Achilles had once led his army to the Trojan plains and laid siege to the city. If Ben could prove that, the world would sit up and take notice.

Eris' treasure could be his saving grace.

The boat passed the silhouettes of low headlands outlined against the sky. Their ferryman murmured something to Eris, who nodded her head, lips pressed tightly together. A pale fingernail of pebbles nuzzled the shore of one of the small bays. As they drew towards the beach, the hull creaked and screeched as the fisherman hefted the skiff up onto the shore. Steadying the boat with one hand, he held the other out to Eris, who primly placed her hand in his and leapt, gazelle-like, to land on the beach. The gnarled old man offered Ben no such assistance, but the war had given the American a lifetime's experience disembarking boats in far less benign conditions than these. He vaulted over the gunwale and landed, surefooted, on the shore.

Without a backward glance, Eris scrambled quickly up the beach towards a small rise where a cluster of darkened buildings sat like a scattering of children's blocks. He strode after her, surprised by how nimbly she managed to negotiate the slippery pebbles in the dark. She darted into a cobbled laneway between two low buildings. Fearing he might lose sight of her, he called out under his breath. 'Eris . . . wait!' She paused, peering over her shoulder without turning around. 'Keep up!' she hissed. 'We must get there before daybreak.'

Citrusy morning light shone through the slatted shutters, reflecting off motes of dust that dipped and darted through the musty air. Ben stood passively in the centre of the room as Eris moved through the space, efficiently whipping covers off furniture and pulling back heavy cotton curtains embroidered with geometric designs in cobalt blue and carmine red.

She spoke without looking at him. 'The kitchen . . . it is through there.' She tilted her chin towards a door at the end of the room. 'In there you should find bread, cheese. Maybe some olives. In the garden is a pump for water. Make a fire in the kitchen and we will have tea.'

'What? No electricity or running water?' Ben asked.

She turned, hands on hips and eyes flashing. 'My family fled this house thirty years ago. So, no. No electricity. No running water.'

'Thirty years? That bread'll be a bit stale then,' he said. 'And as for the cheese . . .'

'The neighbours made the house ready. They knew I was coming. Do you have to argue?' She glared at him.

He raised his hands in mock submission. 'I'll get right onto it.' He paused. 'When do you think I'll be able to see your collection?'

'When I am ready. First, we eat. Then we rest. This afternoon, I will take the objects out to show you,' she said.

'No problem. No problem at all.' He turned and walked towards the kitchen. Although he was beyond impatient, he knew that pushing her would do no good. *Breathe, Ben, breathe*, he urged himself. He knew it would be worth the wait.

'Ben, one moment.' Eris moved towards him and lightly placed her hand on his wrist. 'Please be careful outside. Do not go past the walls of the house. They must not see you here.'

At the time he assumed she was concerned about propriety; a modest woman would not want her neighbours to know she was in her house alone with a strange man. But Ben would have many occasions in years to come when he regretted not asking her who, exactly, she was hiding from.

'Ben!' A sharp rap at his door.

Disoriented, he awoke. Outside a loudspeaker crackled to life from the minaret of a distant mosque as the muezzin readied to call the faithful to prayer. As the lilting song roused him from sleep, he felt the roughness of a starchy embroidered bedspread beneath his fingertips. The room was hot; his hair a sweaty mat stuck to his scalp.

Images flashed through his somnolent mind: the train; a boat; tea and bread with a beautiful woman with pensive eyes in a kitchen flooded by bright morning light.

'Ben! Wake now!' Another sharp rat-a-tat. 'The things you want to see? They are downstairs.'

He sat upright, Eris' words sparking a rush of adrenalin that made his head buzz. Ben's skin prickled with anticipation.

The moment Ben stepped into the dining room that afternoon was one of the most memorable of his life.

Excavating was like gambling and, for any archaeologist, finding something made of metal was the ultimate jackpot. He knew from bitter personal experience that nobody ever left that much of it lying around. From the moment humankind discovered its powers, metal had always been hard won, expensive and treasured. And it was never wasted. He had seen the destructive after-effects of metal-lust. With the beating of the drums of war, temples were stripped of their bronze gods and goddesses for melting down into spears and arrowheads. Victorious invaders seized goblets, platters and cutlery and smelted new coins and reliquaries from their enemies' treasuries. In Crete, he had opened any number of tombs stripped bare by looters who had been there first, often thousands of years previously, and carried away the golden grave goods. So, when he picked at packed dirt with his trowel and used paintbrushes to sweep aside dun-coloured dust, few things made his heart race faster than a glimpse of an instantly recognisable but foreign colour in the soil. Viridian green meant bronze, flaky grey-black — silver. But the greatest prize of all was gold. And while Ben had excavated more gold artefacts than most archaeologists would see in a lifetime, all of it amounted to a mere fraction of the treasure trove Eris had laid out upon the dining table.

He opened his mouth, wanting to say something, but words failed him. Goblets and pitchers; diadems, pendants and rings; figurines of animals and strange anthropomorphic gods. Stacked edge to edge, they reflected a golden light onto the ceiling and cast a rosy flush across the room.

He had travelled here intending to record and document Eris' collection for publication in an academic journal article, and perhaps convince her to surrender her trove to the Turkish authorities. The ensuing publicity and recognition might go some way towards assuaging her concern at the loss of the treasure. His greatest hope was that it would help resurrect his own reputation in the eyes of the archaeological community. But seeing the scale of the collection – its immense value – he knew that no one would part with it willingly.

'So.' Eris stood possessively beside the table. 'Was it worth the trip?'

'Exquisite. Just exquisite,' he murmured to himself as he picked up a spiral-formed armband.

It was overwhelming. The range of cultural material was extraordinary. Ben knew better than most the rich pickings that could be found in this corner of Turkey. It had witnessed the rise and fall of every great Aegean empire, and – at one point or another – played host to most of the civilisations that shaped western history. So to find such a collection wasn't impossible, though it certainly was remarkable. Ben could only imagine that Eris' father had stumbled on a series of ancient burial grounds. That was the only possible explanation for the richness of the array. The thought of what else might be there set his heart racing; he would have to broach the subject carefully but he needed to know exactly where Eris' family farms were located. Any site that yielded treasures like these would be a significant archaeological find.

There were so many artefacts that he decided to sort them into groups to make the task of classifying them easier. On one corner of the table he had grouped a small number of classical Greek and Roman objects including a palm-sized golden figurine of the fertility god, Priapus, who was sadly shorn of what would once have been an impressive phallus; a small marble stele engraved with heavily eroded Greek characters, cracked in two pieces; and a finely wrought golden wreath with delicate tendrils of tiny, scallop-edged laurel leaves. Another corner was occupied by antiques from the Islamic era; a silver haircomb inlaid with intricate geometric patterns in solid gold; a tiny wooden box inscribed with deeply engraved Arabic script highlighted with gleaming gold leaf; and a gold belt buckle embellished with filigree curlicues as fine as threads of saffron. The centre of the table housed Hittite treasures; a serene mother-goddess seated on a throne with lion's-paw feet; a delicate drinking cup with a hooked handle made of solid gold beaten to shape and polished to a rosy lustre; and a small golden juglet with a narrow neck and inscribed with geometric patterns like the designs on a Turkish *kilim*.

But it was the collection gathered at the end of the table that most captured his attention. And it was the cluster of antiquities to which the pendant he had first noticed around Eris' neck belonged. He had studied enough Aegean Bronze Age metalwork to recognise the fundamentals of its manufacture and design. Signet rings, earrings, bracelets and necklaces were wrought with exquisite artistry and design. The motifs were distinctive: statuesque, fine-waisted figures wearing tiered skirts holding double-headed axes aloft; long-horned ibexes and gambolling fat-flanked bulls; delicately winged bees entwined about a pollen-laden blossom. But the artisans who'd made these treasures over three thousand years ago had left their distinctive calling card. Their touch could be detected in the application of the microscopic beads of gold used to embellish their designs. The techniques used to create granulation of this delicacy had been lost to the civilisations that followed.

Ben's heart pounded as he lifted a silver ritual vessel made in the form of a bull's head – now blackened through oxidation – with gilt horns curving in an elegant arc above its brow, a gold rosette on its forehead, and a golden muzzle.

'Look . . . this rhyton,' he said, raising it up to show Eris. 'There are others like it in Crete. But they're all stone. Not silver.' He turned it in his hands. 'And these,' he said, picking up one of the signet rings. 'The figures . . .' Eris was leaning against a tall sideboard, arms crossed in front of her chest, unimpressed. He held the tiny ring closer for her to see. 'Here – see here. It would be easy to think these came from Crete. Yes, there's the Minoan double axe symbol. Yes, the worshippers are wearing tiered skirts. But this was made by an artisan imitating Minoan symbols. I'd put money on it. These are Mycenaean. Not Minoan.'

The Greek woman shrugged her shoulders. 'So what? Why does this matter?'

'This matters because it means this is Mycenaean. And if what you told me is correct, your father found these things near Troy.'

'Yes. I've told you that already. Why is this important?'

'Well, don't you see? Mycenae? Troy?'

'No, I do not see or I would not ask you,' she snapped. 'You do not impress me by showing how clever you are. Instead, you annoy me.'

'Let me explain. *The Iliad*. You know *The Iliad*, yes?'

'Of course I do. That is a stupid question. You saw me reading it on the train.'

'OK, then. Well, Agamemnon was the king of Mycenae – a city in Greece just south of Athens. His brother, Menelaus, was married to Helen. Which was a bit of a problem when she decided to take off to Troy with Paris. Helen – the most beautiful woman in the world . . . the face that launched a thousand ships.'

'Yes. I know all this.'

'According to *The Iliad*, Agamemnon and Menelaus took their armies to Troy to retrieve her. And the things you have here have all come from Mycenae. They date from round about the same time as the Trojan War. So this might just be the proof I've been looking for.'

'Proof?'

'Never mind. Suffice to say – it's very exciting.'

She was silent for a moment. 'So it would be important?'

Drawing a deep breath, he attempted to keep his feverish excitement under control. He rubbed a rough palm across his chin and laughed out loud. 'Possibly more than you can imagine.'

## İzmir, Turkey, 1952

While he pondered the best course of action to take with Eris, Ben began to illustrate and record her artefacts in his field diary, measuring, sketching and describing them in detail.

As he worked, she moved about the room, dusting and straightening furniture and objects dulled by a thick coating of dust. Her anxiety was palpable as she wiped a cloth across the windowsill, eyes flickering nervously between the task at hand and the desk where Ben was working. He couldn't tell whether it was because she didn't trust him, or if it was something else altogether. To distract her and lighten the mood, he changed the subject.

'So, your family left this house in the '20s. Was it after the fall of İzmir?'

'Smyrna. The Turks call it İzmir. To me this city will always be Smyrna.' Out of the corner of his eye, he saw her recoil. 'Yes. I was very young. A small child. I do not remember much. What I *do* recall . . . they are not happy memories.'

'It's a beautiful home.'

'My father – he was a businessman.'

'A businessman? I thought you said he found these things on his farm.'

'He did. He sold Turkish tobacco and bought farms here and in the north-west, around Hisarlik. That is where he found these things, as I told you.' She lifted a kerosene lamp from the mantle above the fire and set to work on it, digging her cloth into its fluted surface decoration; rubbing and buffing away the dirt obsessively. 'We wanted for nothing. Before the *Μικρασιατική Καταστροφή* – the Catastrophe – we lived a good life. We were Ottoman Greeks . . . Ottoman Christians. My family had lived here in Asia Minor for as long as we could remember. It was our home.'

Ben glanced up and caught sight of her wetting the tip of her finger with her tongue to rub away a persistent smear on the lamp's multicoloured shade. She continued speaking in subdued tones. 'This was a city that opened its arms to all people. Our neighbours were also Ottoman, and they were Muslim. But that did not matter. We shared the same homeland. But after Turkey lost the Great War, the government in Greece decided to occupy the city – they always dreamt of taking back the lands of Asia Minor.' She shrugged. 'My father, he was not so sure it would be good for the Greek Ottomans living here. He was right.'

'It must have been a bad time for Turkey,' he said. '"The sick man of Europe". Everyone was fighting for a piece of it.'

She replaced the lamp on the mantle. 'Yes – but here, in this city, it was supposed to be different. Smyrna was a place where Christians and Muslims lived as brothers, side by side. Then came the Greek politician Venizelos and his

"Megali Idea" – the Big Idea. Big Idea?' Eris threw her hands in the air. 'Pah! Bad idea, more like,' she scoffed. 'Smyrna was to be part of Greece, and also most of the coastline of Asia Minor – all the places in Turkey where Greeks lived in ancient times.'

Ben had heard about the terrible things that happened in Smyrna after the Great War. But even to him – a man who had spent more time in this part of the world than most – the reasons for the conflict were oftentimes quite incomprehensible. 'But you were Greeks . . . so that would have been good for you, wouldn't it?'

'You wouldn't know. And you couldn't understand. It was not easy for my family when the soldiers came from Greece. Like them, we were Christians. But they took over the streets and treated us like peasants.' Ben watched her as she gazed at an indeterminate spot in the distance. She took a deep breath and exhaled loudly. 'It was worse for the Muslims. My father tells stories of good people – neighbours, people who worked for him – being forced from their homes . . . killed by the Greek soldiers.'

She rolled her sleeves up above her elbows and ran her dust cloth over the sinuous lines of the polished timber bookshelf. 'It was worse when the Turks arrived in 1922. They would never allow the Greek army to keep the city. And so Atatürk attacked Smyrna with his soldiers and drove the Greek occupiers out. But where did that leave us?'

'I've never really understood,' Ben admitted. 'Were you Ottomans, or were you Greek?'

She laughed wryly, one corner of her mouth curled up. 'We were both. How crazy is that? When I think about it now, it must sound strange to anyone who was not here. We were Ottomans – for hundreds of years, Greek people lived in towns in Asia Minor with the Sultans as their rulers.

But we also called ourselves Greek. Most of all, we were Christians – we prayed to the Orthodox Greek saints and we were christened, married and worshipped in Greek churches here in Ottoman lands.'

She pulled one of the dining chairs out from beneath the table, its wooden legs screeching on the tile floor. She sat heavily on the rush-bottomed seat.

'But after the Greeks and Turks fought over our city, my father knew it could never be as it was before. It was not the Turkish soldiers that frightened him. It was the groups of bandits waiting outside the city that he feared. They were jackals, waiting for the fighting to start.'

Eris picked at her hair absentmindedly and gazed at the floor. 'They hated us for our wealth. Hated us for being Christians. And they wanted revenge for the things the Greek soldiers had done to the Muslim people in the city.' She paused, drew breath. 'My mother and father knew what would happen. Father was at his warehouse, and mother was packing the house with my two sisters. They were eight and twelve. We were to go to our farm near Hisarlik – father thought we would be safe there. But we were too late.'

The room fell silent. Stifling afternoon heat pressed through the heavy stone walls. The throbbing anthem of the cicadas' chorus pounded at Ben's eardrums as he put down his work. Eris sat at the end of the table, fingers entwined together in her lap like a tangled ball of yarn.

'I was five. We heard shouting … screaming … in the street. The sound of things breaking. Mother told me and my twin brother we would play hide and seek,' she continued. 'That we must be very quiet, no matter what happened. We would lose the game if anyone found our hiding place. I remember her smiling. But her eyes, they were clouded – black. Stormy. She took us to her bedroom upstairs and emptied her dowry chest.

We could only just fit. Our knees were tied in knots. My head was resting on my brother's back. The sound of his heartbeat was a hammer in my ears.'

Her voice dropped to a whisper. 'It was so dark. It was difficult to breathe. Then we heard the noises. The floor shook when the door was smashed in. My mother was begging and weeping. Then she started screaming. My sisters were shrieking. There were men's voices, roaring like lions and laughing. I reached for my brother's hand. It was wet with tears. Hours seemed to pass. Then we heard nothing. My head was full of the scent of the lavender mother used to keep moths away.'

'We stayed there,' she said. 'Our legs were numb and our knees throbbed. Dust filled our lungs. We waited. Then we heard a howl from downstairs. When our father cried out our mother's name, we knew his voice. We called for him. He opened the chest and lifted us out, holding us in his arms and pressing his face into our hair. Father carried us downstairs and walked through this room with his hands over our eyes. It smelt of blood and bad things. Our neighbours were Muslims. They helped us escape the city. Father dressed as a woman and covered his face and in Hisarlik, we were safe. We stayed there until we were forced to go to Lesvos in 1923.'

Leaning her elbows heavily on the timber table, she spoke so quietly he had to strain to hear her. 'Many years later, Father told me the Turks raped my mother and older sister then they cut their throats. My other sister they pinned to the door with bayonets. They slit her open and spilled her insides across the floor.' Eris looked up at him with hollow eyes. 'The smell of lavender still makes me weep.'

'And this house . . .?' Ben's voice cracked, his heart aching for the broken woman seated before him.

'Our neighbours – they cared for it. They are Turks and they are good people. They told the soldiers it was their house, and it was left alone. One day they hoped – we all hoped – we could return.' She gestured towards the treasure trove piled upon the table. 'Father could not carry this with us when we fled Smyrna so he left it here, hidden. But things between Greece and Turkey have never improved. It was too dangerous to come back. Now that it seems there will be war in Cyprus, we could not wait any longer. My father is too old, so it had to be me. The only thing that wasn't here was the pendant I was wearing. That was with my aunt in Ankara. This is why I was on the train. But now, I must take all this with me to Lesvos. It is time.'

He looked at the bounty that lay before him. A sense of urgency burned in his gut. 'When do you plan to leave? I don't . . . it's difficult to explain just how important these things are. I really need to record them . . . to publish them. They . . . they mean too much. Not just for me, you understand. For the world. For everyone.'

Pushing her chair back from the table, she began to pace nervously about the room, absently shifting ornaments from one place to the next. 'I have not much time. And I don't care about the world.'

'What I would really like is to return to Eskitepe to collect my camera so that I could photograph the pieces . . .'

Eris spun on her heel and snapped. 'No! That is *not* possible!'

'OK, then. İzmir is a big city. I'm sure there's somewhere there I can buy one . . .'

'You don't understand! There is no time. We kept these things safe so we could one day sell them if we needed money. Now, we need money. We are desperate!' She resumed her pacing, her arms locked across her chest. 'It was a mistake to bring you here.'

Gently standing and placing himself in her path, he lightly rested his hands on her upper arms. 'Please, tell me what's wrong. Perhaps I can help.'

She looked down at her feet. 'It's my father. Well, my brother, really. He has debts with some bad people and he owes them money. Lots of money. My father must pay what he owes. Otherwise . . . I do not know what might happen.'

'No debt could be this great.' He shook his head. 'Eris, what you don't understand is that if you let me write an article about them and publish illustrations in a journal . . . well, as far as everyone's concerned they'll be authenticated. As it is, most people wouldn't know whether or not these are real. But if I write about them, it will make them much more valuable than they would be otherwise. The authorities won't be happy . . . I'll have to think about that one. Maybe we can sort something out – I'll wait until I know you're clear of the country and then I'll go to the police. It's hardly my fault if you disappear and take all this with you, is it? Can't worry myself with the details right now. I'll work that out when it becomes a problem. One thing's certain – your collection will be worth far more if I write about it.'

'But these men, they are impatient. I am afraid of what they will do if I do not return to Lesvos quickly. How long do you think it will take for you to do your drawings?'

'Give me four days.' It would be tight – much less time than he needed. But he could see even that was pushing it.

'And how long until the pictures are in the papers?'

He hesitated. The best outcome for him would be an academic paper in the *Journal of Near Eastern Studies* where he could thumb his nose at his peers on a grand scale. 'Well, it takes some time for refereed articles to make it to print. To be absolutely honest, it might take a year and a half. At least.'

Laughing scornfully, she shook her head. 'One year and a half? Then what is the point for me in waiting? I must sell these things quickly.'

He hesitated. The only other solution he could think of would involve quite a compromise on his part. 'OK. The newspapers. That's how we can do it. I'll take my drawings to the *Illustrated London News*. I've worked with them on some articles before – I'm sure they'll publish a story. That way the pictures will be in print in a matter of weeks. Let me do this. Please.' It wouldn't carry anything near the weight of an academic article. But it would be better than nothing.

Gnawing on her bottom lip, she was silent for a moment, her brow knotted with anxiety. 'Four days and then you will have what you need? And then the pictures will be in the newspaper in a month?'

Four days to complete a job that would, under normal circumstances, take weeks, if not months – it was a big ask. He nodded with a great deal more certainty than he felt. 'Yes. Absolutely.'

'All right. I will stay for four days. You may do your drawings. But then I must go.'

He would need to work night and day to finish the task. But it was worth it.

'Thank you,' he said, and squeezed Eris' shoulder warmly. She flinched and drew away from him.

Time ebbed and flowed from day to night and back again. Ben was stretched to breaking point. But as the hours ticked by and he began to make difficult choices about which of the treasures deserved to be measured and documented and which he should leave aside, the harder he pushed himself.

When his focus began to wane and his back and knees creaked from countless hours sitting in the same spot, he would find respite in the garden. Under a spreading canopy of ancient olive trees with trunks as fat as a man's torso, he followed a worn circuit around the interior perimeter of the moss-covered stone walls that enclosed the house and garden. His senses were revived by the warm and humid air thick with the scent of citrus oil and jasmine blossoms.

On occasion, Eris joined him and spoke of her childhood in Lesvos and the harrowing events that had driven her to its shores. The three-year battle between Greece and Turkey had left tens of thousands dead and countless more displaced and homeless. The resolution to the conflict was clear-cut and brutal. In 1923, Eris and her family, and over one-and-a-half million other Christian Ottomans, were forcibly expelled from Turkey and relocated to Greece. On the other side, half a million Muslims who had been living in Greece for generations were exiled to Turkey.

Like so many of the Greek Orthodox Christians living in Ottoman lands who were forced to relocate to Greece, when they first arrived on Lesvos, Eris and her family were treated as pariahs. She spoke of her father's attempt to start anew on the island with the handful of coins her aunt had stitched into the hemline of her coat – all that remained after their possessions were seized on the docks by Greek authorities when they arrived from Asia Minor. They had been lucky to escape with their lives, and although it was galling to Eris' father to know that just across the water was a hidden cache of treasure that would have made their lives on the island more comfortable, it would be a long time before it was safe to go back and reclaim it.

'It was the politicians,' she explained. 'Always the politicians. They treat us like pieces on a giant chessboard. They forget we are also human beings, like them. But they do not care. They just play with us in their giant game. So many who came to Greece with us did not even speak or read Greek. Yes, they were Christian. But they only spoke Turkish. They had spent their lives in Asia Minor. The houses we left behind were built by our ancestors. Gardens and trees planted by our grandfathers. All deserted. It was a terrible time.'

With the quiet acceptance that allowed survivors of unimaginable horror to endure, she described her family's misfortune in measured tones. Ben was cut of a different cloth. When faced with adversity, he met it with raised fists and a guttural roar. But Eris' gentle acceptance of her fate calmed him, and for the first time since the end of the war, he began to give voice to the visions that haunted him.

'It never felt real – it still doesn't . . . the shock of living in constant fear and discomfort, in conditions you could scarcely fathom before the war – fatigue beyond description . . . hunger . . . physical pain. The stench and filth. Death and horror were part of that landscape – just one face of a hideous mosaic.'

Eris placed a hand gently on his wrist. 'But you are a good man.'

He winced. 'No one can be a good man in war. There's a threshold . . . a point where the person you were is left behind and you're transformed into something hard and cold. Something inhuman. I wasn't any different.'

Leaning against an olive tree's gnarled trunk, he felt its rough bark jab his back through his shirt. He pressed harder against it. The pain was perversely comforting. 'There was a village in the foothills of the mountains. Someone told the Germans it was where the family of one of the Resistance leaders lived. The fighters called him Abaddon – the Angel of the Abyss. The Destroyer. And the Germans wanted him dead. But when he proved too difficult to kill, they went for easier pickings.'

Ben dropped his head forward. 'We knew as soon as we heard the sound of the bombs in the valley. We waited till the soldiers had retreated to their barracks. From a distance, we thought our eyes were deceiving us. Where stone houses once stood, there was only rubble. The trees and fields around what used to be Asos were coated in a shroud of dust. It was all that remained. Other than the dead. We found them in the olive grove. The men of the village. None of them were of fighting age, of course. The fighters were in the mountains with us. The brave Germans slaughtered toothless grand-fathers. Rounded them up, stood them in a line, and shot them. Boys not even old enough to sprout a beard. The young. The slow-witted. The old. White faces caked in dust and blood, dull eyes looking to the heavens. I've never forgotten. There were two boys – brothers. One was older – maybe eleven. The other wouldn't have been much more than nine. Their shirts were soaked with blood, a black stain spreading beneath them across the packed earth. The older boy's arms were wrapped around his brother. Trying to protect him, I suppose. Or comfort him. Either way . . .'

Eris gently squeezed his wrist. 'Ben, I am so sorry . . .'

'That was it for me. After that, I felt nothing.' Tears spattered into the dust at his feet.

He spoke, and her presence comforted him. With a peni-tent's zeal, the words tumbled from his lips as heavy as rockfall. Once he began, it seemed he couldn't stop. He recalled the blind panic he felt as wave after wave of German para-troopers quietly spun to earth under pearly moonlight like schools of Portuguese men-o'-war; his incoherent horror at the charred bodies of infants, their bones and impossibly tiny skulls turned to chalky splinters in the ruins of mountain villages set aflame by German troops wreaking hellish vengeance on the elusive Resistance; and the grievously injured young sergeant they captured and strapped to a tree, leaving him to die screaming as wild dogs tore the flesh from his bones.

The one thing he withheld from Eris was Karina. It felt like a betrayal even to speak her name. He communed with her only in his soul's darkest caverns.

As he began to release the spectral memories that tormented him, he drew closer to the deep pit where dark things lay, long hidden but never forgotten. A leaden veil descended heavily upon his shoulders and he tried to draw back from the precipice, afraid of what he might find when he looked over the edge.

When night fell and he slept, his past returned to him. Ghosts long neglected found refuge in his dreams.

13

## Crete, Greece, 1944

'He has left the brothel and is heading towards the mountain pass.'

Michail stood panting, hands on hips, exhausted from his dash across the foothills. The moon was full, its light shining on the looming peaks and boulders punching black holes in the night sky above the island like defiant fists. The grotto's rock walls resounded with a sharp clatter of weapons shouldered and the thud of worn boots on shale as the fighters prepared to depart.

Ben turned to his comrades. 'Right. You know what to do. Chambers and Ioannis, take your men and head north to take the high ground. One each side of the cutting. Karina, position yourself on the cliff with a good shot of the road. Grigoris and I will blockade the pass.'

'Wait, Ben.' Michail held up his hand, skeletal in the moonlight. 'It isn't like the other times. He isn't alone.'

Commandant Hans Volmer was a tediously regimented

man whose life was scheduled into strictly observed hourly blocks. Since arriving on Crete, three hours every Tuesday evening had been dedicated to an enthusiastic exploration of Heraklion's celebrated fleshpots. Perhaps reluctant to admit to any human weaknesses, when indulging his vices Volmer gave his army-issue chauffeur the night off and drove himself into town. It was the only time during his waking hours that he was not surrounded by a gaggle of attentive acolytes. For the past two months, he had focused his attentions on just one brothel and, as confirmed by the reliable testimony of the madam who also happened to have five brothers fighting with the Resistance, one buxom prostitute in particular who was celebrated for her cushiony derrière.

. Volmer was predictable and this made him an easy target. The plot had been in place for a month: they would abduct the Commandant and rendezvous with a British naval launch in one of the thousands of isolated coves dotted along Crete's southern coastline. From there they would evacuate Volmer to the British base in Alexandria. Ben had engineered the plan to boost the spirit of the beleaguered Cretan populace while also striking a blow to the German occupiers' morale. His commanders in Alexandria were impressed by his initiative and audacity, and the plan was given a resounding thumbs-up. To reduce the risk of brutal reprisals against the Greeks, once the mission was complete an airdrop of leaflets was planned that would claim the abduction as the work of Allied troops with no local involvement, a report that would be corroborated by a BBC news transmission in the days that followed.

The revelation that Volmer was not travelling alone seemed to scupper their well-laid plans.

'Damn. Tell me.'

'It's Garvé.'

'That fucking bastard,' Ben cursed beneath his breath. *I've been counting the days . . . why did it have to be this one?*

The fighters stood silently in nervous clusters, awaiting his orders. Ben turned to his friend and comrade. 'Any views on the matter, Will?'

Tall, slim and with a heavy lock of black hair falling over one raised eyebrow, William Chambers was the very model of the dashing British airman. Will had parachuted onto the Lasithi Plateau in 1942. He'd joined forces with Ben and his fellow fighters holed up in mountain eyries, from where they had managed to become a persistent stone in the occupying force's jackboot. The men had become close during the last two years, hunched at night by open fires as the snow fell around them, raising their voices together in song as Manolis tickled the three strings of his *lyra* with a bow. Other than the blond hue of Ben's hair, which he had to blacken with burnt cork ash any time he wanted to venture into one of the larger towns, there was little to distinguish Will and Ben from their Greek confederates. Dressed in dusty mountain shepherds' garb – knee-high black boots, breeches, black shirt, embroidered waistcoat with a silver-scabbarded dagger jammed into a mulberry silk sash and bandoliers draped across their shoulders – they had also both cultivated the extravagant moustaches for which the Cretan mountaineers were renowned.

'We only planned for one captive, Ben. This brings an unknown element into play that I'm not particularly comfortable with. I think we postpone for a week. We know his routine. It won't be difficult to reschedule.' The Englishman was naturally cautious, which made him the perfect foil for Ben's impulsiveness. 'Perhaps we should check with Headquarters.'

'No time. The car'll be through the pass before we get an answer.' He turned and began pacing. 'Let's think this through. I know Josef Garvé. All too well. We all do.' Ben's Greek comrades murmured their agreement, some cursing and spitting on the ground. 'If anything, he's the worst of the lot of them.'

'He's not military, Ben,' Will countered.

'No. No he's not. But you'll just have to trust me on this. He's a pig.'

Will smiled tightly. 'Sounds a bit personal, Ben. You know what they say? An eye for an eye, and the whole world goes blind.'

'Ah, yes – and a tooth for a tooth, and we all eat soup. But if it is grandmother's *avgolemono* broth . . . I'd be willing to make the sacrifice.' The fighters laughed, more raucously than they might in other circumstances.

Ben continued through clenched teeth. 'I have good reason to target him, Chambers. Remind me when we next have time for a quiet drink by the fireside, and I'll fill you in on that son of a bitch's history on this island.' He balled his fists, fighting back the black fury that rose in his throat at the thought of the Frenchman. 'Think of it this way. He gives us a direct line to Hitler's inner circle. Volmer's just a military functionary. But Garvé – he's become a shill for Himmler.'

A booming voice echoed from the corner of the grotto. 'Ben is right, William. Garvé is a μεγαλες πουτσες. He took as his mistress a young girl from our village.' Grigoris rose to his feet and ambled over to the two men, his brooding face cast into moonlit shadows by the turban wrapped tightly about his head. 'Brother, if you would allow it, I will wrap my hands around his throat, snap his spine then shit in his mouth. But if that cannot be and we must keep these sons of whores alive, I would be happy to help the French arse-licker leave Crete in chains.'

'This is good for us,' Ben agreed. 'Not one, but two of the German hierarchy. And one of them with direct links to Hitler and his slow-witted stooges. It's too good an opportunity to pass up.'

Around him, shaggy heads nodded gravely, gaunt cheeks and hollow eyes a testament to hardships endured over months worming from one hiding spot to another in the mountains, evading detection by the thousands of German troops desperate to break the back of the Resistance. These proud and unflinching people had risen up against the hated occupation, relinquishing their existence as farmers, fishermen and shepherds to fight for freedom. They were Ben's family, and whenever he called on them to put their lives at risk, the sense of responsibility weighed heavily on his heart.

Manolis hoisted a wineskin from a niche in the wall. Like most men of fighting age, the village headman had left Asos and taken up arms against the Occupation. He raised it above his head with the Resistance toast: 'Blessed Virgin stand close to us! May she scour the rust from our guns!'

The night was unusually tranquil as the fighters wound their way through craggy ravines cast in shadow by stands of oleander bushes in flower and ancient olive trees. The fierce southern winds that blasted across the Mediterranean from the African shore with a lion's roar had abated. The only sound was the gurgle of a gushing snowmelt-fed stream wandering its way down the mountainside towards the distant sea.

Ben felt a hand at the small of his back.

'Why do you always keep me away from the fighting?'

Karina had fallen into step beside him. A rush of desire surged through his veins. He could barely remember their life together before the war. Now their marital bed was a hastily packed pad of straw and rushes, the night sky a canopy above their heads.

'You are always at the front of the fighting,' she complained. 'But you never let me stand by your side. We have been doing this for years now, *χρυσέ μου*. What must I do to prove my skills? I think it's because you're afraid something will happen to me.'

'No. It's because I'm afraid something will happen to *me*. You're the best shot we've got, Karina *μου*. That's why I want you on that ridge. If things go badly down there, I want you protecting me. There's no one I trust more.'

'Don't argue, little sister.' For a large man, Grigoris was surprisingly stealthy. He had manoeuvred soundlessly through the line of fighters to join Karina at Ben's side. 'He is right. You make best use of your talents from a distance. Besides. Grandmama needs you to live through the war and go back to Asos.'

'What *γιαγιά* needs, Grigoris, is for us to fight for her home.'

Grigoris enveloped his sister in a bear-like embrace. 'I know, nightingale. And you are also my guardian angel. If you are up on the ridge with the German donkeys in your sights, I know I'll be safe.' He dropped his voice. 'Much better you than any of these other goat-fuckers who can't shoot straight to save themselves.'

Ignoring her brother, she took her husband's hand. 'Still. One day I hope I can show you how good I can be in a fight.'

'And I hope you never have to,' he said as he kissed her forehead.

He lay on his belly in a tumble of gravel beside the road, propped up on his elbows, gun at the ready. Five men lay at his side. In a culvert on the opposite side of the road, Grigoris was holed up with two other fighters, readying themselves to cover the passenger's side of the car. The bright wash of moonlight across the barren landscape left nowhere to hide; Ben was all too aware of just how exposed they were.

If they had been positioned somewhere less isolated, he could have called on the support of the mountain villagers to help them spring the trap and watch their backs. If German troops approached a town when the Resistance fighters had come down out of their mountain lair to collect much-needed supplies, the locals would shout out coded warnings – 'The black cattle have strayed into the wheat!' or 'Our in-laws have arrived!' But out here, Ben and his comrades were on their own.

A treacherous voice of doubt took up a refrain in his mind. What if Volmer had picked up a convoy somewhere between Heraklion and here? Maybe there were more men in the car than just the two of them – maybe Michail hadn't looked hard enough? And what if a German patrol happened by? There was no cover here – in the moonlight they'd stick out like dog's balls. They were sitting ducks and easily outnumbered. What if this was a mistake? *It is a mistake. Will was right. We should have waited. You're an idiot, Hitchens.*

A tawny owl's call echoed from the escarpment above the road – Ioannis' signal that Volmer's car was approaching. The warning was unnecessary; in the deathly silence, the grinding of the staff car's gears and roar of the engine as it laboured up the steep and rocky road was unmistakable. As it came closer, the hairs on the back of Ben's neck prickled and his heart beat faster. But his hand was steady as the gleam of headlights swung round a curve in the road.

He whispered to his men, repeating the instructions they all knew by heart. 'On my signal, Dimitri, you and your boys step in front of the car. Fire warning shots in the air . . . shoot out the radiator if he doesn't stop.'

Karina's cousin smiled grimly. The smuggler's teeth flashed white in the moonlight. 'With pleasure.'

'At the same time,' Ben continued, 'Grigoris and I will take the vehicle from either side.'

The men nodded, black eyes flashing and mouths set in resolute lines.

The car rounded the corner and entered the ravine. Ben raised his hand up in a fist. 'Wait . . . wait . . .' As the distance closed, he could feel the men beside him tensing, ready to swoop, their breath coming in raggedy gasps. Fifty feet. Forty. 'Wait . . .' Thirty. Twenty.

Ben dropped his hand and shouted. 'Now! Go! Go! Go!'

Dimitri and his two comrades sprinted onto the road in front of the vehicle and fired their weapons into the air. Volmer slammed on the brakes. Fishtailing in the loose gravel, the car swerved on an angle before coming to a halt. Ben and his men ran along the ditch beside the road and took up position on the driver's side of the car. Volmer stared out the window in confusion, mouth agape. But Ben was fixed on the baleful menace of the man seated beside him. They locked eyes and Garvé blanched with the shock of recognition. Then he was gone, firing his pistol as he dived out of the passenger's side door.

'Get out of the car, Herr Commandant!' Ben shouted. The German reached for the handle and the door creaked open. He stepped out onto the road and stood defiantly, hands raised above his head. Ben moved towards Volmer and shouted. 'Grigoris? What's happening? Can you see the French bastard?'

Before the Greek could answer, a volley of shots from the rear of the vehicle signalled the Frenchman's location. The shrill whine of a bullet passing close by Ben's eardrum caused him to recoil and drop to the ground. Volmer crouched and scrambled for the back of the car, ducking down beneath the boot to take shelter from the covering fire blazing down from the shooters on the escarpment. Firing blindly into the dark, Garvé and Volmer returned their shots.

Ben scuttled across the road beneath the line of fire, dragging himself towards the culvert on his elbows. He rolled into the ditch out of the pool of light cast by the car's headlights. Hunching down below the level of the road, he ran until he was positioned behind the two men holed up at the rear of the car. He had them in his sights and knew he could bring them down in a heartbeat.

*Less risk*, he thought. *A dead German in the hand is worth two in the bush. And some of those bullets are going to find their marks.* Ben hesitated. But to capture them alive . . . that's what he'd promised, so that's what he'd do. He was damned if he was going to let that French bastard get off that easily!

Both men were wielding Lugers. Counting off eight shots, Ben timed his assault for when he knew they would need to reload.

Six. Seven. The wet slap of a bullet hitting flesh and a muffled grunt followed by the heavy thud of a body hitting the dust. Eight. *That's it. Now.*

Ben couldn't see who had fallen, and had no time to think about it as he sprinted out of the shadows, cudgel raised above his head. Sensing that Garvé posed the greatest threat, he clouted the Frenchman behind the ear and took great pleasure body-slamming him into the side of the car. Volmer spun around and began to stumble backwards, fumbling with his pistol as he attempted to reload it. Ben raised his gun in steady hands. 'Herr General! Drop your weapon!'

'*Nein*!' Volmer roared as the magazine slipped into the grip and he pointed its barrel at Ben's head. There was a deafening crack of rifle fire from above and the German's legs gave way beneath him. He fell into the dust, screaming and clutching his ankle. Gun raised, Ben kicked the men's weapons away from them.

Eyes firmly fixed on the two men at his feet, Ben bellowed into the night. 'Michail? Andreas?'

'Yes!'

'Bring the cuffs. Now! We need to clear the road and get out of here.'

The boy ran over carrying the army-issue handcuffs with three grim-faced companions walking behind, rifles at the ready. 'Behind their backs,' Ben instructed gruffly. With a boot to the back, Garvé fell face-first into the dust as Michail locked his wrists behind him. Volmer was still doubled over in pain, but the men hoisted him to his feet and wrenched his arms behind his back.

Ben could see no further than the halo of light cast by the abandoned vehicle's headlights. 'Come on! Let's go! Let's go!' He turned to the men who now surrounded the two prisoners. 'Christos, Andreas – get in the car and drive it to the ravine. Push it over the cliff – but careful – don't follow it in, mind! We need you back here in one piece. Yanni, Grigoris, take these bastards and watch them as we regroup.'

Michail shook his head. 'Grigoris is gone, Ben.'

'Gone? Gone where?'

Eyes downcast, the Greek tilted his chin towards the side of the road.

Heartsick, Ben walked over to the culvert. Grigoris lay spread-eagled on the roadside, as mighty as a razed oak.

A single bullet had pierced the centre of his forehead. It was an innocuous enough hole, Ben thought to himself, the shock of his friend's death yet to hit him. The wound was no bigger than a small coin and rimmed with black. A line of crimson blood oozed down his cheek and smeared across his chin. Ben didn't need to check for a pulse. The damage to his face was superficial, but were he to turn Grigoris onto his front, he knew that half his skull would be blown away.

The crunch of gravel announced the arrival of their comrades from the escarpment. Ben moved to shield Grigoris' body from Karina. Her face was flushed, triumphant. 'Did you see that shot? Yes, I saved your life. You can thank me later. Now, where's my brother? If he'd been doing his job . . .' She froze, mid-step, as she took in the tableau by the side of the road.

He reached out and grasped her shoulder. 'Karina . . . I'm sorry . . .'

Shrugging off his hand, she dropped to her knees. She filled her lungs, shoulders shaking. Ben steeled himself for the keening wail he was sure would follow. Instead, she released her breath in a shuddering rush. Fat tears coursed down her cheeks as she reached for Grigoris' lifeless hand and lifted it to her lips. 'Oh, dear brother. It is the way it is written. So, you have left us, son of Georgios and Irini. Life to us.' She stood, legs quivering, and wiped her eyes with the back of her hand. 'We have no time to mourn.'

Ben had always marvelled at Karina's strength. Her composure at this moment took his breath away. 'She's right. It's not going to do Grigoris any good if we're caught here flat-footed by a German patrol. Let's go.'

Nikolaos stepped forward, hands clasped before him. 'There's more. Ben, it's Will.'

'What? Tell me.'

'Ioannis is helping him back down. He's taken a shot in his thigh. It's bleeding – not too badly. But he won't be able to walk.'

From the steep incline beside the road, there was an awkward thud and scrabble as Ioannis assisted the wounded Englishman down to the road. Ben flicked the switch on the flashlight hanging from his bandolier and ran towards the culvert. In the beam of light Will's face took on a translucent quality, his head lolling loosely on his neck as he slipped in and out of consciousness. A sheet of sticky red oozed from a tear in his black breeches, the gore bright against Will's milky-white thigh.

Ben knelt beside the Englishman and examined the wound. He was relieved to feel an exit wound, but the bullet had done some ghastly damage on its way out. There was plenty of blood, but not so much as to suggest a major vessel had been breached. He took the sash from around his waist and used it to bind the wound. 'You're a lucky bastard, Chambers.'

Will smiled through lips turned white. 'Exactly what I was thinking.'

'I've been saving this for a special occasion.' Taking a syrette of morphine from his bandolier, Ben cracked it open and lifted Will's shirt, slipping the needle under his skin. 'My gift to you. This should fix you up for a bit. Good news? The wound won't kill you. Not for a while, anyway. But we'll need to get you to a doctor. Quickly.'

He turned to the two men supporting Will. 'Make him comfortable in the car until we're ready. We'll move out soon.'

Ben spun on his heel and kicked at a rock lying by the road. *Who are you to take such a gamble with people's lives, you goddamned fraud? What were you thinking?*

Turning to face the prisoners, he struggled to quell the tide of blood-red rage rising in his chest. Volmer was bent double in the dust, lying awkwardly on his side. His face was porridge-grey and knotted with pain. Treacly black blood oozed from his wound and shards of shattered bone protruded through the slate-grey fabric of his trousers, shredded to ribbons by the gunshot. Garvé knelt rigidly beside him, features frozen with disdain.

'I was wondering when you would crawl out from under whatever rock has been sheltering you, Benedict.'

Fury burst behind Ben's eyes and he cracked his elbow sharply into the Frenchman's temple, knocking him sideways into the dust. 'Shut your goddamned mouth, maggot!'

Ben began pacing, working through the options. 'We could carry the German. But we'll also need to carry Will. It has to be Will. Carry Will *and* Volmer? Maybe, maybe. But then we'd have to leave Garvé behind. And that's not happening. Too big a prize.'

Dimitri had been standing silently behind the two captives, his rifle pressed into Garvé's back. After dissolving his business arrangement with the Frenchman, the smuggler had become one of the Resistance's fiercest fighters. 'Or we could just kill them both. For Grigoris. This cock-licker killed my cousin.' He slid the bolt of his gun forward. 'And I've been wanting to do this for a long time.'

'Dimitri, no!' Ben raised his hand.

'They must not die heroes, cousin.' Karina spoke firmly. 'Kill the sons-of-whores and they will be martyrs. Capture them, parade them in front of their enemies. Humiliate them. Then, they will be pariahs. That's the punishment they deserve.'

Ben had a moment of clarity. 'OK. Change of plans. Manolis and Andreas, use the car to take Grigoris to the village. Leave him with his wife – she'll have to take care of his burial. Then dump the car – but bring it back here to do it. Can't chance the Germans finding it near Asos. The rest of us will split into two groups. There's not enough of us to carry two injured men across the mountain pass. So it's your lucky day, Volmer. You get to stay so we can get Will to safety. We'll take Garvé along as an appetiser for the generals. We'll need to make a pannier to carry Will. Dimitri – you take the general into the mountains and hole up in the caves. Clean and wrap his wound as best you can, though he can rot – literally – as far as I'm concerned. We'll give the go-ahead for the leaflet drop and broadcast as planned. Hopefully the Germans will believe Volmer has left the island already.'

'After that?'

'Once the dust settles we'll arrange another extraction and come back to get him. Shouldn't be too long. A week at the most. Clear?'

The fighters nodded and disappeared into the night.

By the road, Karina was crouching by her brother's body, murmuring prayers and blessings beneath her breath. 'You, who of old did fashion me from nothingness, and with your image divine did honour me, lead me back to be refashioned into that ancient beauty of your likeness. Blessed are you, O Lord . . .'

Ben crouched beside her and gently placed his arm across her shoulders. 'He was a good man.'

'The best. I will miss him.'

'So will I. But Karina . . . we must go.'

'I can't leave when my brother is to be buried,' she said.

'No. This time, you must listen to me. You can't stay. It's not safe. We can return once the Germans stop looking for us.'

They gazed in silence at Grigoris' tranquil face.

'I will pray for him.' The words felt fraudulent as they fell from his lips. It had been a long time since he and God had been more than just passing acquaintances. But to his wife and the devout villagers who were now his family, no other sentiment would do.

Karina said nothing. She rested her head on his shoulder as the melodic buzz of crickets and night insects filled the air.

From the corner of his eye, he could see Garvé staring at them dispassionately, his face an expressionless mask.

Ben shuddered.

# 14

## İzmir, Turkey, 1952

On what was to be Ben's last day, his nerves were frayed. The burning sense of urgency that had been eating at him since he commenced the monumental task of recording Eris' cache was almost unbearable. It was down to the last few hours as he tried to be methodical about triaging which artefacts would have to be excluded from his account. Mental and physical exhaustion had depleted his spirit. The velvety black of night seeped in through the open windows, and the incessant whirr of crickets in the garden irritated him beyond belief.

A gentle touch on his shoulder stilled him. 'Tomorrow I must leave.' Eris spoke quietly. 'And, I think, you will not be able to draw all the things that are left before then.'

Ben laughed as he stood, pushing his chair back from the table. 'Well, thank you for pointing out the bloody obvious. Much obliged.'

'If you are not going to be able to finish it tonight, then you might as well stop now and come and play a game of *tavla* with me.'

'*Tavla*?'

'The English call it backgammon,' she said.

'I know what it is, thank you. I just can't believe you're suggesting I waste time playing a board game.'

'My father always says if you want to live forever, look at the old men playing *tavla* in the cafés. They are peaceful. Content. You know this is true – you have run out of time and will not get all of this done. So come and sit with me.'

He had always prided himself on being the one who kept going until the bitter end. But looking down at Eris' upturned face as she gazed at him with eyes as warm as molten toffee, he knew she was right.

'OK. You're on.' He closed his notebook and slipped it into the bookcase. He then picked up the two broken fragments of a small, marble slab engraved with ancient Greek characters from the dining table. The elements hadn't been kind to it, and the engraving appeared to have been eroded to a point at which it was illegible. Nevertheless, it warranted closer inspection. 'This . . . I've been saving this one till last. Can't ignore an inscription. Archaeologists' rule number one.'

As he placed it on a small side table at the base of the stairs, the light from the lantern struck the marble on an angle and illuminated the text. The lettering became clear. If he held the inscription in just the right position, he might be able to decipher what was written there.

'Eris, did you see this?'

'No, I did not. And now, I have other things to think of. Come.'

Hesitating, he turned the tablet fragment in his fingers.

'Fine. But I'm not going to bed until I've transcribed this. Don't let me forget.'

Eris passed through the arched doorway that led out into the paved courtyard where a lantern shed a warm glow on a backgammon board set up on a small stone table. Moths dipped and spun in the light and a cool evening breeze rustled through tangled garlands of wisteria dripping from a wooden trellis overhead. She turned and looked over her shoulder, her eyes veiled by thick black lashes. 'I will try to remind you. But I cannot promise. We might find other things to think about.'

'Another double six? You have the devil's own luck.'

Laughing, Eris shifted her pieces with a rapid-fire flick of her wrist and a confidence that would have put a Greek grandfather to shame. 'Yes, luck is important. But if you make bad decisions with the numbers you throw, you will lose.' She gestured towards the spread of Ben's own pieces. 'And you? You make some very bad decisions.'

'Story of my life,' he moaned.

She had manoeuvred her pieces in such a way that his chequers were quickly locked out of his home board. Now, just three of her own pieces remained. He braced himself in anticipation of what would be a decisive thrashing.

'So what's your excuse?' he asked. 'It's like billiards – proficiency in a game like this bears witness to a squandered youth.'

'When we arrived on Lesvos after the Population Exchange, my father was one of the only new arrivals who could read and write Greek,' she said. 'Most of the others who came from Asia Minor . . . well, many of them . . . couldn't even *speak* Greek. And so, my father would help them with documents. He would write and translate for them. With the money hidden in the hem of my coat, he had enough to rent a small shop – a grocery. And there he would help the other immigrants. While he worked, the old men would sit with me. They taught me to play.' She laughed. 'I should have warned you.'

'Well, where I come from,' he said, 'if you don't manage to score a single point by the end of a game, you have to drop your pants and run round the table.'

Raising one eyebrow, Eris curled her full lips into a wry smile. 'That would not be very proper, Benedict Hitchens.'

'No, it would not. So out of consideration for you, I will refrain from de-trousering myself.'

They fell into a companionable silence, listening to the secret sounds of the Aegean night. The manic urgency that had been driving him for days subsided, replaced by a languid and very pleasant inertia. His arm was as heavy as a burlap sack of wet sand as he lifted the cup and took what would be his final throw of the dice. After moving his pieces, he dropped his arm to his side and watched as she finished the game with a whoop of glee, her eyes shining with delight at her victory.

'Your husband must love that competitive streak.'

She lifted her left hand. 'In all the time we have been here you have not noticed? No ring. No husband.'

Of course he had registered the absence of a wedding band on her finger. 'A woman as beautiful as you and – forgive me – being the age you are, I assumed you were married but chose not to wear a ring.'

The victorious glint in her eyes was snuffed out. 'You have told me of the things that happened to you in Crete. For me, too, the war was difficult.' She smiled sadly. 'I was betrothed to Xander when I was a girl. He was so handsome. Black eyes and a happy heart. And his beard . . . Ah, what a beard he had. The beard of a strong man. We were married as the Germans arrived on Lesvos. Xander went up into the mountains to fight. He said we did not get rid of the Turks just to welcome more invaders. My family and I lived through the war. It was not always easy, but in our village it was also not so different from normal. Lesvos – it was not important for the Germans. Mostly, they left us alone.'

Plump tears glistened in Eris' eyes. 'Once the planes disappeared from the skies and the sirens stopped screaming, the men began to return to my village. But my Xander did not come home. No one could tell me what had happened to him. And so I waited. Every day I waited, thinking he would appear.'

Reaching across the table, Ben took her hand.

Eris did not look up, but her fingers tightened around his. 'Now, I am the daughter who looks after her father. He is old and he needs me. And I have never met another man who made me stop loving my husband. That is why I have not married again.'

He stood and moved to stand by her side. She leant against him, her head resting on his ribcage. He felt her shudder as she filled her lungs like a swimmer rising to the water's surface. She stood and slipped her hands around his waist, pulling her body towards his. Ben's heart raced as she pressed her breasts against his chest and arched her hips hard against his. Her skin's perfume made his head spin – she smelled of the lingering warmth of sun and the green scent of olive oil soap.

She turned her face towards his. As she fixed him in her gaze, Ben felt the pit of his stomach drop away. His desire was so powerful he was finding it difficult to stand.

'Please, Ben. Tomorrow I must return to my life, but tonight I want to lie with you.'

The desire was so suffocating he was unable to speak. He responded to Eris' plea in silence, taking her heart-shaped face between his hands. As he bent to kiss her, she arched her back and pressed against him, parting her soft, full lips and responding to his embrace with a mendicant's ravenous appetite.

She took his hand. 'Please. Come with me. Upstairs.'

He did not need to be asked twice.

Eris lay on the bed dressed in a simple, white linen slip. He lay beside her, modestly but ineffectually attempting to disguise his state of arousal with a jumble of sheets gathered about his waist. He reached out and stroked her hair, which now fell about her shoulders. Shifting onto her hip, she moved towards him and entwined a leg around his thigh. He tucked her hair behind her ear, and moved his fingers towards the tiny mother-of-pearl buttons holding her shift closed. He expertly undid the fastening and gently eased the linen sheath open, exposing her full breasts. Beneath the shift her skin was as glossy as honey. She was breathing in short gasps, her eyes tightly closed, as he ran his finger across her small nipples. She inhaled sharply. Fearing he had hurt her, he pulled his hand back.

'Eris – are you OK?'

She opened her eyes, her lids hooded and heavy with desire. Her voice was thick and husky. 'Yes . . . Yes. I am good. You feel good.' She pulled at the tangle of sheets between them and found him, hard and throbbing, against her soft belly. 'Please. It has been so long.'

He lifted himself onto his elbow and bent to kiss her, deeply and softly. Raising the hem of her slip, he lightly touched the tops of her thighs as she moaned and raised her hips. Moving his hand towards the soft, dark mound of hair between her legs, he stroked her gently. She reached up and wrapped her arms around his neck. She kissed him hungrily, her tongue playing about his lips as she began to move her hips rhythmically. He slipped his finger inside her and she groaned and guided him on top of her. Placing her hands at the small of his back she positioned herself beneath him. He kissed her, feeling his swollen cock pressing against his belly. It took every ounce of control to refrain from plunging deep inside her.

'Eris? I will be careful. You tell me . . .'

'I need you now.' She shifted her hips and with a swift movement guided him inside her. The unexpected speed took him by surprise, and he clenched his teeth, willing himself to keep control. Eris began to move beneath him, her hands fluttering over her own breasts, now exposed through the gaping front of her shift. She locked into a rhythm as he began to slide slowly back and forth. With delicate fingers, she pinched at her nipples, her head thrown back and mouth open and wet with desire. He could feel himself swelling and pulsing as he moved. Reaching down between her legs he began to stroke her where she was slippery and swollen. She groaned and tossed her head on the pillow as he felt her begin to clench and contract. Crying out, she dug her fingernails into his shoulders and wrapped her legs tightly about his waist as he exploded, his body taut and rigid as he groaned, his mind taking refuge in a sublime moment of rupture.

The room was dark, the only light cast by the moon shining through gauzy white curtains that billowed in the evening breeze. He lowered himself onto the mattress and rested his head on a cushiony pillow. She lifted her head and laid it on his arm as he ran his hand through her hair, now tousled and damp.

Outside, the muezzin summoned the faithful to the mosque for the fifth and final time of the day, the bewitching melody drifting along the town's narrow, cobbled streets as his voice dipped and soared in divine ecstasy.

Ben smiled and gently kissed Eris' forehead.

The piercing cries of gulls heralding the return of the fishing fleet to the town's small port cut through his slumber. Chilled by dawn's arrival, he grasped at the edge of the cotton bedspread, gathered in a knot at the end of the bed. Turning, he reached for her. But where he anticipated a warm and yielding body, he found a void.

Ben swung his legs over the edge of the bed, and felt the rough floorboards beneath his feet. Every nerve in his body surged with an intoxicating afterglow fuelled by the fire of the woman whose touch and scent remained on his skin. He was as dizzy as a drunken man.

He couldn't remember the last time he had felt so strongly for another human being. There had been no shortage of other women since Karina. But this was different. Eris had achieved the impossible: she had managed to revive a branch of his soul he thought had withered away to nothing.

The thought of leaving her was absurd. He knew what he needed to do. For one thing, his professional career in Turkey was dead and buried. But McNeil might have been right – it might be time to give Greece another chance. A change of scenery. He'd never been to Lesvos. But with his qualifications, it wouldn't be hard to find a place at the museum or on one of the excavations on the island. Hell, they'd be pleased to have him. He might even get the chance to study Eris' collection in more detail – if he could convince the criminals holding her family to ransom that they would benefit from the publication of the Mycenaean treasures. And if something blossomed between himself and Eris in the meantime, that could only be a good thing.

Was he rushing into this? Probably . . . undoubtedly. But that had never stopped him before. And this time, he couldn't see that anything but good could come of it. Now all he had to do was convince Eris. *Time to crack out the patented Hitchens charm*, he thought to himself as he walked down the long, narrow hallway towards the staircase.

He called out. 'Don't tell me you're down there making me breakfast in bed. Really . . . you shouldn't have. Hey – I've had an idea. Probably sounds crazy, but let me know what you think . . .'

When he reached the bottom of the stairs and saw the state of the dining room, he knew something was terribly wrong.

'Eris? What . . .'

One of the French doors leading out into the garden had been forced open, and now hung off its hinges. The house was as silent as a tomb.

'Jesus, no.'

In the kitchen, the kettle on the stove had boiled dry, and brittle fragments from a brightly painted teacup were scattered across the terracotta tiles. A balloon of panic rose in his chest as he ran through the house, flinging doors open, one after the other. But the house was empty. He was alone.

The destruction on the ground floor told a grim tale. There had been a struggle. Broken fragments of objects swept from shelves and tables covered the tiled floor, and two of the dining room chairs had been splintered. The table Ben had been using to record Eris' antiquities was turned on its side. Where the night before there had been a collection of artefacts of unimaginable value and beauty, now there was nothing. Most of all, Eris was gone. And he was in no doubt that she had left against her will.

She had warned him of the danger she was in, and as was his way he had ignored her. All he had cared about was his own needs.

Ben clenched his fists, feeling his blunt fingernails digging painful half-moon welts into his palms. 'Please, no. Jesus. Not again.'

He crouched down on his haunches and buried his face in his hands. As Ben tried to make sense of the inconceivable, life in the town continued along its steady routine. Outside the high walls of the garden, roosters welcomed the rising sun, a discordant chorus to the melodic song of the muezzin calling the faithful to morning prayers. He wanted to shout, to scream, to pound the walls with his fists, to make the world stop and listen.

'Why didn't I hear anything? *Why*? It looks as if someone drove a bloody truck through the place.' He spoke aloud, smacking his forehead with his fist. 'What is *wrong* with me?' Perhaps exhaustion and soporific post-coital slumber could explain how he had managed to tune out what must have been a hell of a racket downstairs. Yes, the bedroom was down a long corridor on the second floor and he had slept with the heavy oak door closed. But, still, his ineptitude left him floundering.

Crippling dismay sucked at his limbs like quicksand. The cogs in his mind raced like a malfunctioning clock. He stood and turned towards the stairs, hoping against hope that he'd find something on the upper floor that might help him understand.

In the dim light, he tangled his legs in the side table that had been standing at the base of the stairs but now lay upended on the tiles. Falling heavily, his knees cracked painfully as he landed on the floor. 'Bloody fool!'

Kneeling on the bone-cold tiles, he was struck by a wave of desperate futility. He had lost everything. Eris was gone and the priceless antiquities of which she was sole custodian had vanished with her. And any hope he had for salvation had been dashed. Now he had nothing and no one to bear witness to what had happened.

It suddenly struck him. He jumped to his feet and stumbled to the bookcase. His notebook. It was still there. If nothing else, he still had his written record and illustrations of Eris' treasures, for whatever that was worth. It was proof – to himself, at least – that he hadn't dreamt the whole thing.

He tried to focus. The thought of what Eris might be going through made him feel ill. She had put herself in real peril by delaying her return to Lesvos. The men threatening her family had tired of waiting. It was the only explanation. And if they had lost patience . . . he shuddered to think what they might be doing to her.

There was only one alternative available to him. The police. But he knew it wouldn't be easy to explain what had happened here.

As he turned to go upstairs, he saw something tucked under the edge of a woollen *kilim* that had been shoved to one side of the staircase. He lifted the corner of the rug, not quite believing what he saw. Lying on the tiled floor was the smaller fragment of the Greek stele he had put aside the previous evening.

He bent and retrieved the engraved piece of marble. It was cool and heavy in his palm and carved with Greek characters. It felt real. And at that moment, it was exactly what he needed. It was proof that this had been more than just a dream.

The officer on duty at İzmir's central police station looked as if he had just awoken, his tie askew, suit jacket wrinkled and face puffy from sleep. Corpulent belly straining against the small buttons that valiantly attempted to hold his shirtfront shut, Inspector Hilmi shifted in his seat and tugged at the front of his trousers, trying to loosen the uncomfortably tight waistband. As Ben relayed his story, the inspector took notes, peering at a lined notebook through saggy eyelids and pausing occasionally to raise his eyebrows. Ben concluded his account with a description of what he had found this morning, the only omission from his narrative being the fact that he and Eris had spent the night together in her bedroom.

The inspector had been unimpressed by the marble fragment. When Ben showed it to him, Hilmi turned it over in his hands before dropping it onto his desktop, mumbling something about Turkish cultural heritage and museums. A stack of documents dislodged and tumbled over the tablet, hiding it from view, and Ben cursed himself as he realised he was going to lose the one connection he still had to Eris.

Sighing deeply, Hilmi leant forward heavily on his elbows and flipped back through the pages of his notebook. He spoke slowly. Deliberately. 'So. You meet a stranger. On a train. A Miss Eris Patras. Miss Patras is wearing an old necklace. You notice this because you say you're an archaeologist. Sounds like you're an unemployed one, though . . .'

Ben opened his mouth to protest, but the inspector tutted and raised his hand. 'Please, Mr Hitchens. Miss Patras – a Greek woman – invites you home. You follow her to a house in İzmir. She shows you some old treasures that her *Greek* family has been holding on to. *Illegally*. Treasures they discovered in *Turkish* soil. You stay with her, in her house, while you draw pictures of these *illegal* treasures – the pictures you've shown me. After you finish these drawings, you know she plans to smuggle the treasure out of Turkey. Illegally. Sound about right?'

'The details . . . yes, I suppose it is. But it just doesn't . . .'

'Yes or no, Mr Hitchens?'

He felt helpless and desperate. It was easy to see the inspector reading sinister motives into the situation, with all blame attributed to him.

'Yes. That sounds about right.'

'Right.' Hilmi scribbled another sentence in his notebook. 'Then, you wake up this morning, and Miss Patras and the treasure are gone.'

'With evidence of a struggle . . .'

'Yes. Your "evidence of a struggle". You know, we've got processes here. And in cases like this what I'd do next would be to examine the crime scene. If that is what we have here.'

Ben fought to keep his growing frustration under control. 'Believe me. There has been a crime. Eris – Miss Patras – wouldn't have smashed up her own home and disappeared. No way.'

'So the easiest way for me to work out whether or not a crime has been committed is to visit her house. But that's a bit of a problem, isn't it? Because you can't tell me where that is.'

That morning, Ben had left Eris' home in a frenzy, tearing along a jumbled maze of dusty streets in search of someone who could help him. By the time he stumbled into a small square with wooden tables and chairs arranged under the canopy of emerald-green chestnut trees, he had absolutely no idea where he was and wouldn't have been able to find his way back to Eris' house if he had wanted to. He breathlessly explained to a group of farmers gathered in the teahouse that he needed to speak with the police, and one of the men agreed to drive him to the station in the centre of İzmir. The route they took to the centre of town was circuitous along winding, dusty roads that left him confused and disoriented. When the farmer dropped him at the front steps of the police station, he hadn't thought to ask him where they had come from. It was an oversight he would long regret.

Clenching his fists, Ben spoke through gritted teeth. 'That's right. Miss Patras didn't want me to be seen outside the house. We arrived on a beach somewhere in the dark, and I stayed at the house the entire time until I left this morning. As strange as it sounds, I really have no idea where I was.'

A phone sitting on a filing cabinet behind Inspector Hilmi's desk rang. He spun in his chair and picked up the handset. His back was to Ben. Without thinking, Ben shifted aside the pile of papers on the desk and grabbed the marble tablet from beneath them. It was a risk, but he couldn't lose it. He could only hope the inspector would be distracted enough to forget it had been there at all.

Hilmi hung up, grunted and scribbled some more notes in his book before locking his eyes on Ben. 'So this woman's last name is Patras?'

'Yes.'

'You're sure?'

'Yes. Absolutely.'

'OK, then. Looks like we have another problem. There's no Patras family registered in the district.'

'Ah, that will be because after Miss Patras' family left Smyrna – I mean, İzmir – their neighbours – Turkish neighbours – looked after their home when they went into exile on Lesvos.'

Hilmi raised his verdant eyebrows. 'So, these neighbours. What's their name?'

'Unfortunately, I didn't meet them. Miss Patras didn't want to introduce me to them.'

The inspector looked the American up and down. 'I don't blame her.'

Ben's mind was racing as he tried to find a solution. 'A map – can you get me a map? Of the city?'

Hilmi gestured to the wall behind Ben. He stood and walked over to the framed map of İzmir. 'There – there's the train station. That's where we arrived.' He traced the path they took down to the docks. 'And this is where the fisherman picked us up.' He ran his fingertip out into the blue of the bay. 'We definitely took this direction. The mountains were on our left. So we must have been heading south.' Ben traced the coastline, pockmarked with bays and countless tiny villages. 'It must have been one of these towns.'

Hilmi was standing at Ben's shoulder. 'That's a lot of towns.'

'I know. It was dark. And I wasn't paying attention to where we were going. It didn't seem to matter at the time.' He grimaced. Given his military experience, he was furious that he had been so unobservant.

'Is this normal for you, Mr Hitchens? Do you always follow strange women to strange places? To find hidden treasure . . . it's the sort of thing a child might do. But a grown man?' The inspector shook his head. 'One born every minute.'

At Ben's insistence, Inspector Hilmi agreed to transport him on what the policeman assured him would prove to be nothing more than a wild-goose chase. To Ben's great relief, the Turk had not given a moment's thought to the missing tablet fragment that had disappeared from his desk.

The Turkish officer's stern façade mellowed as they drove along the seaside from town to town. Clearly pleased to be released from the confines of the police station for the day, Hilmi drove at a hair-raising pace along the narrow country lanes, kicking great clouds of powdery dust into the air as he swung the car from one side of the road to the other, honking his horn with relish as he swerved to overtake rickety donkey-drawn carts and bountifully hipped women carrying sheaves of wheat atop their heads.

Through the open window, a blast of air cooled Ben's skin. The world outside smelled of rich, green grass and chalky limestone baking in the sun's rays. It was so different from the parched landscape of the south with which he was familiar. Mounds of fat-leaved grapevines grew wild among ancient fig trees, their spiralling branches heavy with fruit. Snowy-coated herds of goats wandered through the fields, accompanied by the rustic lullaby of bells clanging about their necks.

As the sun began to descend towards the horizon and they passed through yet another small town without result, his hopes began to fade. There had been moments when his heart leapt, certain that he recognised an intersection, an ornately carved fountain spouting a sparkling stream of fresh water into a marble basin, or the shape of a distinctive minaret glimpsed across the rooftops. But closer inspection yielded nothing.

One hand on the wheel, and resting his elbow on the open window, Hilmi stuck the smouldering stub of a cigarette between his lips and inhaled deeply, eyes screwed half shut against the acrid smoke issuing in plumes from the corner of his mouth. He pulled over to the side of the road and turned to face his passenger.

'So. Mr Hitchens. Where to now?'

The inspector tilted his chin towards the road ahead which peeled away from the coast and wound into the low hills of the Çeşme Peninsula. 'West of here, we go inland. To Urla. It's not on the coast so it's not the place you're looking for. Any seaside towns beyond here are too far from İzmir to get to quickly by boat.'

Ben looked back down the road in the direction they had come. 'What about back there? Are there any villages we may have missed?'

He shrugged. 'Yes . . . Ah . . . No . . . Maybe . . . I don't know.' As was the Turkish way, Ben knew Hilmi would say just about anything before he would give an outright 'no'.

Clouds of pollen and insects darted about in the late afternoon sunlight. The whirring cicadas in the soapy green cypress trees along the roadside were so loud it felt as if they had taken up residence in Ben's skull. The sense of urgency that had been driving him since he'd woken that morning had been replaced by a hollow melancholy.

'Perhaps we could drive back through the towns again to check. Just in case I missed something.'

Hilmi sighed, doleful eyes contemplating his passenger. 'Why not. If you wish. We have to go that way anyway.' The Turk spun the steering wheel and gunned the engine into life. He accelerated back down the road towards İzmir.

Ben felt lost. There had been a time when he would have known exactly what to do. Tracking people down. It was what he did. But those dark days on Crete were a lifetime ago, and he had grown soft. He pictured Eris. The thought of what she might be going through blinded him with rage. He might not know exactly what his next move was going to be, but he was damned if he was going to sit around doing nothing.

The reporter from the *Illustrated London News* tapped his pen against his lower lip pensively. 'So this woman. This . . .' he glanced down at his notebook, '. . . this "Eris". She just disappeared. Into thin air. With a king's ransom in treasure.'

'Yes. More or less.'

'. . . And the Turkish police?'

Ben tapped his heel nervously against the timber floor. 'Useless! Worse than useless. I don't think they believed a thing I told them. It's been months since she was taken, and they haven't turned up anything!'

Going to the press was a last resort. Any thought Ben had of salvaging his reputation by publishing news of Eris' treasure had been put to one side the instant she disappeared. All he cared about now was finding her. At first, the interest the Turkish police showed in the case gave him some hope. But once he realised that their only priority was tracking down the treasure he realised he'd have to continue the search for her alone. When his efforts yielded nothing, he decided the only way to get things moving was to publicise his story in an attempt to flush someone out who might be able to help.

Dermott Batey was a seasoned journalist. Judging by the sceptical expression on his face, he had some sympathy for the aforementioned Turkish police. Ben knew he had a hard sell ahead of him.

'After she was taken, I went to Lesvos myself, trying to find evidence. Thought I'd be able to find a trace of her. Her family. Something. Anything.' Ben leant across the table and spoke in hushed tones. Customers at neighbouring tables in the tiny harbourside *lokanta* leant close in an attempt to eavesdrop. 'But I found nothing. Nothing! It's as if she never existed. Combed the church records looking for her marriage certificate. Drove from town to town asking anyone I could find. But she's a ghost.' He grabbed Batey by the wrist. 'Sometimes I question my own sanity!'

'Quite.' Smiling politely, the journalist retrieved his wrist from Ben's grasp. 'Might we just change topic for a moment?'

'Yes. Sure. Certainly.'

'Eskitepe. Tell me about that.'

'It made me. Made my reputation, anyway. The Neolithic levels – well, they gave me the first permanent human settlement ever discovered. They say I changed history. Though that's not why I went there. I went for the Bronze Age deposits. Thought I might find evidence there for the Trojan War. That's where my true interests lie.'

'If it's so important to you, why did you leave?'

*Bloody idiots is why*, Ben cursed beneath his breath. The humiliation still seared. 'Difference of opinion with the Director of the British School. I wanted to open trenches in the Hittite levels. He wouldn't give me the funds to do it.'

'Oh?' Batey's eyebrows shot up. He flicked back through the pages of his notebook. 'Is that right? Tell me – Professor Ethan Cohn? He was your mentor before the war, wasn't he? How's your relationship with him now?'

'Fine. I think. It's been a while since we spoke, though. Why do you ask?' *Where's this going?* he wondered.

'Well, he had some rather – how can I put it – tough things to say about you.'

'Ethan? Can't say I'm surprised.' The curmudgeonly old bastard. 'He's never forgiven me for branching out on my own. Never had anything good to say about me once I started to make a name for myself. He's not very good at sharing the spotlight.'

The reporter's head tilted, considering Ben with a clinical gaze. 'One of the things he said – and I only mention this because I have it from a number of sources – is that you may have staged this whole thing to draw attention away from the fact you were dismissed from your position at Eskitepe under a cloud of suspicion. Antiquities theft, wasn't it? There's no connection between that incident and the story you're telling me, is there?'

Ben stood, knocking the bentwood chair back onto the tiled floor with a clatter that caused the restaurant to fall silent. 'That's got nothing to do with what's happened here! How *dare* you!'

Batey rose calmly to his feet. 'I'm here because you contacted me, Dr Hitchens. But I'm not a journalist for hire. I investigate stories and I write them. And you may want me to write a tale of a kidnapped woman and a lost fortune. But I write the story I find. And the question of what happened at Eskitepe does seem to have a bearing on what you're telling me today.'

'You can't...' Ben's head was whirling, the ground beneath his feet falling away.

'I can, sir. And I will. And this is the one chance you have to put your case forward.'

Ben snatched at the man's collar and crushed it in his fist, pulling him close across the table. 'Fuck. You.'

There are few places more joyless than a bar at midday. The neglect evident in the smoky windows and dingy floors mirrored Ben's mood. The bartender poured him a raki without making eye contact and then resumed pushing grime around the cracked benchtop with a filthy dishrag.

After storming out of the café, Ben's fury at the journalist had abated quickly. Self-interest had driven him back through the *lokanta*'s doors to apologise and attempt to make amends for his outburst. But Batey had gone, and Ben's opportunity for redemption with him.

Of course it was his own fault; it always was. He had nowhere else to go and no one left to care. He could slip between the rotten floorboards and his absence would barely rate a footnote.

The only measure of the amount of raki he had consumed was the onset of double vision and difficulty focusing as the sullen bartender poured him measure after measure, skimping on ice and short-changing him.

He didn't care. Everything he was – everything he had – was gone.

Slumping back against the banquette's sticky vinyl, he shut his eyes and succumbed to a desolate fog of unconsciousness.

# PART 2

# I

## Istanbul, Turkey, 1955

Beyoğlu's steep laneways were slick with the peachy-pink setting sun as Istanbul's night owls began to stir. By the time Ilhan swung open Refik's glass-panelled door and stepped into its smoke-filled interior, Ben was already three sheets to the wind. A small bottle of raki sat before him, its contents almost gone.

'You couldn't think of a better way to spend your ill-gotten gains, Ben? I hope you lined your stomach with some *mezze* before you started drinking.'

Ben shook his head. 'It would have been rude to start dinner without you.'

'So that rule doesn't apply to the raki?'

'Certainly not. As you should know by now, I've no qualms about drinking alone.'

Ilhan pulled out a chair and signalled to the waiter, who brought over a tall, narrow glass, an ice bucket and another bottle of raki. He poured himself a generous slug of the clear spirit and added ice and water.

'Şerefe!' The two men raised a toast, Ilhan with considerably more dexterity than Ben, who sloshed a good measure of his drink on the back of his hand.

Shaking his head, Ilhan handed him a napkin. 'Have you seen the catalogue yet? Mine arrived today.'

'No. Though my mailbox hasn't seen much action for a while. Wouldn't be surprised if the postman had given up on visiting me. Waste of his time.'

'I don't think you understand how big this is going to be, Ben.'

Ben sighed. 'What's to say Sotheby's won't take one look at the statues and decide they're not right?'

'Did you spot anything out of the ordinary when you examined them? If you didn't know any better, would you think they were fraudulent?'

Ben was silent.

'That's right,' Ilhan continued. 'And if you would give your stamp of approval, what makes you think someone at Sotheby's will know any better? You're the expert. Remember?'

'Yeah. How could I forget?'

Ilhan ignored him. 'Besides, auction houses never look too closely – just enough to stay out of trouble. They put our statues in the catalogue based on a physical description, the provenance, and the reputation of the Steigmeier collection. Once they take delivery of the statues, they'll put them on display, and sell them. No questions asked. Hammer falls, they get their cut of the sale price, and everyone's happy. All they care about is that they *look* authentic. And – thanks to you and that little Italian prick – those three masterpieces are extremely convincing.'

'Wow. I am so very, very proud. Might just have to give myself a little pat on the back.' Ben sighed. 'Ilhan . . . seeing the finished statues today . . . knowing where they're headed . . . I don't think you understand. It's everything I've ever fought against.'

'Your conscience hasn't seemed too troubled by what we've been doing until now.'

'The little deceptions we've been engaging in? That's small-time stuff. This is something else altogether. Please leave me out of the execution phase of the operation. I don't really care about the details.'

'You should. Care, I mean. If this works, you'll be a very wealthy man.' He watched as Ben poured himself another long shot of raki. 'Though if you keep that up, you won't be around long enough to enjoy it. So, Ben. Before you disassociate yourself from our project . . . did you bring it?'

'Bring what?'

'You have a very odd sense of humour at times, my friend. The tablet. You remember? The thing you were so insistent we include in this deal with Sotheby's?'

'Yes, I remember. And, no; I don't have it. Not here.'

Exasperated, Ilhan leant across the table. 'They were reluctant to include it at all. Particularly with the terms you insisted on. I don't want them asking any questions.'

'Don't fret. I've every intention of giving it to them. I just . . . I'm not ready to hand it over yet.'

'Ben, you're out of time.'

'There's always time, Ilhan. In my case – too much of it.'

'Well, you'll need to come up with a decent excuse. And you'll have to do it quickly. They're due any minute. Henry Wootton-Jones is playing tour guide for our contact. I doubt that man knows the meaning of the term "running late".'

'Ah, Christ.' Ben rolled his eyes. 'Really? That insufferable cretin? I wish you'd warned me. I would've had a more valiant attempt at polishing off the remaining raki.'

Gritting his teeth and addressing his friend under his breath, Ilhan responded testily. 'You should be more circumspect. Wootton-Jones is, after all, one of the few Westerners left in this city who is still happy to be seen in public with you. Plus, he does have the ear of many influential people – a fact that may be useful to you one day.'

The door to Refik swung open, admitting a fastidiously tidy man with a neatly trimmed sandy moustache and horn-rimmed glasses. The left arm of his suit jacket was pinned neatly across his chest. Henry Wootton-Jones raised his hand and called across the room. 'Benedict! Ilhan *Bey*!' He sidled through the bar towards them.

Ben groaned. 'He may be useful. But he's *such* an ass.'

Following in Wootton-Jones' wake was a young woman. Even through the pleasantly drunken fog clouding Ben's senses, there was no mistaking her appeal. With minimal makeup and blonde hair scraped back into a tight ponytail, she was downplaying her beauty. But her matter-of-fact outfit of khaki pants and long-sleeved white shirt did little to disguise her curvaceous figure. Topped off with a face featuring high cheekbones, full lips and knowing eyes, she was an enticing package.

'A woman?' Ben murmured as he sat up straight in his chair and attempted to smooth his rumpled jacket. 'You didn't tell me Sotheby's had sent a woman.'

'It didn't seem relevant.'

'Look at her! How could it not be relevant?'

'This is just business, Ben. Remember? Behave yourself.'

With a sweep of his hand, Wootton-Jones approached their table. 'Charlotte! Didn't I tell you? Here we have the man himself . . . Dr Benedict Hitchens! Miss Charlotte Fair-weather, may I present the venerable Dr Benedict Hitchens.'

Distinguished by the supine posture and dusty pallor of a man who spent little time away from a desk, Henry Wootton-Jones had accrued the most odious characteristics of the career bureaucrat – a rusted-on sense of petty self-importance and contrived gravitas commensurate with his position at the British Consulate in Istanbul. The only vaguely interesting thing about him was his impressive war wound: he had lost his arm in the Normandy landings. But Wootton-Jones managed to turn something distinctive into a subject of tedium; he wore his injury like a badge of honour and no occasion passed without at least one mention of his lost limb. The man represented everything Ben most despised.

Rising to his feet and swaying slightly, Ben extended his hand. 'Wootton-Jones. What can I say? Delighted?' The grasp in return was flaccid and slightly clammy.

'Benedict, my good fellow. *Splendid* to see you!'

'How many times, Wootton-Jones? It's Ben. Just Ben. Only my sainted mother, wet nurse and school headmaster call me Benedict.'

He turned his attention to Charlotte. 'It's a pleasure to meet you.'

She smiled primly. 'Dr Hitchens. I've heard a great deal about you.' By her tone of voice, whatever she'd heard, it wasn't good.

Wootton-Jones continued his introductions. 'And this is Mr Ilhan Aslan.'

Ilhan took the young woman's hand and lifted it to his lips. 'I have had the pleasure already, Henry. How did you find your visit, Miss Fairweather?'

Charlotte blushed and leant in towards Ilhan, leaving her hand in his grasp longer than was absolutely necessary.

'Oh, it was wonderful, thank you, Mr Aslan. Wonderful. What a marvellous city. If I didn't have to rush back to Sotheby's for the sales, I'd be tempted to stay longer.'

'Just business, you say, Ilhan? Monkey business, more like!' Ben murmured in Turkish.

Wootton-Jones barrelled on. 'Ah, yes. Of course. Completely forgot. You two are already well acquainted, aren't you?' He turned back to Ben. 'Charlotte's here on behalf of the auction house to take delivery of a very important collection of antiquities from Ilhan.' He tapped the side of his nose. 'Very hush-hush, you see. And with the reams of paperwork required to take them out of the country . . . well, I've been giving Charlotte a hand – just the one hand, mind. That's all I've got to give, after all!' Wootton-Jones snorted, relishing his pun.

Ilhan and Charlotte laughed politely. Ben greeted the diplomat's joke with a stony silence.

Charlotte lowered herself gracefully into a chair offered by Ilhan. 'Speaking of which,' she said, 'is it safe to assume that all the items are ready to be transported tomorrow? We've booked freight by air departing in two days.'

'Yes.' Ilhan took the seat beside hers. 'Everything's ready to go. The only object that's been held up is the tablet . . .'

'Really? To be honest, Mr Aslan . . .'

'Please, you really must call me Ilhan.'

'Thank you. Ilhan.' Charlotte smiled coyly, the blush of an English rose rising to her cheeks. 'Well, I was rather perplexed about your insistence that we illustrate the tablet and include such an elaborate catalogue description. Compared to the other three items – which are exceptionally fine – the inscribed stele is . . . well . . . rather modest. The directors weren't at all keen to highlight what is a relatively humdrum object. Given the fuss we've made about it, it would be something of a loss of face if it was withdrawn from the sale. I fear it would land me in a fair bit of bother.'

'It'll be there,' Ben interjected.

'Oh.' A look of alarm passed across Charlotte's face. 'The tablet's coming from you?'

'No, no.' Ilhan responded quickly. 'Don't worry – it's from the same dealer as the three Steigmeier statues. Though it's not from the Steigmeier collection. Ben's just been doing some research on it before it's sold. He'll get it to you before you leave, isn't that right, Ben?' Ilhan smiled tightly.

Marvelling at the speed with which Ilhan had mended the fence through which he'd charged, Ben nodded. 'Yup. I'll be sure you get it.'

Charlotte smiled, evidently relieved. 'Well, that's good to hear. Integrity is so important to the business, you see.' She looked sideways at Ben. 'Provenance is everything.'

Ben sat in the corner, silently brooding as his dinner companions chattered animatedly. He was less than pleased to see Ilhan bombarding Charlotte with a Dresden-scale charm offensive. She gazed at him, transfixed, as he regaled her with colourful stories about his adventures in the Anatolian hinterlands. When the Turk leant forward and grasped her forearm to emphasise a point, she didn't pull away, instead sliding her chair closer to Ilhan's corner of the table. Watching his friend exercise his abundant charisma to great effect, Ben chose to sulk. He knew it was churlish. But he didn't care.

As the waiter cleared the detritus of their meal, Ilhan clapped his hands together and pushed his chair back from the table. 'If you'll excuse me, I now need to prove Newton's theory. "What goes in, must come out".'

'Don't you mean "What goes up, must come down"?' asked Wootton-Jones.

'Not when it comes to raki, Henry. I will return!'

With his departure, the table descended into an awkward silence. Henry Wootton-Jones was the first to speak. 'So, Benedict. I've been meaning to get in touch. Your colleagues at the Institute have been having a God-awful time getting their excavation permits ever since that whole . . . *business* . . . you managed to get yourself caught up in. The missing treasure . . . that woman . . . what was her name? Patras, wasn't it? The Turkish government is treating everyone like thieves. I'm sure it's just as much about loss of face as it is anything else. They just want to be seen to have *done* something. If you'd just let it go, clear the air with the authorities . . .'

'Again, Wootton-Jones, it's Ben. Just Ben. And if I had a penny for every time I've spoken to a goddamned Turkish official over the last three years to try to clear this thing up . . . well, I wouldn't be stuck here, for one thing!' Ben gagged on the knot of fury at the back of his throat. 'As for my bloody so-called former colleagues . . .'

Charlotte cleared her throat, obviously uncomfortable. 'Ah, gentlemen . . . there's that saying about airing dirty laundry in public . . .'

'Let me finish!' Ben snapped. The Englishwoman drew back, eyes widening with shock. He regretted his outburst immediately. 'I apologise for that, Miss Fairweather. Most unseemly. But nothing gets my goat more than this – those lily-livered morons at the Institute . . . where were they when I needed them? When my reputation was being demolished, how many of them vouched for me? Not a single bloody one. Couldn't wait to see me fall – vindictive, jealous pricks.'

'Well, you're not making my job any easier either, old chap,' said Wootton-Jones. 'I'm stuck in the middle, you see – trying to get things done for your colleagues –'

'*Ex*-colleagues!' Ben drew a deep breath. He glanced up at the Englishman's rheumy eyes blinking furiously above his horn-rimmed glasses. 'I am truly sorry it's caused you problems. But what choice do I have? As I see it, I have two options – neither of them particularly appealing. I could lie, and say I made the whole thing up. Or, to get them off my back, I could tell them what they want to hear and admit – falsely – that I was an accomplice to the theft, and accept the penalties imposed by the Turkish authorities. Either way, my career would be beyond resurrection.'

'But if you'd just let it be; stop talking about it . . .'

'Stop talking about it? How would you suggest I do that, Wootton-Jones? Even if you leave my career prospects out of the equation – a woman is missing. God knows what happened to her . . . I can only assume she's dead.' A familiar jab of guilt swept over Ben. 'Can we just let it be tonight, please, Henry?'

'You're not just tilting at windmills are you, old chap? This missing woman. The victim of foul play? All sounds a bit melodramatic to me. Couldn't she just have . . . gone?'

'No. There's no way,' Ben said. 'If she was able to get me a message – to let me know she was OK – she would have. No doubt about it.'

Charlotte broke her silence. 'It *is* a most curious affair, Dr Hitchens. It made all the papers in London . . . That article in the *Illustrated London News*. Everyone was talking about it.'

'That's what I mean! My story was everywhere, more's the pity. Eris would have known. She would have done something to help me. She never would have left me hanging out to dry . . .'

'And gossip. There was no end of gossip,' Charlotte continued. 'You wouldn't *believe* some of the stories that were going round.'

'Yes. Yes I would.' Ben shook his head slowly. He stared at his palms, which were deeply furrowed from years spent digging in Anatolia's parched soils. He spoke without looking up. 'Here's the thing, you see. That bloody journalist. He couldn't have done a better job of burying me if he'd tried. No one back in England believes a word I say. Most people think I either made the whole thing up to make people forget about the mess at Eskitepe, or to prove my claims that *The Iliad* and the people in it were something more than mythological beings . . .'

'But those claims were discredited *years* ago . . .' interjected Charlotte.

Ben slammed his fist down on the wooden tabletop, setting the glasses rattling, and drawing tuts and disapproving stares from neighbouring diners. 'I *had* the evidence.' He inhaled deeply, calming himself. 'I had it . . . in my hands. You've seen the pictures, right? I didn't fabricate them. As you said – they were all over the papers back home.'

Charlotte spoke quietly. 'But they were drawings. Not photographs. Drawings. *Your* drawings. You can see, surely, why people are suspicious.'

'If I hadn't been there myself, I wouldn't believe it either,' Ben conceded. 'The Turkish police – who might be able to help – they don't even believe Eris existed. And they've done bugger-all to try to find her. As for me – I've crisscrossed the countryside round İzmir and scoured Lesvos looking for her. Couldn't count the days . . . weeks . . . I spent trying to find her house in İzmir. Thought I was onto something a few times. But I didn't get a good enough look at the place from the outside while I was staying there. Damned places all look the same as one another from the outside. Wasn't paying close enough attention. My mind was elsewhere. Now, no one will help me. But she lived on Lesvos for so many years – was married . . . had a family business. It's a small island. There should be records. But I didn't turn up a single thing. There's something much bigger at play. It's as if there was . . . I don't know . . . a conspiracy of sorts. In my darkest moments I've even thought maybe she was involved – played me like a patsy. But I can't believe that. It's impossible. Still . . . there has to be a reason. Doesn't make sense, otherwise. She's the key. And if I could find her, you see . . . even if I managed to find something that proved she existed . . . Well, it might go some way towards clearing my name.'

He felt hands resting on his shoulders, and heard the voice of his friend behind him. 'You must forgive him. It has been a trying time for Dr Benedict Hitchens.' Ilhan spoke in measured tones. 'His evidence? Gone. Reputation? Finished. And, as he tells it, the love of his life along with it.'

Charlotte persisted. 'Perhaps it's the auctioneer in me, but I'm intrigued – the thought of missing treasure out there just waiting to be found. I do want to hear your side of the story.'

'No. That's enough from me,' said Ben. 'There are many more interesting things to talk about. The weather, perhaps. Or the looming problems in Cyprus. How about you, Henry? What dramas are keeping you busy at the consulate? "The Consul General has lost his stapler! All hands on deck!" No pun intended, my one-armed friend.' He raised his glass. 'Please, just leave me to my drinking. It's the one thing I seem able to do singularly well these days.'

Ilhan held his drink aloft. 'A toast, then! To Dr *Ben* Hitchens. A hero so tragic he would make Shakespeare weep. *Şerefe*!'

'No. Let's not drink to me.' Ben's head spun and he felt the floor tilting as he threw back his drink in a single hit. 'To Eris.'

*How is it that they aren't having any trouble with the flagstones?* Ben wondered as he staggered and tripped along the narrow lane in the wake of a small group of young men. They had no difficulty negotiating the narrow cobbled footpath that meandered alongside one of Pera's countless anonymous steep roadways.

He had taken a couple of turns up unfamiliar streets after he left the *meyhane* and was now regretting his determined refusal of Ilhan's offer to help him home. He cursed as the laneway took an unexpected U-turn and seemed to be headed back the way he had come.

Trying to get his bearings, he cursed: *Why can't this goddamned city have any straight streets?*

Looking over his shoulder, he looked in vain for his personal police escort, hoping they might be willing to point him in the right direction. Although he hadn't worked out the exact roster, it seemed that someone in the Turkish bureaucracy had decided he wasn't a national security threat once the sun had set. Apparently his routine was so predictable they knew they'd be able to pick up his trail at his apartment every morning, regardless of what he'd been up to the night before. And so now, when he really *did* need them, they were nowhere to be found.

Ahead, he saw three men turn a corner towards where a pool of bright light from a side street seeped across the asphalt. He followed, seeking assistance from the upright of a street sign to swing around the corner. The three men had disappeared into what was, given the late hour, a surprisingly large crowd of people moving along the pavement.

Joining the throng, he was too intoxicated to notice the furtive way the male pedestrians were sidling up the street, hats tilted over their eyes and coat collars turned up like Russian spies in a B-grade movie. The only women in sight lounged in doorways, bare flesh exposed in low-cut satin bodices and through slits in transparent skirts. With faces adorned with cherry-red daubs of rouge and scarlet slashes of lipstick, they pouted and preened for the passing men. Muscle-bound bodyguards loomed behind them and stepped in to negotiate when a passer-by expressed more than a casual interest in one of the women on offer.

It hit him. *Oh, for Christ's sake. Cihangir. That'd be right.*

He slumped down in an unoccupied doorway, oblivious to the disapproving stares of the nocturnal street-crawlers whose passage he blocked with his outstretched legs. Leaning his head against the doorjamb, he shut his eyes, attempting to still the ground that lurched beneath him. Consciousness began to slip away from him, and through the fog he saw her eyes. Golden and impenetrable. Her full lips curled at the corner in a seductive smile, she extended an arm towards him, delicate wrist turning at the last moment to offer Ben her palm. He smiled and reached for her.

'Eris?'

'No. But if you pay me, I will be anyone you wish . . . Are you interested?'

Starting awake, Ben looked into the face of a woman leaning over him, her full breasts cascading over the cups of a tightly cinched black bodice. Her face was pretty but painted on. Cupid's-bow lips, apple cheeks and large, doll-like eyes were framed by hair styled in soft platinum-blonde waves.

He ached all over with loss and longing.

'*Evet.*'

He ran his rough palms over her soft, white skin, feeling the weight of her breasts in his hands. She spoke to him gently, in a lilting and unfamiliar language – Central Asian, perhaps – as she expertly unfastened the buttons of his trousers and lowered them past his knees.

'Wait . . .' he mumbled as he bent to unlace his shoes and step out of his pants. For a moment, he felt ridiculous as he stood there with bare legs and worn boxer shorts flapping beneath the tail of his wrinkled shirt. But then she moved towards him and unbuttoned his shirt, pressing her nakedness against him. She was warm and her curves firm as her breasts pressed against his chest, and she raised her face to his and tilted her head back, lips parted. Bending, he joined his lips to hers, his head spinning as her tongue touched his and she slid her hips against him. He was throbbing; engorged.

The woman placed a hand against his chest and trailed her fingers towards the waistband of his shorts. He groaned as she rubbed him through the worn cotton, slipping her hand inside and grasping him firmly with soft fingers. The sensation of her touch made every nerve in his body prickle. He pushed her back on the bed and pressed his thumbs into her plump thighs, holding her legs apart and probing at her, swollen and urgent. Shutting his eyes, he plunged deep inside her, feeling her warmth and wetness. Ben conjured up Eris' shade in his mind's eye, picturing her as he best remembered her, dark curls tumbling, tangled against starched white sheets, her head rocking from side to side as she pulled him deep inside her and her long, brown limbs locked together at the small of his back. Ben found a rhythm, pumping and thrusting feverishly as desire took hold.

The woman beneath him murmured, a strange amalgam of foreign words cutting through his fantasy and dragging him back to the stark reality of the grimy room. He raised a hand to her lips, stilling the unfamiliar babble. 'No. Please. Don't speak.' He felt her beneath him, bucking and grinding.

The moment was lost; Eris' shade dematerialised. But he was so close. Hips pumping frantically, his hard belly slapped against hers. Nothing languid. Nothing sensual. Urgent and desperate, he finished inside her.

He rolled to one side. Feeling hollow and sick to the stomach, he didn't want to look at the woman. Transaction complete, she swung her legs over the side of the bed. As she moved about the room gathering her clothes, her shoes made staccato clicks on the worn floorboards. Eager to find her way back out into the lane and the next paying customer she dressed quickly and efficiently. Then, businesslike, she walked to the head of the bed and tapped Ben on the shoulder.

'Do not fall asleep. I will need the bed again. There is water in the jug.' Without a backward glance, the woman walked from the room.

As he lay in the steamy room, he listened to the rhythmic thumping and grunts of other commercial couplings in neighbouring beds. The room was cast in a hellish glow from the red light globe switched on to signal to passers-by in the street below that this bedroom was occupied by a woman who charged by the hour. It smelled of sweat, semen and unwashed feet, and turned Ben's stomach.

Dragging himself into an upright position, the room seemed to spin. He lowered his head into his hands and fought the urge to vomit. Staggering to his feet he moved towards the dresser and poured water from a chipped urn. As he splashed it onto his face, its bracing chill quelled his nausea.

A grimy mirror freckled with rust stains like liver spots hung on the wall before him. His reflection captured the type of good looks that had always been described as 'rakish'. Ben's strong features seemed to survive even his most concerted efforts to destroy himself. But as he buttoned his shirt, he looked into his eyes. There was no disguising the damage there. They were mirror-like.

Hollow. Dead.

The muezzin's song rang from the minaret rising like a needle into the early dawn sky. Clusters of old men shuffled past along the cobbled laneway, their leather slippers whispering on the paving stones as they heeded the melodic call to prayer.

Whorls of sea mist swirled through the streets, settling on Ben's skin like beads of sweat. The smell of the Bosphorus filled the air, heavy and limpid. Staggering, he rounded a familiar corner and slumped against the crumbling plaster wall of his apartment building. His landlady, her day's labour already well under way, briskly swept the stairs, a poisonous mutter under her breath her only acknowledgement of the return of her dissolute tenant.

As he passed, he mumbled a greeting. She shook her head and turned her back on him. He leant heavily against the wrought-iron balustrade and dragged himself up the steps towards the front entrance.

Feeble grey light seeped into the foyer. He couldn't be bothered trying to find the light switch so he felt his way blindly, hands creeping along the wall, as much to keep himself upright as to find his apartment. His fingers found the doorjamb. But as he moved forward to grasp the handle, something beneath his foot threw his already compromised balance off kilter. He fell, landing heavily on his hands and knees on the cold stone floor. Hearing the fleshy impact, the landlady peered quickly into the room, shaking her head before resuming her sweeping.

'No, really Belma *abla*. Don't worry at all. I'm fine.' He hefted himself upright. Fumbling with his keys, he opened his front door and switched on the single globe that hung from the ceiling. At his feet in the doorway he could see what had tripped him – a brown paper–wrapped parcel twice the size of a paperback novel. He bent, head spinning, and picked it up, looking at the neatly written address. *Dr B. Hitchens.* He scratched his head. 'Yup. That's me.'

Throwing the package onto the small table in the middle of the room, he staggered over to what served as his kitchen, relieved himself in the sink and swayed towards the bedroom, struggling to quell the sickly ebb and flow of the floorboards beneath his feet.

He slumped heavily onto the mattress and fumbled with his laces, levering off his boots and tossing them with a thud into the corner. As he turned to collapse back onto the bed, he caught sight of a framed photo sitting in judgement on his dresser: his younger self standing proudly in the blazing sunlight on the summit of Eskitepe, one hand jauntily on his hip, the other grasping the long handle of a spade.

Ada had taken the photograph on the last day they spent together on site. As promised, she had stayed in contact over the years. But he knew she still smarted from the perfunctory way he had ended their relationship – the messages on the postcards that arrived from excavations across the Mediterranean and Middle East were affectionate but pointedly platonic.

He sneered at the memento mori of their affair.

*You cocky little shit*, he thought to himself.

A queasy but all-too-familiar wave of shame washed over the American as he fell backwards onto the mattress.

# 2

The phone rang just three times. 'Have you seen the catalogue?'

'Of course.'

'Is it the one?'

'Absolutely. No doubt about it.'

'You're sure? You haven't laid eyes on it for years.'

'Trust me. That's it.'

'What do you think he's playing at?'

'Impossible to say. Maybe nothing. Perhaps he's just moved on. I'd prefer to get my hands on it before it goes to auction, though. Too much can go wrong in London.'

'Wherever it is, he's kept it well hidden.'

'Yes, he has. But it changes everything now we know he still has it.'

'Do you have a plan?'

'Always.'

# 3

## Istanbul, Turkey, 1955

The hammering water pipes kept time with the incessant throbbing in his skull. As he stood and waited for the pitiful trickle of water that would eventually issue from the tap as erratically as an old man's stream of piss, a razor-sharp sliver of daylight cut between the dusty curtains and stabbed at Ben's eyeballs. A hot wave of nausea drove him back against the kitchen bench.

He knew the life cycle of a monumental hangover all too well. But this was one out of the box. Splashing his face with a handful of water cold enough to make his jaw ache, he downed a couple of aspirin and prayed that medicinal respite would come quickly.

The sound of *İstanbullular* going about their lives outside assailed his pounding eardrums – the incessant blipping and blaring of car horns; raucous shouts of street vendors; women chattering and children shouting with glee as another goal was kicked in a spontaneous game of street soccer.

The apartment was a sorry sight. The sheet on his bed was tangled and sweat-stained, and a heavy coating of dust covered every flat surface. Yes, the thought of being trapped inside was most unappealing. But he was in no condition to confront the outside world. Resting his forehead in the palms of his hands, he resigned himself to spending the day in a room that smelled of mildew and desperation. Consciousness beat a rapid retreat and his eyelids dropped, heavy as lead sheets, over chafed eyeballs.

'*Bay* Benedict! *Bay* Benedict! *Orada mısınız? Bay* Benedict! *Derhal kapıyı açın!*'

An insistent battering at the front door shocked him awake.

'*Bay* Benedict! *Derhal kapıyı açın!*'

'No, I'm not opening the door. *Ne istiyorsunuz?* What do you want?'

'*Polis!*'

*Christ almighty. What now?*

Grimacing, he took to his feet. Even in his weakened state, he wasn't stupid enough to ignore the police.

'*Bekleyin! Bekleyin lütfen!* Wait, please!' He staggered towards the door. Unlocking the latch and bracing himself for the effects of the light that would flood the room, he was shoved aside by two broad-shouldered men, surprisingly tall for Turks. They stood side by side in front of the open doorway with arms crossed, blocking the way to the street outside. Little did they realise he would be more likely to vomit on their polished shoes than make a break for freedom.

'Sir – we have come to take you to Superintendent Demir.'

Ben groaned. 'Demir. Shit!' he exclaimed. *Just what I need,* he cursed beneath his breath. *Bloody Ilhan. He said he had the police under control.*

'He is the head of the antiquities bureau.'

214

'Yes – I know exactly who he is. Unfortunately, my relationship with him is far more intimate than I'd prefer.'

The taller of the two officers responded. 'If you could get your mail and bring it with you, please sir.'

'What? My mail? Ah – what mail?'

'A parcel arrived for you yesterday.'

Parcel? He had no idea what they were talking about. What the hell? Ah, yes. The undignified homecoming. He looked towards the small table in the centre of the room where a brown paper–wrapped package sat, its edges a little worse for wear. It bore the telltale re-taping of the wrapping that was the signature of the attentions of the Turkish police.

'That? Seems you've already had a good look at it.'

The two Turks said nothing. The aspirin kicked in and Ben's headache began to subside to a dull roar.

'All right. Let's go.' Taking his aviator sunglasses from the bench near the door – the only defence he had against the burning glare of the summer sun – he followed the two men out of the apartment building into the street.

A bank of traffic was stalled behind a delivery van parked in an intersection, drivers shouting, gesticulating, and punctuating their abuse with screeching horns. The smell of rubbish piled on street corners, fermenting in the summer heat, turned Ben's stomach, and the stifling humidity made him feel like he was suffocating. He would have given almost anything to have been allowed to retreat to his apartment and wait out the day.

But nothing was worse than the growing dread he felt about what might await him at police headquarters.

'I am very curious to see your response to what arrived in your post yesterday, Mr Hitchens.'

Superintendent Hasan Demir sat poised in his high-backed leather chair, gazing dispassionately at Ben across the gilded pate of the obligatory bust of Atatürk that occupied pride of place in the centre of the busy desktop. Hasan emanated a quiet sense of gravitas and world-weariness that matched the seniority of his position. He had climbed the career ladder steadily since Ben had first encountered him in Konya, and wore the air of authority well.

The still unwrapped parcel sat on the desk between them.

'Superintendent . . . although, what the hell – we're old friends now, aren't we? I think I might take the liberty of calling you by your first name. So. Hasan *Bey* – here's the thing – I haven't opened the parcel yet. I was . . . er . . . out till fairly late last night. Though judging by the slipshod repairs to your handiwork, I imagine you know a great deal more about what's contained in that parcel than I do. Perhaps you'd like to enlighten me.'

Hasan was silent, his grey eyes fixed steadily on him. When Ben had first arrived in the superintendent's office and Hasan had offered him tea – the customary precursor to all normal social and business interactions in Turkey – he was fairly sure he was not about to be thrown in prison. They had drunk in silence. But once the niceties had been dispensed with, the police officer had launched his line of questioning.

'Open it, Mr Hitchens.'

'Now, why didn't I think of that?' he asked sardonically, picking up the package and tearing off the wrapping. Out fell a Sotheby's catalogue. A wave of nausea caused by something other than intemperate alcohol consumption made his stomach clench. It was the catalogue containing their three forgeries. And, most worryingly, his tablet.

The floor seemed to undulate beneath him. His mind raced. *Damn him*, Ben cursed to himself. *He's worked it out. Well, that's just great.* If Hasan had connected it to the antiquities missing from İzmir, Ben was finished.

He was grateful for the ceiling fan revolving above his head. Beads of sweat gathered on his forehead as he fought to keep himself under control. He hoped Hasan would attribute his agitation to the lingering symptoms of his hangover.

'I can see that something is bothering you, Mr Hitchens. What is it?'

'Ah, nothing at all. Not feeling very well, you see. Coming down with something, I think.'

Hasan raised an eyebrow. 'Is that so?'

'Er – yes. Might be the flu. It would be best for you to keep your distance. Wouldn't want to catch a bug. Might have had a drink or two too many last night, though there's nothing too unusual about that, unfortunately . . .' He was babbling as his mind raced. He didn't want to show too much interest in the catalogue. It would be bad enough if Hasan had identified the forgeries. But if he had somehow worked out that Ben was selling one of the items from İzmir in the Sotheby's sale, it wouldn't be a stretch to conclude that he had also been involved in the theft and sale of the rest of the collection.

'It does seem curious, doesn't it?' Hasan prompted. 'When I saw the catalogue, at first I thought that perhaps it had been sent to you because it included one of the treasures from the collection you claim was stolen. Perhaps someone wanted to let you know it was being sold. Or perhaps you, yourself, were selling something. But I have committed every detail of your drawings to memory, and I know that nothing in this catalogue is related to the artefacts in the *Illustrated London News* article. Which makes me wonder, why has it been sent to you?'

*Fishing*, Ben thought with some relief. *He's just fishing. He's got nothing.*

'There have been times Sotheby's have asked my opinion on something they're selling . . .'

'Now, really, Mr Hitchens. Given your less than stellar reputation these days, that seems very unlikely. Wouldn't you agree?'

'Maybe it was an accident.'

'An accident? Even less likely.' Hasan sighed, exasperated. 'I don't think you understand the danger you might be in, Benedict. The people who smuggle antiquities out of this country make a great deal of money from their activities, and they kill people who get in their way. Only last week I was called to Diyarbakır to investigate the torture and murder of a sixteen-year-old boy who was trying to cheat the criminal who runs the smuggling racket in the region. They stripped the skin from his body while he was still alive and left him hanging from a lamppost as a lesson to any others who thought to defy them. It was a most unpleasant way to die.'

Despite himself, Ben shuddered at the thought of it. 'You forget, Hasan *Bey* – you call me into your office to recount your little horror stories about the dastardly forces who might do me harm with depressing regularity. And, yet, here I am – still in one piece. I am not in anyone's way. In case you hadn't noticed, I'm old news. Anyway, with my little coterie of bodyguards courtesy of the Turkish government, I don't think I'm at any risk of physical harm.'

It was Hasan's turn to look surprised. 'Bodyguards?'

'Come on, Hasan. You don't actually think I haven't noticed them, do you?' he said. 'Actually, I've been meaning to tell you – your agents are getting sloppy. They're not even trying to hide from me anymore. It's not a good look when your hunters hang about in full sight of your quarry. Not a good look at all.'

'I'm confused, Mr Hitchens.' Hasan shook his head. 'We certainly were watching you in the months after your story was published – I won't deny that. But the bureau hasn't had officers assigned to you since then.'

Ben was momentarily taken aback. 'Ah, come on now, Hasan. Every day. Two men. Bad suits. Dark hair. Moustaches. Actually, to be fair, that could be describing most of the city's population.'

Bending forward over his desk to emphasise his point, Hasan spoke gravely. 'Benedict, we are very busy in the city at the moment with the troubles over Cyprus.'

'Same old story, isn't it?' Ben said.

'Same story, different chapter. Greek Cypriots want to be part of Greece. And Muslim Cypriots would rather die than be ruled by the Hellenes. So they bring their fight to our streets. And the British? As usual, they do nothing. I think they would rather we all just killed each other.'

'As I said – same old story.'

'Quite. But still – these days my men spend more time trying to stop Greeks and Turks tearing each other's throats out than they do working on my cases.' Hasan sat back and placed his hands behind his head. 'So I can assure you – as much as I would like to keep an eye on you, I don't have enough men available.'

'Come on, Hasan. If not you, then who?'

'That, I don't know. Who else might have cause to keep track of your activities? Be careful. In this city, it is not good to have someone too interested in your business.'

Despite the crushing heat and his alcohol-induced infirmity, Ben made the distance between police headquarters and his apartment at a reasonable pace. The dizzyingly steep streets leading from Karaköy to Galata were lined with multi-storeyed, imposing buildings housing banks and trading companies. Sidling past shoeshine boys plying their trade on the footpath, he fought his way through a steady and determined stream of well-suited businessman breaking for lunch and moving downhill towards the fish restaurants lining the shore of the Golden Horn.

Surprised to find he had any reserves of strength left, he took the steps at his apartment building two at a time. His attendants took up position in the lee of the apartment block on the opposite corner, seeking shelter from the fiery midday sun. In the damply cool darkness of the foyer, he fumbled in his pocket to find his front-door key. Slipping it into the lock and turning the handle, he was momentarily surprised to find the door already open until he recalled the state he had been in when he'd left the apartment that morning.

Inside, his heart lurched in his chest and his muscles tensed involuntarily at the sight of the overturned table and piles of papers swept onto the floor. It had been many years since the war – a time when he lived in a state of constant disquiet, expecting exposure or betrayal at any moment – but it had bequeathed him an uncanny ability to sense peril.

Nerves jangling, he took another step into the apartment, instinctively assuming a fighter's stance. Too late he spun on his heel as he heard a floorboard creak behind him. There was a whoosh and a thump as something heavy connected with his left temple. A sheet of blinding white light filled his vision. Then, nothing.

# 4

## Istanbul, Turkey, 1955

The first thing he noticed as he began to wade back through the grey fog of consciousness was the smell of dust filling his nostrils. His head spun as he struggled to lift leaden eyelids. Lying face down on the floor, his cheek was pressed against the rough timber boards and his arms were outstretched in front of him. As his eyes began to focus, he fixed on the little puffs of dust in the air caused by his laboured breathing. With a prodigious effort, he hoisted himself into a sitting position. The sudden surge of blood to his brain threatened to knock him sideways, and he had to lower his head into his hands as pinpricks of light blurred his vision.

The door to his apartment was ajar, his assailant long gone.

The room was in disarray. Threadbare socks and under-pants were strewn across the floor, tossed from the dresser that had been pulled away from the wall, its drawers roughly yanked out and thrown in a haphazard pile in the corner. Books and papers stacked on the desk had been knocked to the floor and cupboard doors in the kitchen were gaping open, jars of sugar and tea upended.

Whatever the intruder had been searching for, it certainly hadn't been his handful of genuinely valuable possessions. The gold signet ring with his mother's family crest on it still encircled his pinkie finger and he could feel the weight of his Achilles pendant against his chest. His satchel lay on the floor beside him, undisturbed, and he could feel the bulk of his wallet in his back pocket.

There was only one other thing in his possession that might attract such unwanted attention. Wincing, he rose to his feet and moved gingerly towards the sink, praying it was safe. The door of the cupboard beneath it had been flung open and the contents tossed out. This, he'd decided, would be the best place to hide the tablet fragment. His instincts had been right – the one thing beneath the kitchen bench that remained in place was the rubbish bin. An interior insert served as a receptacle for the insignificant amount of household waste he generated. Lifting the insert out, he grimaced at the pungent smell of a rotting jumble of orange skins, eggshells and tea leaves.

Beneath the insert at the bottom of the bin itself sat the marble fragment, wrapped tightly in heavy plastic sheeting. Relieved, he lifted it from its resting place, comforted by its cool, heavy weight.

In the years since Eris had disappeared, the tablet had assumed talismanic importance for him. At first, he clung to it, treasuring it as a thread that bound them together. But as it began to reveal its secrets under his dogged scrutiny, it had assumed a significance he could never have imagined when he'd first retrieved it from the ruins of Eris' home. Charlotte Fairweather had been quite correct in her assessment. At first glance, the tablet was a very run-of-the-mill ancient relic with little to recommend it. Though now, Ben knew better. It was the key to a treasure so sublime it was almost inconceivable.

He had discovered its hidden meaning by chance. In the immediate aftermath of his tragic encounter with Eris in İzmir he had studied the tablet obsessively, poring over the inscription, examining every fissure and crack in the ancient stone. He couldn't help but believe that if he could make sense of it; translate the text; discover its source; it would somehow bring him closer to her. Over the course of weeks and months, he had transcribed the eroded text. But all he ended up with was a meaningless jumble of Greek letters.

Knowing that nobody of right mind would waste time inscribing a solid block of marble without good reason, he had concluded that it must have been a coded message. He had put what he had learnt in the war about ciphers to use, but countless days of scrambling and unscrambling the letters yielded nothing. Frustration and desperation took hold, until he found inspiration in a peculiar dream. He was a messenger carrying a secret communiqué to the Spartan king, Leonidas, at the Pass of Thermopylae. The instant Ben awoke, he knew. It was a scytale cipher. Used by Greek commanders, a strip of parchment or leather was twisted along a staff of a specific diameter. Once the message was inscribed on the leather and removed from the staff, it was illegible by anyone other than someone who knew what diameter staff was required to read it. Once the leather was twirled around the correct staff, the message could be interpreted.

Working out that it was a scytale had been easy. The process of finding a staff with the correct diameter was not. A painstaking process of trial and error ensued and he had been ready to give up when he had stumbled across a rod of the right thickness in the crowded Egyptian market at Eminönü. It was one of the fine rolling pins used to make *yufka* pastry, the silken dough that was a staple of Turkish cooking, and as soon as Ben twirled the strip of paper around it, he knew.

When he had read the first line of the inscription, his heart had skipped a beat.

*And so it was that the immortal Achilles, son of Peleus, was laid to rest . . .*

He had worked the remaining strips of text along the wooden rolling pin.

*. . . light of Hellas, his limbs encased in Hephaestus' splendid golden arms such as no other man of this earth has ever borne. Deadly sword and famous shield that caused sons of Ilium to tremble are held against his chest.*

*Androcles, greatest of men, who proved his worth when the hero fell, will be entrusted with the truth. As others worship before an empty tomb, those of his line shall know his fate, the place beyond which he shed his human form and became a god, to live for evermore on the sacred heights of Olympus.*

*Now, warriors, who marched with the stripling son of Thetis to the walls of Ilium; go. Go and lay him with Cybele in the arms of the mother of beasts. Hasten his passage with sad lament, and let him pass Hades' gate. Where the mightiest of the three guardians of Ilium stand, lay him to rest on the father of them all. Take the mortal remains of the son of Thetis to the many-fountained peak where the ox-eyed goddess light-footed made her way to deceive Zeus the storm-gatherer. He lay with her in love in a golden cloud as the Achaeans, beloved of Hera, overran the warriors of Ilium.*

*Lest the sons of Androcles seek to wake the hero from his slumber, a path has been laid . . .*

The text ended there. But it said enough to shock Ben to the core. Even now, as he ran his fingers across the chilly marble, his skin tingled with supernatural awe.

Achilles. Not the Achilles Ben knew so well from the time-honoured lines of Greek poets and philosophers, but something different, speaking of events that occurred after Achilles' death. This spoke of Achilles the man. The marble tablet was no longer simply a tangible reminder of his encounter with Eris. It promised something else – Achilles' final resting place.

The hints were so tantalising. The mention of an empty tomb Ben took to mean the Achilleion, the cultic site recognised in antiquity as Achilles' burial place that attracted such pilgrims as Alexander the Great. If the inscription was taken literally, it implied that the Achilleion had been constructed as a decoy to protect the location of Achilles' actual tomb. As for the location of Achilles' burial place, Ben had recognised the obscure mythological references immediately. To the ancient Greeks, a towering peak on Turkey's north-west coast was sacred to the mother goddess, Cybele, and known as the 'mother of beasts'. Mount Ida.

He might have dismissed it all as a poetic fancy if it had not been for the mention of Androcles. There were many versions of the tale that recounted Achilles' fate. But one of the more obscure variants featured the Achaean general, Androcles. According to that account, when the hero fell, slain by Paris' arrow, the Greek generals began to squabble among themselves to determine who should inherit Achilles' famed armour, which had been cast by the god Hephaestus, and promised its bearer immortality.

Androcles stayed by the fallen man's side and defended his body from those who wished to strip it of its armour. When it became apparent that none of the Greek claimants were willing to give ground, Androcles was deemed to be the one man who could be entrusted with Achilles' entombment, burying with him the armour that caused his comrades to take up arms against each other. At a time when the desecration of a tomb meant the soul of the deceased would be unable to find peace in the afterlife, it hadn't been a stretch for Ben to imagine that an elaborate ruse might have been confected to protect Achilles' final resting place from desecration.

At that point, things became rather more complicated. Why, for one thing, was the location of Achilles' tomb inscribed on a marble tablet that Ben had conservatively dated as having been created at least eight hundred years after the Trojan War? And although he had Mount Ida as a starting point, the tablet had fractured at the place where it seemed it would detail more specific information about finding the tomb. Mount Ida covered an enormous area; to begin a search for a single tomb would be a fool's errand. Ben knew he needed to find the other half of the tablet.

So had begun his mad quest. By offering his tablet for sale at Sotheby's he was ensuring that every antiquities dealer and collector worth their salt would be aware of its existence. He could only hope that the person who had taken possession of the other half of the tablet would look closely enough to realise the two halves belonged together and seek to unite them. The provenance he had fabricated indicated it had been found in a tomb belonging to an ancient Greek family that claimed descent from Androcles – a signal he hoped would communicate the tablet's importance to other interested parties and heighten their desire to acquire it. His plan, flimsy as it was, was to attend the Sotheby's auction and confront the person who bought his half of the tablet. If he could discover where the other tablet fragment had ended up, he could backtrack and discover its source to identify the men who had kidnapped

Eris. And if he found the other half of his tablet, he would have the information he needed to find Achilles' tomb.

Of course, exposing the tablet in this manner was a risk. Not only could it give Hasan the evidence he needed to convict Ben of antiquities theft, there was also a chance that the men who kidnapped Eris would see it and assume he had held on to other pieces from the collection in İzmir. Having seen their handiwork, he could only assume they would be less than pleased to learn he had deprived them of things they thought of as theirs.

The coincidence of the break-in was too great to ignore. The throbbing lump on the side of his head was a brutal reminder that he was tangled up in something dangerous. That he couldn't identify his adversaries made it all the more worrisome.

He stood and returned the tablet to its hiding place, as an afterthought slipping the catalogue into the bin as well.

The sensible course of action would have been to retreat. But Benedict Hitchens had never been renowned for behaving sensibly.

'Hey! You two!'

He roared at the sentinels who remained standing in the shade on the footpath opposite his building. 'Yes! You!' Startled, the two men glanced at each other and dropped their heads, turning their backs on the dishevelled American barrelling across the road towards them. They began to walk briskly in the opposite direction towards the busy intersection at the end of the street.

'Don't ignore me now, you sons of bitches! Tell me who was in my apartment! You must have seen them leave.'

Legs pumping, he broke into a run as the two men picked up their pace. 'Who was it? For Chrissakes! Tell me!'

Glancing over his shoulder, the taller of the men called to his partner and they both bolted, each running in opposite directions at the end of the street. Reaching the intersection, Ben made a split-second decision to follow the smaller man, thinking he would be easier to outrun. It was a bad call. The Turk had the speed and agility of a whippet. He darted up the narrow footpath, dodging the street vendors and beggars on the pavement.

Finding a strength he had forgotten he possessed, Ben pursued the fleeing man up the steep laneway. His boots found purchase on the slippery cobbles, and he was surprised that he could keep pace with the Turk as he weaved between the numerous pedestrians.

Ahead, the street opened out onto a small plaza intersected by tram tracks. His legs burned from the unfamiliar exertion. Gritting his teeth, he pushed harder. He was gaining on his quarry. Fury and blind rage tapped reserves of strength that had lain dormant for years. The smaller man slipped sharply round a corner to the left. Ben charged after him and ran straight into a packed mass of people pouring out of the exit of the Tünel tramcar station. The Turk leapt over the barrier and bolted onto the tram. Frustrated, Ben tried to fight his way through the impenetrable crowd of commuters. Bells chimed on the platform as the tram prepared to depart.

Ben bellowed, 'Get out of my way!'

Arm in front of him, he ploughed through the throng, bursting into the tiled station just in time to see the small carriage begin its descent into the long, pitch-black tunnel. He was too late. Next stop was the terminus at Karaköy.

Hands on hips, he wheezed and sucked air into his lungs. He was furious. But there was no point following him down on the return carriage. By the time Ben disembarked at Karaköy, the man would be long gone.

'Twice in one day? You never come to visit me voluntarily and are always in such a hurry to leave my office, so I must say I am surprised to see you again so soon.'

Ben had forced his way past Superintendent Hasan Demir's assistant and barged uninvited into the Turk's office.

Hasan sat with his hand suspended above a sheaf of documents fanned across his desk, a black fountain pen held between manicured, blunt-ended fingers.

'You need to tell me what the hell is going on, Demir.' Jaw jutting forward and hands clamped aggressively on his hips, Ben knew he presented a formidable figure.

Hasan placed his pen carefully on the desktop and leant back in his chair, arms crossed. With a pensive expression, he considered the man standing opposite him. 'May I offer you tea?'

'Tea?' Ben was incredulous. 'No. I've had more than enough of your goddamned tea. What I want is the fucking truth!'

The Turk sighed. 'Mr Hitchens, please control your temper. Your language is very shameful.'

'Shameful?' He felt his heart pounding. 'I'll give you shameful! Shameful is breaking into my apartment and using my head for batting practice!'

Suddenly alert, Hasan sat forward. 'Break into your apartment? What are you talking about?'

'Don't tell me your flunkies weren't involved, Hasan. They fled like rats out of an aqueduct as soon as I confronted them.'

'As I told you before, Benedict. None of my men are following you.' Hasan gestured towards the worn leather chair on the opposite side of the desk and spoke in the authoritative tone he had developed over many decades spent appeasing irate individuals. 'You are upset. But this is not the way we do things here. You have been in this country long enough to know that. Let us address each other like civilised people. Please. Take a seat and we can talk about this problem of yours.'

Ignoring Hasan's invitation, he remained standing. 'Yes, I am upset. You can't tell me it was just coincidence that the break-in occurred while I was conveniently tied up with you here. And when I arrived home – obviously a little earlier than expected – your man decided my head needed tenderising. Knocked me senseless.'

'I can assure you I had nothing to do with it,' Hasan said. 'Certainly, I would not hesitate to search your apartment if I thought it would be worthwhile. But none of my men would attack you. If they did, they would find themselves assigned to patrol the Soviet border. It sounds to me as if you should make a formal report about this break-in.'

Ben scoffed. 'Why? Waste still more of my time? I think not.' But he was thrown by Hasan's steadfast conviction, free of any of the usual Turkish techniques of verbal evasion. 'So, if it's not you . . . who the hell was it?'

Hasan sighed. 'I know you have always doubted me when I have warned you about the antiquities dealers who would do anything to track down the treasure you smuggled out of the country.'

'For God's sake, Hasan,' he snapped. 'How many times do I have to tell you? I had nothing to do with that.'

'So you say,' conceded Hasan. 'But it doesn't matter whether or not I believe you. If these people think you were involved, then you are in grave danger.' He hesitated. 'You might also look at some of the people a little closer to home.'

'What do you mean?'

'Well, not to put too fine a point on it . . . you do have an associate who has very close ties to some very disreputable people.'

'Associate? You mean Ilhan Aslan?'

'Yes, that is exactly the person I am referring to. You know, if I were you I would ask *him* about the men who have been following you.'

'Ask Ilhan? Don't be ridiculous! Why would he need to follow me? My goings-on are hardly obscure to him. Most days I'm cooling my heels on the couch in his shop.'

'It could be that he's not having you followed to keep track of your whereabouts, but to give you the impression that *I* still have you under surveillance,' Hasan said. 'You have been a very worthwhile investment for him. The last thing he would want you to do is find honest employment again. And as long as you think we're watching you, you're not going to try, are you?'

'That's the stupidest thing I have ever heard,' Ben protested. 'Even if Ilhan did decide to fuel my paranoid fantasies like that, it wouldn't be worth his while to pay two men to track me. Christ almighty! I've had enough of this bullshit!' He turned his back on Hasan and headed for the exit. As he stormed out into the corridor and slammed the door, the superintendent shouted down the hallway after him.

'Why do you think they don't follow you at night? Life is cheap in Istanbul, Benedict!'

Ben rounded the corner and tackled the stairs at the front of his apartment block. From the corner of his eye he saw a figure approaching quickly from across the road. Nerves on edge, he was expecting trouble.

He whipped around as quickly as his battered body would allow. The slight figure standing before him was clad in a neatly ironed short-sleeved white shirt and dark pants and kept a respectful distance. 'Yilmaz! *Merhaba. Nasılsın?* You surprised me. What are you doing here?'

'*Merhaba, Bay* Benedict.' Ilhan's assistant bowed his head deferentially. 'Ilhan *Bey* asked me to come and check that you were all right.'

'It's been quite a day.'

Yilmaz's eyes darted, avoiding Ben's gaze. 'He said that you left Refik very late and he was concerned that you might have had some . . . problems finding your way home.'

'Well, could you please thank Ilhan very much for his concern, Yilmaz, and assure him that I couldn't be better.'

The youth looked Ben up and down dubiously. 'Are you certain?'

Ben winced, feeling the tender lump on the side of his head. 'Quite certain. Thanks. I'll probably drop by the shop tomorrow. Tell Ilhan for me, won't you?'

The boy smiled as he turned and walked back down the street. 'Yes, *Bay* Benedict, I will give him your message. Oh. He also asked me to remind you not to forget you must deliver the parcel to Miss Charlotte tomorrow.'

Ben smiled tightly. How could he forget? 'Yes, I know. Tell him not to worry.'

Yilmaz nodded and raised a hand in farewell.

*It's insane to suspect Ilhan*, Ben thought. He had never been anything but a good friend. He was also the only other person who knew anything about the significance of the tablet. If he had ever wanted to work against Ben, there had been more than enough opportunities to do so over the years. Why would he start now?

Standing on the stoop, Ben watched as Yilmaz reached the end of the street and turned the corner without a backward glance.

# 5

The voice at the other end of the line was strained.

'My men. They didn't find anything.'

'I told you it was a waste of time. We know he has it. You're too impatient. He'll work it out, and then he'll bring it to us.'

'And I think you're too trusting. What if he tells someone?'

'He won't. It's not in his nature. He's too proud to ask for help.'

The line went dead.

# 6

## Istanbul, Turkey, 1955

It was the first time in years he had awoken with the dawn *ezan* without a skull-splitting headache and a grievous case of the dry horrors. Ben lay on the mattress and listened to the muezzin assure the faithful that prayer is better than sleep. Most mornings, he would have begged to differ. But not today. Today, his life had renewed purpose.

Swinging his legs over the side of the bed, he wriggled his toes and threw his arms high above his head, stretching his back until his spine crackled. His body ached after the trials of the previous day, but his mind was delightfully clear.

He stood and pulled back the curtain that concealed the one sash-window in the bedroom, holding his breath in anticipation of the inevitable plume of dust that billowed from the heavy fabric. The pane of glass was filthy; he struggled to loosen the latch on the window's upper sill, which was stiff and unyielding through lack of use. He couldn't remember opening the window once in the three years he had lived here.

With a grinding squeal of protest, the lock succumbed. Outside, the melodic cries of the gulls and swallows dipping and darting about the lofty rooftops chimed along the narrow laneway.

Stripping the sheets off his bed, he stuffed the scattered piles of dirty clothes from the floor into his old army duffel bag, moving methodically through the apartment and righting the disarray left behind by the intruder.

He retrieved the carefully wrapped tablet and the Sotheby's catalogue from the bin. Tucked in an envelope beneath the tablet was a neatly folded rubbing of the inscription, along with a full transcription of the text and the ribbons of code he had used to decipher the hidden message. He slipped the envelope inside his journal and placed the tablet on his desk.

There was no more avoiding it. He had to deliver the tablet to Charlotte at her hotel. But the break-in had made him skittish. Once it was out of his hands, whoever had the other half would have all the information they would need to beat him to the tomb. He had no intention of making it that easy for them.

He scrabbled around under the sink until he found what he had been looking for. Placing the cool slab of marble on the edge of the desk, he steeled himself. It was the only memento he had of Eris and the thought of parting with it made him falter. What he had resolved to do now was even worse.

But as he saw it, it was the only solution.

He lifted the hammer.

'Dr Hitchens, this tablet is not the same as the one illustrated in the catalogue!'

The cool marble foyer of the recently opened Hilton Hotel echoed with the clickity-clack of high heels and excited chatter of international tourists checking in at the reception desk. Upon arrival, Ben had been greeted at the glass doors by the supercilious disdain of a top-hatted concierge, who scrutinised him as Ben imagined he might assess a dog turd on his mirror-gloss shoes. He suspected that without Charlotte Fairweather's intercession on his behalf he would have been asked to leave.

After showing him to a cluster of chairs in a corner of the room where they took a seat, Ben had retrieved the tablet from his satchel and handed it to the Englishwoman. She was not impressed with what she saw.

'. . . This is not at all what I was expecting. It's totally different!'

'I can assure you it's the same tablet. If you compare the lettering . . .'

Charlotte turned the marble slab in her hands. 'But this corner . . . there's a clean break. This happened recently . . . a quarter of it is missing! A sizable amount of the text is gone!'

'Ah, yes. Can't say I'd noticed.'

'Hadn't *noticed*? It's as plain as the nose on my face. A corner smashed right off!'

'Now you mention it . . . you could be right.'

'Of course I'm right! What on earth happened to it?'

'Can't say, I'm afraid.'

'Well, this is just *marvellous*! How am I going to explain this?'

'It's still the same tablet . . .'

'Yes, but it has quite clearly been damaged. *Seriously* damaged. We'll have to put out a saleroom notice. Oh, for goodness' sake. This really is *most* unacceptable.'

Ben was silent. There was no point trying to justify it.

Charlotte continued, her fine brow creased in frustration. 'Look, to be frank, I don't hold out much hope of it selling in this state. Please pass that information on to the owner.'

'I'm pretty sure you'll find a buyer for it, Miss Fairweather.'

'You are, are you? Well, you must know something I don't!'

*That I do*, thought Ben to himself. *That I do*.

'Ben *abi*!'

From his customary perch in the window of his store, Ilhan spotted him as soon as he entered the square. Leaping to his feet, he flung open the front door and strode towards the American, arms outstretched and his usually stoic expression split by a wide, white-toothed smile.

Having surrendered the disfigured tablet to Charlotte Fairweather, Ben had only one thing to do before he departed for London. The chunk of marble weighed heavily in his satchel, digging into his hip. He knew he couldn't risk trying to take it out through customs with him to England. But given the events of recent days he also knew it wouldn't be safe in his apartment. He needed to entrust it to someone else. His first thought had been Ilhan, but after the break-in, he didn't want to expose his friend to any more danger than he was already in.

Ilhan's eyes shone with concern. 'I'm glad you came today. At Refik the other night, I was worried for you.' Ilhan signalled to Yilmaz. 'Boy! Two teas!'

Yilmaz ducked his head. 'Of course, *efendim*.'

'So.' Ilhan took Ben by the shoulders. 'You do look worse than usual. What happened?'

'It's been an interesting couple of days. After I farewelled you at Refik, I ended up in Cihangir.'

Shaking his head, Ilhan tut-tutted like a disapproving grandfather. 'Why do you do these things to yourself, Ben? You know about those women. It is not just that they have loose morals. It is the diseases they carry. Better to lie down with a mange-ridden street hound.'

'Well, thank you for that mental picture.' Ben negotiated around the low-hanging ornaments dangling from the roof of Ilhan's store and manoeuvred his way to the banquette at the back of the shop. The brass bell above the door tinkled as Yilmaz returned bearing a small copper tray with two waisted glasses of Turkish tea. Ben inhaled the fragrant steam as he took a sip. Ilhan sat opposite him on a low stool and rested his outstretched legs on a padded ottoman.

'And how did things work out with the charming English-woman?' Ben asked.

'I thought you knew me better than that, Dr Hitchens. I would never betray a lady's confidence by sharing intimate secrets with you.'

'"Intimate secrets"? That tells me all I need to know. Well, I wish my evening had been even half as satisfying as yours.'

Looking up, Ilhan's forehead wrinkled with concern. 'Yilmaz told me you looked a bit shaken up when he went to check on you yesterday.'

'Yes, well, that was the other thing that happened to me. I had a break-in.'

'Break-in?' Ilhan's brow furrowed. 'At your apartment?'

'Where else? Yes. Copped a whack to the head into the bargain.' Instinctively his fingers probed the swollen spot on the side of his head. He flinched.

'And this is the first I hear of it? Ben – you should have called me.'

'So you could do what? The bastard was long gone by the time I came around. I can only imagine they were looking for the tablet – they didn't take anything else.'

'The tablet? Oh, God . . .'

'Don't worry. They didn't find it.'

Running his fingers through his hair, Ilhan shook his head. 'You were very lucky.'

'No thanks to Hasan's goons. Bloody man said he had nothing to do with it, which I do find rather difficult to believe. Two men standing out the front of my place, brazen as you like, as I'm getting pummelled inside. Just scarpered when I confronted them. Speaking of Hasan, he's on my case. Don't think he knows anything, but he found the catalogue and knows something's going on. That's certainly not helping my state of composure. He's not on your payroll, by any chance?'

'Demir?' Ilhan scoffed. 'No such luck. Not for want of trying, though. Unfortunately he's one of a dying breed – the incorruptible public servant. He might have caught wind of our plans. But I haven't heard anything from my little birds on the force. He's got more than enough to worry about with the boatloads of real antiquities leaving the country without concerning himself with forgeries.'

'I'm less concerned about that than I am about his working out what I'm doing with the tablet.'

Ilhan patted him on the back paternally. 'It will soon be over, my friend. Don't worry.'

'Worried? Me?' Ben smiled grimly. 'Never.'

The glittering tracery of countless fishing lines shone in the clear morning light, strung like a spider's web from the tips of rods held by ranks of fishermen standing along the wrought-iron balustrade at the edge of the Galata Bridge. Water-filled buckets at their feet brimmed with tiny shimmering fish the size of a man's thumb.

Ben stood at the edge with his elbows resting on top of the handrail running along the eastern side of the bridge. Beyond, the mouth of the Golden Horn opened towards the Asian side of the city and a cool, gentle breeze slipped across the Bosphorus' oily black waters.

Ben was troubled. The dead weight of the marble fragment in his satchel tugged at his shoulder, a reminder of the urgent need to find somewhere safe to store it. That he could think of only one person in the city to approach for help was a sad indictment of his circumstances.

At six foot two inches tall, and with a tousled, sandy-blond mop of hair, he stood little chance of blending into the crowd. The passers-by stared at him unapologetically, curious to see a foreigner – a *yabancı* – in their midst. Although now well accustomed to the unceasing scrutiny of the locals, today their rubbernecking unsettled him.

Turning his back on the iconic skyline of Sultanahmet, he reluctantly began the journey towards the northern shore of the Golden Horn and the imposing edifice of the British Consulate.

'Well, I say. Dear chap, I am pleased as punch you have chosen me as your confidant.'

Henry Wootton-Jones' already over-inflated sense of his own self-worth had received an unnecessary boost when Ben had arrived at the consulate and handed the marble fragment over to him for safekeeping.

'Just between ourselves now, Benedict . . .'

'Do me a favour, Wootton-Jones. Now we are partners in crime, can you please make an effort to drop the "Benedict"? Or shall I start calling you "Hank"?'

'Quite. Sincere apologies . . . *Ben*. Goodness. *Hank*? I think not!' The British diplomat winced. His whispery brows were knotted together above watery pale blue eyes, and his mouth contorted into a thin-lipped, white smile. 'Now, as I was saying. About this "crime", as you put it. Given my position and the regard in which I am held in the diplomatic community, it is beholden unto me to ensure I am not going to land in a pickle by getting caught breaking the sovereign laws of this fine country.' He splayed his one hand and pressed it against the desktop. 'Particularly with all the ballyhoo about Cyprus – the Turks are in a terrible flap about that at the moment. I don't want to be responsible for any more trouble. This doesn't involve anything actually . . . *illegal*, does it, Benedi – *Ben*?'

Ben knew he had to be careful. He sighed and shook his head. 'No, Wootton-Jones. You won't end up in any trouble if you keep this here in your desk for me. I'll come and retrieve it as soon as I'm back from the auction.'

Wootton-Jones' eyes lit up. 'Auction, you say?'

'Yes. That's why I'm heading back to the Mother Country.'

'Well, you absolutely *must* get in touch with Charlotte when you're there. She was *most* impressed by meeting you.'

'Impressed? Ha!' Ben laughed as he stood and moved, perhaps a little too eagerly, towards the door of Wootton-Jones' office. 'Could have fooled me!'

Outside the imposing twin pillars of the consulate's gatehouse, a mob of protesters waved crudely painted placards reading, *Kıbrıs Türktür*.

The air crackled with tension and Ben was assailed with the sour smell of anger and adrenalin. He passed through the heavily guarded black iron gateway and tried to shoulder his way through the crowd. Surrounded by a heaving mass of angry Turks, his path was blocked by a broad-chested man with an abundant black moustache who had seen Ben exit the consulate building. Jabbing a finger in his chest, he abused Ben in broken English. 'You, English! English give Cyprus to Greek. Cyprus not Greek! Cyprus Turkey! Cyprus Turkey! Thief. You thief!' The stream of abuse continued in Turkish as Ben tried to push his way past. Fury, along with half-masticated flecks of breakfast, spat between lips white with rage.

In an effort to defend himself, Ben tried to speak reason, addressing the man in Turkish. 'Friend, you have it all wrong. I'm an American. Not British . . . American.'

The Turk spat at the ground. 'American. British. You're all English. All the same. All you do is steal from us.' He grabbed Ben's left jacket sleeve as the other protesters surged behind him. Ben's survival instincts kicked in. He snapped his right arm across his assailant's forearm and broke his grip on his sleeve, simultaneously jerking his knee upwards to catch the Turk sharply in the groin. The man doubled over, clutching his midriff. There was a roar from his confederates, their anger now channelled towards the easy target in their midst.

*Oh, shit!* he thought, and braced himself for a pummelling.

The uniformed guards blockading the consulate gate sensed the protesters' shift in mood. Drawing their batons, they pressed into the crowd. Brutal clouts cracked skulls and bones. The mob was forced back from the gate, men howling in pain and fury. Caught in the melee, Ben's heart slammed against his chest. He fought to keep his feet. With fists and shoulders he drove a path through the crowd. Breaking through the mass of protesters, he sprinted to one of the laneways opposite the consulate and zigzagged through the maze of streets, hoping to shake off any pursuers.

When he thought he might be safe, he stopped, back pressed into an empty doorway, and waited; listening. The dull roar of the mob outside the consulate was audible above the rooftops, but there was no sound of pursuit. The protestors' interest in him had only been fleeting; their rage was directed towards the British Crown.

Ben ran his fingers through his hair and straightened his jacket. Pulling a soft pack of cigarettes from his breast pocket he lit one, drawing the soothing smoke deep into his lungs.

# 7

'It's as we hoped. He's going to London.'

'You're certain?'

'Without a doubt.'

'And the tablet?'

'I'm not sure yet. He's starting to jump at shadows. Either way, we know where it will be by the end of the week.'

'I really hoped to get it before it arrived in London.'

'It's out of our hands now. What next?'

'I've a man over there who's always willing to help without asking too many questions. For a price, of course.'

'It will be worth it. I promise. Oh – you should know – we're not the only ones watching him.'

'More police?'

'Perhaps. But I can't say for certain. I can't ask too many questions. It would raise too many suspicions.'

'Be careful.'

# 8

## London, England, 1955

From the air, London looked like a pernickety architect's working model. Neat, regimented rows of identical buildings sat side by side, surrounded by well-behaved gardens lining orderly streets. It made Ben twitch.

It was so unlike the city he had just departed. Modern urban design had bypassed Istanbul. Thousands of years of history lived on in its streets and it was as incoherent from the air as it was at ground level; needle-fine minarets seemed set to pierce the aeroplane's gleaming fuselage, projecting from a tangled knot of roadways meandering erratically up and down the city's steep hills. Congested bottlenecks funnelled traffic through ancient monumental gates in the city's legendary battlements and the great arches of the Valens Aqueduct. Houses clustered in random blocks, their boundaries dictated by the ancient walls that had sheltered the city's residents for over one thousand years from wave after wave of invaders, walls that were not breached until the arrival of Mehmet the

Conqueror who, at the tender age of twenty-one, brought the Byzantine Empire to an end. The city was chaotic and disorderly, and Ben loved everything about it.

London was another matter. At ground level, his disquiet with its immaculate façade intensified. Even when he'd first landed in the city as a teenager about to embark on his course of studies at Oxford, bursting with rosy-hued idealism, London's grey pallor had sapped the life out of him. He had always felt out of place and out of sorts here.

He slumped on the rear bench seat of a cab as the city streetscape flickered by like a stand of living postcards. The cab drew to a halt at an intersection and neatly dressed and composed pedestrians filed obediently through the crossing like lines of well-outfitted ants. Serried rows of black cabs and lolly-red double-decker buses moved sedately and politely along well-defined lanes of traffic with nary a horse cart or street vendor to be seen. Even the dogs were clipped into unnatural forms. Nothing in London was left to chance.

The cab slowed and indicated a right-hand turn. 'Paultons Square, Chelsea, guv'nor,' the driver announced over his shoulder, his dimpled forearm resting along the back of the front seat.

A lush and neatly maintained fenced garden was bordered at one end by the King's Road, and surrounded on its other three sides by brown-brick Georgian terrace houses painted with gleaming white trim.

'Seems like someone has gone up in the world,' Ben murmured to himself as the cab pulled up at the front of an immaculately presented four-storeyed home.

'Dr Benedict Hitchens. As I live and breathe.' Ada Baxter wrapped Ben in a bear hug.

'Ada, you haven't changed a bit.' It was true. Her turquoise-blue eyes held the same worldly, knowing glint, and her body, pressed against his, felt firm, yielding and immediately familiar to his touch. Her hair smelled of honeysuckle. A sudden surge of desire made the pit of his stomach lurch.

She smiled, eyes sparkling, and stood back, holding him at arm's length. 'Thank you. Wish I could say the same for you, Ben. Hard to believe it's only been three years.'

'A tough three,' he said. He looked around the tastefully decorated entrance hall. A shimmering Tabriz carpet rested on shiny chequerboard marble floor tiles. Hung along the duck egg blue walls was a row of Piranesi etchings of the ruins of ancient Rome mounted in gilt-edged black frames. He raised an eyebrow. 'Tough for me, anyway. But not so much for you by the look of things.'

'None of this is new, you idiot!' She laughed and cuffed him affectionately on the upper arm. 'I just didn't mention it when we met – didn't seem relevant. And you never asked. Besides, I wanted you to fancy me for myself, not for my family's wealth. Fat lot of good that did me in the end, though.'

'Well, you are full of surprises,' he said. 'When you didn't hang up in my ear – which was a surprise itself – and invited me to stay . . . Let's just say I wasn't expecting such salubrious accommodation. Thought I'd be bedding down on a couch in a walk-up flat.'

'If you'd called me two years ago, I would have made you sleep in the gutter,' she responded. 'But I've moved on. Any ill will I might have harboured towards you has matured into a gentle and nostalgic affection.'

Ada opened a door to the left of the flight of stairs leading to the upper floors. 'Come on. I'll get you settled in before dinner. Down here . . . I've put you in the basement.'

Ben laughed. 'Fair enough. That's probably more than I deserve.'

'Don't take it the wrong way – it's a proper bedroom. But there's a separate entrance – thought that might suit you best. I'll give you a key and you can come and go as you please. That way, we won't be getting under each other's feet.'

'Don't worry, Ada,' he assured her. 'I know how it works – house guests, like fish, go off after three days. And I have no intention of sticking around long enough to stink.'

She took his hand and squeezed it affectionately. 'It's lovely to see you, Ben. And you can stay as long as you like.'

After supper, Ada threw open the doors leading out onto the tiled patio and admitted the sounds and smells of London. The gentle summer breeze was crisp and carried with it the scent of roses and geraniums blooming in a riot of colour in the courtyard garden outside. As he reclined on a heavy leather club lounge arranged artfully to make the most of the view of the garden, he nursed a sherry served in a delicately etched crystal glass and marvelled at the utterly unfamiliar sense of order in his surroundings.

Ada moved towards the lounge and he raised his glass in a toast. 'To you – the most gracious host I have encountered in many a year . . . Hell, the *only* host I have encountered in many a year.'

She leant towards him and clinked her glass against his. 'You need to get out more often.'

'There aren't many who would have me these days.'

She sat beside him and stretched out her legs, resting her feet on the glass-topped coffee table between twin stacks of photography and home décor magazines. The sleeves of Ada's white shirt were rolled up to her elbows, revealing a collection of delicate gold chains and bangles on fine wrists. He reached out and ran his finger across the collection of bracelets. It was a barely veiled invitation, and a rather feeble excuse to touch her golden skin. 'These are new.'

Taking his hand between hers, she squeezed it and smiled wistfully. 'Too much water under that particular bridge, Ben. And anyway . . .' She held up her ring finger, revealing a sizable diamond in a yellow-gold setting. 'I adore you, darling. Truly I do. But I'm going to be hitched.'

'Ouch!' He winced comically to disguise his genuine disappointment. 'And it's so obscenely large. I presumed it was costume jewellery! Congratulations – though it's a sad day for single men across the globe – another good woman lost to wedlock. Can't blame me for trying, though.'

'Come on, Ben. You had your chance. But you were never serious about me.'

'I've always regretted how things ended.'

'Can't say the same, I'm afraid. It couldn't have worked out better for me.' Ada reached over the couch and patted his arm affectionately. 'Sorry.'

'So is he worthy of you?' he asked.

'Who?'

'Your betrothed.'

'Andrew Hoyne. He's a good sort. You'd like him.'

'I doubt that. My fragile ego will compel me to despise him.'

'Don't be like that. He's fun. And he's a smarty-pants, like you. Studying neurology.'

'Bet the family approves.'

'They've come around,' she said. 'Believe it or not, they would have preferred I lined myself up with a feckless member of the aristocracy. Even medicine is too much like a trade for Mummy's liking.'

'See – they'd be much happier if you hooked up with me. Remember, my mother has a most noble lineage.'

'That may be true, Benedict Hitchens. But your reputation has been somewhat tarnished of late. Not sure that your family tree would be enough to compensate.'

'Touché, my dear,' he laughed. 'May as well give up, then. So what does your fiancé think about me being here?'

'He's in the States at the moment. Doing his residency at Johns Hopkins,' she replied. 'I haven't told him you're staying. Not sure he'd understand. And what he doesn't know won't hurt him.'

'So – sneaking around on him already, eh?'

She slapped his thigh playfully. 'Don't get your hopes up!'

'Me? Give up on hope?' He laughed. 'Not likely. At the moment, that's all I have going for me.'

'Whatever happened, Ben?'

He pulled his hand away from hers, drawing his arms defensively across his chest. 'God. It's quite a story.'

'It's fine if you don't want to talk about it. It's just that . . .'

'No, it's OK,' he replied. 'Really. You, of all people, deserve an explanation. You were the one left hanging in the breeze when I took off to İzmir.'

'I know the basics of it.' Ada stood and walked towards a glass-fronted Regency bookcase. She bent and took a leather-bound folio from the bottom shelf and passed it over his shoulder, placing it in his lap. 'Here you go. I kept your press clippings.'

Catalogued with an archivist's eye to detail were neatly pasted pages filled with chronologically arranged newspaper clippings documenting Ben's very public fall from grace.

'Couldn't help myself.' She sounded sheepish. 'I'm sorry; I know it makes me look rather desperate. But I was transfixed. It was like watching a slow-moving train wreck.'

He flicked back through the folio to the very first page: the feature article from the *Illustrated London News*. A photo of a stern-faced Benedict Hitchens standing on the İzmir waterfront with arms crossed was printed beside a banner headline: *Disgraced Archaeologist Caught in Web of Intrigue*.

'Much of what's in here is rubbish,' he explained. 'That bastard journalist took a set against me for some reason. Batey . . . I curse the day I heard that name! But the bones of my story in there are accurate. Not that you'd think it judging by the snide tone of the article.'

'But Ben – why couldn't you get any photographs? Everything that came later – well, it was just because no one could take you at your word. It was too far-fetched to believe. It would have been quite different if you'd had photos to prove your story.'

'There was a good reason for it. And it was also the one thing that didn't make it into my account,' he said. 'Eris told me she planned to take the antiquities out of the country. She was in a hurry and couldn't wait for me to get my camera. Little did I know, eh?'

'Half the country thought you made up the part about the woman and that you'd smuggled the treasure out of Turkey yourself. The other half thought the entire story was utter tripe. Even the most charitable of your peers were convinced you were just trying to peddle your theory about the Trojan War.'

'Just wait – the evidence exists. I certainly don't plan to manufacture it myself.' He laughed. 'And if you could see the way I've been living in Istanbul, any suspicion that I'd raked in a pile of ill-earned cash through antiquities smuggling would be very quickly disavowed. Ah, for Christ's sake.' He sighed heavily. 'Truth is – the only reason I've pursued this is that I want to find out what happened to Eris. They can say whatever the hell they want about me.'

'You do know I believe you, don't you, darling? I'm on your side.'

'I know. I don't count you among the ranks of the enemy.'

He wrapped one arm around Ada's shoulder and attempted to give her an affectionate but platonic hug. But the surge of desire he felt as he pressed against her was anything but benign, and he quickly released her.

Blushing, Ada hurriedly changed the subject. 'So. On to less fraught topics. What brings you to town?'

'Fairly mundane matter, unfortunately.' On the flight into Heathrow he had resolved to play his cards very close to his chest. Given the events that had recently befallen him, he had no desire to expose Ada to harm, and the more she knew about what he was planning, the greater the risk to her. 'There's a marble tablet coming up for sale at Sotheby's. I negotiated the consignment on behalf of a collector in Istanbul. He's asked me to come here and oversee the sale.' Ben figured it wasn't a complete lie. It *was* being sold by a collector in Istanbul. It was a minor detail that he and the 'collector' were one and the same person.

'Ha!' Ada laughed. 'And you're planning to venture into that vipers' pit alone? To "oversee" the sale? I say again ... Ha!'

'That was my plan, yes. Why the scorn?'

'Going in there unaccompanied . . . they'll eat you alive, Dr Hitchens.'

'I fail to see what perils might await me, Miss Baxter. It's just a glorified department store for second-hand things, after all.'

'Oh, poor Ben. You have no idea.' She shook her head.

'And you do?'

'The only time my father ever paid me any attention as a child was when he let me join him on one of his many trips to auctions around the country,' she said. 'He's got a thing for old master prints, you see. Get between my father and a copy of Albrecht Dürer's *Melencolia I* and he'll run you through with his shooting stick. He only tolerated me because I did what was expected: I sat still and kept quiet. But I did watch and listen. Very, very closely. And I know exactly what goes on in those places. The one lesson I took away from it all? Don't trust anyone.'

'So how would you suggest I protect myself?'

'You're in luck. Sotheby's has auctions of one type or another most days. I don't have anything planned for tomorrow, so we'll go and sit in on whatever sale they have scheduled. I'll talk you through it. Introduce you to the ins and outs of the auction trade.'

'I'm imposing on you enough already, Ada.'

'I insist, Ben,' she said. 'I'd never forgive myself if those jackals took advantage of you.'

'Jackals? That's being a little harsh, isn't it?'

'I repeat . . . you have no idea.'

# 9

## London, England, 1955

'One hundred and fifty pounds. I have one hundred and fifty pounds.'

With his gavel poised above the flat top of the polished mahogany rostrum, the auctioneer flicked his gaze around the room, scrutinising the audience with hawkish eyes.

'One hundred and *fifty* pounds. Do I hear one hundred and sixty? No? If I hear no further bidding, I will sell this exquisite seventeenth-century Dutch landscape painting for one hundred and fifty pounds . . . No further offers?' He paused. The gavel slammed down with a crack that made Ben jump in his seat.

'Sold! To the gentleman on the aisle!'

'Don't know what you're talking about, Ada,' he leant towards her and whispered in her ear. 'There's nothing to it – it's all fairly straightforward.'

'It is, is it? Interesting. So you think that man paid a fair price for that painting?'

'Well, he was happy to pay more than the other people bidding,' Ben replied. 'It's a competition, and he won. So . . . yes. I suppose he did.'

'There's the problem, Ben. Which other bidders do you mean?'

'Well, the auctioneer was pointing to bids all around the room.'

'Really? It's known as "bidding off the chandelier". There were no other bidders. Just that one man. And the chandelier. Also the vase of flowers back there. And I think the floor lamp in the corner might have thrown its hand up once or twice as well.'

'No. That can't be right!' he exclaimed. 'He was looking directly at the other bidders – nodding and smiling at them. I thought I just couldn't see the other people putting their hands up.'

'Yes – because auctioneers are more convincing performers than most of the actors treading the boards in the West End,' she explained. 'It's all just a show. And the man up the front there would have kept pushing the price until it reached a point where the auctioneer knew the vendor of the painting was happy to sell it.'

'Well, does that matter then?' he asked. 'If the owner wasn't going to sell it for less anyway?'

'In theory, perhaps. But what if the seller is greedy? Or delusional?' she responded. 'If you put the buyer and seller in a room together they could have a chat and work out a price they were both happy with. But like this, the buyer is operating blind. He's just paying what the seller wants. More often than not, that's simply what the auction house has told the seller it's worth, whether that's accurate or not. And that poor man there thinks other people in the room have validated the price he paid because they were bidding at that level too.

Only problem with that assumption? The other buyers
don't exist.'

'Isn't that . . . I don't know . . . illegal?' Ben was shocked by
the flagrant deceit.

'No. *Caveat emptor*, remember? With your background in
Classics, Ben, you of all people should know about "buyer
beware".'

The white-gloved attendant at the front of the room was
now holding aloft a small, dark etching in a black frame
trimmed with gold edging. Bidding had resumed and was
moving at breakneck pace. Hands were shooting up with
such speed that it was difficult to follow the action. Spotters
standing in the corners of the room indicated bidders to the
auctioneer with outstretched arms. The elegantly suited
man standing behind the rostrum progressed the bidding in
increments, moving from one bid to another with the speed
of a Spitfire.

'Now you can't tell me there's any fake bidding going on
here,' Ben whispered in Ada's ear.

'No. There's plenty of real bidding going on. But even that
can't always be taken at face value.'

'Oh, for God's sake.'

'Seriously, Ben. I'm not just being paranoid. These are the
tricks of the trade. Imagine you had built up a large collection
of similar works by the same artist. Or multiples of the same
artwork if you're talking prints.'

'If only!' he whispered.

'Well, how would you go about increasing the value of your
collection? Easy – put one of your artworks in an auction and
get some friends together to bid the price up. Let's say it's
valued before the auction at ten pounds and you and your
allies make sure it reaches a price of one hundred pounds.
Even if you have to buy it back yourself, as the seller you're

going to get most of your money back anyway. Most importantly, now you have a collection of ten works worth a total of a thousand pounds rather than just one hundred pounds.'

'I don't know whether to condemn them or applaud their cunning,' he protested.

'It's nothing new. There's a Rembrandt etching called *The Hundred Guilder Print*, so named because in the 1600s Rembrandt manipulated the auction market to set a price of one hundred guilders for his print – of which he had many copies, of course. If it's good enough for Rembrandt – well, you see what I mean. It's *outrageous* what people get away with.'

Although Ada was whispering, as she spoke her voice was rising in pitch to a level that reflected her righteous indignation. An elderly gentleman seated in front of them turned and frowned, a disapproving finger resting against his lips. She smiled thinly and mouthed an insincere apology.

'Jesus.' Ben was shaking his head in disbelief. 'So there's always a chance you're paying a price that's been pushed up by people who have other motives? Doesn't the auction house know this is going on?'

'Of course they do. But the policy here is, "Don't ask, don't tell". As long as they get their cut of the sale, they couldn't care less, so they turn a blind eye. They get paid a percentage of the sale price, so the higher the hammer price, the higher their fee. The people who do these things are doing the auction house a favour. The auction world is as transparent as a vat of grease. And twice as slippery.' Ada paused, and laughed quietly. 'But there is *one* thing the auctioneers aren't at all keen on. My father used to be part of a bidding ring of people who were interested in the same prints. When something was coming up for sale and they knew they'd all end up bidding for it, they'd come to an agreement before the auction not to compete with each other. That way they could buy it as cheaply as possible. Then afterwards they convened at a local pub to work out who would keep the print – that involved compensating those who didn't get the prize, of course. But it ended up costing them much less than if they'd fought it out in the auction rooms. And that's the only reason the auctioneers try to put the kibosh on that practice – the lower the price, the smaller their fee.'

When Ilhan had assured him the auction staff would not identify their forgeries, Ben had been sceptical. But if Ada was to be believed and wilful blindness prevailed here, everything might very well go as planned.

'This is absolutely stunning. Ben? You *must* come and look at this.'

Ada was standing at the feet of a marble statue he knew all too well. To the crowds of appreciative spectators gathered before the figure mounted on top of the stone plinth, it represented the pinnacle of Archaic Greek craftsmanship and artistry, its apple cheeks and pensive expression as fine an example of ancient Greek art as could be found. The arch smile illuminating the immaculate marble face confirmed it – Raphael Donazetti was a consummate master.

To his great discomfort, Ada continued. 'What a coup to secure the Steigmeier collection. I doubt there is a more perfect *kouros* anywhere in the world. There are so few in existence as it is. But this – this is something else. It has a life and vigour unlike any I've seen before. You're the expert here – what do you think?'

'What do I think?' *You don't want to know*, he thought to himself. 'Ah . . . I've certainly never seen anything like it.

No doubt about that.' He turned away from the imposing statue, insides churning with a strange combination of guilt and grudging pride.

He turned his attention to the rest of the auction room. It had been deliberately and carefully designed to replicate the rarefied and consecrated surroundings of a national museum with its parquetry floors, brass fittings buffed to an opulent gleam, glass cabinets glittering, and typed labels describing the treasures on display. The only feature that distinguished this room from one at the British Museum or the Victoria and Albert was that the antiquities arranged here were for sale.

It was an exceptional display of pilfered treasures. If his stomach had been turned by his own complicity in deception, he felt slightly less culpable as he took stock of the authentic antiquities on display. A slab of limestone engraved with the singular elongated head and almond-shaped eyes of the heretic Egyptian Pharaoh, Akhenaten, seated at the side of his wife, the famed beauty Nefertiti, bore the brutal scars of the chisels and crowbars with which it had been levered from a wall at Amarna. In one corner of the room, a floodlight illuminated a four-foot-high, five-headed, tenth-century stone bust of Shiva, savagely decapitated from a body that presumably still resided in Asia, the head now impaled upon a heavy metal rod embedded in a stone plinth. At the centre of the room stood a flawless fifth century BC Etruscan *hydria* vase, its fat belly embellished with the silhouettes of high-kicking centaurs pursuing winged stallions, no doubt torn unceremoniously from a looted grave in Tuscany.

It was a rogues' gallery of stolen treasures, stripped from their place of origin and disconnected from meaning and relevance. They were, to all intents and purposes, stolen goods, yet here they were presented with a veneer of legitimacy under the auspices of an august and venerable two-hundred-year-old commercial institution. To Ben's way of thinking, the damage to the world's cultural heritage caused by the odd bit of fakery was far less grievous than the wholesale vandalism and pillage represented in the room, though he wasn't so self-delusional as to expect that many people would agree with him on the matter, not least the people unfortunate enough to invest in Raphael's masterpieces.

Clenching his fists into tight bundles of knuckles and nails, he fought to quell his slow-burning anger. *Glasshouses and stones*, he reprimanded himself. *Stay focused*.

Turning towards the back of the room, he worked his way along the cabinets lining the walls. He knew exactly what he was looking for, and it didn't take him long to find it. Tucked away in one of the more modest corners of the room sat a flat, glass-topped cabinet lined with black velvet. A variety of artefacts were arranged in neat rows inside, white labels typed with black lettering pinned alongside them. Near the centre of the array was his tablet fragment, its newly scarred corner gleaming white under the overhead lights.

Ben looked towards the front of the room where Ada stood admiring another one of Raphael's creations: the flawless Cycladic figurine. There was no doubt at all that their three statues were going to attract the lion's share of interest at the auction. But Ben could only hope that the fanfare around the much-celebrated 'Steigmeier' statues wouldn't divert so much focus from the other lots in the sale that the one collector whose attention he hoped to capture would bypass the trap Ben had laid for him.

Only time would tell.

# 10

'My men have been in to see it. I think we may have a problem.'

'What?'

'The tablet is incomplete. It must have been damaged after they took the photo for the catalogue.'

'What do you mean?'

'Exactly what I said. A piece is missing.'

'A significant piece?'

'My men are employed for their physical gifts. Not their intellectual capacity. They'd have no way of knowing – they can hardly read English, much less Ancient Greek. But they said it looks like at least a quarter of it is gone.'

'Christ! Without the full text, we'll be unable to decipher it!'

'The photograph in the catalogue – that's not enough for you?'

'It's too indistinct. I can't see the letters.'

'I see. Do you think he has it?'

'He must. There's no other explanation.'

'Fine. I'll see what I can do.'

# II

## London, England, 1955

A flock of pigeons fluttered and cooed from the eaves above Ben's head as he leant against the brick wall of the building immediately opposite Sotheby's. The street was bumper to bumper with vehicles belching fumes into the air. Tight-lipped pedestrians moving along the pavement with clipped steps cast wary glances at the edgy man on the footpath, cigarette cupped in his weathered hand.

The night before had turned out to be a very pleasant diversion. At Ada's urging, they had dined at Ley-On's restaurant in Soho. She was thrilled by the exoticism of Chinese cuisine. Ben was less enthusiastic about the platters of pork slathered with lolly-pink sweet and sour sauce, and chicken scrambled together with slivers of crunchy but flavourless vegetables the waiter assured him were bamboo shoots. The dish called chop suey was more to his liking. He and Ada fell back into a comfortable and familiar patter as they spoke of things past. It was as close as he had come to feeling normal in more years than he could remember.

It was short-lived. Morning had dawned, and with it a renewed sense of desperation and urgency. His mind was a stopwatch, relentlessly ticking over and counting down the minutes until the auction was due to commence. He attempted to call on instincts honed in the crucible of war and ready himself for what he assumed would be a confrontation. But his senses were dulled by years of self-abuse and all it achieved was to highlight a growing list of his deficiencies.

From the opposite side of the narrow street he watched a stream of elegantly coiffed ladies and dapperly dressed gentlemen alight from cabs and privately chauffeured cars at Sotheby's porticoed entrance. They were oblivious to the gleaming black basalt statue holding court above their heads. Ben had recognised it the instant he'd arrived at Sotheby's imposing headquarters. He guessed it to be eighteenth-dynasty Egyptian – made in the fourteenth century before Christ. Protectress of the Pharaohs and Goddess of War, Sekhmet was known to the Ancient Egyptians as 'Our Lady of Slaughter'. Ben had always had a soft spot for her, in part, at least, because she was the patron goddess of an annual festival that had required her subjects to drink themselves into oblivion. He had no idea how she ended up atop Sotheby's portico. But as he stood at the entrance, bracing himself for what was to come, it seemed strangely appropriate.

He studied each arrival closely, wondering whether he would be able to identify his target at first sight. Would there be something that would mark him as Ben's man? A twitch? A nervous glance over the shoulder as he mounted the steps? Perhaps he would pause just a minute too long at the entrance, tentative. Nervous. Ben knew it was a pointless exercise, but justified it to himself as a way of charting the lay of the land.

Before he went into battle, he liked to know what, exactly, he was getting himself into.

The crowd gathered outside began to thin. It was time. He drew a deep breath and crossed New Bond Street. Sidling past a handful of latecomers lingering on the footpath, he entered the marble-tiled reception area and found his way into the high-ceilinged auction room.

After Ada's eye-opening introduction to the murky auction world, he now saw things in a very different light. Well-dressed men and women fidgeted in their seats as the room buzzed with the monotone murmuring of secretive conversations and the sudden sound of anxious laughter and agitated coughs. The tense atmosphere reminded him of the nervous anticipation among punters taking stock of the horses and jockeys around the mounting yard at Royal Ascot.

At the sound of a door opening, the room fell silent and all eyes spun to the stage. The auctioneer solemnly took his place behind the rostrum, gavel held elegantly between long fingers. The theatrical air of the auction that followed was fascinating enough from an anthropological perspective that Ben was surprised to find himself distracted from his own concerns. The auctioneer himself was an intriguing chimera: a strange mix of orchestra conductor, circus ringmaster and – as Ada had so rightly pointed out the day before – stage actor. The nature of the auction itself was laborious. It would have been easy for buyers to lose interest and concentration in between the lots they wanted to bid on. But the auctioneer kept the adrenalin pumping through their veins and worked his magic to maintain the buzz of tension and euphoria in the room. Well-timed and carefully targeted quips kept the audience amused and engaged when it seemed they might flag, and he modulated his voice like a sports commentator, emphasising the drama as a string of bids lifted the price of each lot higher. Now that he knew something about the tricks of the trade, Ben kept a close eye on what was going on, hoping to catch the auctioneer with a phony bid. But it was impossible. The man at the front of the room was a master of deceit.

The buyers were also intriguing. Each bidder had his or her own set of peculiarities; if they had been playing poker, they would have been called 'tells'. Some buyers disguised their bids from the audience so effectively that it was all but impossible to identify them until the auctioneer pointed them out when the gavel dropped and the bidder held a paddle up to indicate the buyer's number. Other people placed their bids with a gauche ostentation, heads thrown back and paddles raised confidently in the air like a peacock's tail. Some buyers were businesslike, nodding or quietly raising a finger to advance the bidding until they reached the point at which the bid exceeded their price. Then, a sharp and dismissive shake of the head would indicate they were out of the running.

The man who was the winning bidder for the tablet fragment was of the latter variety. Ben had been so entertained by the progression of the auction he hadn't kept track of the advancement of lot numbers until he realised, with a start, that the young man wearing a starched navy apron and white gloves standing on the stage was raising aloft his marble stele. The bidding progressed rapidly with three bidders quickly driving the price up. One dropped out, leaving just two men to face off against each other.

Ben studied them both closely. One of the bidders was in a row towards the front of the room, sitting primly in his chair, white hair surrounding his bald pate like a silvery halo. The other was seated to Ben's right in the row of seats in front of him. The slightly built man had a high, domed brow with receding dark hair slicked back, an imperious nose and a neatly trimmed black moustache. He cast his bids with restrained determination. Nothing in his body language suggested he was going to let the tablet get away from him. When the sharp crack of the gavel announced his victory, the man stood and moved towards the exit. A heavy-set and imposing man who had been seated beside him followed him out.

Rising from his seat, Ben edged past the other people sitting in his row. He crushed toes and whacked knees in his urgency to keep the man who had bought the tablet in his sight. The buyer and his companion moved into the reception area. Ben tailed them, turning his attention to a display cabinet to disguise his intentions. He watched in the mirrored back of the cabinet as the neatly dressed buyer moved towards the counter to finalise his purchase.

Clenching his fists into tight balls, Ben barely managed to restrain himself from charging across the room to pummel the man. *It mightn't be him*, he told himself, over and over. *It mightn't be him.* A mantra to help him keep control of the surging fury that threatened to boil over. *It mightn't be him.*

The buyer finalised his transaction with the receptionist, then muttered something to his companion and spun on his heel, heading for the concealed door to the gentlemen's rest room.

Without thinking, Ben followed him into the bathroom. He had no plan. But he knew he couldn't let him get away. He plastered the most ingratiating smile he could muster as he passed the buyer's companion, and pushed through the heavy oak door.

The smaller man stood with his back to the door, noisily relieving himself into the pristine white urinal. Ben walked towards him as he finished and did up his fly. As the buyer turned towards the sink to wash his hands, Ben grabbed him by the shoulders and slammed him against the wall, crushing his collar and tie in his fist.

'Where the fuck is it?'

The blood drained from the man's face. 'What?! . . . *What?!* . . . I don't . . . Who *are* you?'

'The other half of the tablet you just bought! Where is it?' Ben growled.

'I've no idea what you're talking about!' Shock gave way to indignation, and florid blotches rose to the man's cheeks. 'Who the *hell* do you think you are? How *dare* you!'

'Whoever took the other half is a murderer and a thief! They're also the only other person who'd want this that badly!' Ben hissed. 'Was it you? You'd better pray it wasn't.'

'Murderer? Well, I know nothing about that,' the man responded. 'I didn't buy that goddamned tablet for myself. I'm an agent. I bought it for one of my clients!'

'Who? Tell me who it is!'

'I shan't be telling you anything! I don't give a damn what my clients do. Can't be held responsible for their activities. Are you with the police?'

'No, I'm not,' he said. 'And that should concern you. Because there's nothing I won't do to get the information I need.'

'You're a fool!' the man scoffed. 'You saw my friend outside? He's there for a reason. In my business, threatening louts are par for the course. I'm not afraid of you!'

'You're not?' Leaning forward, blood thumped in Ben's ears. He whispered menacingly and tightened his hold on the man's throat. 'Really? Well, you should be.'

The door opened behind them. Before he had the chance to break away, Ben was airborne, hurled into the toilet cubicle by the scruff of his neck. As a pair of balled-up fists began to pound his skull, a constellation of stars burst before his eyes.

Bent double, he fought to protect his ribs from the assault of steel-capped boots smashing into his side.

'That's enough, Curtis.' Through eyes squinted shut with pain, Ben saw the man brushing himself off and rearranging his tie.

Ben curled into a foetal position on the floor of the cubicle. The buyer stood above him. 'Consider that a warning! Curtis? Good fellow. You've earned your keep today.' He addressed the man as he would an obedient dog. 'Let's go!' He strode towards the exit.

The door swung shut. Ben groaned and used the toilet bowl to pull himself upright. Wincing, he looked at his battered reflection in the mirror above the sink. Feeling for broken teeth, he probed the inside of his mouth and prodded the split corner of his lips with his tongue.

'Shit,' he exclaimed to the now empty room. He bent and splashed his face with cold water and ran his fingers through his unruly hair.

*Well*, he thought wryly to himself. *That went well.*

Straightening his shirt and tucking it back into his pants, he rearranged himself into a vaguely presentable state. He couldn't let the buyer get away. If he was meeting up with his client in London, Ben had to be there. To do that, he needed to find out who the man was. But he wasn't expecting to find him still on the premises. It was going to require some creative thinking.

'Excuse me?'

The woman seated at the Sotheby's reception desk was crowned with a backcombed beehive hairstyle as impenetrable as a stork's nest. She glanced sternly at Ben over the top of cat's-eye tortoiseshell spectacles. 'Yes?'

'Ah – I was just in the bathroom and the gentleman in there with me dropped a notebook.' He took his own notepad and waved it before the receptionist's unwavering gaze. 'There's no name in there, I'm afraid. But we were chatting and he mentioned he was a buyer's agent. Shortish. Dark hair. Moustache . . .'

'That would be Mr Spencer Scott. He's one of our regulars, sir.' The woman pursed her lips and held out her hand, palm up. 'He'll be back in a little while to collect his purchases from today's auction; if you would like to leave it with me, I will make sure it's returned to him.'

'Actually, I would feel better if I returned it in person,' he said. 'Can you tell me how I can reach him?'

'Suit yourself. You should find him at his bookstore.'

'And that would be where exactly?'

The receptionist looked him coolly up and down. 'The Fulham Road.'

He tucked the notebook back in his pocket. 'Thank you. Much obliged.'

As he turned away from the desk, he had an inspired thought. 'Ah, excuse me?'

The receptionist looked up from her work. 'Yes?'

'I was wondering, would it be possible to speak with Miss Charlotte Fairweather?'

'Do you have an appointment?' She raised an eyebrow archly.

'No. No, I don't. If you would kindly tell her Dr Benedict Hitchens would like a moment of her time, I'm fairly sure she'll see me.'

'Is that a fact?' The woman raised the handset of the gleaming telephone resting on the desk.

He wished he felt as confident as he sounded.

Ben sat in a high-backed and disagreeably ossified leather chair in the reception area, nervously tapping his toes inside his boots. The news that his tablet had yet to leave the building had buoyed his hopes. It meant that if Scott was meeting his client in London, he had not done so yet. If the exchange had not taken place, it gave Ben a chance to get Scott's client's details from Sotheby's. But he couldn't do it without Charlotte.

He had one shot at getting this right. In days gone by, he had no doubt he would have been able to find a way. But to say his espionage skills were rusty was a monumental understatement.

At least he looked the part. His morning ablutions had been unusually thorough; he had gone to great effort to make himself look presentable, shaving and anointing his skin with an expensive aftershave, ironing his one passable shirt, and buffing his well-worn boots to an impressive shine. But he still felt out of place. Everything about the building oozed luxury, money, taste and style, from the snap of bespoke shoes on polished marble floor tiles, to the gleaming lustre of the polished doorhandles and the lavish botanical display on a plinth in the centre of the expansive foyer. Given his privileged upbringing, he should have felt right at home. But the truth was that places like this always made him feel inadequate.

He identified the spiky click of her heels before he laid eyes on her.

'Dr Hitchens?'

He rose to his feet and extended his hand. 'Good day, Charlotte. And, please. Call me Ben. I'm sure we are familiar enough to venture into first-name territory.' The vague shadow of distaste and suspicion that crossed her brow and the noncommittal way Charlotte offered her hand confirmed what Ben suspected; he had made quite an impression when they met in Istanbul, but not a good one.

'Thank you for making time for me,' he said.

'Well, out of respect for your friend, Ilhan, who negotiated what's sure to be the highlight of the sale for us . . . it would have been churlish for me to refuse.'

Ben smiled, attempted small talk. 'It really is a remarkable collection you have on show. Where do these things come from?'

'Collectors, mostly. Europeans developed a taste for antiquities during the Renaissance. And after Napoleon's fleet arrived back in Paris from Egypt at the turn of the nineteenth century groaning with Pharaonic treasures, it became a race to see who could accumulate the most impressive collection.' Charlotte spoke with an authoritative tone, clearly enjoying the opportunity to flaunt her expertise. 'Greece . . . Italy . . . North Africa . . . India . . . the Near East. As you'd know better than most, those regions are absolute treasure troves for connoisseurs. Now that the prices for these things are beginning to head for the heavens, we get all manner of gems turning up.'

She lowered her voice and spoke conspiratorially. 'Though we do have some – how can I put this? – *unconventional* things arrive on the doorstep as well. Just last week I had a call from Victoria at reception to tell me she had a man waiting to show me something quite unique. She could barely control her laughter as she was speaking to me . . . "He believes he has the Holy Grail!" she told me. Priceless! It was nothing more exciting than a mass-produced pewter tankard. But he was quite convinced. I sent him on to Christie's – told him it was too big a sale for us to handle!'

Ben laughed politely.

'Now.' Charlotte checked herself, lowering the professional veil again. 'My time is rather limited. How can I help you?'

'The tablet I brought you in Istanbul . . .'

'Oh, for goodness' sake! You're not going to make a fuss about that, are you? You should be happy we agreed to sell it at all, given its compromised state.'

'Yes, I'm sure the owner will be thrilled. But it's something else.' Ben did his best to sound relaxed. If he seemed too eager, too desperate, she would question his intentions. 'It's possible that it's more important than I realised. And I foolishly forgot to transcribe the inscription before I gave it to you. So I have two questions. Am I able to take a rubbing of it now, before it's collected by the new owner? And would it be possible for me to have the owner's details so I can contact them in the future if I manage to decipher the text?'

'Certainly not!' Charlotte snapped. 'Out of the question! It's company policy. We never hand out the details of our buyers or our sellers.'

*Dammit*, Ben cursed to himself. He had another thought.

'OK. Right. Well, could you perhaps write them a letter asking them for permission to put me in touch with them? They may be willing to cooperate.'

She paused. Ben willed her to concede.

'Yes. I suppose I could do that.'

'And may I take that rubbing?'

'Yes, yes. Though you'll have to be quick. I don't know when it's going to be collected.' She smiled tightly and ushered him towards a recessed door tucked behind reception. 'Through here.' Her voice was clipped, her demeanour resentful.

Ben was apprehensive; she didn't trust him, and that meant he would have to keep his wits about him if he was to get the information he needed.

Charlotte led the way into the hidden bowels of the building. If the façade Sotheby's presented to the world conveyed the impression of wealth, respectability and grandeur, backstage was another matter. As he strode after Charlotte's rapidly retreating form, Ben glanced into room after room where earnest Sotheby's worker bees were bent double over dusty ledgers and surrounded by paintings, sculptures, packing crates, bookcases, and teetering piles of antique furniture.

Charlotte stopped outside a door. 'Right. This is us.'

Inside a large room filled with stacks of open metal shelving, she checked the lists taped to the end of each row until she found the one she was looking for. Striding halfway down the dimly lit aisle, she reached up to a shelf set at shoulder height and retrieved something. Ben recognised it immediately. His tablet.

She returned and placed the marble upon a thick piece of green baize that sat in the middle of a ponderous oak table at the apex of the room. His heart raced. He needed the next part of his hastily concocted plan to work.

Smiling grimly, Charlotte indicated the tablet. 'Look. The only reason I'm doing this is out of a sense of obligation to your friend. I'm putting my job in jeopardy – there are many here who would seize on any excuse to demote me to reception or the typing pool. That's where we women belong, of course,' she said bitterly. 'And if the buyer were to find out what I'm doing, I'd have hell to pay. Once that hammer fell, it belonged to the new owner. This shouldn't be happening – not without their express permission. The quicker we can get this over and done with, the better.'

'Right. Yes, of course,' he responded. 'I'll get right to it.' He paused. 'And that letter?'

'I'll write it while you're doing that.'

Opening his satchel, he drew out some folded sheets of paper and a draughtsman's pencil.

Charlotte reached for an enormous, leather-bound ledger resting beside a typewriter on a small desk. Flicking through the pages, he could see her scanning through the auction records.

'Right. There we go.' She studied the page and laughed. 'Well, I needn't have worried about the buyer being here today.'

'Why's that?'

'Can't be specific, but they're not locals.' Leaving the ledger open on the desk beside her, Charlotte fed a sheet of paper into the typewriter. The keys clattered and clacked as she set to her task.

Ben bent over the tablet and began to run his pencil across the paper, making a carbon copy of the ancient letters engraved into the stone. He guessed at how far into the letter Charlotte had progressed.

Holding his breath, Ben pressed down hard on the pencil. The lead broke with a loud snap.

'Dammit!' he exclaimed.

Charlotte looked up. 'What now?'

He held his pencil aloft. 'No lead in my pencil . . . so to speak. Snapped in two. Don't happen to have any spares, do you?'

'Oh, for Christ's . . .! Yes. I'm sure we do.' She picked up the handset of the phone sitting on the desk beside her.

Ben's blood ran cold as he heard the ringtone. This wasn't going according to plan.

'Victoria?' she snapped. 'We need some spare drafting pencil leads up here . . . What? Yes . . . yes, I know it's busy down there . . . I don't care, to be honest. There must be a store-man who can run some up . . . Fine. Whoever. Thank you!'

The handset slammed back into its cradle. 'Stupid cow!' Charlotte cursed beneath her breath. She gathered herself. 'They'll be up in a moment.'

'Terribly sorry for the bother, Charlotte. I'm such an idiot.'

'Not a problem,' she said through gritted teeth.

A knock at the door, spare leads delivered, and with them the dashing of Ben's hastily concocted plan to copy down the address when Charlotte left the room.

He replaced the lead and finished the rubbing, his mind running through his fast-diminishing options.

Charlotte pulled the paper out of the typewriter and signed it with a flourish. Neatly folded, she slipped it into an envelope. 'All done?' She stood and walked to Ben's side.

'Ah, yeah. Finished.' He slipped the rubbing into his journal. Slowly. Awkwardly. Buying time. As she strode towards the door he edged back towards the open ledger still sitting on her desk.

The phone rang. Ben flinched.

Charlotte pushed past him and grabbed the handset. 'Yes?' Her face blanched. 'Tell him I'll be right down.' She slammed it back into the cradle. 'Jesus. That was close. He's here.'

'The buyer?'

'Yes. I mean, no. Not exactly. It's his agent.'

'Spencer Scott?'

She looked up at Ben, startled. 'You know him? How do you know him?'

'Does it matter?'

'I suppose not. I'm just surprised. I wouldn't have thought the two of you moved in the same circles. Anyway – no more time for dawdling. Let's go.' She fixed him in an unwavering stare. Any vague hope he harboured that he might be able to sneak a glance at the book disappeared.

Burning frustration made his ears ring.

She walked in brisk, economical strides along the corridor. Holding the door open, Charlotte ushered him through. 'You'll be right from here, then?'

Mindful that the man he'd recently pinned to the wall of the restroom was standing in the reception hall, Ben edged out of the door as furtively as he could, keeping his back to the room. But he needn't have worried. Sotheby's determination to shield the messy inner workings of its commercial machine from public view worked in his favour. A column of elaborately arranged flowers stood on a plinth immediately in front of the entrance to the back-of-house and hid the door from general view. If Spencer was standing in reception, Ben couldn't see him and he could only assume the dealer couldn't see Ben.

'Thank you for your cooperation, Charlotte. I really am most obliged.'

'You're welcome.' Her narrowed eyes and set smile said otherwise.

As Ben saw it, he had only one choice. As Charlotte made her way into the room, he saw just what he needed – an upholstered Victorian occasional chair left against the wall for waiting customers. With the measured yet frantic activity in the room, nobody thought to notice the tall man in the rumpled suit bend to pick the chair up before slipping back through the door that led to Sotheby's storerooms.

He knew if he happened to encounter anyone in the corridor they'd be unlikely to think he was out of place and challenge him if he looked like he belonged. And a man carrying a piece of furniture would not look out of place. He could only hope the flimsy subterfuge would work. If it didn't, he was out of ideas.

Holding the chair at shoulder height, its solid back shielding his face from anyone he might bump into, he strode along the corridor. All good . . . so far. The door to the room he'd been in with Charlotte lay ahead.

'You!' a voice rang out from behind him.

*Christ!* 'Ah . . . yes?'

'That for the furniture sale?' A stubby man wearing an apron and spectacles perched on the end of his nose stood behind him.

'Furniture sale?' *Go with it.* 'Yes. That's right.'

'In here. We're cataloguing.' Tight-lipped, the man indicated a door beside him. Shaking his head, he addressed someone in the room. 'I swear to God, Matthew. These temporary workers brought in during sale time? They'll be the death of me.'

Ben placed the chair on the floor. The man snatched it up and carried it into the room without another word.

He spun around and strode back down the hall. The storeroom door was open, the ledger still sitting on the desk. Heart pounding, he grabbed his notebook and pencil out of his satchel and smiled grimly as he copied down the buyer's details. Lesvos. He'd always known this would lead him back there. Three trips to the island after Eris disappeared had yielded nothing. But as he'd found his way from one village to another, he'd grown suspicious of the repeated denials and reached the conclusion there was a conspiracy of silence contriving to stop him finding out what had happened to her. This seemed to confirm it.

He looked down at the name and address he had transcribed into his notebook. *Mr I. Adler.* The only real surprise was that it wasn't a Hellenic name.

Ben had always assumed Eris' brother was in trouble with other Greeks, but perhaps there was more to it.

Footsteps clicked down the corridor. He had no doubt who it was. Stuffing the notebook back into his satchel, he deliberately dropped the pencil onto the floor.

Charlotte walked through the door to find Ben on his knees. '*You* again? What the hell are you doing?'

He stood, holding his pencil aloft. 'Bloody thing – left it in here!'

'Is that so?' she said, sceptically. He knew she didn't believe him and he didn't care. 'Might be time to invest in another,' she snapped.

'Another what?'

'Pencil.'

'Ah. I see. But this one has sentimental value, you see.'

'Well, I can't keep Spencer waiting any longer. I'll be very happy to see the back of that damned tablet. It's been far more trouble than it's worth. You should be relieved some idiot was silly enough to buy it.'

'Yes. I'm sure the seller will be delighted.' They fell into awkward silence. He held out his hand. She took it reluctantly. 'Thank you, Charlotte.'

'Not at all.' The insincerity in her voice was palpable.

'Well,' he said. 'You never know. I may have reason to run into you again sometime.'

The look of distaste on her face suggested that Charlotte Fairweather would be quite happy if she never laid eyes upon Benedict Hitchens again.

Ben was past caring. And he had somewhere else to be.

# 12

'We got it.'
          'Was there ever any doubt?'
'No. Not really.'
'The price?'
'No more than we expected.'
'And the other piece? I won't be able to do anything without it.'
'Leave that up to me.'

## 13

## London, England, 1955

From a table in the window of a pub diagonally across the road from Spencer Scott's antique book emporium, Ben had a clear view of the interior of the shop. Scott's bodyguard was seated in a leather armchair flicking through the sports news. At the rear of the store, the dealer was engaged in an animated telephone conversation. Brow furrowed and gesticulating tersely, Scott was clearly not a happy man. The thought that he may have contributed to the dealer's discomfiture made Ben smile.

His heart raced each time a vehicle slowed in the proximity of Scott's store. But none of the passengers who alighted onto the pavement opened the door and entered the shop. If the mysterious buyer was planning to visit the dealer, he was yet to appear.

Traffic was light on Fulham Road at this time of day, and Ben was able to keep a close eye on Spencer Scott as he moved from one side of the store to the other. The dealer walked halfway through a doorway, and seemed to be speaking to another person in a rear room. As he turned and strode back into the main gallery, a slight and bookish young man followed on his heels, a stack of leather-bound volumes clutched to his pigeon chest. Scott gestured to the leather-topped partners' desk positioned in one corner of the store, and the young man carefully placed the pile of books in a single column on the edge of the desk. Judging by the interaction between the two men – Scott speaking with his forefinger raised in the air as the younger man listened attentively – Ben could only assume that the third man was the dealer's assistant.

The one-sided conversation continued for five minutes. When Curtis stood, neatly folded his sports paper and tucked it into his jacket pocket, Ben took it as a signal that Scott was about to make a move.

There was little risk of being spotted from this distance, but Ben's bruised ribs were a painful reminder of what would happen if either man caught sight of him. He wasn't going to take any chances. Sidling towards the darkest corner near the bar at the back of the room, he moved away from the windows facing the street.

In the gallery, Scott retrieved his trilby from the hatstand and lifted a small, brown suitcase from the floor beneath the desk. Turning back towards his assistant, Scott issued a final order before waiting as Curtis reached out and opened the door for his master with fingers as fat as Bratwurst sausages.

The two men stepped out onto the pavement and crossed the road, heading straight for the pub. As they weaved between the cars and black taxicabs moving sedately along Fulham Road, Ben pressed his back against the wall. His heart was pounding as he frantically looked round the pub for a refuge. The men's room. If they were coming in, that would have to do.

The men slowed to a halt outside and spoke. Ben nervously wiped beads of sweat from his forehead. Scott stepped onto the kerb and faced the stream of traffic. He turned and addressed Curtis, who nodded his head obediently and walked out onto the road, raising his right hand in the air.

'Taxi. Christ,' Ben murmured to himself under his breath. 'He's catching a taxi.'

Bolting for the front door, he ducked out of the building and screened himself from the two men behind the pub's colonnaded entrance. He was close enough to hear Curtis' laboured wheezing. Crouching down, he edged towards a sickly looking hedge in a planter box and peered through its sparse foliage to where Scott and Curtis were standing.

A glossy black taxi drew up beside the two men. The bodyguard leant in the window and barked at the driver, 'Heathrow. And make it snappy.' Scott cut an elegant figure as Curtis opened the door for him. The dealer handed his case to his companion and ducked into the back seat of the cab. After stowing his boss' bag, Curtis levered his large frame through the door and joined Scott in the back cabin. The cab eased into the slow-moving traffic and headed west.

Ben waited until the taxi had disappeared, then stood and exhaled slowly. *Heathrow*, he thought to himself. It looked like Scott's client wasn't in town after all. Ben was fairly sure he knew where he was headed.

Glancing over at Spencer Scott's store, Ben saw the assistant seated at his desk.

He smiled to himself. *But it might do to confirm it. And I bet I can make him tell me.*

A small brass bell suspended above the door tinkled cheerily as he entered Spencer Scott Antique Books. The walls were lined from floor to ceiling with ornate mahogany book-shelves packed with neat rows of leather-bound volumes. A stepladder on wheels suspended from a gleaming brass rail provided access to the volumes stacked in the uppermost shelves. The room smelled of beeswax, aged leather and old parchment – the distinctive aroma of antique stores. It was a perfume Ben found intoxicating, perhaps because it trans-ported him back to his nicer childhood memories.

'Good afternoon, sir.' The young man who had been working studiously at the desk rose to his feet with an ingratiating smile. 'How might I help you?' His top lip was embellished with an extravagant and carefully tended black moustache. It suggested a personal vanity that seemed out of place in such an arcane world. One look at him confirmed what Ben had already suspected – deceit would be a far more effective way of getting information out of this man than the threat of violence. The latter would just make him go to water and any information he might give him would be of dubious use.

'I am looking for a copy of Alexander Pope's translation of *The Iliad*,' Ben explained.

'Ah, Homer. One of the greats. Are you looking for yourself, or is it a gift?' the younger man asked.

'It's a gift.'

'I'm not absolutely certain that we have Pope's version.' He turned and walked towards the stepladder, sliding it towards one end of the enormous bookcase. 'Are you interested in Homer yourself?'

'Ah, yes – you could say that.' Ben smiled.

'A most extraordinary new translation has just been published by an American scholar – Richmond Lattimore.'

Carefully mounting the steps, the shop assistant continued. 'It's very contemporary. Very exciting. I read Classics at Cambridge, you see. If you like your Homer it is worth tracking down a copy.' He ran his fingers along the row of books, scanning the titles. Reaching for one, he slid it off the shelf and flipped to its title page. 'Well, look at that. You're in luck, sir.' He handed the book to Ben, who turned it over and ran his fingers down its spine, the reptilian texture of the aged leather cover oddly appealing.

'Great. Really. This is perfect,' he said. He hadn't expected to find a copy of Alexander Pope's celebrated translation, and had only suggested it as a means of opening a conversation with the shop assistant. But it would be the perfect gift to thank Ada for her hospitality. It was exactly the sort of thing she would appreciate.

'Wonderful,' the assistant crowed. 'Would you like me to wrap it for you, sir?'

'Yes. Please. It's made it through two centuries in one piece, so it would be a shame if it didn't make it home without damage.'

Lifting a roll of heavy brown paper from the desk, the shop assistant used a pair of scissors to shear off a large sheet. As he neatly folded the paper around the fragile book, Ben continued. 'So, I was wondering whether Mr Scott might be about today?'

'No. I'm afraid he's not,' the man said. 'Are you a friend of his?'

'Ah – I know him from around the traps.'

'Well, in that case it's a shame you weren't here five minutes earlier. Mr Scott left only a moment or so before you arrived.'

'What a pity,' exclaimed Ben, conscious of keeping any hint of insincerity from his voice. 'When do you think he'll be back?'

'Unfortunately he's just headed off on a business trip. International. He won't be returning until next week.'

'Would that be the trip to Greece he was planning?' Ben asked, fairly sure of the answer. 'Lesvos, wasn't it?' he asked casually.

'Ah, yes. I believe that's where he is going.' The young man looked up at Ben, a veil of suspicion clouding his gaze. 'But I was under the impression it was a last-minute trip. This afternoon was the first I heard of it. How did you find out about it?'

'Well . . . when you put it like that, I can't rightly say. Perhaps Scott mentioned it to me at the auction . . . No. No; can't remember, I'm afraid.' Ben picked up the brown paper parcel from the desk, opened his wallet and handed over a wad of banknotes. 'There we go – that more than covers it. And don't worry about the change.'

Bobbing his head, the shop assistant smiled thinly. 'Thank you, sir. I trust that the gift recipient is suitably grateful.' No amount of money was going to allay his suspicions.

But Ben didn't care. The man had already given him what he needed.

Ben knew something was wrong as soon as he neared the corner of Paultons Square and Kings Road.

The corner-store proprietor was a man who was built like a bowling pin and whose principal occupation seemed to be the obsessive sweeping of the pavement outside his shop, an activity broken only when a customer arrived. He was also an impressively loquacious man. When Ben had stopped by that morning to buy a newspaper and a packet of cigarettes, the shopkeeper had subjected him to a disturbingly frank and protracted account of his elderly dog's intestinal failings.

The man was standing by the door to his shop, leaning heavily on his well-worn broom, flatulent canine at his side. Every time Ben had passed him to date, he had hailed him with a cheery greeting. But today, the storekeeper barely glanced up. His attention was focused on something in Paultons Square.

As Ben drew closer, the rotund man shook his head. 'Terrible times we're living in. Terrible times. I'll tell you that for free.'

Ben felt the ground falling away from his feet. A bank of police cars had drawn up haphazardly outside Ada's home. Two grave-faced police officers stood on the footpath taking notes and interviewing passers-by and neighbours.

'What's going on?' His heart was racing but he tried to appear indifferent.

The shopkeeper tut-tutted again. 'Never would have happened back in the day. Not to a lady. Crims – even they had lines they wouldn't cross. But these days? Pah! Bloody animals. A young woman lives down there – comes in here most days to buy her milk, bread, paper . . . whatnot. They reckon she must have disturbed a burglar.' He shook his head. 'Police wanted to know if I'd seen anything. No such luck, I told them. They would have rued the day . . . I would have given the bastards what for – pardon my French.' He paused, remembering. 'Say . . . didn't you . . .?'

But Ben was gone.

As the Georgian terrace grew in his vision, he tried to untangle his thoughts and get a grip on runaway panic. *Ada. This is my fault.*

'You'll need to move along, sir. Nothing to see here.'

A portly bobby blocked his path.

'My name's Benedict Hitchens, officer. What's happened? Miss Baxter is my friend. Is she all right?'

He looked Ben up and down. 'You'll need to speak to the family, sir. Not our business to pass out that sort of information.'

'I'm her house guest.'

The policeman stepped back, eyebrows raised. 'House guest, you say? Well, that changes things a bit. I imagine the DCI will be wanting to have a word with you. Right this way, sir.'

A heavy-set man in a pinstriped suit glanced up at Ben as he entered his basement bedroom. He extended his hand. 'You're Benedict Hitchens, then? Detective Chief Inspector Dunbar.'

'Ada . . .' Ben felt his knees give way. 'Is she all right?'

'Hard to say, sir. They gave her a fair whack to the head. She was taken off to the hospital a while back. So you're the lodger then? Looks like your room bore the brunt of it. How long have you been staying with her?'

'Just a day or two. We're old friends. And . . . ah . . . former colleagues.'

'You don't say. Well, if you'd just look over your things for me. See if anything's missing. For my report.'

'I didn't have much with me. Don't think I left anything of value here.'

Dunbar indicated the doorway to the street outside. The lock had been torn from the timber. 'Looks like they jemmied the door and didn't get much further than this room. We're presuming Miss Baxter disturbed them when she came downstairs – neighbours heard a scream and called us.'

'Ada didn't tell you what happened?'

'Unfortunately she was unconscious when we arrived.'

*Unconscious? Christ!* 'Where did they take her?'

'Take her?'

'Ada. Where is she?'

'Ah. St Mary's, I believe.'

'Any idea who did it?'

'No. 'Fraid not. Looks like a garden-variety break-in. You don't have any thoughts on the matter, do you?' The detective fixed him with a steady and unsettling gaze.

Ben flinched. 'No. None at all. Just bad luck, I guess.'

'Yes. Bad luck. Could call it that, I s'pose.' The detective paused and drew breath, locking Ben in a steely gaze. 'Just for the record, Mr Hitchens, where were you earlier today?'

'Me . . . I was at an auction. At Sotheby's.'

'Auction, you say?' Dunbar asked. 'Plenty of people see you there, then?'

'Yes. Yes. I'm sure they did . . . Miss Charlotte Fairweather. She's an employee there. She'll vouch for me.' As soon as he said it, Ben regretted it. He was already in Charlotte's bad books. Adding a police interview to his ledger wouldn't help his standing with her. But he had no choice.

Dunbar nodded then scribbled something in his notebook. 'Might just have a chat with her, then. Just to get our facts lined up.' He handed Ben a card. 'Anyway, here are my details. In case anything else comes to mind. You'll need to find somewhere else to stay tonight, but let me know where I can find you. And don't go leaving the city. Righto?'

Ben walked along St Mary's whispery halls past rooms that reeked of disinfectant and grief. In his hand he held a sorry bunch of white roses, all he could find at the small florist at Paddington Station.

At the end of the corridor, a stiff cluster of people stood outside the closed door of one of the wards, struggling to stifle their feelings. A tall, rod-backed man with a full head of snowy-white hair and a profile like a Roman emperor stood with his hands clenched firmly at his back beside a woman in a mauve twin-set whose short, salt-and-pepper hair was styled into loose waves and kiss curls about her face. Her eyes were rimmed with red.

'Mr and Mrs Baxter?'

The older man turned and fixed Ben with a suspicious glare.

'Yes. And you are . . .?'

'My name is Benedict Hitchens, sir. I'm a friend of your daughter's. We worked together at Eskitepe. In Turkey.'

Baxter drew a deep breath. 'Hitchens, you say? Yes, name's familiar. Well, as you've obviously heard, unfortunately there has been an accident . . .'

'Yes. The officer at her home told me. It is terrible news, sir. I've been staying with Ada.'

'So *you're* the mysterious house guest. We had been wondering. Ada hadn't mentioned anything to us. Then again, she never tells us much about her social life. Thought Andrew – Ada's *fiancé* – might have known, though. He had no idea she had someone staying with her. Have you met Andrew?'

'Ah, no, sir. I can't say I have.'

'Well, it did strike us as rather peculiar . . . A strange man staying in the basement . . .' Baxter was silenced by a swift retort from his wife. 'Rodney! Leave it alone! I'm sure Ada will explain herself once she recovers. This is neither the time nor the place.'

'Quite, dearest,' Rodney Baxter responded. 'But it does seem quite a coincidence, that this tragedy has befallen our daughter when she has a stranger staying with her . . . a *male* stranger.' He paused, brow screwed into knots as he sifted through buried memories. 'Hitchens . . . Hitchens . . . Benedict Hitchens . . . I know you! You're that thief – the archaeologist! Saw you in the papers. Well, well. Quite the publicity hound, aren't you? Didn't anyone ever tell you that decent folk only appear in print three times? Birth, marriage and death notices! Bloody Americans! What on *earth* was Ada thinking? No wonder she didn't tell us about you! Seems to me that trouble and you are close acquaintances!'

Ben flinched; tried to justify the unjustifiable. 'We're not strangers to each other, Mr Baxter. We're old friends. Ada offered me a place to stay. And now . . . well, I just wanted to check up to see how she was.' He handed the flowers to Mrs Baxter along with the brown parcel containing Pope's *Iliad*. She took them from him with limp fingers and held them as if they were a bunch of wet socks.

'Sir; madam. I'm sorry to have bothered you. If you could just pass on those flowers and the book to your daughter, I'd be most grateful. And please give her my best regards once she's up and about. Tell her I'll be in touch.'

'I shouldn't bother, if I were you.' The old man turned his back on Ben and stalked away, shoulders hunched.

It was an unreasonable attack by a father crippled by sorrow. It shouldn't have stung so badly. But it did.

Ben stepped into the street to hail a cab, white fury burning in his eyes.

'Where to, guv'nor?'

He slung his satchel onto the seat beside him. 'Heathrow.' His heart was thumping against his ribs, the furious acid burn of bile rising in his throat. He had no doubt who was responsible for this. It had to be the same animals who'd broken into his apartment in Istanbul. Staying in London wouldn't bring him any closer to finding them. And the longer he stayed, the greater the risk the trail would run stone cold and he would lose what chance he had of tracking them down. The police involvement in Ada's break-in further complicated matters. If they started casting a wider net, there was a risk he would be caught up in it.

He had to get out of the country. *If it isn't already too late*, he thought to himself. The police would be able to block his passport. And if he didn't contact Dunbar soon, he knew he would become a suspect, if he wasn't already.

The longer he delayed, the greater the chance he'd be trapped here.

The line of passengers shuffled towards a small desk at the back of the departures hall. Ben's anxiety mounted with every step.

A low-flying jet rattled the windows as it flew over the airport building with a deafening roar. The customs officer sat, stiff-backed, and flicked through each passport, scrutinising the pages through spectacles perched at the end of his nose. As he checked each passenger's travel papers, he consulted a list on a clipboard.

Airline stewardesses in tailored suits walked in a gaggle through the cavernous space, floral bouquets of perfume billowing in their wake and momentarily driving away the sickly smell of jet fuel and cigarette smoke filling the hall.

One step closer.

A couple stood in front of Ben, matching luggage by their sides, hips touching and fingers intertwined. Ben had them pegged for honeymooners.

They approached the customs officer and handed over their documents. The woman giggled and lifted her left hand to adjust her hair unnecessarily, tilting her wedding and engagement rings in the overhead light so they glittered and sparkled. Murmuring something to the official, the man cocked his head proudly and placed his hand possessively at the small of his new wife's back. The officer smiled, thin-lipped, and stamped their passports with a flourish. They moved through to the departure lounge.

It was Ben's turn. He handed over his travel documents.

'Mr Benedict Hitchens?' Frowning, the man looked at Ben over the top of his glasses.

'Yes. That's me.'

The customs officer was silent. He flipped through Ben's passport then looked down at the list by his side. Squinting, he lifted the passport closer to his eyes.

'So. Mr Hitchens.'

A pit opened up in Ben's stomach. 'Yes.'

'You've spent a bit of time in Turkey, then.'

'Ah . . . yes.'

'Saw some action there myself as a young chap. The Great War. Gallipoli. Damned shame I never got to see the sights of Constantinople. Always meant to go back. Might head over there with the missus when I retire.' He stamped Ben's passport. 'Bon voyage, then.'

Ben felt indescribable relief as he walked through the doors towards the departure gates.

Hoisting his satchel across his shoulder, he sighed deeply. Travelling light. As usual. It seemed apt. As he approached the small line of travellers waiting to board the plane parked outside on the tarmac, he was – as always, these days – utterly alone.

# 14

'They searched his accommodation in London. There was nothing there.'

'Damn. Well, assuming he broke the tablet intentionally to make things more difficult for us, he won't have discarded it. He'll have the rest of the inscription with him. Otherwise it's useless to him as well. So what do we do next?'

'I've spoken to Mr Scott. And Scott will lead him to us.'

'How do you know Ben's watching him?'

'I've got people keeping an eye on him. But I will have to make sure Scott waits so Hitchens has time to pick up his trail once he gets to the island. He's very put out, by the way. Claims this last minute trip to Lesvos is a terrible inconvenience. And Hitchens shirt-fronted him at Sotheby's. Got in a punch or two. With the retainer I have him on he still had the gall to ask for more "compensation"!'

'He's useful.'

'True. But what if Hitchens doesn't come – what if he decides to give up on it?'

'He won't. And it's probably a good thing that we involve him now. He'll find it much quicker than I ever could.'

'He finds it. We take it.'

'Seems cruel.'

'Such is life.'

# 15

## Lesvos, Greece, 1955

The clatter and clunk of the ferry's engine woke Ben at dawn. They had left Piraeus late the day before. After embarking amid the steamy chaos of Athens' major port, he'd met a group of itinerant workers on deck who were returning to their homes in Lesvos after three months in the Greek capital. They shared a bottle of ouzo as they watched a fiery sun dip beneath the horizon into the wine-dark waters of the Aegean.

After a restless sleep in an airless cabin, Ben found his way up onto the deck. As the sky in the east shone coral pink behind the ragged and improbably lofty peaks of the Turkish mainland, he felt something akin to relief. This part of the world felt like home to him. *Hell*, he thought to himself. *It's probably as close as I'll ever get to having a home.*

He leant on the top handrail and hung his head out over the water, watching it slip like molten gold beneath the ferry's rusty hull. The Aegean was satiny smooth and still as the ship chugged through the narrow stretch of water between Lesvos and the Turkish mainland. In the peachy dawn light, the island seemed to hover, suspended, above the surface of the sea. As they drew closer, he could see picturesque buildings painted azure blue, sunflower yellow and rose-madder pink crowding the harbour. Floating above the town's roofline was the empyrean dome of the Saint Therapon church.

Despite the idyllic scenery, he couldn't shake the feeling of uneasiness that had been stalking him since leaving London. Even now, the hairs on the back of his neck prickled. He shut his eyes and tried to relax as the sticky sea air settled on his skin. His plan had worked and he should have been pleased that his enormous gamble had paid off. In a matter of hours he should have the evidence he needed to prove his story and clear his name. But his preoccupation with Eris' fate meant he was unsure what would be left of himself once he found answers to the questions that had haunted him for so long.

The ferry pulled into port between banks of small, recently docked fishing vessels. Craggy-faced fishermen with stringy arms and bowed legs hefted wooden crates onto the boardwalk. The boxes spilled over with a slippery, shimmering bounty: tiny silver sardines; fat-armed octopi; silken squid; plump sea bass; and the exposed bellies of alien-like skate. Groups of women dressed in black waited on the shore – hungry crows, jockeying for position to make sure they secured the pick of the catch.

Ben disembarked, assailed by the pungent olfactory soup of rotting fish guts, stagnant seaweed and diesel fumes. It was a rude awakening. Edging his way past the vocal and combative customers in the fish market, he walked back down the pier towards the boulevard that ringed the harbour. He moved slowly, eyes panning from one side of the road to the other, looking for warning signs; the glint of binoculars as someone followed his route along the waterfront – far-fetched, he knew. Or – more likely – someone paying him closer attention than the inevitable scrutiny of locals when a foreigner arrived in their midst.

All along the waterside, two-storeyed buildings served as tiny cafés, with timber tables and wooden chairs placed neatly along the footpath. His stomach rumbled at the smell of grilled meat spitting juice onto open coals. Knowing the menu would not differ from one café to the next and figuring the best place to hide was in a crowd, he chose the one that had the greatest number of customers. Seating himself at a table dressed with a blue and white checked cloth, a small terracotta pot of tiny-leafed basil, and two stoppered glass jugs of emerald-green olive oil and vinegar the colour of rosé, he read the menu scrawled in Greek on a chalkboard hanging by the front door.

His fellow diners stared at him unapologetically. A waiter approached, his substantial gut ballooning beneath an apron tied tightly about his midriff. He looked down his beak-like nose with a cool disdain.

'Είσαι Αγγλος? English?'

'Όχι. Είμαι Αμερικανός. American.'

'Αμερικανός?' The waiter's resplendent, jet-black eyebrows shot up and he cocked his hands as if he were holding two Colt 45s. 'John Wayne, cowboys and Indians, bang bang!'

'Yes. America. John Wayne.' The language of Hollywood was universal. Ben reverted to Greek. 'I would like some breakfast, please.'

The waiter looked at him dubiously. 'I don't cook English breakfast. If you go to the big hotels where the foreigners stay, you can find some bacon and eggs there. I only serve Lesvos village breakfast. *Soutzouki*, fetta, yoghurt, tomato, olives, bread and honey.'

'Good. One Lesvos breakfast then, please.'

'Suit yourself.' Shrugging, the waiter slammed a jug of water onto the table then disappeared into the kitchen.

While he waited for his meal, Ben began to work through his plan of attack. He had the address in the village of Molyvos where he expected to find the person who had bought his tablet. He could only hope the same person had the other half. The thought that this might be just a wild-goose chase had occurred to him more than once as he'd crossed the Mediterranean. But it was the only lead he had; there was no choice but to follow it.

He had spent enough time on the island to know the distance between Mytilene and Molyvos was around forty miles. The interior of the island was extremely mountainous. Where the peaks plummeted into the sea along the coast, the roads clung to the edge of perilous cliffs. It was a circuitous and dangerous route, and he had no car. He had resigned himself to the fact that he would need to hire a private driver to get him there. Although small buses regularly travelled the roads between the major towns around Lesvos, what should have been a journey taking no more than three hours could last most of a day with all the detours to pick up and drop off passengers in tiny villages off the main roads. And he didn't have any time to waste.

The waiter reappeared with his breakfast. The smell of the garlic and cumin in the grilled *soutzouki* made his mouth water. The slices of sausage were still sizzling as he popped them into his mouth. They burned, but they tasted so good. The mound of food stacked high on the plate was daunting. But he knew he would need all the sustenance he could get. He tucked into it with gusto.

Stomach distended after his enormous breakfast, Ben sauntered along the Mytilene foreshore. As he walked, he gazed at the shadowy silhouettes of lumbering sea turtles moving languidly in the water, snapping at schools of tiny fish.

Ahead, a cut-in along the road served as a proxy station for a chaotic tangle of taxis, private charter cars and tiny buses. Crowds of people gathered on the pavement, jostling and shoving to get a seat on the next bus destined for their town. A cluster of people stood to one side of the road, transfixed by something going on in their midst.

An irate voice rang out above the heads of the gathered crowd. 'This is bloody ridiculous! You cannot tell me that nobody here speaks any English at all!'

*Spencer Scott*, Ben marvelled. *Well, what do you know?* Given the Englishman's head start, Ben had thought he'd be long gone.

Ducking behind a parked bus, Ben sidled towards its windows and found a concealed vantage point. The buyer's agent was standing with his shirtsleeves rolled up beside a black car, utterly ill at ease as its driver sat nonchalantly on the bonnet with a cigarette dangling from his lips, arms crossed indifferently. Scott's high-pitched voice bounced off the stone façades of the buildings ringing the harbour. He was gesticulating wildly in a futile attempt to communicate with the driver. 'MOLYVOS! I. Need. To. Get. To. Molyvos! You. You drive. Wait. Then drive!' Arms outstretched, Spencer mimicked driving with his hands clutching an imaginary steering wheel. 'You. Drive. Me. Drive me back here. To Mytilene.'

The driver was unimpressed and unresponsive. He gazed at Scott dispassionately and shrugged his shoulders. 'No English. Me no English.'

'Saints preserve me!' Scott slapped his thighs with frustration. Ben noticed now that Curtis was standing beside him, scanning the crowd, his arms hanging ineffectually by his side. 'For Christ's sake! How hard can it be?'

The concierge from one of the small hotels on the waterfront came trotting across the road, summoned by one of the bystanders. Hands clutched before his chest ingratiatingly, he spoke to Spencer Scott in broken English.

'Sir. Welcome Lesvos. You English, yes? English, I speak a little. I help, yes?'

Scott let out an audible sigh of relief and mopped the perspiration from his brow with a silk handkerchief. 'Thank you! What a relief. Could you please explain to this gentleman that I would like him to drive us to Molyvos, and then wait for us – we will only be in the town for a short time. Then we will need him to drive us back here to the ferry.'

'I try tell, sir.' The concierge turned to the driver and spoke to him rapidly in Greek. The driver barked out a response. The concierge interpreted for Scott.

'He say yes. You pay petrol. Also food, water for drive. Is long way Molyvos and back Mytilene one day.'

Nodding his head impatiently, Scott signalled for Curtis to open the rear door of the car. 'Yes. Yes. Of course. I don't care what it costs. All I want is to get out of this godforsaken place as quickly as possible!' He turned to climb into the cabin then stopped himself, taking a handful of coins from his pocket and handing them to the concierge. 'Thank you for your help.'

'You welcome, sir.' The concierge dipped his head. 'Hope have good drive. Hope enjoy Lesvos.'

'I seriously doubt that!' snapped the Englishman.

The surly driver pulled away from the kerb. Show over, the crowd of spectators dispersed as the concierge pocketed his tip and walked back across the road. Ben moved towards the cluster of vehicles to approach another private driver. He had already decided it wasn't necessary to tail Spencer Scott's car; the Englishman would stick out like the proverbial sore thumb and it wouldn't be difficult to find the dealer once he arrived in the very small seaside town of Molyvos. Besides which, he already knew where they were headed.

The road hugged the footings of the Byzantine fortress looming above the village, its sharply crenulated battlements standing out starkly against the summer sky. Ben's driver followed the road as it narrowed and began its descent down a steep slope towards a scatter of finely built stone houses over-looking the harbour's gentle arc. The channel of ink-black water separating the Greek island from the Turkish mainland was so narrow that Ben could make out small villages and the wake of fishing boats on the opposite shore.

As they entered the town of Molyvos, the driver slowed and drew to a halt beside an old man sitting hunched on a wooden stool, pipe clenched between toothless gums. His gnarled hands were ravaged by rheumatoid arthritis and rested on a polished olive tree branch that served as his cane. The driver greeted the old man and asked directions for the address Ben had given him.

The car negotiated the narrow cobbled streets slowly and laboriously, easing past flocks of goats and hay carts and villagers who would stop in the middle of the road for no reason other than to stare at the approaching vehicle. The progress was torturous.

'C'mon, c'mon,' Ben murmured beneath his breath. He knew there was no real need to rush. Another minute or two would make no difference. Yet now he was so close, the sense of anticipation was almost unbearable.

Rounding a sharp hairpin curve, the car turned into a wider road edged on one side by a waist-high stone wall and, below that, the lapping waves of the Aegean, and on the other by a long row of two-storeyed stone houses. The driver stopped and indicated a steep and narrow staircase leading up the hill between the houses. 'Up there. You'll find the house up there.'

Ben climbed out of the car. The sun on his back burned through his cotton shirt, and the sound of cicadas was deafening. The only other motorised vehicle in sight was Spencer Scott's car, which was parked beneath a shady tree further along the road. Ben approached the laneway and passed beneath the stone archway at its entrance. Ahead, the street wound steeply up the hill beneath a lattice of ancient wisteria, tendrils growing from mighty trunks as thick as wine barrels. Beneath the canopy, the air was cool and fragrant.

He didn't need to look at the enamel number plaques on the buildings to know which one he was headed for. Compared with the other buildings in the town, the house that dominated a rise at the end of the laneway was a mansion. Most of the buildings were constructed with their entrances opening directly onto the street. A few of the more affluent homes had small walled gardens at the front. But this house was surrounded by a ten-foot-high stone wall enclosing a piece of land that would have accommodated at least ten of the village houses. The feathery tops of canary palms peeked above the top of the wall, and the garden visible through the wrought-iron double gateway was manicured and well tended. The house itself was two storeys high with a double row of windows with blindingly whitewashed painted surrounds and brick-red timber shutters.

*I've got you now, you bastards.*

Backtracking down the lane, he found a small *kafeneion* nestled in a courtyard, its small, blue-painted wooden tables and chairs arranged haphazardly in dappled shade. He selected a table where he was shielded from the eyeline of people passing by on the laneway, but where he could still observe them from behind as they walked down towards the waterfront. The seat also had a clear view of the mansion's entranceway.

He ordered a coffee. As much as it irked him, the only thing he could do now was to wait. Spencer Scott was no use to him anymore, and with what Ben had planned, the Englishman – and, most importantly, his bodyguard – would only get in his way. He resolved to wait for them to leave before approaching the house.

Once he knew the dealer had left, he would make his move.

He was on his third drink when the slight figure of the English dealer appeared through the gate with Curtis' imposing bulk bringing up the rear. The two men exited and began their descent down the cobbled lane. Ben hid his face from view.

He glanced over his shoulder and watched the two Englishmen retreat down the hill. They turned the last corner at the end of the lane and disappeared into the shade of the stone archway.

Although Ben knew it would be wiser to wait until he was sure they were back in their car and well clear of the town before he approached the house, impatience made him incautious. He had waited long enough.

His heart was pounding and fury buzzed in his ears as he strode towards the gateway. The iron gate was heavier than he expected. Grasping one of the upright bars, something ruptured the dam of pent-up anger massed inside his chest and he flung the gate open, smashing it into the brick upright.

He had no recollection of how he got to the front door. He watched himself from above as he pounded the weathered timber with balled-up fists. The plan had been to charm his way inside. But any chance of disguising his intentions from the people in the house dissolved as he bellowed incoherently and smashed at the door like a madman.

Through a red blaze of fury he heard footsteps inside the house echoing along a long hallway. They hesitated, briefly. Then came the click of a latch and the door swung open.

Just two words, and his world fell apart.

'You came.'

# 16

## Lesvos, Greece, 1955

S he hadn't changed.
  His last night with Eris had replayed on a never-ending loop in his mind over the years. He knew her face as well as he knew his own. But even as she stood before him, his mind refused to accept what his eyes were telling him.

The ground seemed to shift beneath his feet. As she reached out and gently took his hand, Ben lost his grip on reality. So many times his imagination had transported him to a world where he could gaze once more into the burnished copper depths of her eyes. As the spectre standing before him lifted her hand to his face and cupped his cheek in her palm, he knew her scent; sweet rosewater and the woody musk of olive oil soap. The impervious barrier between dream and reality was splintering. He was losing his mind.

'Ben. Come.' She took a step inside and tried to draw him to her.

He was transfixed, rooted to the stone step. 'But . . .'

'Not here. Come inside. Please.'

Lifting leaden feet, Ben submitted.

'I have a story to tell you.'

Eris led him into a large room lined with French doors flung open to admit the warm breeze. The bucolic vista was a surreal counterpoint to the tumult spinning like a thresher in his mind.

'I thought you were dead.' He felt Eris' soft fingers entwined in his and feared he might faint. 'Why didn't you tell me you were alive? I've been going insane. I don't understand . . . why? Where have you been . . .? I searched for you . . . Looked everywhere. Drove myself half mad . . .'

'I am sorry.'

'Sorry?' His heart raced as fury began to pound behind his eyes. 'Sorry for what? For not being dead?'

'Ben . . . Please. I must explain.'

'Explain? Really? How do you plan to do that, Eris? Explain why you destroyed me?' His voice was shaking. 'You must've known what happened to me. And you did nothing! Nothing at all. You could have helped me! Why? How could you do this to me?'

'It was not like that, Ben.' She placed her hand on his forearm. 'When I saw what happened to you, my heart . . . it was broken. But I could not help you. I had to hide. It was too dangerous. They –'

'"They"? Who the hell are "they"?' Bellowing, he snatched his arm from her grasp. 'For Christ's sake, Eris! Enough riddles!'

She sighed deeply. 'When we met, I didn't tell you the whole truth.'

'No fucking kidding.'

'I was ashamed.' Her voice was quiet. 'I told you we needed the treasure to pay my brother's debts. But that was not true. It was my father.'

'Father ... brother. What fucking difference does it make? I don't care anymore. All that matters is that you left me – let me make a fool out of myself. What an *idiot* I've been!' A furnace of rage exploded inside. He slammed his fist onto a marble-topped side table.

Eris started, shocked. 'All I can do is say sorry to you, Benedict.' Fat tears glistened along her lower eyelids. 'But my father needed me. Now, he is gone. And when I saw the other half of my tablet in the catalogue, I knew you had found it in İzmir and taken it with you. It was a terrible accident when it was left behind. I never thought I'd see it again. But you found it. It was you, wasn't it?'

'You can't seriously be asking me that. Who else would it be?'

'Ben, I know you are unhappy with me ...'

'"Unhappy" doesn't even begin to cover it.'

'... but now you understand how important that tablet is.'

'At the moment, that's the last thing on my mind. I can't ... how ... how could you do this to me? Why not send me a message? Tell me you were alive? I would have left you alone if you'd asked me to.'

'I couldn't. The risk was too great as long as my father was still here. I am sure after what happened the police would have been watching you.'

'Police? Watching me? You don't know the half of it. My life has been – what am I talking about? – *is* a complete mess. I've been living under a microscope for the past three years!' The magnitude of what had happened struck him. 'Jesus Christ. I could fucking kill you.'

She took his hand and looked up at him through a tangle of thick lashes, her eyes gleaming with tears. 'You would never do that.'

He shook his hand loose. 'Don't bet on it.'

'Ben, this doesn't all have to be bad. I have discovered the secret of the tablet, as I am sure you have, too. Achilles. We can find him. We can work together – use the information we both have.'

'Work with you? You've got to be kidding.' White rage filled his vision. Nothing made sense to him. All he knew was that the woman he thought he loved had betrayed him. At this moment, nothing else mattered. 'I've got to get out of here.' He spun on his heel and left her in his wake. She called to him, but he couldn't hear anything through the furious buzzing in his ears.

The ancient eyrie's crumbling battlements tumbled beneath his feet towards the tiny fishing village below. He had clambered up to the Byzantine fortress, her words still ringing in his head. A chill wind whipped about his ears and he shivered, whether from the cold or a rift in his grip on reality he couldn't be sure.

Everything had changed. He had been the knight valiant – forsaking all in his quest to seek vengeance upon those who had ripped Eris from his arms, as once, a lifetime ago, he had lost Karina. Ada had been gravely injured thanks to his folly, and he had dismantled his life in the vain hope that it would lead him to the woman he now knew had betrayed him. He had sacrificed everything for what he believed was a righteous cause. He had been a fool.

Above his head, gulls dipped and whirled in the swirling air currents. He spread his arms wide and shut his eyes.

She had slit him open and scooped out the remnants of his soul.

He had nothing left.

# 17

## Lesvos, Greece, 1955

He returned to her as the sun was approaching the horizon. The blind fury had gone from his eyes. Reason, and a shadow of the burning ambition that had once defined him, had won out. Eris had the other half of the tablet, and the key to finding Achilles' tomb. Nothing else mattered now.

'So. Tell me.'

'I was taken. That is the truth. But what I did not tell you was that my father was an antiquities smuggler. After we came here from Turkey, it was how he made a living. And when I was old enough, I helped him in his business. When we met on the train, I didn't tell you. It is not the sort of thing I usually tell people.' Eris indicated the house with a flick of her wrist. 'But we did well. The money we made, it bought this. We were very successful.'

'What do you want me to say? Do you want praise . . .? My admiration? Because you won't be getting it.'

'No Ben. I just want you to understand.'

A vein pulsed in his temple as he struggled to maintain his composure. 'Understand? There's a saying about cold days and hell.'

'What do you mean?'

'Nothing.'

She continued in a hushed voice, eyes downcast. 'My father made an agreement with some dealers in Athens and Turkey. Very bad men. We had debts and needed the collection you saw to pay them. When I did not return to Lesvos quickly because I was with you, they came to find me. They broke into the house in İzmir and took me away . . . held me until my father agreed to do more work for them. They stole the collection too, of course. The only reason I still have the other half of the tablet is that they needed me to decipher it for them. They are greedy men and know nothing about archaeology. When I told them about the tablet's secret, they were very angry that they lost the other half. I hoped with all my heart you had found it and one day it would bring us together again. They . . . I . . . have been waiting all this time.'

'But after everything that happened to me . . . Jesus, I made such a fool of myself. You must have known. Why didn't you contact me . . . tell me you were all right?' He shook his head. 'I thought you were dead, Eris. It almost killed me.'

'I can only say I am sorry,' she said. 'But I had to do it for my father. After you were in the newspapers – well, you were right, and your article proved our antiquities were real. The men who stole them from me made a great deal of money selling them. But I knew that after that article, you would be watched. I couldn't write to you. You described me – and the Turkish police were looking for me. I knew they would open your mail. If they found me, they would find my father,' she said. 'He was an old man. He went through many hardships.

To go to jail – it would have killed him. But now he is dead. Now, it does not matter so much.'

'Are you saying the police here didn't know what you were doing?'

'That's right. We live quietly here and are known by different names . . .'

'Different names? Great. So even your name is bullshit, then?'

'No. Not bullshit. You have a name for me . . . Eris. To keep doing what we do, we had to be chameleons. Nobody knows our profession except those we do business with. And they have no desire to tell anyone else what they – or we – are doing. So we lived a respectable life. I couldn't expose my father to danger. But after you and I were separated, I always thought we would see each other again, one day. I kept the tablet – I studied it – because it seemed to connect me with you. When I saw the other half in the Sotheby's catalogue, I knew it was time.'

She moved closer to him and took his hands in hers. 'It was always going to bring us together again.'

He flinched, fighting the desire that welled up in him as he caught her scent and felt the soft touch of her skin on his. She started as he shook his hands free and took a sudden step backwards, his hip crashing into an oak sideboard. 'Christ almighty, Eris! The fear . . . guilt . . . that I hadn't been able to save you. You just needed to tell me you were all right. That's all.'

She stepped forward again and encircled his neck with her slim, brown arms. 'Ben . . .' Pressing against him, he felt her full breasts against his chest. '. . . Please?' He hated himself for it, but he wanted her.

As her hands slipped behind his head and began to draw his face down to hers, he leant hard against the sideboard, feeling its blunt corner bruising his hipbone. He tried to move his hands to her waist, to push her away. Instead, they found their way around her hips, feeling the crisp linen of her skirt crinkle beneath his fingers.

'For Christ's sake, Eris. It's not that easy . . .'

'Why not?' Her voice was thick with desire. 'Ben, we're both lonely . . .' She tangled his hair in her fingers and pulled his mouth down to hers.

'That's not enough.' It was a lie, and he knew it. Whatever internal battle he was fighting was lost. He grabbed her waist and turned her, thrusting her back against the hallway table as he dropped his head and kissed her hungry lips. They clawed at each other's clothes, fingers grasping and grabbing. She tugged at his belt and unbuttoned his trousers as he hoisted her skirt above her waist and lifted her onto the edge of the table. As she arched her hips and shed her underclothes, he tore open her shirt with fumbling fingers.

Beneath his greedy touch, her skin was as satiny and supple as he remembered. Surprising him with her strength, she gripped his thighs with her knees and slid rhythmically against him as he ran his hand down her arched back, dipping his fingers into the silken groove at the base of her spine. It was almost too much to bear; he felt himself pulsing, hot and swollen against her. She kissed him ravenously, tongue slipping between his lips.

Her fingers fumbled with his boxer shorts, gripping him through the thin cotton. He lifted his hands to cup the swell of her full breasts as his hot, swollen shaft pressed against the cool mound of her belly. Wrapping her strong, lithe legs about his hips, she guided him into her. As he slipped inside her, she kissed him deeply, her small, dark nipples hardening as they brushed against the coarse hair on his chest. He responded, entangling his fingers in her hair and pulling her face closer as he began to slide inside her. Moving with him, she rode him, moaning as he pumped his hips and ground deeper within her, reaching around to grip her from behind.

She cried out, her voice thick with ecstasy. 'Ben, yes!'

As he felt her wetness pulsing, he began to throb and surge, the blinding whiteness of release momentarily suspending him from conscious thought.

Outside, the mournful gulls' cries echoed along stone-lined streets as the warm breeze ruffled palm fronds in the garden. Eris relaxed, slumping against his chest. She shivered and released a deep sigh as he ran his hand along her spine. Gazing at him from beneath hooded eyelids, she murmured. 'I missed you, Ben.'

A hollow pit opened up in his belly. He said nothing.

Ben watched the smouldering embers as he drew deeply on his cigarette and felt the comforting burn in his lungs. His boxer shorts bunched up beneath his thighs as he extended his long legs in front of him. A white square of sunlight hit the tiled floor and warmed his feet as he gazed out at the glittering Aegean and, beyond that, the bruised and jagged Turkish coastline.

Eris took a seat beside him and rested her hand on his naked thigh. He didn't try to dislodge it. 'Ben, I hope you can forgive me one day. All I can do is apologise to you. I never knew it would cause you so much pain when I disappeared. It is a surprise to me. In our time together, well – you did not seem to be a man who would worry too much about the women he meets.'

The cicadas in the trees outside were deafening. He shook his head, slowly. 'You were different. I told you things I've never spoken of to another person. Things I've tried hard to forget.'

'I thought maybe you might say these things to women like me to get sympathy.'

'Sympathy?!' he scoffed. 'Even at my lowest ebb, I've never had to stoop that low.' He leant forward and dragged deeply on his cigarette. 'I had a wife.'

She pulled back, took her hand from his leg. 'A wife? You are married?'

'I said "had" a wife. Past tense. I lost her. In the war.' He clenched his fists and felt his knuckles crack. 'When you disappeared, I lived through it again.'

'I didn't know, Ben.' She wrapped her arm around his shoulder. 'I am so sorry.'

'Would it have made any difference?'

'Yes. Probably.'

'Well, it's a bit late now.' He stood, shrugging off her arm. 'The damage is done.'

Retrieving his clothes, he stepped back into his pants and buttoned his shirt. 'And if there's one thing I can salvage from this sorry mess, it's what I think that tablet is telling me. If you're really sorry for what you've done, you'll help me with that.'

'You mean Achilles' tomb.' She stood and moved to his side. 'You know?'

'Yes. It is a scytale cipher,' she said.

He laughed. 'You worked that out for yourself?'

'I have been doing this for many years with my father. I did not study at a university and I have no degree. But there are many things I have learnt from him and the people we work with.' She didn't attempt to disguise the pride in her voice.

'So, the tablet. Do you know where it came from?' he asked.

'Of course. Androcles. In the Trojan War he was an Achaean general –'

'Who defended Achilles' body. Yes, I know all about him.'

'Well, the tablet was taken from a fifth-century tomb belonging to a family of Androcles' descendants. But you must know this. It was in the catalogue. How did you find out about it?'

'Educated guess. There weren't many other reasonable explanations. And I wanted to send you a message. Whether or not my guess was correct, I thought it would catch your attention. I was right.'

'Yes, you were. But I did not know any of this in İzmir. I only started trying to find out more about it after that, when I spoke with my father and we contacted the people who gave us the tablet,' she said. 'After Achilles' death, Androcles built a tomb for him somewhere in Asia Minor with an army of warriors. All except Androcles sacrificed themselves once the tomb was finished so the secret would die with them. The instructions for finding it passed down through his family. That is how it came to be written on the marble. And the Achilleion . . .'

'A ruse. A decoy.'

'Of course.'

A surge of excitement coursed through his veins. 'So. Your translation. Bring it to me.' He checked himself. 'Please.'

Eris walked barefoot over to the French doors. Leaning against the shutters, the breeze ruffled her long hair. 'Is this something you have to do right now, Ben? He has been there for many thousands of years. Achilles is not going anywhere. We are the only two people who know how to find him.'

She turned and moved back to his side, grasping his shoulders and gazing up at him with limpid eyes. 'I have an idea. Let's go somewhere together. I have money. Lots of it. We can get a boat. Go from island to island. We can disappear . . . start all over again. We will have many years to find Achilles.' A gentle smile bloomed at the corners of her full lips. Her eyes opened and she looked deeply into Ben's own. 'You know, your eyes stayed with me. I always remembered. They are the colour of the sea when a storm is coming.' She touched his cheek. 'Ben, come with me.'

'My work was my life, Eris,' he replied. 'Without it, I'm nothing. Thanks to you, my career is finished. This is the one chance I have to resurrect myself in the eyes of the archaeological community.'

'So this is more important to you than us.'

'"Us"? There is no "us", Eris. Never was. And right now, all I want to do is to get to work.'

She flinched, stung by his words. 'As you wish.' She hesitated. 'But before I give you what you want, I ask one thing.'

He clamped his hands on his hips. 'I don't think you're really in a position to ask anything.'

'The tablet. The men who kidnapped me – well, one of the men – he knows I have it. He only agreed to let me keep it because he knew I could translate it, and he could not. But he has arranged an important sale when we find the tomb. He wants Achilles' shield. He is a cruel and greedy man. And if he does not get what he wants, I am afraid of what he might do to me . . . and to you.'

'Why in God's name would I do anything to help you, Eris?' Ben scoffed, scarcely believing her gall. 'And while I'm at it, why should I believe anything you say? To say you're not factoring into my thinking now is something of an understatement. Knowing you're associated with the people who've been making my life hell doesn't help . . . I've been followed. And attacked. And in London, an old friend of mine had her house broken into while I was staying there. She ended up in hospital. Sound familiar? Something your "friends" might do?'

Eris dropped her eyes and shook her head. 'He cares little for people. Only money. It would not surprise me. I am sorry to hear about your friend. Is she all right?'

'I don't know. I hope so.' The guilt still burned.

'It is the sort of man he is. And what he wants now is the shield.'

'What *he* wants? To be frank, I couldn't give a fuck what "he" wants, whoever he is. Fact of the matter is, we don't even know if we'll find it there anyway.'

'If it is there, then it is very important that you give it to me.'

'And if it is there, giving it to you will be the last thing on my mind.'

'Ben, by doing this, we are partners. And I ask only this one thing of you.' She gazed down at the floor for a moment, deep in thought. 'But I will trust you. I believe you will do what is right.'

Ben watched as she strode to a bookcase. He was under no illusion. No matter what she had done to him and how deep the sense of betrayal he felt, he knew that he couldn't deliberately place her in harm's way. And, right now, he hated himself for it.

Eris slid open a drawer. The two halves of the tablet sat beside each other, nestled on a bed of thick felt. She carefully removed them, placing them side by side on a small table. 'Here. And I will save you time.' She took a small, weathered notebook from the bookshelf and handed it to him. 'This is the translation I made of the cipher.'

'What did you use for the staff?'

'A rolling pin for making phyllo pastry.'

Ben laughed. 'I used a Turkish *yufka* rolling pin. It's like I've always said about Greece and Turkey – two sides of the same coin.'

He retrieved his own notebook from his satchel and opened it at the page where he had transcribed the inscription from his own half of the tablet. 'So. This is my half, including the fragment I broke off for safekeeping. Clearly, it's talking about Achilles and how Androcles laid him to rest. As to *where* that was . . . "the many-fountained peak" . . . the place "where the ox-eyed goddess light-footed made her way to deceive Zeus the storm-gatherer" and they lay together "in a golden cloud as the Achaeans, beloved of Hera, overran the warriors of Ilium". Pretty straight forward, really.'

Eris looked puzzled. 'Straight forward? How, exactly?'

'Do you still have a copy of *The Iliad*?' he asked.

She ran her fingertips along the bookshelf and pulled out a tiny, leather-bound book. 'Of course.' She tossed it to him. 'Here.'

Ben caught it in an outstretched hand and leafed through the book until he found the spot he was looking for and handed it back to her, pointing. '"The many-fountained peak where the ox-eyed goddess light-footed made her way to deceive Zeus the storm-gatherer" . . . *Dios apate*. The goddess Hera's deception and seduction of Zeus on the peak of Mount Ida. The mightiest of the Olympians watched the Trojan War from the summit of the mountain. When Hera wanted to give the Greeks the upper hand in the battle, she seduced Zeus and they made love in a golden cloud at the summit of the mountain. While Zeus was distracted, the Greeks overran the Trojans. Mount Ida. I'm sure it's talking about Mount Ida.'

Reaching for Eris' notebook he opened it to her translation. 'So. My half tells us where to look for the tomb.'

He flipped open Eris' notebook. 'And yours, I hope, will tell us how to find it.'

Reading with eyes gleaming, his lips moved as he read the words.

> . . . *When you call the leader of men once more, sing of his valour and summon him from the underworld. Walk in the footsteps of the great man who fled till Phoebus Apollo forsook him, and the greater man who pursued him. Following the waters, pass the blessed twin springs of serpentine Xanthos the son of Oceanus, one rising as from flame, the other in summertime running as snowmelt. Fill a pitcher from the spring that runs hot from Hades' fire.*
>
> *At the topmost peak at the altar where Zeus, master of bright lightning, alighted as an eagle, his beloved Ganymede in his talons, fell tall oaks and split the beams. With the rising sun behind, set a funeral pyre below Zeus' blessed altar where the four axes meet. Anoint the altar with a stream of Xanthos' life-giving waters heated on the pyre. As the flames exalt Zeus on high, be prostrate before the fire as Phoebus Apollo in his chariot rises above the horizon, his light at your back.*
>
> *When summoned, godlike Achilles will rise from his tomb and once more shine his light upon mankind. His armour borne by the best among men shall vanquish the shadow as it falls across the earth.*

Ben laughed aloud and slapped his thigh. 'Look at that! Mount Ida! This confirms it! No doubt about it!' he stabbed the page with his forefinger. '"Walk in the footsteps of the great man who fled till Phoebus Apollo forsook him" – that's Hector, son of Priam and Prince of Troy, favourite of the god, Apollo . . . "and the greater man who pursued him" – that's Achilles, of course, who chased Hector along the Scamander River. "Serpentine Xanthos the son of Oceanus". Xanthos – Scamander – was a river god and the sworn enemy of Achilles. But the *actual* river Scamander – its headwaters are on Mount Ida.'

Eris nodded her head. 'Mount Ida. Yes. That makes sense.'

'Makes sense? Of *course* it makes sense! And then there's the boy Ganymede – "the loveliest born of the race of mortals". Zeus took the form of an eagle and carried the boy to his altar on Mount Ida to serve as his cupbearer. Well, there's a sanctuary dedicated to Zeus near the mountain's summit – and that's where we'll start our search.'

He pointed towards the hazy mauve outline of the mountains on the Turkish mainland visible through the open window. 'It's right there. I'll swear to it. So – will you be able to find someone to take us across the strait?' he asked.

'Yes – I am sure one of the fishermen could. But it would be better to take a car. Getting into the mountains is difficult. You would not want to walk – it would take too long. But if you drive to Mytilene you can catch the ferry from there to Ayvalık and then drive to Mount Ida,' she said. 'I have a jeep here you can use. It was my father's. He bought it from the Americans after the war. It has only ever been used here – never in Turkey. Nobody will recognise it.'

'I notice you're saying "you". Not "we". You're not planning to come with me?'

'To keep you safe, I think it is better if I stay here. I think this man has people watching me. If I am here, I can speak with him on the telephone as I always do, and he will not think anything is wrong. I hope. But he will probably have people following you. Once you go back to Turkey, it is possible he will know what you are doing so it is best that you can move quickly.'

'If I go through Ayvalık, the border police will notice my arrival,' he protested.

'I think the Turkish police will be only a small problem for you. If you are quick, they will not have time to catch up with you. But this man . . .'

'Yes, yes. I get it.'

'The other thing that is good for you – the jeep. It was used to bring antiquities here from other places in Greece. It has many places to hide things that the police never discovered, even though it was searched many times. I think this will be useful for you.'

'I suppose I should be grateful that I have an experienced smuggler to call on for advice,' he said tightly, bitterness making his throat constrict.

Eris turned to gaze out the window, her arms crossed defensively in front of her chest.

He began to prepare for his departure. He was begrudgingly grateful that Eris' chosen profession meant she had on hand all the things he needed.

Other than the small set of hand tools in his satchel, he packed only what he would usually take if he was going on an archaeological survey: a collapsible entrenching spade, a pick, a coil of heavy-duty rope and a metal bucket. As his intention was simply to discover and – if he was honest with himself – loot a site, he didn't bother with any of the things needed to properly document and record an archaeological find. The prospect of ignoring archaeological convention and embarking on a treasure hunt was perversely thrilling.

At the back of the house, Eris swung open the weathered doors to a tumble-down stone building. Parked inside was the military-issue green jeep, a little rusty about the edges from years of exposure to the Aegean sea air, but otherwise in pretty good shape. She showed Ben the various modifications that had been made to its chassis to store contraband. She was right. The hiding places were so ingenious that short of dismantling the entire vehicle, he couldn't imagine a circumstance in which a border inspection would reveal what was hidden.

Hefting a jerry can of fuel into the jeep's open back, he ran through a mental checklist. As a foreigner, his presence on the Turkish coast would not go unnoticed. But to avoid drawing attention to himself, he would avoid as many official encounters as possible. Eating at *lokantas* and engaging in conversations with the locals was out of the question. With enough food to last a week, and blankets to sleep rough so he wouldn't have to stay in village inns where his arrival would be registered with the local police, he would hopefully be able to keep off the radar.

*Well, that's the plan, anyway*, he thought to himself wryly.

He had intended to depart before nightfall, but the light outside the double doors was softening as dusk approached and the cries of birds roosting for the night declared it a futile hope. He resolved to sleep in Molyvos and leave early in the morning to catch the first ferry of the day in Mytilene. When he told Eris, he resented the delight that sparkled in her eyes.

The heavy purple velvet of night had fallen across the island. The cacophony of village life gave way to the echo of barking street dogs yapping and scrabbling along cobbled lanes and the soothing sound of waves licking at the pebbled shore like the trickle of rain on a slate roof.

At a timber table set under weeping wisteria fronds, they ate dinner in silence. Ben rebuffed Eris' attempts to make conversation, choosing instead to study the complete inscription and try to unravel the hidden meaning of the instructions outlined on her half of the tablet. The language was obscure – the meaning more so. But he knew he would crack it, given time. He was so absorbed in the task that when Eris stood to clear the table, he scarcely noticed. When she stepped behind his chair and placed her hands on his shoulders, bending to kiss the nape of his neck, he started, shocked at her touch.

'Ben. We have one more night together. Will you stay with me in my bed tonight? Please?'

He splayed his hands upon the tabletop, feeling splinters and grit beneath his fingers and willing himself not to reach up and return her embrace. 'What happened before, Eris . . . it was a mistake.'

'It did not feel like a mistake to me.'

'It did to me. It will . . . it would . . . take a long time for me to forget what you did to me.'

She pulled out a chair and sat at the very edge of the seat, leaning towards him to grasp his knee. 'That is why we should go. Now. Let's just take everything with us and go.' He felt himself weakening, intoxicated by her proximity, her touch. 'We can become other people. And, in time, we can return to Turkey and we will find Achilles. But if we leave now, we can learn to be with each other again, and one day you might be able to forgive me.'

He stood abruptly, knocking his chair onto the stone terrace with a clatter. 'No! No, Eris. I'm not going to do this again. This is my one chance to fix things. I'm not going to let you scramble my mind. I'll sleep down here. On the couch.'

'You will be cold. And uncomfortable.'

'I will also be safe. And sane.'

Cold morning light raked across the tiled rooftops, banishing the night's frosty breath. The jeep was parked on an expanse of gleaming white gravel at the back door of the house, its tailgate lowered as Ben checked his supplies again. He knew he couldn't be too careful. If he forgot something and had to track it down in Turkey, it would waste valuable time and, more disturbingly, draw unwanted attention to him.

Eris walked out of the house beneath a tumble of vermilion bougainvillea blossoms which cascaded over the rough stone portico. The warm morning breeze ruffled her hair as she crossed the gravel to where he stood. She extended her hands towards him. Resting in one palm was a black revolver; in the other, a box of ammunition. 'Please, Ben. Take this. I am afraid for you and I want you to be safe.'

He slammed the back of the jeep shut. Taking the gun from Eris' hand, he placed it on the dashboard as he climbed into the driver's seat. 'You don't need to worry about me. I can look after myself. But, thank you. It can't hurt. Well, not me, anyway.'

He started the engine and gunned it to life. He leant out the jeep's rusty window and raised a hand in farewell. As he eased the car into reverse, Eris grabbed his forearm.

'You know, Ben, that I did not want these things to happen to you. If I could have made things different, I would never have left. Do you know that?'

He didn't know what to say, so he said nothing. Eris' eyes filled with tears. 'Be careful. You are a good man.'

'Good? No. You must have me confused with someone else.' He gave her a tight smile. 'Now – it's time for me to go.'

Pulling his arm from her grasp, he backed out of the courtyard onto the cobbled street outside without a backward glance. The vehicle's interior smelled of hot engine grease and mildew and the metal frame of the seat jutted through its worn canvas cover, jabbing into the back of his thighs. But he barely noticed. As he negotiated the narrow lanes of Molyvos, he thought only of his destination.

In the distance, the ferry made its stately way towards Mytilene from the Turkish mainland, its prow casting cotton-white spume across the cerulean sea.

Ben leant against the bonnet of the jeep, holding a cigarette between chiselled fingers, eyes squinting against the shards of sunshine reflecting off the harbour's mirror-like surface. He was one of a long line of waiting passengers. A lackadaisical young street vendor made his way through the crowd, offering fresh almonds chilled on nuggets of glistening ice from a huge tray balanced atop his head.

He inhaled the searing cigarette smoke deep into his lungs and tapped his foot restlessly. The bucolic vista of the picture-perfect Greek seaside town was no help – he couldn't ignore the sense of urgency eroding his gut. There was nothing out of the ordinary to signal danger, but a grim sense of apprehension wormed beneath his skin like a parasite.

As the bone-jarring shock of Eris' reappearance began to settle, it was a peculiar sensation to find that the one thing that had defined his existence for years had been as insubstantial as a mirage. Yes, he was still angry – furious, even – about her betrayal. But if he hoped that finding out the truth might have given him some relief at the knowledge that his worst fears amounted to nothing, he was horribly disappointed. Instead, he felt hollow and strangely cheated. He hated himself for it, but he couldn't deny that finding Eris dead might have been preferable.

All he could do now was make the best of a stinking bad situation. Finding Achilles' tomb would be his salvation. And throwing himself into the search would take his mind off the anger that still boiled within him and the questions he had about the glaring inconsistencies in Eris' story. That would come later. But first, he had a few other things to work out.

From the corner of his eye, he saw the distinctive logo of the Hellenic Post building on the waterfront. By his reckoning, it was at least forty-five minutes before the ferry arrived and discharged its cargo onto the docks to accommodate the cars and passengers waiting in Mytilene.

He tossed his cigarette butt onto the pavement and ground it beneath the heel of his boot. *That's plenty of time*, he thought to himself. *I can't leave without knowing.*

'Hello. It's Benedict Hitchens speaking.'

His greeting was welcomed with stony silence.

'Ah, I'm a friend of Ada's and I was just calling to check –'

The voice travelled down the telephone line with the staccato violence of a submachine gun. 'Friend? You're no friend of Ada's. This is Andrew Hoyne, her *fiancé*! You have some nerve calling after the way you took off. I don't think I'm speaking out of turn to say that I doubt she has any desire to talk to you.'

The anxiety that had been making it difficult to breathe as Ben had waited for the call to be placed to London evaporated. 'Oh, that is such a relief. That she is speaking, I mean.

Not that she won't talk to me. It's just . . . well, I'm really pleased to hear she's OK.'

'She was very lucky, Mr Hitchens. No long-term consequences, no thanks to you. You know, I've half a mind to –'

Ben hung up. Ada was fine. That was all that mattered. He didn't need to hear anything else, least of all what her fiancé had half a mind to do to him. Whatever it was, he knew it couldn't be good.

As the line of cars edged slowly onto the ferry's lower deck, Ben nodded and smiled vacantly at the attendants directing the traffic, playing the stupid foreigner and completely ignoring their instructions as he jockeyed for position to make sure he would be one of the first vehicles to disembark when they arrived in Ayvalık.

The deck shifted as the water ebbed and flowed beneath the ferry's hull. The ear-splitting crank and grind of the motor pulling up the anchor bounced around the amphitheatre-like curve of Mytilene's harbour as birds soared above the ferry's wake, dipping and diving to scavenge fish from the water. A surge of excitement swirled in Ben's chest at the sight of the purple peaks on the Turkish mainland. He knew he was on the right track. Every nerve in his body tingled with anticipation.

He had stored the gun and ammunition in the glove box in the hope that he wouldn't need them. Still, he was very grateful they were there. Just in case.

# 18

'He's on his way.'
'He's not going to have a sudden attack of conscience, is he?'

'No.'

'You sound fairly confident.'

'Not without reason.'

'I don't trust him. He's becoming unpredictable. I'm going to keep my men close on his heels.'

'Just make sure he gets it before they step in. We'll never find it without him.'

'Don't worry. They're just there to make sure he doesn't get cold feet. They won't interfere unless it looks like he's not bringing the shield back to you.'

'He told me your men attacked his friend in London. Is that right?'

'Sometimes they get a little over-enthusiastic. Don't worry. We won't be implicated.'

'I'm more concerned about what they might do to him. He's not one to submit quietly.'

'They know what's at stake.'

'I just don't want to see him hurt.'

The other caller fell silent for a moment. 'You're not losing perspective, are you?'

'Me? You must be joking.'

'That is a relief. Because it would be unfortunate. He doesn't deserve your concern. He's far too narcissistic to warrant it.'

'I'll bear that in mind.'

'I just spoke with the woman. He's on the next ferry. Are you in position?'

'Yes. Of course. As you instructed.'

'Let me make this perfectly clear. You are to keep your distance. Do not, under any circumstances, let him see you.'

'We understand.'

'Consider yourself fortunate you're being given another chance after the mess you left behind in London.'

'I already told you –'

'I'm not interested in your excuses!' the voice snapped. 'Just do your job.'

# 19

## Mount Ida, Turkey, 1955

Ben savoured the cool rush of air through his sweat-soaked shirtsleeves as he drove up the steep mountain range that ran like a jagged spine along Turkey's Aegean coast. A jade-green canopy of beech and chestnut leaves soared above the road like the ribbed archways of a Gothic cathedral, casting dappled viridian light across the forest floor below. The dirt road wound erratically through a deep river valley, past sparkling waters rushing seaward across drifts of smooth pebbles and past stands of bright green poplars and willows, their switches dangling like fishing lines in the fast-running waters.

It was difficult to believe the landscape's sudden transformation as Ben left the coastal plains and began the long journey up to Mount Ida. He had endured the shambolic disembarkation at Ayvalık among the shoving and pushing hordes of passengers eager to make their way ashore. His irrational fear that his name would be recorded at all border crossings amounted to nothing; the number of people on board the ferry meant the police paid little attention to his travel papers, making note of his name and passport number and absent-mindedly waving him through. Despite the ease of his passage across the Turkish border, a lingering pall of dread hung over him. Although he accelerated through the raised barrier into the hectic seaside town with a great deal of relief, his nerves were on edge as he side-eyed and scrutinised every other vehicle on the road.

It was market day, and so the streets of Ayvalık and its surrounds had been chaotically busy and so dusty it was nearly impossible to see where he was driving. The heat was stifling. Sweat poured down his back, sticking his shirt to his ribcage and soaking the waistband of his trousers. Although the traffic cleared as he drove north along the coast road, the air was still oppressively hot. His eyes flicked constantly to the rear-view mirror, scanning the other cars on the road. A *dolmuş* tailgated him for twenty minutes, its driver invisible behind a haze of dust. Heart pounding, Ben slammed on his brakes and took a sudden turn up a side road to shake him. Blipping his horn in disgust at nothing more than Ben's dangerous driving, the *dolmuş* driver tore down the road away from him without a backward glance.

It was only as Ben turned away from the sea and entered the pine forest at the foothills of the mountain range that the atmosphere became cooler and he began to feel more at ease. Cedar-scented air blasted into the car, and even over the ear-splitting roar of the jeep's over-taxed engine a boisterous chorus of birdsong could be heard echoing through the tree-lined canyons.

He had avoided stopping along the well-travelled route between Ayvalık and Altinoluk before turning off the road to the north into the foothills of Mount Ida. But he would soon reach a point where he would have to ask for help. It was a risk, but he knew that any attempt to find the right route into the massif without local knowledge was a fool's errand. All the roads were little more than dirt tracks. They were unmarked, unmapped, and generally followed the meandering routes taken by shepherds and their flocks as they travelled into the high pastures. He was heading for the tiny village of Zeytinli in the shadow of the mountain's peak, where he could ask someone to point him in the right direction.

He could only assume that the police would have been alerted to his arrival in Turkey and would soon be on his tail. And if what Eris told him was true then other, more sinister, forces might turn up at any moment.

He knew it was bordering on lunacy to make this attempt unaided, given what he might have to confront in the hours ahead. But he had no choice. He was on his own.

Ben was in a race against time. And it was not one he intended to lose.

# 20

'We followed him to the turn-off to Zeytinli.'

'As we expected, then.'

'What should we do now?'

'Keep track of him. But don't get too close. Don't scare him off. If he makes a break for it before he finds the tomb, we're finished. Do you understand?' The voice was sharp and commanding.

'We'll be careful.'

'I expect nothing less. And remember – he's ex-military. Don't expect him to cooperate willingly. When it comes time, use whatever force is necessary.'

# 21

## Mount Ida, Turkey, 1955

A sharp corner led to a narrow, rutted lane on the outskirts of Zeytinli. On either side, the road was lined with two-storeyed stone houses identical to those in Molyvos. The street led to a large, open square bordered by bent-armed pines and broad plane trees. At one end of the square was the ubiquitous village mosque painted hospital-issue green, its single minaret made from hand-hewn stone and its low dome clad in dull lead sheeting.

As Ben pulled to a halt on the opposite corner, the cluster of men gathered outside the mosque watched his arrival warily. A tall, lean man edged towards the front of the group. With his head thrown back atop squared shoulders as he flicked his *tesbih* beads with a flourish, Ben knew straight away that – in the hierarchy of the town of Zeytinli at least – this was a man of some importance.

'Selamın Aleyküm.'

'Aleyküm selam.'

'*İsminiz?*'

'*Adım Ben. Sizinki nedir?*'

The Turkish man raised his eyebrows, surprised that the foreigner could speak Turkish.

'My name is Mehmet. I am the *mukhtar* of Zeytinli. Are you English?'

'No. American.'

'Welcome to our town.'

'It's a pleasure to be here. It has been a long journey and I would like to refresh myself. Where is the tea garden?'

'Please, you will be my guest. Come.'

At the other end of the square, men wearing cloth caps played *tavla* and threw back small glasses of Turkish tea at a jumble of small tables laid out in the shade of a chestnut tree.

They took a seat at one of the vacant tables. The teahouse's proprietor scurried over deferentially with a small, brass tray upon which he balanced two steaming glasses of golden-brown *çay*. Ben took his tea and dropped one tiny white sugar cube into the glass. The two men sat in companionable silence as they sipped their drinks, accompanied by a cacophony of cicadas in the tree above them. The waiter returned with a gilded dish containing chickpeas, pistachios and hazelnuts, and a white plate stacked with fat, rosy slices of watermelon. Ben's stomach rumbled as he scooped a small handful of nuts out of the bowl. Food had taken a tumble down his list of priorities today and he had forgotten how hungry he was.

'Why have you come to Zeytinli?' Mehmet gazed at Ben curiously. 'We don't have many foreigners visit us here.'

'I'm not really a foreigner. I live in Istanbul.'

'Have you come for our olive oil? In this district, we are very famous for our olives.'

'Well that explains the town's name, anyway. "Zeytinli" . . . "with olives". No. I'm not here for that. I'm an archaeologist – I want to visit Zeus' altar on the mountain.'

Mehmet's dark eyes widened beneath his thick brows and he rapped the wooden table sharply with his knuckles to ward off evil spirits. *'Bismillah.* That place is cursed. Why would you go there?'

'It's my job. I am here to examine the site.' *Not exactly a lie.*

Mehmet's face was grim. 'The forests around the altar are home to many jinn. Those who have been there speak of hearing voices and they are driven mad. Two shepherd boys took their flocks to the mountain pastures. There was a storm that night the like of which I have never seen – rain falling in sheets so heavy it collapsed roofs, and lightning . . . the night was bright as day. The old women in the village said the ancient gods were angry. And the shepherds? They were never seen again. May Allah's mercy be with them.'

*Evil spirits, devils and ghost stories*, Ben thought. A haunting was the least of his worries.

Ben smiled. 'Nevertheless, I really must see the site. Could you please tell me which road to take to get to the mountain? I am more concerned about getting lost than I am about mountain spirits.'

The *mukhtar* tut-tutted. 'A wise man does not ignore the voice of the mountain.' With visible reluctance he indicated the road branching off the square and leading northwards. 'If you follow that path you will find the altar. There are some intersections – always take the right-hand turn.'

Ben stood and shook Mehmet's hand. *'Allaha ısmarladık.* Thank you, Mehmet *Bey*. I will stop here and join you for tea when I return. And buy some of your olive oil.'

*'Maşallah.* God willing. *Güle güle.'*

# 22

## Mount Ida, Turkey, 1955

As he passed through the forest, Ben caught glimpses of the summit of Mount Ida looming above him. Unlike the abundant forest cascading down its slopes like a green hoop skirt, the conical, windswept peak was barren.

On the road ahead, a small handwritten sign nailed to a tree trunk pointed the way to Zeus' altar. Ben had read of this site years ago in an outdated academic survey of western Anatolian archaeological sites. It was dismissed as an unremarkable and minor Classical temple with little to see worth justifying the arduous trek required to get there. Turkey was so rich with extraordinary ancient sites like Ephesus and Pergamon that this place wasn't even mentioned in the tourist guides.

For Ben, the most exciting thought was that it had never been excavated. Whatever might be hidden here had never been found because nobody had ever looked.

The potholed dirt road veered to the right before stopping abruptly in a small clearing. Another sign pointed the way into the forest.

He packed some food in his satchel and looped the rope across his chest. Jamming a blanket in the bucket, he strapped the pick and spade onto his back and began the climb up the steep and overgrown path.

The struggle uphill was arduous. Yet even as he was battling his way through tangled vines and matted undergrowth, he was at work. Despite valiant attempts to blunt his senses with drinking and debauchery over the years, it was reassuring that he hadn't lost his capacity to see. Without even thinking, as soon as he began to walk the trail his eyes were glued to the ground, panning from side to side on the lookout for irregularities in the soil.

Within minutes, he saw it. It was nothing much to look at – just a white-slipped pottery fragment protruding from an eroded hillock. But to Ben, it meant everything. 'Fifth-century BC Classical temple complex, my arse!' he murmured to himself. The strap-handle and terracotta-red paintwork of Mycenaean fineware, circa 1200 BC, were unmistakable.

Heart pounding with excitement, he heaved air hungrily into his lungs. The oxygen-starved upper altitude was taking its toll. Pushing forward, his eyes scanned the terrain as he searched for more ancient markers.

'Christ!' The corner of a monumental worked stone block emerged from behind a sweeping spray of fern fronds, most of it buried beneath the earth.

'It's the size of a *car*!' Ben exclaimed to his feathered companions chirruping and singing in the branches above his head.

341

He threw down the bucket and tools and swept the ferns aside. The chipped and pitted face of the stone was rough and covered with a heavy patina. He whispered a silent prayer. *Please don't make this a pedestrian Classical Graeco-Roman wall. No straight edges. Please.* Whereas the Classical Greeks and Romans had been masters of the plumb bob and constructed their monuments with straight-edged masonry that put twentieth-century builders to shame, what Ben wanted to see were the irregular joins that were characteristic of Mycenaean architecture.

Using the edge of his shovel to peel away the soil covering the side of the massive stone block, he exposed another vast monolith resting on top. It was strangely satisfying to spurn decades of archaeological training. Under normal circumstances he would have spent hours recording, measuring and collecting all the material packed in the earth around the boulder. But today he was no better than the looters who once tore holes into his site at Eskitepe. And he was enjoying it. Shoulders straining, he hacked at the earth, severing the thick roots of the plants growing from the top of the wall like the Hanging Gardens of Babylon until he'd exposed two yards of the mortar line separating the two boulders.

He was right! The edges were not squared off and the mortar line didn't follow horizontal and vertical axes – it was perpendicular. 'I *knew* it! A Cyclopean wall. Might as well have left your damned calling card! You were here, you bastards, weren't you?' He whooped with excitement.

There was no point in exposing the entire wall. Whatever it was – and just judging by its scale, it was a fortification wall of some sort – it was part of a much larger complex. The wall might well have something to do with Achilles' final resting place, but the inscription on the tablet pointed him towards Zeus' altar as the place to commence his search. This was just a sideshow.

Returning to the path, Ben resumed his climb towards the summit of the mountain. The already precipitous slope became steeper still. He was forced to hoist his tools up the hill ahead of him, throwing them into dense beds of fern and bracken to free his hands so he could grasp sturdy branches and thick vines to assist his ascent. The ground was slippery and intersected by knotted roots and sticky clumps of rotting leaves. Catching his boot beneath a tangle of undergrowth, he slipped and landed heavily on his knees, scrabbling with his fingers to find purchase in the soft, friable earth. He leant against a tree trunk and caught his breath, chest heaving.

From the dizzying height, he looked back down to where he had left the jeep. Far below, the late afternoon sunlight glittered off the Aegean Sea. The indistinct outline of the island of Lesvos hovered in the misty haze. He unclipped his canteen from his belt, unscrewed the lid and took a deep swig of water as he measured his progress. Ahead, as the bald peak of the mountain grew closer, the dense forest was thinning.

Resuming his laborious progress up the path, he began to discern forms in a small, flat clearing ahead; the straight lines and geometric silhouettes were unmistakably man-made. The slope below the clearing had eroded so much he had to negotiate a vertical climb up to what appeared to be the edge of a course of flat paving stones. He clambered up the incline, levering his weight against tree trunks and branches, and heaving himself up towards the pavement. With a herculean effort he hefted his tools up and over the lip of the platform and gripped the edge with his fingers, boots kicking and feeling around blindly until he found two rocks embedded in the dirt wall that he could use to propel his weight up and over onto the paving. He landed heavily on his aching knees.

Standing on unsteady feet, he found himself at the edge of an open paved courtyard extending about sixty by thirty feet into the clearing. There was no doubt at all that it was a sanctuary – an ancient religious precinct. Running around its external perimeter was a continuous row of thick stone slabs that seemed to serve as a retaining wall to buttress against the encroaching mountainside. Immediately ahead was a raised stone plinth placed along the courtyard's central axis about twenty feet from the platform's edge. Ben walked over to it and ran his hand across its pitted surface. The elements had not been kind to the altar, but fragments of what would have been an ornately worked lip along its edge remained. On its top, two worn stubs were all that was left of twin horns of consecration – upright stone arcs that mimicked bulls' horns and were a typical feature of Mycenaean altars. At the centre of the otherwise flat surface, pine needles had accumulated in a shallow circular depression about twelve inches in diameter and an inch deep, which would have been used to collect blood flowing from the necks of sacrificial animals. A curious feature was the deep channel that ran from the depression across the top of the altar and down its side, terminating at the marble slab upon which the stone plinth stood.

Ben leant against the altar and considered his options. The sun was now well below the tree line, its golden light blinding against the shimmering shale on Mount Ida's summit. The tall pines at the edge of the platform cast long shadows across the wide expanse of marble paving. Leaving now was out of the question. And the thought of clambering back down to his jeep for the night, only to have to confront the climb again tomorrow morning, was less than appealing.

*Lucky I packed the ouzo*, he thought to himself. It was going to be a long night.

As the lavender light of dusk dimmed, the forest came alive with scuttling sounds as creatures scrabbled through the undergrowth. The sound of wolves baying a little too close for comfort was a reminder that not all Turkish fauna was benign. Taking the revolver from his satchel, Ben flipped the cylinder open, double-checking it was loaded.

He placed the weapon on a narrow stone ledge within arm's reach next to the mattress of pine needles gathered on the stone pavement that would serve as his bed for the night.

The mountain air was crisp and clean, and the sky so clear it seemed he could see every crater on the moon's pearly pockmarked face as it rose above the tops of the trees. Its strange light was so bright that it cast sinuous shadows across the forest floor. The orange glow of the fire he had coaxed to life within a small ring of stones flickered, illuminating the crumbling ruins around him.

He had eaten a filling but unsatisfying tin of bully beef for dinner, and chased it down with most of the contents of his hipflask. He stretched his legs out by the fire, hooked his hands together behind his head and tried to relax. For a time in his life, most nights had been like this. The smell of the pine forest, the crackling campfire and the soaring dome of the night sky overhead recalled the mountains of Crete. But missing were the grunts and snores of his comrades settling in to sleep in the fire's lee, and the coughing and murmurs of men assigned watch as they scanned the tree line and shared stories of love and war. Most of all, he missed Karina at his side, curled beneath the blanket with him, her fingers entwined in his. On this lonely mountain, his only companions were ghosts.

In the moonlight, Ben saw the trees further down the mountain begin to sway as a light breeze drifted up the slopes from the plains below. In the surrounding forest, branches began to creak and rub together and leaves rustled as the sea winds reached the summit.

At the same time, a low and menacing moan sounded from the tree line to his east, then petered out to almost nothing. He started. 'What the *hell?*' he exclaimed.

From the opposite side of the sanctuary another, deeper cry sounded out. It lifted in pitch and swelled, then died out abruptly.

Ben leapt to his feet and grabbed the gun in one hand and his torch in the other, slowly panning the torchlight across the sanctuary. 'Who's there?' He knew it was a pointless entreaty.

Another ominous growl came from the east.

'Screw that!'

He cocked his gun and ran full pelt towards the source of the noise. As he burst through the tree line, he narrowly avoided colliding with a marble column. Realisation dawned.

*Well, that explains Mehmet's tall tales about the jinns in the trees*, he thought to himself. The column was a marvel. Many thousands of years ago someone had carved the stone and pierced it like a musical instrument so that it caught the wind as it blew. The craftsman who had made it had carved a series of holes on other angles so that it would catch the wind regardless of its direction. Although the stone was eroded and worn, it still worked despite the passage of thousands of years.

*They sure went to a lot of trouble to discourage people from coming here*, he thought to himself. *It's the perfect way to keep curious neighbours away. Start a rumour that a place is haunted.* He knew no one would bother going to that amount of trouble unless they had something to hide.

Stretching out beside the fire, he tried to relax. His was a restless mind; the only sure-fire technique he had found to quiet the tumult within was to addle his brain with alcohol.

When compelled to abstain, his thoughts turned to a raft of things best forgotten.

So many ghosts.

As he closed his eyes against the dizzyingly expansive night sky, the wind began to blow and the moans and groans from the ancient musical devices picked up again. As he drifted off to sleep, Ben imagined them a chorus of those he had wronged and those he had lost.

# 23

## Crete, Greece, 1944

S taccato flashes of light from just above the horizon line signalled the impending arrival of the motor launch.

The radio operator translated the sequence of dots and dashes in his notebook. 'They'll be here in five minutes, sir.'

'Thank you.'

A shadowy cluster of figures waited on the shoreline at Will's side. The grievously injured Englishman lay prone on the makeshift stretcher they had fashioned from olive branches bound with torn strips of canvas. He wasn't moving, but even above the loud hiss of waves on the pebble beach Ben could hear his ragged breathing.

At his approach, Karina moved to Ben's side. 'He has a fever.' She took her husband's hand in hers and squeezed it. 'And the wound?' she whispered. 'It has begun to smell of death. I don't know else what to do. I am afraid . . .'

'You have done your best, my love. He'll be off this beach and under medical care soon enough,' he reassured her.

An accented voice came from the shadows. 'Your friend will lose that limb. And given the sepsis, he's unlikely to live. I can smell his leg from here.' Josef Garvé, cuffs tightly secured behind his back, stood awkwardly at attention with the barrel of Yanni's gun jammed into his ribs.

'Shut your trap, filth,' snarled Ben. 'He doesn't need to hear that from you.'

Garvé continued. 'Look at his eyes. He does not hear a thing. He currently resides in a nowhere land untroubled by human voices. Pain does the most extraordinary things to a man's mind.'

Ben grabbed Garvé's shoulder and dragged him down the beach away from Will.

'I said . . . Shut!' cuffing the Frenchman sharply across one ear, 'Up.' And the other.

Ben fixed his gaze on the distant horizon, watching as the silhouette of the landing vessel moved through the water, a white wake at its prow. *All I have to do is control myself for two more minutes*, he counselled himself. Two more minutes and he'll be someone else's problem.

'Poor man. You don't understand, do you?' Baleful eyes fixed on Ben's face. 'They won't imprison me. My connections – those in your army who are indebted to me – are too powerful. I'll feed your superiors a bit of useless information about the German plans and they'll let me go. You know – all you have achieved here is to waste time. And lives.'

Ben tightened his grip on the locked cuffs behind Garvé's back, fighting the impulse to shove him face first into the sand. 'No. That's where you're wrong. Serving you up to the tender mercies of military intelligence is worth it.'

'You don't regret your brother-in-law's death, then?' His eyebrows arched sceptically as he looked towards Karina where she knelt in the sand beside Will. 'You are more ruthless than I suspected. What of your wife? What of Karina? Would it be worth *her* life?'

Ben jerked Garvé's wrists towards his spine, straining his shoulders against their sockets. The Frenchman winced and inhaled sharply, pain washing yellow across his pale skin.

'Don't you mention her name! Don't you even *think* her name!'

Through thin lips drawn tight across teeth pressed together in agony, Garvé continued to speak, a viper's hiss. 'It is good that you convinced her to leave with you. There is a lieutenant in Heraklion – Schubert. Torture is to him what music was to Mozart. There is no boundary he will not cross. And if you had left your Karina there, I would have got him word . . .'

Ben silenced him with a fist. He slammed Garvé's mouth with such force that he scraped his knuckles raw on the Frenchman's front teeth as they popped through his lips. Hot blood pounding in his eardrums, he drew back and pummelled Garvé again. Ben felt the cartilage shatter in Garvé's nose. A geyser of blood gushed from his nostrils and splattered onto the ground in a lurid vermilion fountain.

Garvé's face was a gruesome mask of gore. He spat on the ground, a bubbly mess of blood and spittle coagulating on the sand. 'As I was saying. Schubert. He will be looking for me. And for that idiot Volmer. If he found your Karina . . .'

Ben turned and called his comrade, afraid of what he might do next. 'Yanni! Yanni!'

'. . . he would introduce her to such pure pain. He would have his men take her. Over and over and over again. I've seen it before. Hours – no, days – of violation. She would die with your name on her lips and a German cock inside her. She would betray you. They all do. Would *that* be worth it?'

When Yanni had taken charge of the Frenchman, Ben stumbled down the beach away from the pool of light cast by the fighters' torches. In the heavens above, the stars shone like beacons. His breath came in shuddering gasps.

'Do you feel better now?' He felt Karina's arms encircle his waist. 'You shouldn't feel bad, my love. It's no more than he deserved. If it had been me, I would have broken his legs as well as his nose.'

'Feel bad? Not likely. He has a whole lot more than that coming to him.' He took her in his arms, and the turmoil in his soul quietened. 'Please promise me you'll stay away from him. That man is poison. You'll go to Alexandria on the frigate. It's a bigger ship – you'll be safer. I'll go with Garvé on the launch. I don't want you anywhere near him.'

She rested her head on his chest. 'And we will meet at the base of the famous lighthouse of Alexandria, one of the seven wonders of the world. I have always wanted to see it.'

'I've got some bad news, *ζωή μου*. It's long gone.'

'Then you will have to find some other way to entertain me.'

He pressed his face into her hair. 'I'm sure I'll be able to work something out.'

It was always expected that the launch would cover the distance between Crete and Alexandria faster than the larger frigate. It was only when the new day dawned and its berth at the docks remained empty that Ben began to worry. News of the vessel's fate reached him as he kept vigil by Will's bedside.

The HMS *Defiant* had been attacked by two German torpedo boats just ten nautical miles from the Cretan coast. The crew and passengers escaped the sinking ship in life rafts and were taken into custody.

As soon as he heard of his wife's capture, Ben sought passage back to the island, determined to find her and free her but terrified of what he might find when he arrived.

The lights of Asos shone like fireflies in the mist-shrouded valley as Ben descended from the craggy mountains. Grim portent weighed heavily in his chest. Even before he crossed the threshold of their home, he knew he was too late.

Her family had laid her body out upon their marital bed, her white shirt torn and bloodied from the volley of bullets shot by the firing squad. Livid bruises and welts stood out against her ashen skin. 'She told them nothing! So she was no use to them,' her grandmother sobbed, spindly fingers digging into Ben's back as she sought his embrace. 'When they tired of her, they murdered her.'

His knees gave way and he caught himself on the side of the bed, grabbing at Karina's arms, her face, her legs. Where once he knew silken skin and the warmth of her breath he found the chill and unyielding pallor of death. An animal keening filled the room, piercing and fearsome. He watched himself from above, his beastly cry carrying him above the heads of Karina's family as they clutched at each other and wept.

'Those demons – they slayed two souls.' Reaching for him, stroking his hair, γιαγιά wailed. 'She didn't want to tell you yet – it was not yet three months. But she was to give you a child.' She crossed herself, murmured a prayer beneath her breath.

A child. His child. He dropped his head forward into the crook of Karina's neck and felt the tendrils of her hair feather against his face. He remembered nothing after.

He buried her in the snowy white gown she had worn on their wedding day. Her grandmother returned the tiered golden necklace he had given Karina when they were courting and he fastened it around her neck. He kissed lips as cold as granite and laid his hand upon her belly to farewell the tiny being he would never know – never hold in his arms. Twirling his fingers in her hair, now groomed and picked clean of the tangles and burrs of war, he lifted it to his face to breathe in her essence for the last time.

As her coffin was lowered into the stony ground beneath an achingly perfect Aegean sky, he knew what it was to be broken.

Grief was replaced by a white-hot fury that carried him up into the labyrinthine ravines and cave systems that peppered the mountains like honeycomb, where Dimitri and his fighters had managed to keep General Volmer hidden, despite the Germans' best efforts to retrieve their commander.

His comrades said nothing as Ben affixed chains to the German's legs and dragged him behind Karina's tractor along stony mountain roads until it was impossible to distinguish shreds of uniform from torn ribbons of flesh. He went under cover of dark to the wishing tree outside Asos and hung the German's scourged and naked body among the strips of linen and cotton.

Over the months that followed, Benedict Hitchens became a blight on the German occupation. Fearing for Karina's family and his other kinsmen, he made sure the women and youngest children left the village to join their men in the mountains. The old men and young boys stayed in Asos to care for the livestock. Nobody thought the Germans would visit revenge upon the innocent. But they were wrong.

When the Nazis learnt of Ben's connection with Asos, they slaughtered its remaining inhabitants and razed the village to the ground. All it did was stoke his fury. His cruelty and ruthlessness became legend and a bounty was put on his head. It achieved nothing.

His comrades regarded him with equal measures of awe and fear. They gave him a name – Abaddon. The Angel of the Abyss. The Destroyer.

As Josef Garvé had predicted, he was subjected to little more than a cursory interrogation once he arrived in Alexandria. Shadowy operatives interrupted the interview and passed on an unequivocal command from the highest levels of government to release the Frenchman without further delay. Word found its way to Ben in the mountains and his anger knew no bounds. He vowed vengeance.

The story of Ben and his comrades' daring capture of a German general seized public imagination at a time when morale, dampened by war fatigue, was in desperate need of a boost. For that alone, the British Army deemed the operation an outstanding success.

After the war, Ben left the island and never returned.

# 24

'Where have you been?'

'There was nothing to report. We spoke to the villagers in Zeytinli. He spent the night up at the sanctuary.'

'You're certain?'

'Yes . . . well, as certain as I can be without going up there to check for myself.'

'There's no other way down off the mountain?'

'Not if the village *mukhtar* is to be believed. One way up, one way down. We've parked ourselves in the village square. There's no getting past us.'

'You'd better be right. We can't afford to lose him.'

# 25

## Mount Ida, Turkey, 1955

The sky began to blush with a rosy glow as the sun rose in the east behind the steep mountain peak.

Ben started awake from a troubled sleep. The marble beneath his back was deathly cold and dawn mist had settled upon his skin and clothes. The nightmares had been particularly vivid, whether as a symptom of Ben's sobriety or Eris' shock reappearance, or revival of his grief about Karina, he couldn't be certain.

He had worked so hard at pushing his memories of Crete deep into the impenetrable fog of his subconscious that he was surprised by the aching sorrow that caused him to wake with tears upon his cheeks. He seldom allowed himself to think of her. Since the war ended he had sent whatever money he could afford to Karina's remaining family. But he never included a return address and so he couldn't be sure whether or not they received it. At first he sent it thinking that it might be used to tend her grave. But now he wasn't even sure why he bothered.

Rolling onto a stiff hip with bones creaking with cold, he groaned and heaved himself up into a sitting position. He cut a hunk out of a loaf of bread and smeared it with a layer of honey. Stoking the fire into life, he poured some water and tea leaves into a bucket and placed it on the coals to boil.

Birds chirruped in the trees, heralding the arrival of the sun.

He warmed his hands on the tin mug. A shudder ran along his spine as a breeze picked up and tickled his skin. The ghostly sentinels in the forest resumed their eerie anthem and broke into his melancholy reverie.

He had a great deal of ground to cover, and he was running out of time. If Eris was to be believed, there would be a gang of criminals breathing down his neck before he knew it. He also hadn't forgotten his old friend, Hasan Demir, who was sure to have been notified as soon as he crossed the Turkish border. It wouldn't take any of them very long to track him down. Anyone arriving in Zeytinli would be told the story of the crazy American who had spent the night at Zeus' altar.

With a heart still weighed down by his nocturnal apparitions, he drained his cup, stood up, and brushed the seat of his pants.

No point putting it off any longer.

# 26

## Mount Ida, Turkey, 1955

The morning passed slowly as Ben scoured the mountainside, crisscrossing the surface in a grid-like formation with his eyes fixed on the ground, looking for hints of subterranean structures.

It was a painstaking and frustrating exercise. He saw nothing of note other than surface finds of broken pottery and finely worked stone tools that only confirmed what he already knew: that Mycenaeans had built this sanctuary over three thousand years ago. Yes, it showed they had been here – within spitting distance of the walls of Troy – at the time the Achaeans came to these shores from Hellenic lands and laid siege to King Priam's city. That was groundbreaking historical evidence in itself. It was also testament to Turkey's rich cultural heritage that no other archaeologist had bothered to look closely enough at the site to discover what Ben had found in a matter of hours. But that wasn't why he was here. He was searching for a much bigger prize.

As he scoured Mount Ida's slopes he found nothing to suggest that an entrance to a tomb had been carved into the mountainside. The only man-made structures he had found since he arrived were the sanctuary itself and the monumental Cyclopean wall he'd discovered the day before. Desperate to see whether the wall was more important than he'd initially thought, he scrambled down the slippery sides of the summit and circumnavigated it at the same elevation as the forti-fications. As far as he could tell, the wall continued all the way around the peak. But it seemed to run in an uninter-rupted ring around the mountain without any distinguishing features or breaks that might have suggested an entranceway.

He cursed as he slipped yet again on the loose tumble of shale cascading down the mountain slope. The knees of his pants were already abraded and torn from the sharp scree. In desperation, he dropped to his hands and knees and crawled up to the sanctuary like an infant.

Breathing heavily, he sat with his back braced against one of the upright stones surrounding the sanctuary's paved area. He knew he was looking for a Mycenaean grave. That usually would mean a *tholos* tomb – the subterranean beehive burial chambers reserved for the wealthiest and most powerful corpses. But *tholoi* were conical hillocks of earth that stuck out like a proverbial sore thumb where they occurred in a flat landscape.

He took stock of his surroundings. It was possible that Achilles had been buried in a simple pit grave, but it seemed unlikely. For one thing, other than the sanctuary, there was no flat ground in which to dig a grave. And although the flat slabs of stone in the paving would be ideal capstones for a pit burial, the ancient Greeks had an exceptional sense of occasion. It was difficult to believe that they would have placed their greatest hero to rest in a simple hole in the ground.

'Think, man! Think!' He screwed his hand into a fist and smacked his forehead. He flexed his legs in frustration and pushed back with his feet on the paving, grinding his back into the flat slab of stone behind him. As he did so, it shifted with a grind and crackle.

'Christ! That moved!' Leaping to his feet, he grabbed the top edge of the stone and pressed his weight against it. With an almighty heave, he dragged the slab away from its foundations. It dislodged and tumbled backwards, then crashed onto the paving with a smash, shattering into pieces.

On his hands and knees, Ben scuttled over to the gap left in the row of stones by the dislodged slab.

Nothing. There was nothing behind it other than a densely packed mass of the same shale that covered the entire mountain.

'Dammit!' he cursed, and kicked at the packed scree. Loosened, a torrent of tiny stone chips cascaded onto the pavement with a sound like wind blowing through a stand of bamboo. Disheartened and frustrated, he grabbed a handful of the stones and flung them into the forest.

As he saw them flying through the air, another, more rational, corner of his mind was at work. *Those pieces of stone are too regular . . . too small to occur in such volume in nature*, he thought to himself. *And the scatter shouldn't be that deep. It's a mountain.* There should have been solid stone or earth underneath the loose fragments. Not *more* pieces of broken stone.

He looked up at the domed summit of Mount Ida.
*Surely not.*
He bent and picked up some of the loose stones.

The scree covering the mountain's slopes was not natural. It was man-made: chips of stone – rubble – left over from a monumental construction. And that rubble formed an immense, conical mound. A mountain-sized mound.

He had been looking for man-made constructions *on* the mountain. But it was the mountain itself – the entire summit – that was man-made.

The portent of his discovery struck him like a sledge-hammer. He leapt into the air, punching at the sky with upraised fists. 'Jesus H. Goddamned Christ!' he shrieked.

The tomb wasn't *on* Mount Ida. The mountain *was* the tomb.

Ben's euphoria waned as he began to contemplate the complexity of the task that lay before him. It was one thing to find Achilles' beehive tomb. It was another thing altogether to get into it.

Once more he navigated the steep sides of the *tholos*. Now that he knew what he was looking for, he thought it might make it easier to pinpoint the features that would reveal a hidden entrance.

*No such luck*, he thought to himself as he completed his survey.

'Right. What now?' he asked nobody in particular.

Figuring he might as well start at the beginning, he sat on the pavement and dragged his satchel towards him. Carefully folded inside his notebook was the transcribed inscription from the tablet. He drew it out, opened it and read it again. Much of it was descriptive, directing the reader to Mount Ida. He focused on the words that seemed to give instructions on how to find and open the tomb itself.

*. . . Fill a pitcher from the spring that runs hot from Hades' fire . . . fell tall oaks and split the beams. With the rising sun behind, set a funeral pyre below Zeus' blessed altar where the four axes meet . . . Anoint the altar with a stream of Xanthos' life-giving waters heated on the pyre . . . As the flames exalt Zeus on high, be prostrate before the fire as*

*Phoebus Apollo in his chariot rises above the horizon, his light at your back.*

Follow the instructions. Ben laughed. *Well, there's a thought. Do as I'm told. First time for everything, I guess.* It couldn't hurt, and it wouldn't be the craziest thing he'd ever done. Not by a long shot.

## 27

## Mount Ida, Turkey, 1955

Ben cleared the accumulated debris from the stone pavement to the east of the altar. He wasn't sure exactly what he was looking for, but hoped there might be evidence of an ancient hearth to indicate where he should set his fire.

The surface of the paving stones was worn and pockmarked with age; three thousand years of exposure to the elements had taken their toll. But as he slowly moved from one side of the pavement to the other, there was a distortion in the sound of his steps on the stone; on the perimeter of the paved area his tread was solid, but in the centre of the pavement the stone seemed to reverberate with each step.

*As if I were walking on something hollow*, he thought to himself, his throat constricting with excitement. *Why didn't I notice this before?*

He filled his pockets with stone fragments from the shattered slab and began to stamp across the pavement, placing a marker at the point where there was a transition from what sounded like solid ground to a cavity beneath the stones. By the time he had finished, he had delineated a long, rectangular area extending the full length of the pavement and about twenty feet wide.

He knew immediately what it was – a void. A big void beneath the stones. But how to get in there was less clear. Using the spade as a lever, he tried to loosen the paving. The stones didn't budge. They were enormous, and couldn't be shifted without mechanical means or a large crew of workers, neither of which Ben had on hand.

He vaulted onto the top of the altar to look for any irregularities in the pavement. Nothing stood out. But then, he saw it. The dull grey patch on the stone hadn't been evident at ground level. Nor were the eroded symbols carved into the pavement. But there was no missing them from an elevated height.

As he ran his hands across the ashen patch on the stone he knew it was the remains of a hearth. But what made his heart race were the symbols incised into the stone. They were indistinct and rough-edged. But they were also utterly unmistakable.

*. . . set a funeral pyre below Zeus' blessed altar where the four axes meet.*

The outline of four double-edged axes were inscribed on what looked to be the cardinal points of the compass, their heads converging on the circular area that had – at some point in time – been used as a hearth. He took his compass out of his pocket. As he guessed, the axe shafts were aligned to the north, south, east and west.

'Christ almighty. This is real.'

Ben stood, hands on hips.
What next? he wondered.

Ben sat on a fat, gnarled log he had dragged over to the paving
and watched as the flames from his pyre to Zeus licked at the
midday sky, waiting for his bucket of water to boil. It sat in
the coals at the edge of the bonfire – his proxy for the hot spring
water called for in the inscription. When the water began to
steam, he used a branch threaded beneath the handle to carry
the metal bucket over to the altar. Sweat pouring down his
forehead, he sloshed the boiling hot water into the depression
on top of the altar.

As quickly as he poured, the water ran into the narrow
channel running across the top of the altar and down its face.
But when it hit the pavement, it didn't pool and disperse
across the stones as he expected. The steaming liquid seemed
to defy physics – it simply disappeared, apparently into thin
air. Ben dropped to his knees and examined the point where
the channel met the paving; on closer inspection, the deep
groove in the altar continued below the stones. The water
had been directed in a stream to a hidden point beneath
the pavement.

He couldn't be sure whether he felt it or heard it first.
A booming metallic clang reverberated from beneath the
paving stones and a vibrato tremor rippled through the soles
of his feet.

Running back towards the fire, Ben tried to find the source
of the sound. But the ground began to tilt beneath his feet.
Impossibly, the edge of the pavement nearest to the altar was
heading skywards, and the end upon which he was standing
was plummeting downwards like a colossal seesaw.

He didn't have time to think. He slipped and began to slide down the steep gradient. Ripping his fingernails to the quick, he tore desperately at the stones. The log that had been sitting by the fire was teetering on the edge of the abyss. He grabbed at it in an attempt to slow his fall, and sharp splinters dug into his palm. The branch caught on the stone lip. For a moment, he thought he was saved. But his weight was too much for it, and as it gave way, the log joined him on his voyage into the dank depths of the mountain.

# 28

## Mount Ida, Turkey, 1955

As he slipped over the end of the tilting slab into what Ben could only imagine was a bottomless abyss, he managed to grab the stone edge. Heart pounding, his biceps burned as he supported his weight, feet kicking in empty space. A fierce knot of mortal fear burned at the back of his throat. He hazarded a look down.

Of all that was sent cascading down the slab as it tipped, one of the things he had the good fortune to avoid was the roaring fire. It was good luck rather than good management that the pyre of burning logs and coals had not ended up on his head. But now they served another, more useful, purpose. The remains of the fire were still smouldering, and they illuminated a dirt surface just inches below his dangling feet.

He released the edge of the stone slab and dropped down to the floor. As he did, the slab began to right itself with an ominous rumbling and grinding crunch of stone grating against stone. Relieved of the weight of his body, the slab was tilting back into its original position. If it swivelled shut, he would be trapped inside the mountain. Ben grabbed a smouldering beam from the floor and hefted it up into the gap between the stone slab and the surface pavement, burning his fingers and singeing the hairs on his arms. He rammed the log into place near the pivot. It was enough to stop the stone swinging shut.

The first thing he needed to do was disarm whatever it was that had held the stone in place for so many millennia. Edging his way past its bulk, he moved towards the end of the passageway beneath the altar.

'You clever bastards,' he murmured.

The locking mechanism set into the marble-faced back wall of the corridor was ingenious. The stone wall was a continuation of the altar on the pavement above; the deep channel along which the water had flowed ran down the wall and terminated in a narrow spout, which fed the water into a deep bronze basin suspended on four heavy chains. Ben ran his hand down the bronze rod, which was connected at one end to the chains, and at the other to a hinge on an L-shaped latch. When in place, the latch would hook into a bracket set into the edge of the slab, locking it in a horizontal position. The weight of the water in the basin caused the hinged rod to drop down and pull the latch back. It was impossible to trigger the lock from above without the weight of the water in the basin, but Ben was relieved to see that it would be easy to activate it from below if the brace he had jammed in the slab's hinge didn't hold.

He moved back down the otherwise featureless corridor towards the central axis of the stone slab. A cylindrical stone beam extended across the underside of the paving. It rested in a U-shaped stone channel running horizontally from one wall to the other like a door's hinge. He took his torch from his pocket and shone it on the pivot stone.

*What the hell?* he wondered.

The stone glistened in the torchlight. He reached out and touched it, and was surprised to find the surface warm and tacky. The entire beam was coated in a thick layer of something warm, sticky and gummy.

*And it's right below where I was instructed to light my fire.* Ben laughed and exclaimed out loud. 'I'll say it again . . . you clever, clever bastards.'

The fire had warmed and softened the adhesive, loosening what would otherwise have been a fairly firm grip on the pivot, while the water had triggered the latch mechanism and allowed the entire slab to tilt. Ben knew that if he had been following his instructions to the letter, he would have been 'praying' and prostrate on the eastern end of the slab, which would have resulted in a much less perilous descent.

Flicking the switch of the torch hanging from his belt, he examined his surroundings. The corridor was long and, beyond the patch of light that shone through the gap onto the dusty floor below, pitch black. He gathered his satchel and tools from the floor where they had fallen, looped the rope across his body and strapped the spade and pick to his back.

The air in the corridor was cloyingly cool and full of the musty smell of earth and stale things. The passage into the artificial mountain was relatively spacious. The walls of the corridor were made of the same monolithic irregular stones used in the wall running around the base of the *tholos*. Ben plotted the layout of the tomb in his mind's eye – the wall he'd found in the forest must have been a retaining fortification at the base of the mound to contain the mountain of debris piled on top of the burial chamber.

As he moved carefully along the passage, the torchlight picked out two indistinct forms on the otherwise feature-less floor. He moved closer. A shock of recognition caused him to start. He was looking at two small human skeletons, their bare bones blindingly white in the torchlight. Both lay on their side in the foetal position, their remains bearing no obvious signs of violence.

He knew right away. The missing shepherd boys from Zeytinli. *A wet night . . . they light a fire on the wrong spot . . . rainwater runs down the altar into the basin. You poor bastards*, he thought.

As he continued to move along the otherwise empty corridor, he scanned the floor and surface of the walls for any clues about what might lay ahead. He was disheartened but not altogether surprised to see that the corridor terminated at a blank wall.

'Damn.'

He took a step forward. A deafening crack sounded beneath his feet. He threw himself back onto the floor. Landing awkwardly, the surface he had been standing on disintegrated and disappeared. He flipped over and shimmied away from the collapsing floor on his belly like a serpent. A cloud of dust filled the air. As the murky billow of debris descended upon him, he buried his mouth and eyes in the crook of his elbow.

After what seemed an eternity, the thunderous roar of collapsing stone and wood abated. Where once there had been solid floor, now a gaping void at least fifteen feet wide ran across the entire corridor from one wall to the other. Crawling warily towards its edge, he shone his light down into the cavity. His first thought was that it was a trap engineered to foil any potential grave robbers. But the beams of timber that underpinned the floor had been substantial. By the look of the stubs that remained, they hadn't been made to collapse. It looked as if age, burrowing grubs and damp had weakened them. He picked up a pebble and tossed it into space. The faint echo when it landed – a disturbingly long time after it was dispatched – was chilling.

The end of the corridor was tantalisingly close across the void. Ben had no choice. He had to find a way to get across.

He examined the wall. It wouldn't be easy, and mountaineering had never been his forte, but there were enough deep gaps between the stones to serve as foot and hand-holds. If his luck held out, he'd be able to scale the vertical face to the other side of the man-made ravine.

Securing one end of the rope around the pivot stone beneath the paving slab, he tested his weight against it and tied it firmly beneath his armpits. The anchor seemed strong enough. The first few feet across the ominous black void were easy. There was no shortage of places to wedge the toes of his boots, and the stones were irregular enough that he could force his fingers into the crevices between them. *Walk in the park*, he assured himself nervously.

His confidence was short-lived. Just beyond the point of no return, the muscles in his arms and legs began to scream. His shoulders and biceps burned with such intensity it felt as if acid was pumping through his veins. His calves and thighs began to convulse. As he inched across the wall and moved closer to the other side of the chasm, he relaxed slightly and dropped his weight back to give his arms some relief. With the shift in momentum, his left hand slipped. He scrabbled to get a grip on the friable surface. As he floundered, he made the mistake of looking down between his splayed legs. The dire black chasm and the horror of falling into the void set his heart thumping. A burst of adrenalin surged through his veins. Fear pushed him forward. But his mind stalled. A wave of crippling dread rose deep inside his chest. He clung to the wall like a limpet. He was finished.

But then he heard her voice.

*No, Ben. Not like this. Not today.*

Karina.

Smashing through the terror he pressed forward. He moved spider-like across the stones. When he was within reach of the other side of the chasm, he propelled himself off the wall and collapsed onto the floor.

He landed on the hard, stone surface face first. For a moment, he lay there in the dirt, panting like a marathon runner. The air was stale and dusty. But he was alive.

Raising himself up on shaky legs, he shone his torch towards the blank stone wall at the end of the passageway. At first glance it was exactly the same as the three other wall surfaces in the subterranean corridor.

*That's peculiar*, Ben thought as he panned the torchlight across the wall's surface.

The rocks that made up the walls on either side of the passageway were rough-edged. But the stones at the short end were quite different. He ran his hands across them. Although from a distance the stones had looked similar, the surface here was smooth – it almost looked as if they had been polished. The gaps between the boulders were barely wide enough to slip a sheet of paper through, unlike the mortar lines between the stones in the rest of the passage, which had been wide enough to accommodate his fingers and the toes of his boots.

He tapped the stone with the end of his torch. The boulder rang with an unmistakable hollow clang. It was another decoy. Like the pavement in the sanctuary above, there was a hidden cavity behind it.

Running his hands around its perimeter, he searched for a latch or trigger of some sort to open the false wall. Nothing.

The clock was ticking. He had to find the tomb, and he had to move fast. If it was behind the stone slab, there was only one way through.

He unstrapped his pick from his back, hefted it above his head and went to work.

# 29

'Any movement?'
        'Not yet.'

'You're sure he hasn't found another way down from the mountain?'

'Positive.'

'I'm concerned about the others. Have you seen anyone else since you've been there?'

'No. I would have noticed. There aren't many places to hide. Trust me.'

'What about the Greek police?'

'Not that I've heard. But then again, I wouldn't, would I?'

'Speak to me like that again and I'll make sure you regret it.'

'I apologise.'

'Don't bother. Just do your job. I want to make sure we're the only ones with a horse in this race.'

'Trust me. I've got it under control.'

'We'll see about that. In the meantime, I'm on my way.'

'You're coming here? But I thought . . .'

'I'm not paying you to think.'

# 30

## Mount Ida, Turkey, 1955

The dust cleared and the deafening clangour of his pick smashing into the rock subsided, leaving a ringing in Ben's ears. He inspected his handiwork. If the wall had been made with boulders as big as those used in the retaining wall at the base of the *tholos*, it would have been impossible to break through without TNT or a bulldozer. But he was in luck. The wall was constructed from irregularly shaped pieces of flat stone, and his blows were making an impact. At the centre of the stone panel, a starburst of fissures radiated out from a tiny hole the size of a chickpea, through which Ben could see a black void beyond.

He knew he was almost there.

Raising his pick again, he focused his energy on the small breach in the wall. Now that its integrity was compromised, progress was easier. Blow after blow and the stone began to crumble until there was a space large enough to admit the beam of light from his torch. He took a deep breath and shone his torch through the opening.

The collapse of stone onto the floor in the space beyond had cast a cloud of dust into the air. The torchlight refracted and reflected on the thick pall. He couldn't see anything.

'Dammit!' he cursed out loud.

He attacked the broken slab again. Heavy blows made his biceps burn. Hairline cracks in the stone began to widen and splinter. Discarding the pick, he leant into the fracturing wall with his shoulder. The sound of large chunks of stone falling to the floor echoed from inside the chamber. He gritted his teeth and pressed against it with all his might. There was a slight shift and his boots slipped on the dusty floor. Suddenly, the stone broke into myriad fragments with a bone-crunching crack. It exploded inwards, carrying him with it. He curled into a ball and tucked his head against his chest defensively, rolling across the shattered stone as sharp-edged fragments ripped into his back and hips.

The air was thick with dust; it chafed his lungs and made him cough uncontrollably. Covering his mouth with his sleeve, he lifted himself up onto his elbows and shone his torch into the gloom. As the dust began to settle, forms started to take shape.

He held his breath.

## 31

## Mount Ida, Turkey, 1955

He couldn't believe his eyes.

Soaring above Ben's head was the monumental Mycenaean edifice he had imagined in his dreams. Over three thousand years ago, massive blocks of stone had been carefully and painstakingly assembled to create a beehive-shaped dome. It was a masterpiece of design and engineering.

At the centre of the circular room was an elaborately carved rectangular platform large enough to contain an outstretched body. Circular plinths were arranged around the perimeter of the tomb. But they were empty.

His heart seemed to stop in his chest. A wave of disappointment and disbelief smashed into him and left him hollow and floundering. Disbelieving, he stumbled over to the platform and rapped its side to see if it had any hidden secrets. Nothing. It was solid to the core. Whatever had been placed in the tomb was long gone – most likely looted soon after the *tholos* was sealed.

'Goddammit!' He kicked at the loose fragments of stone about his feet.

At the sound of rumbling from above, his blood ran cold. A chunk of stone the size of a football crashed to the ground just to his left. The hairs on the back of his neck stood on end. A large slab landed on the floor a foot from where he stood and broke into a volley of razor-sharp fragments that barrelled into the leg of his pants like shotgun pellets.

He scrambled back towards the jagged-edged hole in the wall. A sinister creaking and groaning filled the chamber. Tripping across the fallen stone, he struggled towards the corridor outside.

The engineering of the stone-lined tomb meant that each and every piece of rock performed an important structural function. The beehive design had been chosen to evenly distribute the phenomenal weight of the stones across a carefully aligned network. The removal of a single stone – such as the one he had whacked out to gain entrance to the sepulchre – had a domino effect that could send all the other stones tumbling.

And that was exactly what was happening. In the tomb chamber, the ceiling began to collapse at an exponential rate. The shriek and shatter of stone fracturing on stone was deafening. He ducked and weaved to escape the deadly deluge. As the massive capstone plummeted to earth it exploded on the central plinth. Ben dived for the tomb's opening just as a rain of murderous stone fragments flew through the air.

Throwing himself through the entrance, he ran for the black void in the centre of the corridor. He leapt into space. Arms extended, he dived forward and smashed into the opposite side of the pit. Bracing himself, he anticipated the wrenching tear when the rope around his chest reached its full extension. A thick cloud of airborne debris pursued him down the shaft. Gratingly sharp pieces of dirt filled his mouth and lungs. He grabbed blindly for a handhold as he plummeted into the depths of the mountain. Finding the rope, he wrapped it around his wrist and clamped it in his fist. When he reached the end of the rope and his freefall was broken, the rope was torn from his hands, ripping skin and flesh. The loop around his chest snapped tight and constricted his lungs. It burned like a branding iron across his back and beneath his arms.

He dangled in open space like a hanged man. The detritus from the collapsing tomb continued to billow down the shaft. Despite the strain, the bowlines connecting him to the beam above held tight.

Squinting against the dust, he looked for the dim patch of light shining far above his head. The puzzle of why the tension on the rope hadn't sent him smashing into the wall according to the laws of centrifugal force was easily answered. As he had jumped, the rope had hooked itself around the butt-end of one of the beams that had supported the collapsed pavement. So now he was suspended in the centre of the shaft like a pendulum.

By his estimation he had fallen about thirty feet down into the void. The rivulets of sweat that had saturated his hair and the back of his shirt while he swung the pick now ran cold. He shivered uncontrollably, chilled to the bone and in shock. In the pit it was pitch black and the air was clammy and frigid. The oppressive weight of the mountain above made the space feel more constricted than it actually was.

Ben's heart began to race. He tried to reach for the torch clipped to his waistband. It wasn't easy. The excruciatingly tight makeshift harness ripped into his armpits and constrained his movements. But the thought of the black nothingness beneath him made him grateful for its painful embrace. With a monumental effort he managed to get his hand down to his belt, where he fumbled with the torch, eventually getting a grip around its shaft. He switched it on, relieved to find it still working.

It hurt to laugh. 'It's not *all* bad news, then.'

The feeble torchlight illuminated the walls of the chasm. The stones used to line the pit were virtually un-worked. There were plenty of crevices and small ledges he could use to clamber back up to the surface. Spinning around, he inspected the four walls to determine which offered the best way out.

The one thing on his mind was escape, so at first he thought his eyes were playing tricks on him. But as the swirling plumes of dust began to clear, he knew he wasn't imagining things. He pedalled his legs in the air to keep himself facing the eastern wall – the wall located immediately below the empty tomb above.

*It can't be*, he marvelled. Every nerve in his body tingled. The portent of what he was looking at was almost beyond comprehension.

There was no mistaking the twin lions rampant. Set back inside a shallow recess was a monumental, near-perfect replica of the great Lion Gate on the citadel of Mycenae. But unlike the edifice on the Greek mainland, the stone here had not been exposed to the elements. The carving was pristine. The extraordinary realism achieved by the ancient sculptor was remarkable; the two figures stood proudly on the gate's pediment, sinuous tendons and ropey muscles glistening.

He dropped his torch back to his side and began to swing his legs back and forth. As he built momentum, he stretched his arms as far as he could, grasping for the lower edge of the niche. When it was within reach, he dug his fingertips into the rough-edged stone lip. Jamming his feet into a narrow crevice in the wall, he halted his pendulum-like swinging and heaved himself over the edge and into the alcove.

The lintel of the massive double stone gates was at least ten feet above the threshold, and the twin lions loomed above that inside a triangular pediment. What he saw at the apex made him smile. *Well, that answers that question, anyway*, he thought to himself. Not for the first time in his life he wished for a camera.

The lions in the famed Mycenaean gate had lost their heads in antiquity and for decades archaeologists had debated what the sculptures would have looked like intact. He now had the answer. The twin creatures were sphinxes, with lions' bodies and human heads.

Untying the rope from his waist and jamming it between two stones on the ledge, he moved tentatively towards the immense stone doors. His nerves were frayed. The ground felt solid, and there was nothing to make him suspect there might be a trap. But he wasn't going to take any chances.

His skin prickled in the frigid air. The flat stone surface of the double doors was cold and waxy. Ever the optimist, he pushed, hoping they might yield. But the doors showed no sign of giving way, and with his pick buried under tons of collapsed rubble above his head, his options for getting the door open were limited. He reached for his knife.

If the doors were held shut by a basic latch, it would be a simple task to trigger it. He slid the blade into the crack between the two doors and ran it up the join until it encountered a hidden obstacle on the other side. He then ran the blade downwards until it met the top of the obstruction. At four inches wide, it was too broad to be a latch.

*Dammit!* he cursed to himself. *They've bloody well barred it shut.*

As he poked at the obstacle with his blade, the tip of his knife embedded itself into the hidden beam.

*Wood.* He sighed, relieved. *It's wood. Thank Christ.*

Unstrapping his entrenching tool from his back, he made a silent prayer that its flat spade would be thin enough to work its way through the chink between the two doors. There was no way he could exert enough force with the knife to budge the beam. But with the spade's heftier gauge, it might just be possible.

The end of the shovel slipped into the breach. He tackled the beam from below on the assumption it was held in place by brackets on the other side of the door. As he yanked the shovel up, he felt a slight movement, but it wasn't even close to being enough to shift the beam entirely.

Presuming the wood would be in a similarly decomposed state as the framework of floor joists that had given way above, he changed tack. Shifting his shovel to a point above his head, he jammed it through the gap and brought it crashing down on top of the beam. A splintering thud sounded through the doors. He lifted the spade and slammed it down again. The ancient timber groaned and creaked. Once more, he smashed the shovel down. This time, the metal end wedged firmly into the wood. He rocked the blade back and forth through the gap, weakening the decaying timber. He pulled the shovel back and started slamming it into the beam from the outside. With a final moan of protest, the wood gave way.

The immense double door swung inward, emitting a draft of deathly cold, stale air. Ben leant into the massive stone panels with his shoulder and pushed them open, gritting his teeth at the grating sound of stone grinding on stone as the doors swivelled on their pivots.

The space on the other side of the entrance was as black as tar. He stepped across the threshold and raised his torch. A featureless stone corridor led to another gateway, but as far as he could see, no barrier blocked the entrance. The oppressive gloom seemed to sap the torchlight as it travelled down the long passageway. But beyond the portal, the feeble illumination caught on something. A shaft of light reflected back like a starburst. He shifted the spotlight slightly; another blinding gleam like the rays of the setting sun shot out from the space at the end of the corridor.

His throat constricted with excitement. The staccato thumping of his heart pounding in his chest drove him forward. Any concerns about potential perils in the corridor ahead were forgotten. The vast second doorway loomed above him and filled his line of sight, its simple post and beam construction decorated with elaborate geometric designs and covered in colours so vivid it looked as if the paint was still wet.

Hands shaking, he lifted his torch. When he saw what lay in the beam of light, he dropped to his knees.

## 32

**Mount Ida, Turkey, 1955**

B en couldn't be sure quite how long he knelt in the dust.
But it felt like an eternity.

A lifetime spent sifting through the soil to discover buried
civilisations amounted to nothing in the face of what lay
before him. The splendour was overwhelming. Everywhere
he looked he saw the glint of gold. It was a struggle to focus
and his hand trembled so much he had trouble directing the
torchlight. His mind seemed to be stuck on a loop. The only
words that came to mind were those uttered by Howard Carter
upon first opening Tutankhamen's tomb. His companions
had asked if he could see anything inside the sepulchre. 'Yes.
Wonderful things.'

*Wonderful things.*
*Wonderful things.*
*Wonderful things.*

The immense beehive-shaped roof was almost completely
lined with gleaming sheets of gold pressed into raised spirals

and geometric designs and embellished at intervals with rosettes the size of Ben's outstretched hand. The only break in the gold panelling was where a band running around the wall had been covered in plaster and painted with a vividly coloured narrative mural.

He knew. He had always known. Achilles was here. A man mourning a fallen comrade . . . The same man in a chariot dragging a lifeless body behind him beneath the battlements of a walled city . . . Now felled by an arrow shot by an archer high on the city walls.

*Achilles. These are scenes from Achilles' life story.*

*He is here. I have found him.*

The torchlight reflected off a multitude of shimmering gilt surfaces, filling the sepulchre with a golden glow. The massive underground vault was a storehouse for the afterlife. Three thousand years ago, the man who was laid to rest in this most noble of tombs was furnished with all he would need in the world beyond the grave. Ten circular plinths were arranged around the perimeter of the room, each covered with a bounty of golden platters and cups that would have carried the dead man's final offertory banquet. Leaning against the walls were banks of weapons and chariots, their wheel hubs clad in gold and inset with precious stones. Wooden chests sat in rows, inlaid with carved ivory lozenges worked into the forms of deer, lions and bulls galloping and gambolling in bands around the well-preserved timber panels.

A ring of immense funerary kraters was set inside the circle of offertory plinths, their surfaces painted with simplified linear likenesses of prancing horses drawing chariots, proud warriors, and goddesses with breasts bared and arms aloft. Ben had uncovered many Mycenaean vases in excavations over the years, but he had never seen a single example as colossal or as impeccably preserved as these.

He took a tentative step forward, and stumbled on something beneath his feet. Lying on the tomb's stone floor were three horse skeletons, the gilded buckles and fixtures of their bridles and harnesses shining in the dust.

*Xanthus, Balios and Pedasos?* Ben wondered to himself. Achilles' three horses. The immortal beasts, Balios and Xanthus, were gifted to Achilles' father, King Peleus, by the God of the Sea, Poseidon. When his son was departing for the Trojan War, Peleus gave them to Achilles to draw his chariot. As Homer told it, when Achilles' companion, Patroclus, was felled by Hector, the two horses stood stock-still in the heat of battle and wept.

Ben stood and raked the light further into the tomb. What appeared to be hundreds of human skeletons lay stacked upon each other in rows like a grim display of fallen dominoes, armour still clinging to their bones and shields resting on their chests. Hollow eye sockets peered out from beneath boars'-tusk helmets. The carefully regimented way they had fallen showed they had gone to their death willingly. Ben edged carefully around the remains of the men who had laid Achilles to rest in this peerless sepulchre that – once it was known to the world – would eclipse even the famed tombs of the Pharaohs.

At the centre of the room, set beneath the dome's pinnacle, a monolithic platform stood surrounded by a tier of stone steps. Its summit loomed above Ben's head and was surmounted by a massive golden bier.

He began to climb. The weighty silence in the tomb was overwhelming. Blood rushed, buzzing, in his ears as he reached the top step of the platform and directed his light across the flat top of the golden funeral bier. He held his breath. Lying in state beneath the ethereal golden dome was a man born of legend.

An electrical bolt of superstitious awe ran along his spine as he reached out and placed his hand tentatively on the masterfully crafted golden greaves covering Achilles' shins.

*'The glorious arms wrought by Hephaestus, so splendid. No man has ever worn the like on his shoulders. If I could but hide him from death's gaze when his hour is nigh, so surely as I can bequeath him armour that will astound the eyes of all those who behold it,'* he whispered beneath his breath, reciting Homer's immortal words. *'He marvelled at Achilles' strength and beauty. He was as a god to see.'*

He could think of nothing else to say.

A death mask beaten from a sheet of solid gold lay over Achilles' face. His noble, aquiline nose descended from a strong forehead above full lips, their corners turned up beatifically. The ancient craftsman had pressed into the soft metal with a fine point to fashion delicate whorls of hair in mimicry of a trimmed beard hugging a chiselled jaw and cleft chin. Resting on the bier beside Achilles' gilded skull was his helmet, wrought in solid gold, silver and bronze. Across its brow, a sphinx flew aloft, clutching in arched talons the flailing and thrashing men who had failed to answer her riddle. The breastplate encasing Achilles' chest was broad and formed to cling to the swelling muscles that once covered a ribcage of strong bones, now exposed and brittle. A fierce lioness breathed tongues of flame as she leapt, claws unsheathed, towards a muscular colt fleeing across the curved cuirass. And lying by the fallen warrior's side was his mighty sword, its broad blade wrought with golden, lofty-antlered deer, their spindly legs galloping in flight from a prince atop a surging horse, bow raised and hunting dogs baying at his side.

Resting across Achilles' midriff was the most precious object of all. His shield – the stuff of myth – was so magnificent

Ben's breath caught in his throat. On sheets of gold, silver and bronze, the maker had captured the divine cosmos and the world of men in forms so fluid and animated it truly did look to be the work of the gods. It was beyond imagination.

The shield and all it represented was too meaningful to pass into one person's hands. It should belong to everyone, and to no one. The splendour of what he had found was deeply humbling; by comparison, his – and Eris' – needs and desires were meaningless.

He placed his hand at the centre of Achilles' chest.

*'The immortals live free of care, yet the path they lay for man is wrought with sorrow.'*

# 33

'Still nothing?'
    'No.'
'Right. It's been too long. Move in. Find him. Now.'
'Consider it done.'

# 34

## Mount Ida, Turkey, 1955

For Ben, nothing would ever be the same again.

Compared to the perilous descent to the tomb, the ascent to the surface seemed effortless. The greatest hurdle he had to overcome was tearing himself away from Achilles' side. He was transfixed, and so filled with superstitious awe that he feared it would all prove to be nothing more than an apparition that would disappear once he turned his back upon it.

However, Ben was confident that if he covered his tracks and reset the seals at the entrance to the burial complex, no one else would be able to find the tomb without his help. Still, the thought of deserting this priceless bounty was almost too much to bear.

Logistics dictated that he would be hard-pressed to take anything with him other than the shield. The prospect of a vertical climb out of the shaft with a disc of solid metal strapped to his back was daunting enough. Besides which, there were a limited number of hiding places in Eris' jeep. He had escaped close scrutiny at customs in Ayvalık but knew he might not be as lucky second time around, particularly if Hasan had got word to the border.

There was one other thing he could take with him without any great risk to life or limb. Ben had never been much of a praying man, but still he murmured words of thanks and atonement as he bent and eased the great seal ring off Achilles' skeletal hand and slipped it onto his own finger.

'It's just a loan, my friend. I will return it and make sure you are paid proper homage. I promise.'

He found his way to the tomb's floor and trod carefully around the splintered bones of the men who died there. Outside the entrance, the rope that would be his way out lay where he had left it against the shaft's stone wall. He fashioned a harness to hold the shield against his back like a tortoiseshell, and began to climb.

Adrenalin no longer played havoc with his reason as he methodically found purchase in wide cracks between the masonry. Once he'd adjusted to the awkward weight of the shield, the climb was fast and easy.

In the ancient corridor beneath the sanctuary's paving stones, a shaft of light guided Ben's way as he clambered back up into the world. He heaved aside the branch that had kept the stone slab from tilting shut and triggered the devices that had kept Achilles' resting place hidden for so many years. Scattering dead leaves and pine needles across the paving and buffing away the charred patch on the stone that was all that remained of his fire, he knew all traces of his presence had been erased.

There was no doubt that the detachment he felt after he left Achilles resting atop his gilded pyre made what might have been an insurmountable task achievable. But now the prospect of returning to the world of men was both daunting and exhilarating. The evidence he had been searching for had been found. It had been a transformative experience. But at the same time, he knew what was to come – the avalanche of attention that he both relished and resented.

Ben found his way back to the jeep and navigated down the mountain on autopilot. But his senses sharpened as he drew closer to the road that would lead him through Zeytinli. Every glint on the track ahead, every unexpected movement in the dense undergrowth on either side of the road, made his nerves spark.

It was a short trip back to Molyvos, but there were plenty of things that might get in his way. And he planned to be ready for all of them.

He had no need to stop in the town. There was more than enough fuel left in the tank, and he had plenty of food and water. Given what was strapped into the false bottom of the jeep's metal tray, he planned to avoid all unnecessary pit stops.

The town's rough-hewn stone houses and pencil-like minaret appeared in the distance. Unfortunately, he knew there was no avoiding the central square. The only route back down the mountain passed through the middle of town.

*Here's hoping I've timed my arrival for afternoon prayers*, he thought to himself.

There was no way to sneak stealthily through town. The only modes of transport in Zeytinli were four-legged, and the cacophony of sound as he drove down the mountain track was as subtle as a twenty-one-gun salute. The jeep's engine roared and the chassis clunked as it clattered across the town's rough cobblestones. The clamour rebounded from wall to wall. His approach would have been audible from miles away. As women in floral headscarves peered out from around colourfully painted doors and a gaggle of barefooted children took up the charge and ran along in Ben's dusty wake, he knew any hope that he would pass through the village unnoticed was futile.

Ahead, the laneway opened out into the shady town square. Beads of sweat accumulated on his forehead. He gunned his engine. Rounding the corner he accelerated towards the road leading south. Out of the corner of his eye, he saw movement. Bolting like a jack rabbit, Mehmet crossed the square, waving his arms. Before he could escape, Ben's path was blocked. The long-limbed village chieftain stood in his way, a broad smile across his face. Ben's only choices were to mow him down or stop.

'Jesus H. Goddamned Christ,' he cursed through gritted teeth, which he bared in a forced smile. He wound down his window.

'*Bay* Ben! *Hoşgeldiniz*. It is a relief to see you have returned.'

'*Hoşbulduk*, Mehmet *Bey*. It is good to be back. It seems the jinn weren't interested in me after all.'

'I had to stop you to tell you – your friends are here. They arrived yesterday.'

His blood ran cold. 'Who do you mean, Mehmet *Bey*?'

Mehmet gestured up one of the side streets leading out of the square. 'They were just leaving to go up the mountain to meet you there. They're getting their car.'

Ben didn't wait to hear another word. He slammed the jeep into gear and jammed the accelerator to the floor. The vehicle lurched towards the other side of the square, jolting across the rough cobblestones. The sudden forward momentum whipped Ben's head back and to the side. His skull smashed into the doorjamb. Stars burst in his field of vision. He battled with the steering wheel, directing the jeep towards the narrow laneway. In the rear-view mirror he saw a grey car shooting out of one of the side streets at breakneck pace. Mehmet threw himself into a doorway out of its path.

Ben catapulted the vehicle into the lane. He slammed his fist onto the horn to clear the path ahead of him. A boy leading a donkey with a bundle of firewood strapped to its back pressed against a wall. Ben charged past as far to the right-hand side of the laneway as he dared. He winced as the side mirror was torn from its socket with a wrenching metallic screech as the jeep scraped its side along a low wall.

He looked over his shoulder. His pursuers were in a wider sedan that was too large to squeeze past the donkey. The man in the passenger's seat leant out the window, cursing at the boy. Ben manoeuvred along the crooked street like a rally-car racer, pleased to extend the distance between himself and his pursuers.

He burst out of the rough gateway marking the edge of town and sped down the steep track. He knew his respite would be short-lived. It wouldn't be hard to work out where he was headed. There was only one path down the mountain.

He could lead them a merry chase and try to backtrack along some of the other roads leading into the forest, Ben thought, mind racing. But he'd just as likely end up getting lost himself and trapped up a dead end.

An engine screamed behind him. He spun the wheel to avoid a gaping pothole in the centre of the road and didn't let up on speed as he hit a deep ditch. The jeep's worn suspension rammed the axle into the chassis. The impact slammed up his back, crunching the base of his skull against his spine.

Ben tore past the glittering pebble beach he had passed the day before, where village women scrubbed clothes on the lake shore. A row of dripping-wet young boys clambered out of their swimming hole and stood, slack-jawed, staring as he roared past them. He cursed as the steering wheel reeled to the left, wrenching his arms from their sockets. Struggling to keep control of the jeep as the front wheels eddied in a drift of gravel, the car fishtailed and slid towards a vertical drop. He turned into the skid, drawing the vehicle back into the centre of the road.

The grey car loomed in his rear-vision mirror. He mentally backtracked along the mountain road and could see only one option. The risks were incalculably high. But the men on his tail weren't going to stop. On the rough mountain tracks, his jeep had the advantage. But once they hit the open coastal road, the sleek sedan would have no trouble running him down. He had to shake them. And he had to do it now.

Ben looked through the dusty windshield. Timing was everything. A hairpin turn looped through the forest ahead. He took a deep breath and braced himself in the hard-edged metal-framed seat. As he approached the first curve, he suddenly spun the steering wheel to the left. The jeep propelled off the road and plunged into the undergrowth. He lost control of the car as it became airborne. With a crushing jolt the jeep smashed to earth and began plummeting down the mountain as he fought to avoid massive tree trunks looming in his path. He looked behind and saw that his pursuers had – as he had hoped – followed him. It was an unwise decision. As difficult as the terrain was for the jeep, it was made for rough conditions. The sedan was designed for roads.

Ahead, the forest was thinning. He braked hard. The car decelerated and he steeled himself as it shot over the low escarpment edging the mountain road below. The car landed on the gravel with a bone-shattering crash. He lifted himself from the seat to reduce the impact. His teeth came together with a crunch and he rose so high in his seat that his head hit the jeep's steel roof. The car smashed to ground on the track, and he dragged the wheel to the left.

As he tore back down the road he looked in the rear-view mirror. The driver of the grey sedan had not anticipated the road ahead, far less the river canyon beyond that. They hit the escarpment at full speed and, airborne, overshot the track. Soaring across the road, the car clipped the canyon's jagged edge and plummeted towards the watery chasm.

Ben gunned the engine and accelerated along the track. He winced at the shattering smash as the vehicle behind him impacted on the jagged rocks below.

A long line of vehicles snaked towards the waiting ferry anchored in Ayvalık, its engines churning the aquamarine water. Ben sat in the sweltering hot jeep, eyes on the coast road – watching and waiting. He knew they were gone. Most likely for good. But he didn't want to assume they were travelling alone. He had seen nothing suspicious on the road between Zeytinli and here. But that didn't make him any less apprehensive.

He was exposed and vulnerable. Yet all he could do now was wait. He sat with his elbow resting on the open window, eyes shaded by his sunglasses, tapping the blisteringly hot steering wheel with the fingertips of his other hand. His foot jiggled nervously on the accelerator pedal.

The afternoon heat was oppressive. A customs official in a tight-fitting uniform signalled vehicles and embarking passengers with brisk hand movements, dark sweat stains spreading in circles beneath his armpits. Ben held out hope that the man's desire to find his way back into the shade and drink a cool glass of *ayran* would override his attention to detail.

Ben wasn't a superstitious man, but he crossed his fingers anyway.

'*Pasaportunuzu verin lütfen.*'

'*Tabii derhal efendim. Buyrun.*'

He handed his passport to the heavily perspiring officer, who took it in his pudgy hands and flicked to the front page. With barely a glance, he stamped the passport and waved Ben through the barricade.

*That's it?* Ben marvelled, scarcely able to believe his good fortune.

*Bang!* He started, looking in the rear-view mirror. The customs official whacked the jeep's tailgate impatiently with an outstretched palm, an abrupt reminder to drive forward. Ben needed no further urging.

The ferry sounded its horn. He joined the long line of passengers and vehicles snaking towards the ramp feeding into the ferry's gaping belly. Despite the ease with which he had crossed the border, dread and anticipation put his nerves on edge. Every movement in his peripheral vision made him flinch, and every sudden sound sent a jolt up his spine. He knew he wouldn't be able to relax until the ship left port.

With a rattle and clunk, he drove onto the deck as the ferry's engines churned the bay's mirror-smooth water. A rivulet of sweat ran between his shoulder blades and his heart raced as he watched the last cars work their way up the ramp in an excruciatingly slow procession.

On shore, the Turkish officials gathered in the shade, their work done for the day. Ben stretched, raising his arms above his head to ease the tension coiled like a death adder in his chest. The crew was dashing about the deck and moving along the shoreline, loosening ropes and preparing to cast off.

*Almost there . . . almost there*, he thought to himself, the reassuring mantra repeating in his mind.

The last of the ropes was let loose and beneath the deck the engines picked up pace, setting the jeep's floor shuddering as the ferry readied to pull away from the dock. Ben began to relax. He settled back in the cracked canvas seat and shut his eyes, feeling relief for the first time in days.

A harsh cry from shore jerked Ben back to wakefulness. The ferry's engines idled and he heard the unmistakable metallic clang of the gangplank being lowered, hidden out of his sightline behind the walls of the ship's cabin.

*Oh, Christ. Not now. Not when I'm so close.*

His mind worked furiously. There was nothing he could do but wait. If someone had boarded looking for him, there was no point hiding. There was no way off the boat other than to swim. *Is that what I should do? Jump in and swim for shore?* There seemed little point. If they had boarded with the intention of finding him, there would be others on shore watching.

An unmistakable figure stepped through a doorway and Ben's heart sank. It was the rotund customs officer who had so breezily waved him through just moments before. He peered about the deck, eyes shielded from the sun by a pudgy hand. Catching sight of Ben's jeep, he extended his arm, finger pointing in his direction. He turned and addressed someone standing out of sight behind him.

The customs officer began to sidle through the passengers gathered in curious clusters on the deck. He was headed straight for the jeep.

'Shit!' Ben cursed beneath his breath. He leant over and retrieved Eris' gun from the glove box. *What the hell do you plan to do with that?* he thought to himself as he checked the barrel and tucked it into his waistband. *Getting into a gunfight – oh, yes. That's a brilliant idea.* He knew it was incautious, but the weapon lent him a sheen of bravado.

The officer stood at the driver's window. During their previous encounter, his eyes had been glazed with ennui and fatigue. Now, they gleamed with nervous tension, a fox catching scent of its prey.

'*Beyfendi, benimle gelin.*'

'No, I won't go with you. This is a Greek vessel. I don't have to do anything you say,' Ben protested in Turkish.

The customs agent placed one hand on the holstered revolver at his hip. 'You don't know what you're talking about. We're still docked in Turkey. Which means I can do anything I bloody want. So. I will ask one more time. Please leave your vehicle here and come with me.' He flicked his holster open and wrapped his hand around the gun's grip, finger hovering above the trigger.

Ben wasn't sure enough of maritime law to press the point. He felt the chill metal of the gun's barrel digging into his hip and toyed with the idea of pulling it out and forcing his way off the ship. But common sense prevailed. Escalating the conflict could only work against him.

'*Tamam. Tamam.* I'm coming.' Ben climbed out of the car and slammed the door, fists clenched in frustration.

The policeman gestured brusquely towards the ship's cabin, his other hand still resting on his holster. 'That way, please, sir. I will follow.'

Ben followed the man's directions and ducked his head to enter the cabin. His heart sank. A familiar figure stood before him.

'So, *Bay* Benedict. You have a thing for Lesbians, do you?'

# 35

## Ayvalık, Turkey, 1955

Superintendent Hasan Demir leant against the doorjamb, legs crossed and cigarette dangling between his fingers. 'Two visits to the island in a week. I'm intrigued. What is so very enticing over there?'

Ben's heart thumped. Feigning nonchalance, he leant against the bulkhead. He thought fast. 'It's quite simple, Hasan *Bey*. It's pork. The lure of bacon. The enticing sizzle of souvlaki. It's the one thing the Greeks offer me that I've yet to find a substitute for here in Turkey. If I have to look at another plate of lamb *döner*, I think I'll throw up.'

'They are filthy creatures, you know,' Hasan laughed. 'Pigs, I mean. Not Greeks.'

Ben forced a smile and ground his teeth. 'So what brings you to these parts, Hasan?'

'You do, Ben.'

'Me? I suppose I should be flattered.'

'There are very few people who would inspire me to drive halfway across the country at this time of year. With the troubles we've been having with the Greeks lately, I really should be in Istanbul. But here's the thing. For so long, your routine was so predictable. Now, within the space of a week, you travel to London, then to Lesvos, back here, and now? Off to the island again. You know what we look for? What good police work always starts with?'

Ben looked at Hasan blankly.

'Breaks in routine. And your behaviour lately has been anything but routine.'

'I promise you, Hasan,' he said. 'It's nothing to worry about. Once I have my fill of grilled pig, I'll return to my usual, mundane, predictable patterns.'

Hasan's expression gave nothing away. 'What do you have in the car, Ben?'

Ben's stomach lurched. Hasan continued. 'Given your – how shall I put it – *reputation* . . . we do need to make sure you're not taking anything from Turkey that should remain here.'

'If I had any pride left, Hasan, I might take offence. But you're in luck. Skin as thick as a rhino's hide these days.' As he spoke, Ben slipped his hand into the breast pocket of his jacket and took out his packet of cigarettes, deliberately fumbling and dropping them onto the ground. As he bent to retrieve them with his back to Hasan, he quickly slipped Achilles' seal ring off his finger and dropped it into the cigarette packet. It would be the end for him if Hasan spotted that. Ben stood and drew a cigarette out of the soft pack, lighting it and inhaling deeply. He crossed his arms before his chest and hoped Hasan wouldn't notice his heel tapping nervously in his boot. 'I've got nothing. Nothing that will interest you, anyway.'

'Then you won't mind if we have a quick look over your vehicle?'

He knew immediately that the Turk was bluffing. 'Here's the thing, Hasan. Your friend here claimed you have the right to do what you want here . . . that I have no rights as long as the ship is docked in Turkey. But that doesn't sound right to me. It's flying a Greek flag. Now, what say I ask the captain and his men what they think about a Turkish policeman telling them what to do?'

Hasan was silent.

'I thought as much.' Ben dropped his arms. 'So, no. You can't search my car.' He turned his back on Hasan and strode back towards the jeep.

'If you have found her again, Dr Hitchens, be very careful.'

Ben paused. 'I've no idea what you're talking about.'

'I could arrest you . . . for something. Anything. It wouldn't matter. But I'd rather see what's going to happen next. You're careless. You'll do something wrong. And I'll be waiting for you. There's one thing I know for certain, Dr Hitchens. This won't end well for you.'

# 36

'He should be on the ferry. I want you to take it from him. Do whatever's necessary.'

'Isn't he giving it to the woman?'

'That was the idea. But there's been a change of plan. That's none of your concern, however. Just do it.'

'What about the others?'

'I suspect something went wrong on the mountain. I haven't heard from them.'

'And the woman?'

'As I said – not your concern.'

# 37

## Lesvos, Greece, 1955

Ben wasn't able to relax until the ferry pulled away from the docks and he watched Hasan's hawkish silhouette diminish in the distance. But once he found himself on the open water, with the ragged purple profile of Lesvos on the horizon, he felt he could breathe again.

Leaning over the rusty guardrail at the edge of the deck, he let the cool wind ruffle through hair still damp with nervous sweat. The pendant slipped out of the neck of his shirt and swung like a pendulum, glittering in the sun. He took it between his fingers and toyed with it absent-mindedly. Ben had always found it comforting having a constant reminder of Karina with him. But today was different.

The thought of Eris awaiting him in Molyvos filled him with conflicting emotions. There had been a moment before he left the sanctuary on Mount Ida when he thought he would turn right at the coast road rather than left, take Achilles' shield to Istanbul and turn his back on the woman he knew he could never forgive. But it had been a passing whim.

As the ferry's engines laboured beneath the deck and carried him closer to her, it struck Ben that he had no idea what he planned to do next. When Hasan confronted him on board the ferry, it was his opportunity to fix things. He could have shown the superintendent the shield, told him about the tomb and it would have been the first step on his path to professional redemption. Ben had no doubt that Hasan would have turned a blind eye to the fact he had attempted to take the shield out of the country because the importance of such a find would have made Ben's digression irrelevant.

Instead, he was returning to her. And he had no idea what he'd do when he saw her again. He had no intention of letting go of the shield. But he was shaken by the realisation that he didn't want to let her go, either. His body ached for her, even as he knew he could never trust her again.

Ben sat in the jeep on Mytilene's pier as customs officials in the Greek port prepared to lift the barrier and admit the waiting cars and passengers to Lesvos. Travel papers had been checked and stamped. Resting his elbow on the window Ben felt the warm sea air settle on his skin. The sound of gentle waves slapping against the breakwater and sloshing beneath the dock's ancient beams lulled his frayed nerves. He shut his eyes.

'She's got spirit, that woman of yours.'

Ben started. The bright afternoon sunlight raking across the town's terracotta rooftops made it difficult to see as his eyes adjusted to the glare. A figure stood by the jeep's window, backlit by the sun's rays.

'Excuse me?'

'Your girlfriend in Molyvos,' the stranger said. 'She has spirit. She struggled. But you don't have much luck with your women, do you, Dr Hitchens?'

Lightning-fast, Ben slid the revolver out of his waistband with one hand and opened the door with the other. Sliding out of the car in a fluid movement, he confronted his assailant. Surprised by his speed, the stranger stepped away from the jeep. Ben advanced on him, gun clamped against his thigh where the man could see it but where it remained hidden from the guards at the gate ahead. The man backed away from him. He was slightly built with gingery hair slicked back from a prominent forehead and pale brows above watery blue eyes.

Ben snarled. 'What the hell did you say?'

'You heard me, American. You should take better care of your women.'

'You goddamned son of a bitch!' Ben sprang towards the man as he turned and bolted like a rabbit towards the red and white barrier blocking the road. He grabbed the crossbar with one hand and vaulted over it, landing deftly on the other side. Heart pounding, Ben ran after him and jumped the barrier, landing awkwardly on the other side. The man weaved through the traffic on the harbour road, heading for the maze of narrow streets that wound up the hills surrounding the harbour. Ben raced up the pavement in his wake. Horns blared and brakes squealed as he darted across the road.

The man disappeared into a dark alleyway. Ben sprinted after him, ragged breath tearing at his chest. The sound of the man's rapid footfalls echoed along the cobbled street.

'Get back here, you damned coward.' His fury was blinding – red rage roared behind his eyes and made his throat burn. Ben brandished the revolver. Given half a chance, he would blow the man's brains out.

The stranger was out of sight, but his voice rang out, mocking Ben. 'Me . . . a coward? I wasn't the one who left her here alone.' His words echoed along the stone canyon between the tall terrace houses.

Ben bellowed. His legs pumped as he willed himself to run faster. The ringing sound of the man's flight receded into the distance. Ben reached a branch in the road. He slowed and listened. He was fairly sure he could hear the man's steps echoing along the alley to the left. But as he progressed further along the lane, the sounds faded. Ben backtracked and tried the other street. Nothing. He raced up the hill, pausing as he went, straining to hear something – anything – that would help him find the man. One laneway then another branched off the road he was following up the hill. He peered into the shadows. A clucking group of old women seated on low stools stared at the stranger in their midst as Ben ran past. He stopped.

'Excuse me, grandmother,' he asked the most senior of the gathering. 'Have you seen a man run past?'

The old woman clicked with her tongue and raised her eyebrows. No.

Ben nodded. 'Thank you.'

The man was gone. Now all Ben could think about was getting back to Molyvos. Quickly.

*Why did I doubt her? What have I done?* he berated himself.

The jeep stood, abandoned, on a wharf now empty of other vehicles. It wasn't until he was standing by the driver's side that he noticed the rear door was open. A chill ran down his spine as he moved to the back of the car.

Whoever had been waiting here while he was lured away from his vehicle had known where to look. The false bottom in the tray had been levered open and stood gaping like a raw wound. The hiding place beneath it was empty.

Ben pounded his fist into the roof. 'You goddamned idiot!' He yanked the metal plate out of the back of the jeep, threw it to the ground with a clatter and kicked it clear across the jetty. Achilles' shield was long gone.

He slammed the jeep's rear door shut with a smash that rebounded off the wharf's stone buildings. The iron tang of blood flooded the back of his mouth where he had bitten down on his tongue. Fury propelled him into the driver's seat and he turned the key in the ignition. Slamming the accelerator to the floor, the car spun out of the port in a cloud of dust, the rubber on the tyres burning in a blue smoke haze as he tore along the asphalted road towards Molyvos.

The sun had already set as Ben approached the outskirts of town. After he'd left Mytilene he had driven the coastal road at breakneck speed, haunted by a grim sense of foreboding. When he saw the lights of Molyvos twinkling in the lavender light of dusk, a strangely detached horror at the thought of what might confront him at Eris' stone house washed over him.

The streets in the town were still and quiet. Gravel crunched beneath the tyres as he drove into the driveway at the rear of her house. Crickets buzzed in the undergrowth and the heady, sweet smell of jasmine filled the night air.

As he drew to a halt at the rear door, his heart leapt to see a light shining at the front of the house. He threw the jeep's door open and stumbled from the car, grabbing the revolver as an afterthought. He placed a hand on the heavy wooden door. It swung open. He crept inside, gun cocked and ready. Other than the light in the front room, the house was as black and silent as a tomb.

He crept carefully along the corridor. The sound of a slow, rhythmic but muted banging punctuated the silence. The door into the front room was ajar. Carefully pressing his face to the crack, he peered inside. Coaxing it open slowly and carefully, he braced his muscles, ready to respond if the ancient hinges betrayed his presence.

He drew a deep breath and raised the gun to shoulder height as he stepped into the room.

# 38

## Lesvos, Greece, 1955

A shutter slammed in the evening sea breeze. On the dining table rested a neatly addressed envelope.

*Dear Ben.*

His head was spinning.

*Dear Ben.*

Not the words of a woman in peril.

*Dear Ben.*

He turned the envelope in his hand. The paper was heavy. Expensive. The handwriting was elegant and well formed. He held his breath as he slipped his finger beneath the sealed flap of the envelope and tore it open.

*Dear Ben,*

*Words at moments like these count for little. But, for what it is worth, I am truly sorry.*

*I apologise for the anguish I caused you when we first met, and I am sorry for the pain and confusion I am no doubt inflicting now. The reason I am writing is to ensure you do not suffer this time as you suffered before.*

*There was no father. There was no brother. There was only ever me. The kidnapping in İzmir was a set-up. The man I spoke of was not my kidnapper – he was, and is, my business partner. Nothing more. As for you, I needed someone to publicly authenticate my collection of antiquities. He suggested we target you and we concocted the plan together. That is all.*

*Why the deception? My partner believed that if I had simply disappeared in İzmir, you might not have persisted with the article's publication, but if you thought I had fallen victim to foul play, you would be more likely to pursue it. Your actions proved him right. But my business transactions are only ever about money. My intention is never to cause real harm. I was unaware of the effect it would have on you. When I told you that I would not have left you in the manner I did if I had known about your wife, I was not lying.*

*Our time together in İzmir changed me. My life and what I do depends upon deception, but I struggled to maintain the façade when I was with you. There were things I spoke of that I have never shared with anyone else. The chapter of my imagined story where I once lived in İzmir with my family was untrue. But although it happened far away from Turkey, the death of my mother and sisters and its effect on me occurred exactly as I described it. I'm sharing this with you because I do not want you to think any less of me than you already do. That probably makes no sense to you, but it's important to me.*

*So now the shield is in my possession. I have a buyer for it, and I can assure you it will be in good hands. You will hear no more from me. Whatever remains in the tomb is yours. It should be more than enough to rekindle your career.*

*Please do not waste your time looking for me. I have spent a lifetime mastering the art of anonymity, and I do not wish to be found.*

*I thank you for not giving up on me, even though I did not need rescuing and did not deserve it anyway.*

*Despite what you say, you are a good man, Benedict Hitchens.*

The letter bore no signature, simply an 'X'. It smelled of her: rosewater and olive oil soap.

Ben remained at the table, clutching her letter until his knuckles turned white and the waves of fury abated and were replaced by a stinging sense of humiliation.

He could have taken off in pursuit of her – but it was impossible to know how much of a head start she had. She might still be on the road between Molyvos and Mytilene. Or she could be at the port with the shield, awaiting the morning ferry to Athens. There were only so many ways she could get off the island. But he was drained. Even if there had been an opportunity to catch her, he had no reserves left to draw upon.

And so he fell into the arms of an old friend. He finished off the bottle of ouzo in the drinks cabinet and passed out in Eris' soft featherbed, his face buried in pillows that still bore the intoxicating scent of her hair.

# 39

## Lesvos, Greece, 1955

The morning sunlight speared through the lace curtains like shards of glass, tearing at Ben's eyes. The sound of someone rattling at the French doors downstairs drove him from the bed. Head throbbing, he grabbed the handgun from the bedside table.

Downstairs, a dark shadow passed before the shutters. He edged towards the door out to the terrace and grasped the handle. When the shadow moved past the door, Ben shouldered it open with a crash.

'May the Good Lord preserve me!' A frail, elderly man stood hunched over a bucket, hands raised.

Ben lowered his weapon. 'I'm sorry. I thought you were somebody else.'

The old man's face was ashen. 'No – forgive me, sir. I was told the house had been vacated. I'm the caretaker. Nikos. Just here to tidy the garden. Before the owner returns.'

'Owner? She's coming back?'

The caretaker looked confused. '"She"?'

'The owner. Eris Patras. Do you know where I can find her?'

'No sir – the owner's name is not Patras. It's Dimitropoulos. And it's not a "her". It's a "him". He's a doctor – lives most of the year in Athens.'

'Then who was the Greek woman who was living here? Was it his wife?' Even as he said it, his heart sank.

'His wife?' The old man shook his head. 'No, no. God rest her soul – she passed away ten years back. He hasn't remarried as far as I know. The woman who was here – she was just renting the house for the summer.' He looked up at Ben, black eyes gleaming. 'You know her, you say? Didn't talk to me much. Kept to herself. All sorts of curious comings and goings, between you and me. Greek, was she?' The caretaker raised his eyebrows and shrugged. 'Maybe. Maybe. Strange accent, though. Had her pegged for an Arab.'

Ben was the only passenger to take a seat on the top deck of the ferry as it cut through the water towards the distant Turkish shore. In no mood for human companionship, he stayed away from the oppressive mass of people crammed into the steamy confines of the enclosed lower deck.

The bright sunlight reflected in blinding beams off the golden surface of Achilles' ring, which he spun absent-mindedly on his finger. Other than the letter, the house had been stripped bare of everything personal. She had left behind nothing of herself. If it were not for the ring and Eris' letter, the events of the past few days might have been nothing more than the imaginings of a deranged mind.

He slumped lower in his seat. The sun's rays toasted his scalp and sent streams of sweat running down his back.

He took the letter out of his pocket, as starchy and sharp-edged as the message it contained. The words she'd written were now committed to memory. There was nothing there – no hidden message, no mysterious subtext – that made it easier to understand.

Shrieks of delight from the deck below clawed him back to the present. A pod of dolphins gambolled in the waves on the boat's starboard side, leaping and flipping in glistening arcs.

The roar of an outboard motor reverberated off the ferry's metal hull as a sleek launch pulled alongside and kept pace with the larger vessel, the dolphins cutting through its foamy wake. The ensign fluttered at the stern – two horizontal stripes of sky blue with a white band in the middle and a sun at its centre. *Argentinian? That's odd*, Ben thought to himself.

He gazed at it absently as it sounded its horn.

A crewmember in a blindingly white uniform stood on its deck, steadying himself with one hand on the gunwale, his other cupped above his eyes to shield them from the white-hot sun.

'Hitchens?' he shouted above the sound of churning water. Ben thought he was hearing things. 'Benedict Hitchens?'

*What the hell?* He stood and moved to the railing at the edge of the deck. The man on the launch caught sight of him. 'You Hitchens?'

'Who's asking?'

The man ducked back into the cabin.

It had been more than a decade since he had last seen him, but Ben would never forget the face of the man who stepped out onto the deck of the launch. The same homburg perched jauntily atop salmony-orange hair. The same fleshy, white face pierced by shark eyes. 'Garvé?' he whispered as his heart began to pound in his chest. His mind was whirring.

It struck him – a starburst shock of realisation. Eris' mysterious business partner. The business partner who knew too much about Ben for it to be a coincidence. The business partner who told Eris exactly who she needed to be to blind him and make him lose his reason, who knew exactly how to destroy him.

'Garvé!' he howled across the waves. 'I'll fucking kill you!'

The Frenchman raised his hand in a wry salute and said nothing. He smacked the roof of the cabin and the motor launch sped away, cutting towards a sleek yacht on the horizon. But not before Ben caught sight of the vessel's name emblazoned across its stern.

*Karina*.

# 40

## Áyvalık, Turkey, 1955

Ben joined the slow-moving train of vehicles disembarking the ferry. A familiar figure stood at the exit.

Hasan sauntered to where the jeep sat idling and leant in
the open passenger's side window. 'Oh, dear. That's not the
face of a happy man. So, she has done it to you again. You
know what they say. Fool me once, shame on you. Fool me
twice, shame on me.'

Ben pulled to the side of the wharf. 'Not in the mood,
Hasan.'

The Turk shook his head. 'You didn't let her get away,
did you? If we weren't on the verge of war with our Greek
neighbours I wouldn't have bothered with you. But the waters
between Turkey and Greece are fairly frigid at the moment.
My peers across the Aegean aren't even interested in speaking
with me. They certainly weren't going to let me head over
there and start asking questions. So I was hoping you would
do the job for me and bring her back to me.'

Hasan opened the passenger's door. He took a handkerchief from his pocket and swept the accumulated dust and debris from the frayed canvas seat before sitting down. 'I did try to warn you.'

'No, you didn't. Not in as many words. You warned me about shadowy smuggling cartels. You didn't tell me she was as bad as – probably worse than – any of them.'

Hasan smiled. 'Ah, but you would never have believed me. And I couldn't tell you because I needed you to encourage her to break her cover. If you had known who she really was, you would have given up your search years ago. Besides, ever since I met you in the Hotel Sefer with that bandit, Ilhan Aslan, I've known you were quite comfortable flirting with criminal behaviour. I've never been entirely sure about how involved you were with that woman and her operation. So I've always been very judicious about what I've told you.' He shook his head sadly. 'I had such high hopes, Ben – I was sure you would draw her out of her hiding place. Her scalp would have won me accolades across Europe. Why do you think I have spent so many years – invested so much of the department's money – watching you?'

'So it *was* you.'

'Of course. Did you ever doubt it? Ah, Ben,' he sighed. 'She had you from the moment she targeted you on the train. After you published your article, she had no trouble finding buyers for her stolen goods. But I never lost hope. I always knew she'd get back in touch with you. You were too valuable to her.'

'Why didn't you just tell the Greeks – let them arrest her?'

'And lose the chance of catching her myself? Not on your life. I wasn't going to let those Greek bastards get all the glory. A little short-sighted and petty of me? Without a doubt.

Besides, as I explained, the phone lines between Athens and Istanbul aren't exactly aglow with the spirit of fraternity and cooperation at the moment.'

'What do you know about her partner?'

'Partner? As far as I know, she usually works alone.'

'Well, I've got that one over you, anyway. Josef Garvé.'

'You mean Atlantis Maritime's Josef Garvé?'

'One and the same.'

'I've heard rumours about drug connections and people smuggling – especially down to Palestine. With that fleet of cargo freighters crossing the globe . . .' Hasan nodded his head thoughtfully. 'Antiquities. Why not? It would answer the question that's always plagued me – how she manages to move her purloined treasures around the world without detection. Having a global shipping company in her back pocket would certainly help. First I've heard of it, though.'

'Trust me. He's involved,' Ben responded.

'That's good information to have. Thank you.'

'It's my pleasure. Believe me.' He paused, the sun warming his hands on the Bakelite steering wheel, his mind whirling with images: thick, raven tresses falling on honey-brown shoulders; enigmatic amber eyes; fingernails as flawless and smooth as a seashell's underbelly. 'So, where did she come from?'

'Nobody really knows. She first started to make waves just after the war.'

'Is she even Greek? The caretaker of her house in Molyvos seemed to think she's an Arab.'

Hasan shrugged. 'An Arab? Could be. No way of knowing, really.'

'Either way, she spins a good yarn. What's Ilhan got to do with it?'

'Ilhan? Nothing at all,' Hasan replied. 'Just a ploy on my

part. Sorry about that. I needed to draw you out on your own. If Ilhan had been involved – well, he wouldn't have fallen for her lies.'

'Are you saying I'm gullible?' Ben laughed. 'I feel like I should be insulted.'

'When it comes to that woman, you seem to lose all sense, Benedict. She must be quite something.'

'You have no idea.'

'So what did she get you caught up in this time?'

As Ben saw it, there was just one option available to him.

'It might not be all bad. It may be that I can lead you to something that will benefit the both of us. A consolation prize of sorts. But it will require you to do some work on my behalf.'

'You're not in a position to demand anything.'

'Don't be so hasty.' He extended his hand. 'See this?' Achilles' ring glittered on his hand.

Hasan peered down at the heavy golden circlet. 'Looks Mycenaean.'

'It's a whole lot better than that. I took it from Achilles' hand.'

'Achilles? *The* Achilles?' Hasan looked up, eyes gleaming. 'Not some old man playing *tavla* in Mytilene?'

'No. The one and only. I've found his tomb.'

'But that is . . .!' Hasan tripped and floundered as he sought the right words.

'Overwhelming? Astonishing? Momentous? Yes. You've no idea. I've never seen anything like it. Not even close.'

'You're sure?'

'Without a doubt.'

'Why couldn't I just retrace your steps and find it myself? Shouldn't be too hard . . .'

Ben laughed. 'Trust me. You won't find it without my help. But if you exert your impressive influence at all the right levels and get me permission to excavate again . . . well, we'll both be credited with what I can promise you will go down as the greatest archaeological discovery of the century.'

'Might make up for letting one of Europe's most wanted slip through my fingers.' Hasan gazed out at the docks. 'Fame and professional redemption for you. And glory and recognition for me.'

'As I see it, that's the best I can hope for at this stage.' Ben extended his hand. The two men shook on it.

Ben pictured Achilles, lying in repose deep beneath the mountain.

He smiled. 'And if I'm honest, it's a reasonable trade-off.'

# 41

## Istanbul, Turkey, 1955

The bell above the door of Ilhan's shop tinkled merrily as Ben swung the door open.

His friend was seated at the counter hunched over a tray of silver rings. He spoke without looking up as he slipped the jewellery back into the display cabinet. '*Buyrun*! Good afternoon, and welcome . . .' Ilhan glanced up, his eyes gleaming when he saw Ben standing on the threshold. Arms spread wide, he nodded his head and smiled in the warm but restrained way Turks express delight to see a cherished acquaintance.

'Brother. *Selamın Aleyküm*. Welcome. It has been very quiet around here without you.'

'*Aleykümselam*. Then you'll be very pleased to have me back, I'm sure. How are you, Ilhan *abi*?'

'Good, good. But I've been worried about you. In all the years I've known you, there have been many times I've wished for you to shut your mouth. But when you fell silent for such a long time . . . it was unusual. I always thought you were too big and too loud to disappear. But I was wrong.' He ushered Ben into the shop, concern weighing heavy on his brow. 'And then I hear from Charlotte that you were in London. You left Istanbul so quickly and never told me you were going. Why?'

Ben didn't know where to begin. 'It's a long story.'

'A story that has something to do with the marble tablet and your mysterious Greek woman? Have you found her?'

'As I say – it's a *very* long story,' he responded.

The Turk raised his eyebrows and shrugged resignedly. 'For another time then. Did you see the results?'

'Results?'

'Of the auction.'

Ben was puzzled.

'The Sotheby's auction. Our statues.'

'Oh. Christ. I'd forgotten.'

'I'm very happy to say that God has been kind – even to an infidel like you. You are now a wealthy man. Wealthy enough, even, to go and visit your wife's grave in Crete. You should go and pay your respects to her family, Benedict.'

'I'm a little too late for that, Hasan,' he said. 'And enough with the "Benedict".'

'It is never too late. And I will call you Benedict when you need to be spoken to like a child.'

'Perhaps they don't want to see me.'

'Perhaps you should let them make that choice.'

'We'll see. It's good to know I can afford to make some improvements to myself, anyway.'

'Well, you're certainly wealthy enough to replace those terrible trousers. That will be a good start. You look like a beggar.'

'Yes, I might need to call on your sartorial expertise to fit me out with a new wardrobe,' he said. 'What, with all the publicity I'm going to be getting in the near future, I do need to look the part.'

'Publicity?' Ilhan sighed. 'What have you been up to?'

'That's another chapter of the long story. But don't worry – this time it's all good. I've been on Mount Ida – Kazdağı. And I've found something . . .'

'Ah, that's very good to hear. Will this be good for me, too?'

'Don't think I can cut you in on this one, brother. It's going to have to be all above board. It's just too big.'

'Come now. Never say never.' Ilhan turned to grab his keys from the glass top of the display cabinet. 'Let's go and discuss it over a meal. I can't believe you'll turn your back on an old friend when God smiles on you.'

Ben laughed. 'Let's just wait and see, shall we?'

# Epilogue

## Washington, USA, 1955

Not a single man she passed could resist turning their heads to follow her with hungry eyes as she walked through the airport. Smoothing a close-fitting powder-blue skirt over her curves, she ignored their appreciative stares, her gaze fixed directly in front of her. She flicked her head. It was a dramatic transformation, but it hadn't taken her long to adjust to the platinum blonde soft waves hugging the lines of her sharp jawline. Two porters scurried along in her wake. One pushed a cart laden with a matching set of brown Louis Vuitton suitcases. The other trolley supported a single raw timber crate. Four feet square and two feet deep, it was stencilled with bright red lettering: *FRAGILE*.

On one side of the concourse, a wide, open doorway surrounded by ornately etched glass led into a darkened bar. She walked towards the entrance, signalling to the porters. She tipped them and positioned herself on one of the high-backed, brown leather banquettes lining the wall.

A waiter drifted towards her, eyes skimming up and down her shapely form. Reluctantly, he dragged his gaze from her deep cleavage and took her order, returning to the bar to mix her a Manhattan.

All she had to do now was wait.

She took a long draught of her cocktail. It did little to dispel the sense of disquiet that had clung to her since leaving Greece. The life she had chosen for herself required solitude and self-reliance. She had always worked hard, followed her personal code to the letter, and made sure she was amply rewarded. She could not recall when she last had occasion to become dependent upon another human being for anything, least of all emotional succour. Harsh lessons learnt early in life had taught her that reliance upon other people inevitably resulted in disappointment and pain. She thought she had excised the base emotions that would leave her vulnerable. But the doubt that had beset her since she'd sealed the envelope and left it resting on the table in Molyvos persisted and surprised her with its intensity.

When she had successfully completed a project in the past, she celebrated. Quietly, and alone. This time was different. As the dark outline of Lesvos had disappeared behind the clouds as her plane ascended into the heavens, the emptiness had persisted, and a bitterly sharp, hard-edged kernel of regret had taken up residence deep in her heart. She was in no mood to celebrate.

Over the years, the web of deceit that surrounded her had become more and more complex. It was difficult to unravel which threads were still connected to something resembling truth. She had assumed so many different personas and swathed herself in a veil of emotional artifice for so long that the horizon line between what was fact and what were lies seemed to be disintegrating. Her life had taken her to many places and she had experienced many things. Truth found its way into many of the tales she told. But it was getting harder to work out where the lies began.

The American had touched long-dormant corners of her heart. It was a surprise, and not an altogether welcome one. She had targeted him at Josef Garvé's urging, and the background information the Frenchman gave her showed Benedict Hitchens to be easy prey. His blind ambition and much-publicised disregard for convention could be exploited. From a professional perspective, everything had gone according to plan in İzmir. But her heart was fickle, and her feelings towards him had grown quickly despite her determination to remain emotionally aloof from him.

If the lines had been blurred in İzmir, she'd lost all perspective when they reunited in Lesvos. It had been a shock to learn that Ben had been married and his wife died under what she could only assume were tragic circumstances. It explained so much about his false bravado and drive towards self-destruction. She'd been quite sincere when, in a moment of weakness, she suggested he should leave with her. They were both damaged and lonely people and the temptation to escape to a place where they could help each other heal was, for a moment, utterly irresistible.

Now that she was aware of how she had amplified Ben's suffering she carried a heavy burden of guilt. Her stock in trade was deception but the only torment she usually inflicted on others was financial. She liked to keep things neat and clean. Nobody ever really got hurt from her operations. This was altogether different. And she wasn't entirely comfortable with it. She had no way of knowing whether or not the role Garvé had contrived for her to play was modelled on Ben's wife and had been designed to break his heart. But it seemed likely that the two men had a history she had been unaware of.

When she looked back on it, the Frenchman's knowledge of Ben's personality and peccadilloes seemed too intimate to have come from a third party. For the first time in their very long association she had pause to question her partner's motives. She knew he was ruthless, greedy and determined but she had thought he was otherwise fairly uncomplicated.

Her relationship with the Frenchman had always been remote and professional. There had never been a reason or occasion to ask him about his past. It wasn't that sort of association. He was a means to an end for her. Nothing else. And if she were honest with herself, she had to admit she knew next to nothing about him personally. She took great pride in her ability to read people. Could it be that she had misjudged this man? It was a cause for concern. But they had already advanced too far into their next scheme to dissolve their partnership. There was too much at stake and she would be putting too many things at risk. She now knew she wouldn't be able to let her guard down for a single moment.

Either way, it was much better that Benedict Hitchens now lay in her past. She had suffered a momentary lapse of judgement, and it was far better that she was back in control. But if that was the case, she couldn't help but wonder why she felt so bereft.

'You are far more glamorous than I expected.'

She glanced up. A tall woman stood before her, glossy black hair styled into a distinctive back-combed bob that would – in years to come – be mimicked the world over. Her warm eyes were set wide apart above high cheekbones, and full lips curled into a gracious smile. A heavy-set man wearing a black suit stood behind her.

'Mrs Kennedy?' She stood and extended her hand.

'Yes. It's good to make your acquaintance in person. Did you have a pleasant flight?'

She nodded and smiled. 'Uneventful.' She indicated the banquette beside her. 'May I offer you a drink?'

Mrs Jacqueline Kennedy smiled and shook her head. 'Thank you, no. I have an engagement this evening and really must be getting back. I saw the newspaper coverage of the tomb's discovery. They're making quite a fuss about it, aren't they? No wonder, I suppose. There was no mention of the shield, of course. I shan't ask how you managed to get it out.'

'It wasn't easy.' She smiled tightly. Fierce regret gripped her heart. 'But I had some help.'

'Well, you did what you promised to do. And as agreed, I've transferred the money into the bank account you nominated.'

The blonde woman nodded and gestured towards the trolley with the timber crate. 'I assure you that you will not be disappointed. It is more magnificent than I could have imagined. Truly the work of the gods.'

Mrs Kennedy signalled to her driver, who manoeuvred the trolley out of the corner.

Before the senator's wife left, the woman broke her own rule of never asking questions of her clients. 'Why this, Mrs Kennedy? What is so important about getting this? You might have acquired almost any ancient artefact in the world for a fraction of the cost of Achilles' shield.'

Jackie Kennedy paused, watching the passing parade of harried passengers rushing along the concourse. 'My husband is only a senator, but he is far more ambitious than that. He wants to change the world. No man gets to where he is headed without making enemies along the way. I am an avid student of human history, and I know the power in that shield is probably nothing more than fable and folklore. But even if it is only symbolic, I would rather it lies in his hands than someone else's. It will make him strong. And where he is going, I fear he is going to need all the help he can get.'

She watched as Mrs Kennedy turned and walked towards the exit without a backward glance, the driver hefting the trolley along in her wake.

Draining her cocktail, she ordered another. Eris Patras no longer existed. The initial stages of her next project were already in place and it was time for her to become somebody else. But first, she needed to permit herself a moment to mourn the life – and the man – she had left behind.

# Sources

My husband, Andrew, has a favourite saying: 'Don't let the truth get in the way of a good story.' That sentiment is probably one of the reasons I have wound back my career as an academic – there's no room for embellishment and tall tales in the hallowed halls of academia. And where's the fun in that?

The one thing my experience as a historian has bequeathed me is a deep appreciation for the lessons of history. So while *The Honourable Thief* is a work of fiction, it didn't spring, fully formed, from my imagination. Specific historical events provided a springboard for a story that then developed in my mind and primary accounts gave me context and colour for the worlds I created. For those of you who would like to know some of the sources I used as background for my story, I hope the following may be of interest.

The kernel of the story was planted in my mind by the extraordinary account of the downfall of archaeologist James Mellaart. As described in the 1967 book by Kenneth Pearson and Patricia Connor, *The Dorak Affair*, Mellaart was on a train when he spied a woman sitting opposite him wearing an ancient piece of jewellery. He was invited to the young woman's home where she showed him a collection of other artefacts she claimed her family had unearthed in tombs by Lake Apolyont near the town of Dorak in north-western Turkey. The woman, who gave her name as Anna Papastrati, wouldn't allow Mellaart to photograph her collection, so he stayed at her home for several days documenting her collection during which it's suspected they embarked upon a short-lived sexual liaison. When Mellaart left Anna's home, he asked for the address of the building in which they had been staying. This was the last he would ever see of the woman and her cache of ancient treasures.

In years to come when Turkish authorities attempted to find the woman, they could find no trace of her, or even identify the address Mellaart claimed was her home. Mellaart's story was ridiculed by his peers, and his case was not helped by the appearance of a letter purportedly written by Anna Papastrati that gave permission for the publication of the drawings of her artefacts. It was most likely written on a typewriter at the British Institute of Archaeology in Ankara – at the time, Mellaart's Turkish wife, Arlette, was employed there as the Institute's secretary.

Turkish authorities suspected Mellaart had been involved in a plot to smuggle Turkish 'national treasures' out of the country. He was never permitted to excavate in the country again. But James Mellaart stuck to his guns. In 2012 at the age of 86, he went to his grave without retracting or revising his story. To this day, no material evidence of the Dorak treasure has ever appeared other than in Mellaart's own written account.

Benedict Hitchens' wartime exploits on Crete were inspired by the experiences of Sir Patrick 'Paddy' Leigh Fermor, who was – amongst many other things – a major during

World War II. Leigh Fermor's involvement in the abduction of the German military governor on Crete, General Heinrich Kreipe, in collaboration with the Cretan Resistance and a fellow British officer, Captain William Stanley Moss, is an engrossing real-life story of wartime daring. For background on this, I consulted Leigh Fermor's hugely entertaining *Abducting A General – The Kreipe Operation*, and W. Stanley Moss' *Ill Met By Moonlight*. Unlike Ben's experiences in *The Honourable Thief*, Leigh Fermor's adventure was a very British affair, with Fermor and his captive finding common ground when crossing the snow-covered Cretan mountains. General Kreipe recited a line in Latin by the poet Horace to which Leigh Fermor responded – also in Latin, of course. Leigh Fermor was, himself, an extraordinary man who became a revered travel writer and raconteur; his book, *A Time of Gifts – On Foot to Constantinople*, recounting his overland journey – yes, on foot – across Europe, gave me a window into the world inhabited by Benedict Hitchens.

During the war, American and British archaeologists in Greece were recruited by the military and fought side by side with the Greek Resistance. British recruits worked within a department in the War Office known as MI(R) – Military Intelligence (Research) – and were active with the Cretan Resistance during what's often described as some of the war's fiercest conflicts. American fighters were recruited by the Office of Strategic Services (OSS), a story recounted in *Classical Spies* by Susan Heuck Allen, who gives a fascinating account of the activities of American archaeologists fighting in Greece. Anthony Beevor's *Crete: The Battle and the Resistance* gave me invaluable insights into the wartime experiences of the civilians and soldiers fighting against the German occupation.

The suffering of the people of Crete during World War II as depicted in *The Honourable Thief* is also, sadly, based on fact. The 2005 documentary, *The 11th Day*, directed by Christos Epperson, provides a harrowing account of life on the Aegean island during the war, including the German destruction of the village of Anogeia and other towns in the Amari Valley in part as retaliation for the villagers' collaboration with General Kreipe's kidnappers.

To less sombre sources: Other than the opening line of the epic poem which is reproduced in Greek, the English quotes from *The Iliad* used in *The Honourable Thief* are not word-for-word because I've always assumed Benedict Hitchens translated Homer's *Iliad* himself. As a wet-behind-the-ears undergraduate studying Ancient Greek at the University of Melbourne, even I had a stab at translating the odd passage of Homer – and did a terrible job of it. I have no doubt Benedict would have been all over it. But as my starting point I used an original nineteenth-century copy of Alexander Pope's *Iliad* from my library, and tweaked his translations – so sincere apologies to Mr Pope for the liberties I have taken with his exquisite work. As for the most beautiful translation of *The Iliad*, my favourite is that written by Richmond Lattimore. His interpretation of Hector's farewell to his wife, Andromache, brings me to tears every time.

The shadowy world of forgery and the peculiar motivations of forgers have fascinated me for years – what I have learnt along the way spawned the character of Raphael Donazetti. For a primer, Noah Charney's book, *The Art of Forgery*, is entertaining and well-researched, as is *False Impressions: The Hunt for Big-Time Art Fakes* by Thomas Hoving. One of my other favourites on the subject is the 1961 publication by Frank Arnau, *3,000 Years of Deception*, which opens with the completely hilarious line: 'According to the enlarged edition of his oeuvre catalogue, Corot painted over 2,000 pictures. Of these, more than 5,000 are in the United States.' If you want to delve into the mind of a forger, the autobiography by Eric Hebborn, *Drawn to Trouble*, is also a remarkable resource.

The descriptions of Istanbul are my own, and inspired by the ridiculous amount of time I've spent in that city over the years. Charles King's beautiful book, *Midnight at the Pera Palace* gave me the time machine I needed to find my way back to mid-twentieth-century Istanbul.

I can blame no one other than myself for the descriptions of archaeological excavations and art auctions. Although I've shifted things chronologically, everything described is based on my own experience of those worlds. Though I've never bailed up an art buyer in the men's restroom and I've certainly never stolen and on-sold artefacts from an excavation. Not personally.

# Acknowledgements

T his book is the product of good times shared with more brilliant people than I can count, far less list here. But I'll have a stab at it.

To my dear Turkish friends who over many years of acquaintance have tolerated my embarrassing attempts to speak their language and made their home, my home: Hasan Selamet, Metin Tosun, Cansin Sağesan, Umut and Canan Alkan, Bahadir Berkaya and Chris Drum-Berkaya. Thank you. I hope I have done your beautiful country proud.

Throughout my academic career I have enjoyed the mentorship of a raft of brilliant teachers and scholars. Their inspiration finds voice in this story, though they are not accountable for any inaccuracies contained therein. Thanks, in particular, to Professor Jaynie Anderson and Associate Professor Christopher Marshall who have been supportive colleagues and friends, and to Professor Chris Mackie who encouraged my love of the Classics. But my greatest debt of gratitude is reserved for the late Professor Tony Sagona, who introduced me to the world of archaeology at the University of

Melbourne and, with his brilliant wife, Claudia, was director of uproariously fun excavations in the far east of Turkey that gifted me a lifetime of memories . . . and a husband.

Invaluable linguistic assistance was offered by Cansin Sağesan, who made sure my Turkish was in keeping with the period and vaguely comprehensible to anyone with a working knowledge of the language. Thanks are also due to the wonderful Linda Petrone and Pepe Montemurro who taught me how to swear like an Italian.

Thanks, also, to my friends and former colleagues in the commercial art world, who shall remain nameless lest they be associated with the rather jaundiced (but as they'd all attest if they were being honest – completely accurate) portrait of the auction business I have presented in *The Honourable Thief*.

Coaxing a publishable manuscript out of a writer is an art form that lies in a realm somewhere between black magic and alchemy and I've been lucky enough to have some of the best wordsmiths in the business help me massage *The Honourable Thief* into printed form. Cate Paterson, my publisher, is a truly extraordinary and inspirational person who's a registered force of nature (I've seen the certificate). Not a day has gone by when I haven't given a quiet word of thanks for having her on my side from the earliest days of the conception of *The Honourable Thief*.

It's such a leap of faith for an agent to take an unproven writer on board and I'll always be thankful for the day Clare Forster of Curtis Brown Australia took the plunge and signed me up. Clare is insightful, brilliant, determined and the supreme diplomat – but she's also ferocious in her representation. The velvet hammer personified. I would be lost without her guiding hand.

Fighting the good fight for *The Honourable Thief* internationally are Dan Lazar at Writers House (US) and Gordon

Wise at Curtis Brown UK. Their belief in the story – and in me – is valuable beyond measure.

My editor at Pan Macmillan Australia, Alex Lloyd, has been unstinting in his support and enthusiasm for my work and asked all the right questions to help me to whip *The Honourable Thief* into shape. Brianne Collins cast an exacting eye over the story and was enormously helpful at highlighting roadblocks and inconsistencies while offering incredibly useful suggestions to clear the detritus. Thanks also to Geordie Williamson and Claire Craig who offered invaluable feedback in the early days of the manuscript's development.

Without my bibliophile mother, Loretta, whose fierce support of my creative endeavours meant I was never pigeonholed into a conventional career, I'd just as likely have ended up being a lawyer – and a horribly miserable one, at that. For that I'll always be indebted to her. Thanks also to my wonderful sisters, Victoria and Phoebe, and Andrew Batey, Adrian, little Stella superstar, and Jim and Dianne. And to my dad, Willie, who'd be relishing all this if he was still around.

Roman and Cleopatra – my two pretty-damned-close-to-perfect children – thank you for your love, humour, enthusiasm and support, all of which make our home a wonderfully happy and often hilarious place. Thank you for indulging the attention this book has demanded from me, even when it eats into 'Cards Against Humanity' time. You're both extraordinary human beings – wish I could claim any responsibility for that, but the truth is you were both born that way. Though the one thing I do hope I've managed to teach you is that if you do something you love, one day you'll find a way to make a living out of it . . . and end up a great deal happier as a result.

And then there's Andrew. My best friend and love of my life. You have never doubted or questioned my dreams and ambitions and encouraged me in my professional wanderings. You have always helped me believe I was capable of this. It's not that I doubted my own capacity to write, but when I announced I was going to pen a novel, a single word of doubt from you about the wisdom of that decision might have punctured my confidence. I'm just lucky you're as big a dreamer as I am. These stories are borne of the adventures and experiences we've shared together – here's to many, many more. And to one day owning that Greek windmill on the cliff overlooking the Aegean, though I've no idea how we'll furnish a home with curved walls. I love you, husband. Thank you.